PIMIKO AND THE UNCHARTED ISLAND

BY FORTHRIGHT

FORTHWRITES.COM

Amaranthine Saga, Book 6
Pimiko and the Uncharted Island

Copyright © 2022 by FORTHRIGHT
ISBN: 978-1-63123-078-3

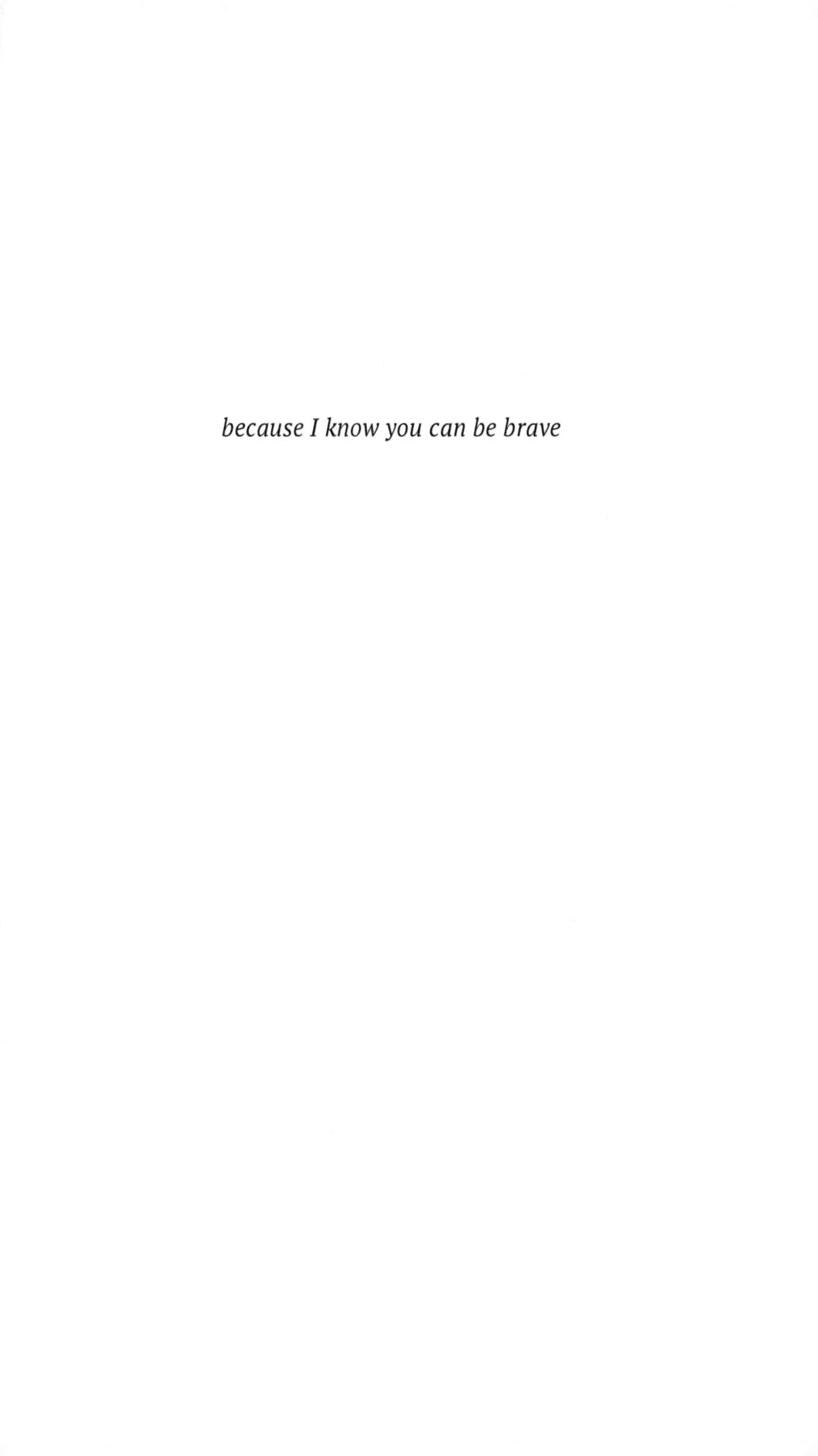
because I know you can be brave

Table of Contents

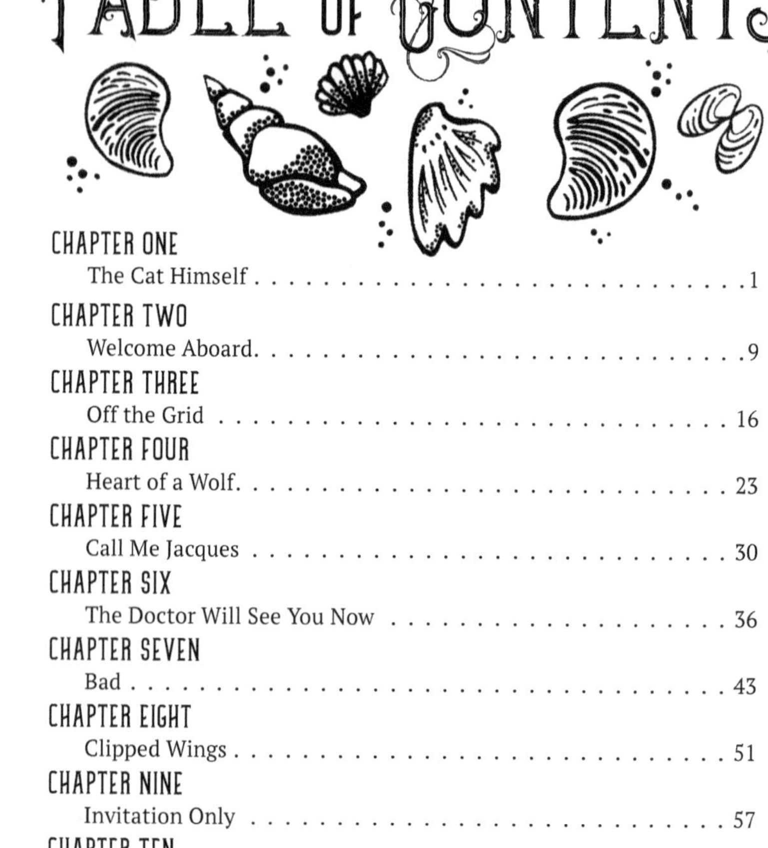

A MESSAGE FROM FORTHRIGHT

RECOMMENDED READING

Over the course of their writing, the books in the Amaranthine Saga *and the short stories in the* Songs of the Amaranthine *collection have been overlapping in interesting ways. Each informs the others, and new details are always coming to light. The same can be said of* **Lord Mettlebright's Man** *(Amaranthine Interludes, #1), which is currently being serialized on my blog. That story (in 100-word chapters) runs behind the scenes of the Amaranthine Saga, beginning after the events of Book 1, all from the perspective of Jacques Smythe.*

If you want to catch the significance of all the allusions in this book, I suggest brushing up on the Saga & Songs before you proceed. At the very least, I recommend these three titles:

Lord Mettlebright's Man
Bathed in Moonlight
Flattered by Flowers

And if you haven't yet explored the option, reading (and rereading) is truly a pleasure with the audio editions, narrated by Travis Baldree.

PIMIKO
AND THE
UNCHARTED
ISLAND

1

THE CAT HIMSELF

isoka Twineshaft had come to appreciate solitary moments. They were rarer than remnants these days and just as precious. With a secretive smile on his face, he skipped lightly along the hall, tapping the toes of his hearth slippers on the creamy flowers that decorated green carpeting.

He hummed a snatch of melody that belonged to a long-ago game. What were the words again?

In a space that was distinct, yet as close as his next thought, a voice supplied the lyric he was lacking:

> *High are the branches,*
> *Reaching for a star.*
> *Deep are the root paths,*
> *Delving for a song.*
> *Sweet are the flowers,*

Calling for a breeze.
Bright are the sweet fruits,
Longing for a home.

It was simple, even childish. A sing-song chant his sister had invented to please the pair of stars who used to hide amidst Hiroki's branches whenever the skies were too blue for their liking.

"It had slipped my mind," admitted Hisoka.

"I will not forget," promised Novi.

"Thank you." And because it was unusual for his starry friend to call out to him during daylight hours, Hisoka asked, "Has something happened?"

With a pleased lilt, Novi answered, *"You have mail."*

"I always have mail."

Indeed, Hisoka had several staff members entirely dedicated to receiving his mail. They hailed from all four of the moth clans, which meant fluency in every known language. And a few forgotten ones. The scribes took pride in their meticulous sorting and stacking, and in many cases, they dealt with responses on his behalf. Official mail involving Council business was handled by Isla, whose own staff managed their appointments and public appearances.

Few letters arrived with the kinds of seals that demanded privacy. When they did, Canarian brought them to Hisoka's bedroom, setting them on the small table where he sometimes welcomed friends to his hearth. However, when Hisoka reached the hushed room, no letter awaited.

"Novi?"

"Here."

Hisoka launched himself toward the large, circular opening in the ceiling, where trailing plants and tree branches turned the late summer light green-gold. Slipping through slanting sunbeams, Novi met him partway, and hands clasped.

Bound as they were by shared years, shared grief, and shared vows, Hisoka could hear this star's voice without needing the contact. But it was friendlier this way.

Their foreheads touched, and Novi said, *"It is time. It is now. Or nearly so."*

"For …?"

"Nemi."

Hisoka's heart lurched. Was their search finally at an end? "What can you tell me?"

Because his star never *could* tell all. He wasn't a messenger in the truest sense. More of an unofficial informant with friends in high places.

"The place you are needed next is the place you most want to be."

"Maker bless," he breathed. "Will we find her at last?"

"That is the shape of my hope," murmured Nemi's twin.

"Where?"

Novi lowered his gaze. *"There is a letter. An invitation. One you must accept."*

Hisoka nodded. "Go on."

"This chance is fleeting." A pleading edge entered the star's voice. *"You* must *accept."*

"Then I cannot refuse." Hisoka repeated, "Where?"

"Make haste to the room where mail is sorted. There will be a silver envelope with the Moonprowl crest. Rescue it."

Usually, Hisoka strolled through the halls of his home at an easy gait. That one, simple thing reassured his staff and guests alike. People expected him to be calm. They needed to believe he had things well in hand. But when a star said, "make haste," Hisoka wasn't about to dawdle.

Though this house was now more embassy than home, it had once been a family estate, and Hisoka knew every parlor and passage, especially the hidden ones.

Dropping lightly into the lowest level, where deliveries were received at all hours of the day and night, Hisoka strode through rooms he hadn't entered in decades. Not since giving Yulwen Dimityblest and Revic Nightbide their initial tour.

Clerks and scribes nodded respectfully as Hisoka passed by. Heralds brightened and bowed, surprised by this glimpse of the cat himself. But he didn't slow to greet them by name—though he could have. Or to grant the courtesies to which every person was due—though he meant no insult. For the wording of Novi's message worried him.

A fleeting chance.

A rescue?

Hisoka arrived in the sorting room with enough speed to stir paper. And to startle his apprentice, who sat hunched on a stool, grimly feeding packets into a paper shredder.

"Isla," he greeted. "Since when do your duties bring you here?"

"Sensei!" She stood and tucked her hands behind her back. "I could ask you the same."

"Isla," he repeated softly, chidingly.

She flushed and folded. "This isn't one of my duties, *per se*. I sometimes pitch in. Yulwen knows, and he doesn't mind at all."

Hisoka stepped close enough to check the provenance of the neat rows of thick envelopes clearly destined for destruction. "What have we here?"

"Junk mail," Isla blurted.

He couldn't let that pass. "On such fine paper? Every one of these packets clearly benefits from moth craftsmanship."

"Unsolicited mail, then," she amended unhappily. "It's just the usual, Sensei."

"Ah." There had been an uptick in such deliveries over the past few years. He dearly hoped this wasn't where he was meant to search for Novi's foretold letter.

Ever helpful, ever thorough, Isla went right on. "Most of these are bids for your attendance upon the ladies of the feline court. However, there are quite a few applications for paternity from reavers." She stiffly added, "You don't need them."

"And so you shred them?"

"Sometimes." With a haughty tilt to her chin, Isla said, "It's therapeutic."

He chuckled. "You are your mother's daughter."

"I am myself," she insisted, not for the first time. "But ... why are you looking through them?"

Hisoka ran his thumb up the nearest stack, lifting enough to catch a glimpse of each sender's name. "Something important may have become mixed in with the rest."

Isla's brows drew together. "They're all the same, Sensei. And you have a standing order to refuse all offers of this nature."

"I do."

She pulled one from the pile and pointed. "See? Yulwen stamps them here. This mark means that the usual letter of refusal has been issued."

"All very orderly," he agreed, still riffling.

"I'm only shredding them because that's been done!"

"I haven't accused you of anything, Isla."

"But ... what are you looking for?"

"Something important may be here," he murmured distractedly. Several of the envelopes in this stack could have qualified as silvery, and that slowed his search. "Didn't I say so? I'm sure I did."

His apprentice reluctantly offered, "Maybe I can help. I'm familiar with all clan crests, even those of the feline courts. They added three dozen this past Dichotomy Day, which is remarkable, given the Waning. Many of them are probably represented here, since each Lady Mistress wants to ornament her hearth with quality consorts."

There was an edge to her tone. Not scorn, exactly. Isla wasn't the sort to think less of a clan because of their culture. Indeed, she'd always been fascinated by their many variances.

"You disapprove?" he asked.

"Right. Well. I mean ... you can't deny it's a waste of paper."

In the next pile he checked, the very one Isla had been pulling from, he found an envelope with a silvery shimmer and an unfamiliar crest. It felt correct. "Hmm."

"Let me see." Isla tried to tug it from his hand.

He didn't release it. "I'm not familiar with this crest."

"No surprise, since you don't watch television. Pop culture is one of your weak points."

"I rely on those around me to demystify current trends." He was having difficulty keeping an even tone. "Will I need to call in Yulwen, or can you oblige …?"

"Moonprowl," she said crisply. "That is the crest of Pim Moonprowl."

"Ah, yes. The American actress."

Isla folded her arms tightly over her chest. "The first openly Amaranthine actress on American television. She's outspoken about Amaranthine rights. Although feline, she was cast as a wolf tracker on *Pure Instinct*, an award-winning crime drama that's in its final season. She also models for her own line of lingerie. Put together, she's more famous than you in the States."

Hisoka really wanted to return the envelope to its place in the pile. Or slide it directly into the shredder. No wonder Novi had been so uneasy.

"She's done so much for peace," Isla added softly. "Kimi's a big fan."

"High praise," he managed, tucking the packet under his arm.

"You're keeping it?" Catching his sleeve, she asked, "Why *hers*?"

"I hardly know myself." He slipped free, eager for retreat. "I'll notify you if there will be any change to my schedule."

"Sensei?"

Hisoka stopped and half-turned toward the young woman who reminded him so much of Michael, yet wasn't.

"Couldn't *I* ...?" But she lost courage.

The unasked question hung between them, and not for the first time, Hisoka left it unanswered. And calmly, slowly fled.

2

WELCOME ABOARD

im felt a tempest coming on. She understood the need to keep the peace and sublimate her better instincts, but this was asking too much. "I do not sleep with strangers!"

The avian—ship's captain, if the braid on his uniform was any indicator—cleared his throat and studied the sky. The reaver—meek thing—blushed to her roots and studied the floor. The healer—definitely part of the hoof-and-antler set—actually snorted.

"Are you really going *there*? I'm not talking about creative dalliance with nameless bedmates!" She shook her itinerary at them. "*Nothing* in these materials mentioned that I'd be expected to go deep."

"All part of company policy," the captain said apologetically. "To preserve the very secrecy that ensures your privacy."

"I'm not tired!" Pim's tail lashed. "I replenished beforehand, like any sensible person would!"

The healer's hands framed a plea for peace. "I have the means to induce sleep."

Pim narrowed her eyes. "I have *very* specific requirements."

"My people will do their best to accommodate you, but we won't depart until you're resting comfortably." The captain smiled thinly and added, "Welcome aboard."

"This way, please," murmured the reaver.

Although Pim gave her a few paces head start, she did follow. "I'll be reviewing my contract before submitting to anything."

The reaver girl ducked a nod and kept walking.

Pim took in scents and cast a critical eye over details, but all the while, she was churning over this new hitch. Many contracts had hidden loopholes or unexpected interpretations, and she was usually quick to suss out the pitfalls. Had she let hope get ahead of sense? Was it too late to back out? Did she really want to?

No.

But that didn't mean she'd go along nicely. Pim knew *so* many ways to make suffering mutual. It was all in the attitude. And application.

"Are there other guests on board?"

The reaver's step faltered. "I really couldn't say."

Given the ship's size, there was room for several more passengers, but Pim wasn't sure how the clinic managed its clientele. She wasn't picking up signs of anyone else on board, but it was impossible to miss the teasing taste of sigilcraft on the air.

"Does the ship employ a ward?"

"Yes, of course. She'll be available to secure your cabin to your satisfaction."

"And you are …?"

"One of the cossets assigned to you for the journey." The woman stopped before a cabin door. "Please, accept our hospitality. Your comfort is our duty and delight."

It occurred to Pim that nobody had handed her a key to her room. Glancing back the way they'd come, she asked, "What other amenities are available?"

The door swung wide, and that meek smile was back. "Everything you'll need has been provided."

Pim peered into a spacious cabin with a suitably expansive bed. The cushions, sheer drapery, and many mirrors were in line with current trends in the feline courts. But the sunlight drenching the space came from a series of skylights. None of the walls had windows, which was mildly disturbing. Pim's luggage waited before a wide hearth that was definitely ornamental … but reassuring, nonetheless. They were attempting to cater to her preferences. Unless she wasn't the first.

"Do you get many cats?" she asked.

"I really couldn't say." The reaver gestured for her to enter.

Pim only hesitated for a moment, then prowled the room's perimeter. "Have the rest hated this as much as I do?"

"I really couldn't …."

"I'm not investigating you or anything." Pim hopped up onto a cushioned massage table and crossed her legs. "We need some pittance of trust if you expect me to accept your hospitality."

The woman took the standard receptive posture.

So very proper.

Pim supposed this could be interesting. Again, she asked, "Have the rest hated this as much as I do?"

"More or less," she admitted softly.

Now they were getting somewhere. Pim lowered her sunglasses and peered over them. She liked how the blue-tinted lenses set off her eyes. She was famous for her eyes. With one look, she could cause hardened criminals to bare their souls and confess their crimes.

Pim asked, "Am I safe?"

The reaver's moment of hesitation was hardly reassuring, but she nodded. "In this room, yes. I can promise you that much."

With a touch of purr, Pim asked, "And you'll do your best to ... *accommodate* me?"

"I'll do whatever I can."

Hardly inspiring, as far as vows went, but Pim was prepared to coax better assurances out of this crew. "For starters, bring in the other cosset. And the ward. And the healer. Hmm. Is there a lawyer?"

"A secretary of sorts. He handles all of the arrangements."

Pim stiffened. "A male? That goes against my *explicit* instructions."

"No males are permitted on this entire deck. Not without your express permission."

Having already made a concession for the ship's captain, she supposed that was a reasonable boundary. If only she could be sure these people would honor it. Going deep meant leaving herself entirely vulnerable.

She spared the bed a glance. "Sleep is not easy. And it should be sacred."

A soft chuckle startled her. The reaver shyly asked, "Is that Pim Moonprowl's opinion on the matter? Or Aloora Longstride's?"

Ah, fame. "You're familiar with my work?"

"Never miss an episode."

There was enough admiration in the woman's glance to cheer Pim somewhat. Perhaps she *could* rule over this hearth in the manner of mistresses. "Summon the girls, and we'll make a beginning."

Pim dawdled and dallied in true feline fashion, ordering increasingly decadent foodstuffs from the kitchen and commanding the full attention of the four females she kept locked up in her rooms.

By the second full day, the captain was sending increasingly cranky messages, and Pim's cortege was more than a little infatuated with her. As was appropriate.

Only the healer interrupted Pim's fun with occasional reminders that there was an island filled with finer diversions awaiting her. "Nobody goes there without a reason. Have you forgotten yours?"

"Nooo," Pim sighed, drawing a painted silk robe a little higher on her shoulders. "Is that secretary person still hanging about somewhere? I suppose I could give him an audience."

Word was sent, and Pim arranged herself on a mound of pillows while her girls hastened to straighten the room. Within minutes, a soft tap announced a satisfactorily prompt arrival.

Moths were easy to peg—diminutive, drab, and unfailingly polite. The male who stepped into the cabin was predictably arrayed in creams and beiges, as befit every pencil-pusher she'd ever met. But something was off, and it put a twitch in her tail.

He was too thin. While moths were usually slim, this one was gaunt. And he was heavily warded. The bracelets at his wrists were tasteless things, deeply etched and about as appealing as shackles. Was the poor wretch one of the Broken?

His eyes were too bright, almost fevered.

Or was he actually on the verge of tears?

Pim felt certain these clues added up to suspicious. Maybe she should hash through the legalities with this fellow and abandon the venture. This whole thing was putting her back up.

With a soft clap of hands, the secretary quietly declared himself. "Greetings. My name is Linlu Dimityblest, and I am at your service. May I approach?"

She beckoned him forward, as courtesy demanded.

But when he presented his palms, there was a small crystal on one of them. Intrigued, she covered his hands, triggering the ward that would ensure their next words were private.

"Have you been mishandled, Kindred?"

His laugh was a whispery, humorless thing. "Does it show?"

"Am I safe?" she demanded.

Linlu didn't answer. Instead, he announced, "The stars have been singing to me of the convergence of two moons. You are surely one of them."

"Stars?" she echoed. "You can't mean the Hollywood variety."

"The celestial clans, long lost," he solemnly corrected. "I do hope you will continue on this course, reckless though it may be. You need us, Pimiko Moonprowl, and we need you."

3

OFF THE GRID

Boonmar-fen surfaced in a featureless expanse of sea, heaving for air. A minute passed as he waited to see if there were any discernable changes. Still nothing. So he pulled himself onto his surfboard and flopped to his back, staring at the stars as he caught his breath.

It was said that Elderbough trackers could follow a moonbeam straight to its source, chase the scent of a miracle to its Maker, and taste the beginnings of a soul-bond long before it had the chance to form. But Boon didn't feel much like one of his pack's finest right now.

He was breaking one of Hisoka's longstanding rules by being off on his own, which had forced a pile of responsibilities onto his brothers and his teammates.

Penny was probably peeved. Make that *definitely* peeved. Boon knew he was in for one hell of a dogfight once he got home.

Possibly worst of all, he'd called in a favor. Yeah, it'd guaranteed Mettlebright's support, but Boon had dragged Akira into this mess. Irrevocably. But unnecessarily. That old fox would have helped anyhow, once Boon fished Inti's voice out of the ether.

It had been faint, and it hadn't even been meant for him. Inti had been reaching for Argent.

"Try, try, try again," had come the monkey crosser's sing-song voice. *"Are you listening?"*

Boon had been in the water at the time, looking for a way under the barrier. He'd surfaced, panting and panicking, looking for any sign of a boat. But the litany of nonsense had no visible source. Which meant it was coming from inside the barrier he'd run up against, smack dab in the middle of nowhere.

Risking discovery, Boon responded as he would to any Kith or Kindred of the packs. But his words weren't reaching. So the speaker wasn't a wolf or a dog.

Even so, there was a hesitant answer. *"Someone is near?"*

With little other option, Boon focused on that whispered plea and responded with a silent howl.

"You are, you are, you are!" babbled the voice. And with heartbreaking hope, he asked, *"Good doggie?"*

It was silly to be insulted, but Boon had as much pride as the next wolf.

"Sorry, sorry, sorry."

"No sweat. Some of my best friends are dogs." Boon could only try to infuse his next push toward the voice with friendly feelings. And his efforts were rewarded.

"Wolf, wolf, good wolf. Stay with Inti."

"Aw, hell. What are *you* doing way out here?" The shock of recognition must have filtered through their tenuous connection.

"Wolf knows Inti?" And the ridiculous kid started listing clans.

His incredulity faded as the monkey crosser started from Highwind and worked through the packs that had spun off from the First Wolves. He reacted on cue when Inti reached Elderbough, and the kid impressed him all over again by listing Adoona-soh's children in birth order. It didn't take long to peg her third son.

"Boon. Inti needs help."

"I'm here," he'd growled, but words wouldn't reach. "There's a barrier between us."

He flung himself at the boy, trying to show his frustration at being kept away. The connection gained strength, and Inti's voice was clearer. It was a little like the connection Boon experienced during tending, especially with Hallow. Inti was half-human ... or more accurately, half-reaver, and that gave them just enough compatibility. If Inti hadn't been a crosser, this might never have worked.

"There is a dragon."

"I knew it!" Boon pounded against the barrier, dragging his claws over its unrelenting surface. "I knew I was close."

"Yes, yes, yes. Argent wants them, too." Inti wearily chanted, *"Dragon, dragon, dragons."*

Their one-sided conversations had continued for days, while Inti performed an orderly debriefing, entrusting Boon with his discoveries.

An uncharted island.

A hoity-toity resort.

Experimentation on crossers.

Exploitation of Impressions.

Along the way, Boon learned that the monkey crosser had tried a classic technique: messages in bottles. Though the messages were smuggled remnant stones or sigilcraft, and many of his bottles were test tubes smuggled from a lab that Inti would only describe as *bad*.

At best guess, the plastic bottles had collected at this point, probably bobbing unseen on the other side of the barrier. Those in glass containers must have cracked and sunk, creating a concentration of small stones and sigilcraft at the barrier's base, all of which combined to boost Inti's signal.

Boon's presence raised no alarms, so he kept as close as he could. Two guys, passing acquaintances, both way off the grid, both in need of help. Some nights, Inti sounded so fragile. Boon had hated to leave him, but he needed to do more than keep the kid company. So even though he knew it'd probably frighten the crosser, Boon took action.

He left.

There was a string of islands in the vicinity. Not close-close, but close enough.

Weeks later, Boon was still commuting between the two.

Belly to board, he grimly paddled toward the faint light already showing on the eastern horizon. By mid-high, the sun had dried his hair and fur, and he caught a wave and rode it past a barrier that had been tuned to him since way back when he'd first learned to surf.

His approach had been noted.

Two ladies waited for him on the beach, one with arms folded and scowl firmly in place, the other waving her whole arm in cheery welcome.

Dealing with females was usually a no-go, but Boon wasn't in any position to be choosy. It did help that these two were … safe. Priska wasn't even remotely canine and only eyed him with distaste. And while friendlier, Reaver Navarro was both entirely professional and excessively pregnant.

"Boon! Welcome back!"

"Hey, there, Lupe." And with a nod to her companion, he added, "Priska."

"Anything from Inti today?" asked Lupe.

"Hard to say." Boon looked off the way he'd come. Inti hadn't been showing up every night anymore, and it worried him. "I placed that chunk of green in a pretty little reef near the bearing you set. How many more before the array is complete?"

"One last stone," she promised. "Then I should be able to get a better sense of what you're dealing with."

He grunted and shifted into a respectful posture. "Any other sorts of communication?"

These islands were uncharted for good reason, and Priska hadn't appreciated him dropping by unannounced. She was also the only person with the authority to get messages out. There had been a steady stream of them, but they were relayed the slow way. Hardly better than a message in a bottle. Boon knew the system was in place to protect this enclave and its people. And they *were* making progress.

Sinder unraveled the resort's complex application requirements.

Argent sniffed out their supply lines and booked a suite.

Twineshaft would arrive any day now, and Jacques and Akira weren't far behind.

One last stone, and they'd be as ready as they could be on this end.

"Boon?" Lupe was studying him. "You're severely depleted. When is the last time you slept?"

He firmed his stance and waved off her concern. "That's real nice of you to ask, but I'll be fine. Been catching naps. I'm used to making do."

She traded a look with Priska, who only shrugged. Lupe repeated, "Was Inti able to pass you any messages last night?"

Boon rubbed the back of his neck. "Most of what Inti's said is on the gibberish side of sensible."

"Is he using code?" Lupe asked.

"Could be, I suppose. Maybe he ran out of things to say. Or it could be he's been dosed. Or dream-addled. Or hampered. Or hurt." Boon hated to think of it. Hated being kept from the kid. Hated feeling useless.

"What did he say?" Lupe pressed.

There'd been some strange messages. Or pieces of messages. But ever since the last one—*the winds have abandoned them*—this woman had wanted to hear them all. Boon didn't see the harm in sharing.

"Guess there were a couple," he admitted, dragging his toe through warm sand. "The kid said, 'two moons and a beam.'"

Priska snorted.

"More impressions," murmured Lupe.

Boon considered and nodded. Ever since Inti's retreat from

sensible reports, he'd been dropping hints about lorefolk. "Definitely a recurring theme."

Priska suddenly volunteered, "He could be starstruck."

"What would that be?"

She made a face. "It would be a little like being pollinated. Close contact with *any* imp can be … affecting."

Boon glanced at the thick jungle beyond the sloping beach. "Stars, huh?"

"You disbelieve?" Priska challenged.

"Nope. Wolves just know more about moonbeams than they do about the other sky clans." Boon grit his teeth and casually asked, "Where are we on your calendar?"

"It's nearly November," said Lupe. "But what else did Inti pass along?"

Tail low, mood lower, Boon relayed the kid's latest message. "Do you hear the stars crying?"

Ч

HEART OF A WOLF

Pim strolled down the gangway, scanning the picturesque harbor with its black sands and turquoise waters. The heat had a caressing quality that was sultry enough to make a swim sound appealing. Beyond the beach, lush jungle crowded steep slopes, and through the dense foliage, graceful rooflines showed—pastel stucco and fluted tile, wrought iron over stained glass.

No one else disembarked with her, which perpetuated the sense of being the island's only guest. It made her uneasy.

Or maybe it was Linlu Dimityblest who'd made her uneasy, with his wistful smile and his cryptic plea. This was exactly how the most thrilling cases always started, and Pim knew without a doubt that Aloora Longstride would have acted to protect the moth. Indeed, she rather hoped this represented a fresh mystery.

After filming wrapped, Pim hadn't wanted to lose touch with

the person she'd become for the cameras. For nearly a decade, she'd immersed herself in wolf culture, embracing their attitudes and ideals. Even off-set, Pim tried to adopt wolvish ways. The experience had become increasingly transformative. After a couple of seasons, she'd traded the temporary sigil at the base of her spine for a permanent tattoo, determined to never again put away her tail.

Of all the awards she'd been presented, the thing she treasured most was a brief note from Adoona-soh Elderbough, spokesperson for the wolf clans. She'd congratulated Pim, thanking her for giving the packs a place in the American peace process. But the reason Pim had framed the letter was a single comment, made in closing. *"You have the heart of a wolf."*

Pim suspected that she wasn't a very good wolf. Wolvish customs kept getting tangled up with feline instincts. But she could aspire. In her heart of hearts, Pim's home was no longer a hearth. It was a den.

One path lay before her, and she followed it through a set of sliding glass doors. Cool air swirled, and she removed her floppy hat and sunglasses to peer at the lobby. Here, finally, there were signs of other people.

Quiet conversations hummed just out of view. A pianist teased soft melodies from the baby grand tucked in one corner. Ice clinked against glass in the direction of a lounge. And Pim would have sworn there was a cosset somewhere nearby, skillfully blanketing the place in serene vibes.

There was no front desk, and her shipboard cortege hadn't mentioned anything about check-in procedures. What to do?

Just then, a set of doors across the way whooshed open, and a woman hurried through, spotted her, and hastened over with a funny little skip-jog. "I'm so sorry! I'm a teensy bit late, but it's so easy to lose track of time here. One of this place's finer qualities, I assure you!"

"You work here?"

"I started that way, and they still like me to pitch in, especially when there are newcomers to greet. I'm assigned to incoming Americans, which is why you're getting me."

The woman was about Pim's own height, with sun-streaked brown hair in a messy bun, a wide mouth tinted by gloss, and wideset brown eyes. She wore seashell jewelry, and Pim could see the straps of a swimsuit under her sundress. For the most part, she smelled like sunscreen and salt water.

Thrusting out a hand for an entirely human handshake, she said, "I'm Elara."

Pim hesitated.

Elara leveled the hand so it was palm up, somewhat more in accordance with Amaranthine tradition. Pim rested her fingertips there, as courtesy dictated, but she wanted to bring up her requirements. Which had been very specific.

"Is there a problem?"

And just like that, Pim made up her mind that there wasn't. Sliding her fingers between Elara's she curled her tail around the woman's ankle and took a receptive attitude. "There's no problem whatsoever."

"Great. So! I know this place backward and forward. Do you want a quick tour, an extensive tour, or no tour at all?"

"What do you recommend?"

"How about I show you all of my favorite spots, and you can decide if that makes us friends."

An offer of friendship? Was this part of the resort's usual operations? Or did Elara have a personal agenda? Pim wanted to be sure of her footing. "Are you a fan?"

Elara didn't even hesitate. "Isn't everyone?" she asked brightly.

Pim gave in with grace. "All right. Show me around."

"Say … are you comfortable with touch? Not everyone is, but I am."

"A strange question," Pim said lightly. Their hands were still clasped, and Elara *had* to feel the fur tickling her ankles.

"Granted, but … I'm still holding off until you make up your mind about me."

"I'm entirely at fault." Pim averted her gaze and eased closer. "Apologies. Have I hurt a sister?"

"Oh," Elara said, sounding awed. Her free hand came to rest lightly against Pim's back, the beginnings of an embrace. "Not actually, but … oh, could you say that again?"

Ah, Pim did like to be asked. Rubbing their cheeks together, she purred, "Sister?"

Elara chuckled. "I bet everyone falls in love with you. Like, immediately."

"Usually. Were you hoping for a romantic entanglement?"

"Let's start as friends." Her expression was open, and her scent was bright.

Pim had somehow expected to be in seclusion for the duration of her stay. Friendship was a pleasant prospect. "So you're comfortable with touch?"

"Casual kinds. A total hugger." Elara quietly confessed, "I'd waste away if it weren't for the massage therapists and hairdressers here. I *need* to connect."

Pim tucked her arm through Elara's and leaned into her. "Am I making you nervous?"

"God, yes. But in the *nicest* way. Don't stop. Ever."

Elara ushered Pim out the same doors through which she'd arrived, leading her along a covered breezeway that looked out over a Zen garden. Elara pointed to various entryways as they went, listing, "Saltwater pool, heated pools, walking trails, path to the beach, path to the overlook. Oh, this one's important. I'll show you the best spot to get coffee."

They took a turning, which led into an inner courtyard with shops selling luxury items and gourmet foodstuffs. Elara sashayed right up to one of the counters, greeted the barista by name, and invited Pim to choose a beverage. There was indeed coffee, but other drinks featured on the menu board were works of art, poured over ice and fruit in tall, slender glasses. They even added tiny umbrellas. Pim was beginning to feel properly pampered.

Once they were tucked away at a table for two under a flower-draped pergola, Pim lobbed one of her favorite conversation starters. "Are you aware that my clan has a reputation for promiscuity?"

"Right to it, then?" Elara toyed with her straw. "I try not to give credence to gossip, even if it titillates. I mean … just because your clan has a rep doesn't mean you're that kind of girl."

Pim hummed.

"Unless that was your way of telling me you're that kind of girl." Elara's smile didn't waver.

"I'm not typical." That was blatant understatement, but Pim wasn't ready to go into further detail.

Elara scooted to the edge of her chair and said, "I might not put much stock in gossip, but I *can* be nosy. May I be nosy?"

"Questions? Fire away. I've probably heard them all before."

"You get crazy ones?"

"All the time."

She reached a hand halfway across the table. "Do ladies of the cat clans *really* keep harems filled with pretty-boy felines?"

"Most do acquire a few consorts."

"You don't?"

Pim shook her head. "I prefer the company of females."

Elara's gaze turned dreamy. "*I'd* like a few consorts. Any chance you'd acquire a few, then share them with me?"

It was a joke, but the subtext made it even easier for Pim to relax. Elara liked boys. Pim liked girls. That would make friendship uncomplicated.

"I like flirting," Pim warned.

Those big brown eyes widened. "Are you going to flirt with me?"

Pim couldn't help laughing. "You *want* me to."

"So much!" Drumming her fingers over her heart, she said, "I'm all aflutter, and it feels *good*."

"Nobody around here has the good sense to smuggle you into their harem? I'm shocked."

"I'm not sure anyone here is sensible." Elara eased away, slouching into her chair. She plucked the tiny umbrella from her drink and stuck it into her bun. "And I'm under certain restrictions."

Pim frowned at the sudden mood shift. "Is that an employee policy? Your bosses don't want you to … comingle?"

Elara shook her head. "You'll see after your appointment with Dr. Kodoku tomorrow. We all get a list of dos and don'ts. It's lengthy and ridiculously detailed, but not onerous."

Wait.

Wait, wait.

"You're one of his clients?"

Elara tapped her nose. "Samesies! We're in this together, girlfriend."

5

CALL ME JACQUES

Jacques stretched out an arm and twiddled his fingers to get Akira's attention. His nephew waved back, turned to the three dowagers he'd somehow befriended, and apologized profusely for abandoning their shuffleboard game.

Hurrying over, he knelt beside Jacques' lounge chair.

"Good boy," he drawled.

"Yeah, yeah. For you, I'll be good."

"Having fun?"

"Sure. I was in last place, though. Never played before, and it's harder than it looks."

Jacques smirked. "I'll make inquiries, see if his lordship wants to add leisure sports to the grounds. Perhaps alongside a croquet lawn and cricket pitch."

Akira smiled faintly. "Is that why you called me over?"

"*Non*. It's time to reapply. Or to retreat."

"I vote retreat."

"Right." Jacques stood and reached for his dressing gown. "Shall we?"

The cruise ship was a vast thing, filled to the brim with Hawaii-bound vacationers. In theory, they should have been able to blend in, lay low, and relax before they jumped ships. But Akira kept making friends, and Jacques saw no harm in letting him ease into the role he'd have to play.

It also gave Jacques time to get into character. Which was turning out to be wretchedly revealing. He'd made promises to Argent involving a temporary shift in his devotion. For the foreseeable future, Jacques belonged entirely to Akira.

Every instinct had rebelled at the seeming betrayal, and yet Jacques surprised himself. He hadn't realized that he *could* devote himself to someone other than Argent. Which begged the question … did he want to?

While they waited for the elevator, Jacques pulled his boy-toy against his side.

Akira came easily, glancing up with an amused smile. Which was all wrong for the relationship they were meant to have. Three days of vacation would have to be enough. It was time to get serious.

"I'm starting now," Jacques warned.

"Okay …?"

Which was frustrating enough to make Jacques pull his hair. They'd be among Amaranthine soon, and within the clans, nuance was everything. Akira might be able to posture like a wolf and interpret innumerable avian head-tilts, but they needed a different kind of body language now. Something entirely human. Something that *had* to look natural.

So Jacques kissed him. Or tried to.

Because his pretty-in-pastels partner immediately developed a case of lock-jaw, complicated by deer-in-the-headlights syndrome.

The elevator dinged, and Jacques hustled him inside, employing the keycard that would give them a priority ride to the executive suites on the top floor.

"S-sorry, Uncle Jackie," Akira whispered. "That came out of nowhere, an–"

"Lesson time," Jacques decreed. "And get used to calling me *Jacques*. Uncle Jackie will be waiting for you at the end of all this."

Akira pressed into his side in a common—and entirely clannish—plea for shelter.

"There's a start. Every time you do this, put your hand here." Jacques guided him. "Pinky and ring finger under the waistband, please."

He could tell Akira was trying not to look shocked.

Anyone could tell he was trying not to look shocked.

"We're not playing house with little crossers. Nobody will believe I'm the rake and you're my debauched darling simply because we say so." Jacques held Akira's hand in place. "You can go all shy, but only because you're self-conscious about letting others see how much you want me."

Akira looked ready to protest, but the elevator dinged again.

Jacques took him by the hand and led him gently. Inside their suite, he gave Akira some space. "I reasoned with you. I warned you. I pacted with you. And yet I've shocked you?"

"I didn't mind the flirting."

"Flirting is harmless." Jacques made up his mind. "I suppose I'll have to seduce you."

"I don't think ...." Akira gestured vaguely between them. "I've never really ...."

"Lord. I know. How long do you think I've been watching over you and Suuzu? You're a couple of innocents. And I *told* Argent as much, but he did insist, and so must I." Jacques did pull his hair then, because he hated himself for the harm he could cause. "Look, I think we'll be fine if you trust me a lot and fall for me a little. I'll make it easy."

"But we're family."

"Consider yourself temporarily disowned."

Akira dropped to a seat on the edge of the bed. "You didn't mention this part when Suuzu was around."

"Can you blame me?" Jacques sighed. "He knows, though. In fact, I think Suuzu understood what would happen better than you did. Strike that. Better than you *do*."

"We talked about the mission. I agreed to do my part."

"That was talk, and as they say, talk is cheap. This is where things get expensive." He hesitated to ask. "Please, tell me you kissed *him* first?"

"Uhh ... yeah. Once."

Jacques sighed and came to kneel in front of the bed. "You can be yourself. But I need a version of yourself that's intrigued by what I'm offering. And open to exploring a budding attraction."

"I'll be terrible at this."

"Yes." Jacques touched his knee. "But I can make up the difference."

Akira was definitely having trouble breathing.

"Lord, don't cry. We're not a bad match, as couples go. I'm flippant, and you're earnest. Those are attractive opposites."

Akira's eyes widened, then watered. "So we'll have balance?"

"In our own way, yes." Jacques scooted a little closer. "I'll keep it light. We'll have some fun. You can even ask me for advice. Very practical for an eventual reunion with your lovelorn phoenix."

"Don't call him that," Akira grumbled. "He's been patient with me. And he's being brave right now."

Jacques was relieved by that spark. Akira was rattled but rallying. "Entirely true. We should choose a codeword for him, so we can mention him casually. Does he have a pack nickname?"

"*Of course* he does," Akira mumbled. "Don't you *dare* tease."

"Now, now. I'm the flippant one. Remember?" But Jacques leaned up to kiss Akira's jaw in wordless apology. "Keep it a secret. Anything will do."

But Akira's face crumpled, and he whispered, "Earnest. The packs call him Earnest."

Jacques covered his eyes. Of all the dumb luck. "Do they mean in general, or do they mean about you?"

"Both. Probably."

"Wolves. They do tend to define people by their attachments." He eased his arms around Akira's waist. "You do see the compliment?"

"*Now.*"

Jacques chuckled. "It is my good fortune to be bound as I am, to two earnest boys. Remember that I'm not trying to come between you. I'm simply vying for a place in your hearts."

"Stupid," Akira grumbled. "You know we love you, Uncle Jackie."

"This I know, and know full well," he agreed softly. "But Uncle Jackie is not here. You must deal with *Jacques* and his considerable devotion."

Akira just sat there, bewildered.

"Intrigued," Jacques coached. "Open. Curious."

"Yes, Jacques. I'm ...." His voice caught, but he said, "I am willing."

6

THE DOCTOR WILL SEE YOU NOW

The rap on Pim's door came before sunrise. Unusual in human circles, but hardly surprising among the Amaranthine, who generally passed their nights in other activities besides sleep. At the door was a female of some indeterminate clan with bobbed purple hair tucked behind her ears.

"Pim Moonprowl." She glanced between her clipboard and Pim, perhaps comparing her to a photograph. "If it is convenient, Dr. Kodoku will see you now."

Without another word, she led Pim along hushed halls. A keycard was needed for both of the security doors they passed through along the way, as well as an unmarked office door. The interior was surprisingly lavish, rich reds predominant. Sheer curtains stirred at tall windows that stood open, welcoming in all the heat and humidity of a tropical night.

A soft tinkling brought her attention to a series of tiny windchimes hung at intervals before the windows. Their movement puzzled her until she realized that it was being caused by an oscillating fan, which hummed discreetly behind a potted palm. Wherever the thing wasn't pointed, the air felt unnaturally close and still.

"Here she is!" called the doctor she only knew from their correspondence. "Mistress Moonprowl, we are delighted that you have placed yourself in our hands."

He was half a head taller than Pim, which meant he couldn't have been six feet tall. Glasses perched on his thin nose, and they shimmered faintly with sigilcraft. His ensemble was tastefully eclectic and impossible to pinpoint, not traditional to any clan she knew, and not displaying any identifying crest.

Her attention snagged briefly on his shoes, the soles of which were suspiciously thick. He probably only had an inch or two on her and was self-conscious about his middling height. Her opinion dropped a notch. Height wasn't important. Force of personality was key.

The room was dimly lit by a series of illuminated crystals in glass lanterns. Pink and amber, they bathed everything in warmth, lending flattering color to pale skin, but making it difficult to discern other colors. His long hair was simply dark, and his scent was obscured by the heady perfume of flowers, which must have been blooming right outside.

She offered her palms, expecting an exchange of greetings.

He clasped her hands and drew her to one of a pair of chairs facing his desk. Sitting beside her, so close their knees touched, he said, "You did well to trust us."

Pim was elated to hear it. "May I know your name, Kindred?"

"Oh, we shall not stand upon formality here. Simply call me Dr. Kodoku."

She would. Of course she would. But ... on some level, she knew he was being rude. Many of the oldest and most traditional of Amaranthine accused her generation of being too hasty, forever cutting corners instead of giving proper time to courtesies.

Dr. Kodoku cleared his throat.

Whoops. She'd been tuning him out, and he looked faintly annoyed. Well, he'd been rude first. Pim sweetly asked, "Yes?"

"Shall we try that again?"

She merely arched her brows invitingly.

He smiled and said, "You will answer my questions."

Pim almost rolled her eyes. Of course she would. Wasn't she forever answering questions? It was all part of being famous. All part of being an ambassador for peace.

"Tell me your name."

"Pimiko Moonprowl." She pursed her lips. Normally, she didn't hand out her full name. These days, she was always Pim.

"Do you have consorts?"

"No." Not that it was any of his business. But he was going to be her doctor. These were probably standard questions.

Dr. Kodoku still had her hand cradled between his, and his thumb was caressing its back. "Have you a partner?"

"I am not bonded."

He hummed. "What I meant to ask is ... are you sexually active?"

"Not with males." She pulled her hand free and fixed him with a glare that dared him to comment.

From across the room, the other female—a nurse, perhaps—acidly remarked, "Perhaps *that* is the source of her Waning."

"Pay no mind to Futari," the doctor murmured, his gaze never leaving Pim's face. "Have you never coupled with males."

"I have."

"And you did not conceive?"

She bared her teeth. "I did."

Dr. Kodoku rose and crossed to his desk, pulled a file around and flipped through its contents. "Here it is. Oh, I see! Two mis-carriages. What did the healers have to say?"

Pim swallowed hard. She was used to sympathy or pity. He only seemed intrigued, as if her situation were some new twist in his research. Lip curling, she grudgingly answered, "Nothing helpful."

His nurse quietly said, "She is resisting."

He raised a hand, as if to block her out. "Never mind that. How long since you last attempted to conceive?"

"Not since the second miscarriage."

"Really? How odd. I thought felines were more … insatiable."

She wanted to slap him.

The doctor eyed her warily and spoke more firmly. "Best never mind *that*, as well. Come now, Mistress Moonprowl. You *know* I am only asking because I must."

Yes, of course. Doctors did need intimate details and honesty. She needed to trust him. He was studying the Waning, after all. Looking for solutions. Fulfilling hopes.

"Would you be willing to take bedmates who are not feline?"

Elara's face came immediately to mind. "Yes."

"Adventurous!" he murmured. "I wonder which could be persuaded. Moonlight would suit you best, but males are few and far between. The stars are withdrawn, and the rainbow … impossible thing."

"Do you mean Impressions?" she blurted, feeling silly now that the notion was out in the open. Fairy tales were lovely. Some were even sexy. But they weren't likely to give her the baby she longed to hold.

Dr. Kodoku surprised her. "If it comes to that, yes. There are arrangements I can make."

He sounded serious.

Pim's heart beat faster.

"What about endorsements?" he asked. "Should we manage to leave you with child, would you be willing to—discreetly, you understand—share your experience with others seeking ways to overcome the Waning?"

"*If* you succeed, I would consider it, but I make no guarantees. Just as you have made none."

"Fair, fair," he murmured. "Tell, me, Mistress Moonprowl. Tell me the secret that most shames you."

"I could not protect my children." She felt ill enough to vomit.

He returned to the chair by her side. "That was not your fault."

She could only believe him. So many others had said the same. But it didn't help.

"Now, tell me something less terrible. Something that might give someone like me sway over your future choices."

What did this have to do with her medical history or current health? But Pim felt she *should* answer. "A secret?" she asked, putting off the inevitable.

"Yes." His hand caressed her cheek, and he brought his face close. "What have you never dared to tell anyone? What have you been hiding from the world?"

"I want to be a wolf."

"Is that right?" He looked at her over the lenses of his glasses. His eyes were so red.

She blushed, because it wasn't entirely right. And she suddenly really wanted to speak the truth. "I identify as a wolf. I'm a wolf."

"Useless," remarked the nurse.

"Futari, the curtains," he ordered.

With a sulky look, she began pulling heavy drapes across the windows.

"Pim," Dr. Kodoku crooned. "*May* I call you Pim? You are rather out of practice, are you not? But rest assured, I will have you ready to receive in no time."

Something in those silken words screamed a warning.

"Come along, Pim. We must make you comfortable." With an innocent smile, he said, "An exam is only natural, yes?"

"Yes." But this wasn't the sort of room in which doctors worked. And the examination table he made her sit upon was draped in red silk.

Again, she was looking into a pair of lovely, lurid eyes, and Dr. Kodoku said, "An hour should do. Sleep for an hour, Pim."

That sounded nice. She teetered, and he lowered her gently. There were pillows waiting, and that voice she so wanted to trust loomed near.

"A wolf?" he asked. "I suppose that explains the tail."

The nurse said something, but Pim couldn't quite hear. Sleep was what the doctor wanted. She should sleep. But sleep was so difficult for her. She had very particular requirements.

Futari's monotone came from closer quarters. "She is resisting."

"Sleep now, Pim. You must," he urged, his fingers in her hair.

Yes. A good idea. Wonderful, even.

Just as she was drifting off, he spoke again. And she wanted to hear, since Dr. Kodoku had the most extraordinary voice.

"A wolf," he repeated, sounding amused. "I wonder, will our kitten howl?"

7

BAD

oke. Poke, poke. Poke.

Pim woke to the gray light of early morning, a clinging fog that dripped through nearby greenery, and raucous birdcalls. There was a white beach umbrella overhead, and a faint hum drew her attention to a discreet box that no doubt hid a pool filter. Recognition gradually dawned. She was beside the large saltwater swimming pool Elara had pointed out during yesterday's tour.

A finger poked her cheek.

Slowly, she dragged that detail into alignment with the others. Pim was being poked. That's what had woken her. But when had she dozed off? And why here?

Those answers came unbidden.

A restless night. An early morning swim. Because the clinic had world-class amenities, and she'd wanted to enjoy them.

She fumbled for—and found—a plain white robe and drew it

more tightly around her body. Something was wrong. Had she gone for a swim? Her skin felt prickly and unpleasant. From the salt water? Pim couldn't think what else might have happened, even though this wasn't like her. She hated salt water. The hot pools were more to her taste.

Another poke.

Pim turned her head and gazed into a pair of round amber eyes under startled brows.

"Awake?" he asked.

She tried to move away and found that she was reclining in a lounge chair.

"Hush, quiet. Hush, calm. Hush, lady." The male, who looked barely older than a boy, raised both hands and a thick tail covered in gingery fur. "No harm. No hurt. Only Inti."

"You're ... Inti?"

He crouched a small distance from her, probably arm's length, given the poking. She appreciated that he stayed where he was. Something about their relative positions left her feeling vulnerable.

Presenting his palms with childlike gravity, he said, "Inti is Inti."

"I'm Pim."

His gaze softened, but his tone stayed light, almost silly. "I know."

"You're a crosser."

"Halves and wholeness." Tapping his chest, he said, "Inti is a silly monkey boy."

She shifted uncomfortably. "Do you work here? I thought there were no males in this section."

"No harm. No hurt," he repeated. "Watch Inti. Please?"

From an inner pocket, he produced a lump of clay, which he

kneaded and smoothed before flattening it on his palm. Pulling a sharpened twig from behind his ear, he began to poke and pierce the stuff.

"Are you making something?" Pim sat up straighter, trying to see.

"Crafty, crafty, sigilcraft." He peeped at her, almost shyly, and said, "Inti likes wolves."

"You mean Aloora Longstride?"

"No, no, not know. Inti means Pim." Another stolen glance. "Pim identifies as wolf, and Inti is glad. Inti likes wolves."

"How ...?" Pim struggled with a vague memory of someone wresting away her secret.

"Inti listened at the window. Inti heard."

That was unsettling. "You were at the window to my room?"

"No, no. The red room."

Red. She didn't like red. Never wore it. And right now, she couldn't bear to think of it.

The crosser kept his gaze firmly fixed on his handiwork. "Pim was told to never mind. Pim was told to forget."

She growled weakly.

"Pim does not remember?"

"I don't."

He gave her a longer, more searching look, then gently said, "That might be for the best."

It was a different tone than before, a truer one. This monkey boy presented himself as simpleminded and silly, but the sigilcraft forming under his hands held a subtle strength. He smiled faintly, and she felt the force of a personality that so many males lacked.

Doctor Kodoku's face surfaced hazily in her memory.

"Have you forgotten everything, wolf?" Inti asked. "Have you forgotten Linlu?"

Pim narrowed her eyes. "There *was* a moth."

"Yes." Inti smiled encouragingly.

"A secretary or lawyer or something. And he talked to me. He wanted me to come here."

"Yes, yes."

"And he spoke of two moons."

"Yes, yes, yes." Inti gently poked her arm. "Moon, moon, Moonprowl. The stars sing of you, that is what Linlu says."

"Are you Linlu's friend?"

The twig still flashed against clay. "Inti is the friend of many lost things—moths and men and trees and stars. Lost things and little ones. Crossers like Inti, but not like Inti. But most of all, Inti is the friend of wolves."

"You want to be my friend?"

"Inti needs friends. Friends need Inti." He held out the clay.

The pattern was startlingly intricate, and Pim could sense its strength. "Are you a ward?"

"*This* is a ward." And from an inner pocket, he produced a second clay disk, but this one had hardened, giving more permanence to the sigilcraft. "Same. See? My sigil. My heart. No harm. Take, take, take."

She accepted the hardened disk, turning it over in her hand. The medallion was definitely his handiwork, full of mischievous intent and simple intensity. She was drawn to it. This sigilcraft—like its maker—felt safe. "What's it for?"

"For the flowers and for the stars and for the sway. Inti wants to protect his wolf friends." Tail flipping into a question mark, he took a more serious tone. "Has it begun to work?"

Pim wasn't sure what he meant. But gradually, her senses sharpened, even though she hadn't realized they were dull. Jumbled memories began to straighten out, but she shied away from them. "What *is* this place?" she whispered.

Inti nodded once and said, "Bad."

"We should leave."

"Cannot. Would not. Not alone." His tail flipped around, and he hugged it to his chest. "Would you go without Elara?"

The question was so easy to answer. "No."

"Inti *likes* wolves." Dipping into another pocket, he pulled out a packet of what first looked like blue dental floss ... but the labeling indicated it was surgical thread. "Ward, please. And truest form. Shift, shift, shift."

Pim rarely appreciated bossing, but the crosser's request implied trust. Many were wary of Amaranthine from the predatory clans. Cats, especially, had the reputation for toying with friends and enemies alike.

"Make room," she said, finding her feet.

Inti took two steps back, crouched again, and beckoned for her to hurry.

With a quick glance to assure herself that they were alone, Pim took truest form.

The crosser's smile was sweetness itself. "Blue, blue, blue eyes. So nice. Inti knows another wolf with blue eyes."

She nosed his forehead, accepting the compliment ... and his easy acceptance of her clan preference, even though he was barely a whisker's length away.

He showed the clay sigil, now strung on blue thread. "Wolves like necklaces."

Clever monkey, to call it something other than a collar. Pim licked his ear.

Carefully pushing past long white fur, he looped her new jewelry around her neck. "Many wolves have blue eyes, but the nearest one's are yellow. He is good. He can help."

Pim wasn't sure how she felt about that. Another wolf? Would he hear her claim and scoff?

Inti finished his knotting and stepped back, hiding his hands behind his back. "Thank you for your trust, Pim-wolf."

When she returned to speaking form, the necklace disappeared from view, but she could still feel its effects. "Good idea," she said, touching her throat. "Nobody can take it from me."

"Tricky, tricky, trickster," he agreed.

"This other wolf, the one with yellow eyes. He's on this island, too?" she asked.

A moment later, it registered what she'd said. The *other* wolf. Because *she* was a wolf. She'd said it right out loud, that secret hope, her secret truth.

"Soon. Stars say soon," said Inti. "Stars know secrets. Secret stars."

"Do you mean Impressions?"

"Yes." He looked her right in the eye. "Kodoku keeps them in cages."

Suddenly feeling conspicuous, Pim sank to a seat at the foot of the lounge chair. Inti crouched before her, an expectant expression on his face, putting her in familiar territory. In danger and in charge. Well ... this wasn't the set of *Pure Instinct*, and she didn't have her team. But wouldn't the general approach to a case be the same in real life?

"So, you need my help. I can do that. What are our goals?" she asked. "To free the imps?"

Inti nodded, shook his head, and nodded again. "There is a barrier. And a … zone. You can feel it if you go down by the water. Inti will help break the barrier."

She remembered episodes like this. As the team's tracker, she was essential in such operations. "Cut it off at the source, right? Where's the anchor?"

"Not sure," he admitted. "Many doors, many locks."

"Doors have knobs, Locks have keys," she said wisely.

The crosser chuckled. "Inti likes Pim."

Which was a start, but not much of one. "Barriers before cages, then? Do we try to get the information out of Dr. Kodoku?"

Inti shook his head. "Swaying dragons."

That gave her pause. And shifted matters into terrible clarity. "That's bad."

He scratched at a thick sideburn. "One wolf is good; two wolves is better."

"Your yellow-eyed wolf?"

"Soon." Inti cocked an ear, listening to something. His expression shifted, and his tail slunk around her wrist. "First, first, first. Elara likes you? Elara trusts you?"

"Yes. We get along."

"Elara *needs* you."

Pim tested the air, at a loss. "How do you know?"

"Stars try. Stars hope. Stars help."

Which was less than she wanted to know, but enough to go on. "Where is she?"

Inti grimaced. "Red room."

8

CLIPPED WINGS

You were listening outside the red room earlier."

"Yes."

Pim tried to pull details out of the haze of her memory. "The windows were open."

"Yes, yes."

That made things easy. Stupidly easy. "So I can drop into the garden outside his office and go in that way."

Inti pointed up. "The barrier."

"Even if there's a ceiling, I can fly under it."

"Have you tried?" His tone took that turn into sobriety. "Everyone on this island has had their wings clipped."

Pim wanted to argue, but it was easier to just prove Inti wrong. However, the lift that was usually as effortless as thought simply didn't come. And that scared her. Until it angered her. "I want that barrier *gone*."

"Yes, yes, yes."

But there were more important things to deal with first. "You didn't need to fly to reach those windows."

Inti shrugged. "Trees."

"I can climb," she said, flexing manicured claws.

"Follow, follow," he urged, loping away and leaping into the branches of a nearby tree.

Though it was harder than it would have been without the drag of gravity, Pim had no trouble keeping up. In truth, she found their brief chase through the treetops invigorating. Predatory instincts were stirring, and a growl was building in her chest.

Inti drew up short, and she alighted nearby. He held up his hands and walked along the tree limb to where she poised. Was he speaking to her? It was hard to hear over the rushing in her ears, the rumble in her throat.

"Hush, hush, softly." He pressed his hands to her cheeks. "There is bad, and there is worse. Pim must be calm and quiet."

She sucked in air, exhaled through her nose, curled her tail around her ankles, and nodded.

Inti dropped to the ground. Pim followed, landing beside him. He scampered forward on light feet and peeped through the window for a few moments, then beckoned for her to join him. Knowing just what was needed, she dove right through the window, rolling into a wary crouch.

The fan whirred back and forth. Papers fluttered on the desk. Soft notes came from one of the windchimes overhead.

"Where is she?" Pim muttered.

Her companion slid through the window, rose to his full height, gaze darting around the room. Then he strode to one of the heavy red drapes and pulled it aside, revealing an alcove.

Elara lay on a low bed, partially draped in a silk robe, red patches and running makeup on her cheeks. Pim hurried to her side, hissing through her teeth at the scents that assaulted her, and patted Elara's cheek, calling her name in hushed tones.

Inti dragged a sheet over her legs.

Pim asked, "Why would he do this?"

"He plays with his favorites." Inti grimaced. "He likes his little experiments."

"Why hasn't he been reported? Why hasn't he been stopped?"

"Kodoku is a dragon."

"Is this clinic some kind of con?"

"No. No, no." Inti sighed. "Many babies are born here. He can give you a child."

She flinched. That *couldn't* be the answer to the Waning. "Me and a dragon ...?"

"There are imps. There are trees. There are seeds."

Pim bit her lip. "And we're all in cages."

Inti's thin lips twisted into a smile. "Cages have doors. Locks have picks."

Just then, the office door opened, and the nurse from earlier stepped into the room. Her gaze immediately fixed on Pim, who growled a warning.

"I told him you would be trouble." Closing the door, she leaned against it, looking wholly unconcerned.

Pim glanced Inti's way, but the crosser had gone missing. Adopting her best imperious air, she asked, "What's wrong with her?"

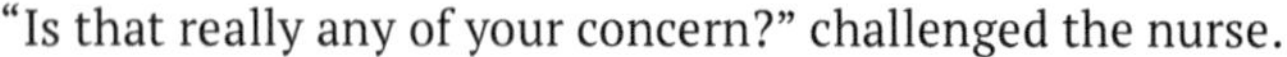

"Nothing."

"She won't wake."

"Is that really any of your concern?" challenged the nurse.

"We forged a bond of sisterhood."

"In one day?" Arms folded, hip cocked, the female muttered, "How nice for you."

Turning her attention to her friend, Pim shook and patted and even pinched. "You did something."

"He did."

"But you were here." She remembered that part now. "The whole time."

"Unlike some, I do as I am told." Flicking her fingers toward Elara, she added, "Dr. Perrine is here as part of a contractual arrangement. Father performs many tests and exams, and he sometimes collects samples."

"Not anymore. Elara is under my protection."

"Really?" The nurse drifted closer. "Are you taking that one as a consort?"

"I'm not her lady mistress. I told you. She's a sister."

"Is that not a *feline* tradition? I thought wolves were all about packmates."

Pim couldn't very well declare Elara her packmate. She had no pack to share. Were there rules for forming one? Every day, Pim ran up against things she simply didn't know about wolf culture. And who was she supposed to ask?

"I wonder what you will do?" The nurse was right beside her now, hugging herself as she peered at Elara. "You say you want a child. Will you abide by clan custom and bed a feline? Or will you chase your convictions and seek a partner from the packs? Would a wolf even consider you?"

"That's none of your business."

"I am only wondering if you had thought this through." She spared Pim a glance. Her eyes were red. "Choices like these always have consequences."

"Who *are* you?"

"Futari."

"Why haven't you screeched for the doctor?"

She shrugged. "Why should I?"

Pim tried again. "Why won't Elara wake?"

Futari sighed. "Let it never be said that I do not understand a bond of sisterhood." Then she calmly said, "Dr. Perrine, wake up. It is time to go."

Elara groaned, low and husky.

"Will you tell the doctor?" Pim demanded.

"I will tell him a truth." Futari nodded toward Elara. "This one is becoming resistant to our influence. Waking ahead of schedule is a sign of increasing unsuitability."

Pim bundled Elara in the sheet, lifted her, and stalked to the window. "I'm keeping her with me."

"You can try." Futari didn't seem to care one way or the other. "But you will be endangering anyone you keep close. They will be used to ensure your compliance."

A threat. They were threatening her? They thought they could push her? Defiance swelled in her soul ... until Elara whined in her arms.

"You are in greater danger than that one," said Futari.

Pausing with her foot on the windowsill, Pim demanded, "Why?"

"My father has plans for you."

9

INVITATION ONLY

isoka leaned against the railing of his cabin's private balcony, watching the water churn away as the ship cut along, trailing a foaming wake. For the first time in many a decade, he had nothing else to do.

The invitation he'd accepted had come with conditions—no cortege, no companion, no outside communication. But in exchange, Hisoka had been promised entrance into a tropical paradise where the whims of the world-famous were made into reality.

Anything one fancied could be provided. For a price.

And Hisoka had been on Pim Moonprowl's wish list.

In the manner of many feline mistresses, she was treating herself to a posh vacation, during which toms of good reputation and noteworthy stamina would see to her every need. While none of these males would be officially bound to Mistress Moonprowl as a consort, she was after more than casual dalliance. All pleasures would be procreative in nature. Pim hoped to be blessed with a child.

The lady didn't interest Hisoka, but the promised paradise did.

"Novi?"

"Here."

"Have you any news from home?" Hisoka wasn't used to being incommunicado.

"Trust the ones you claim to trust," suggested his friend.

"I do. I will." He would have to. "Are we getting close?"

"I could not guess."

"Can you sense her?"

"If I could, I would have gone to her ages ago."

"Not without me."

"We are together in all things."

"Until our promise is fulfilled." Hisoka scanned the uninterrupted horizon line. There was nothing here. Nowhere to search. Nowhere to hide. "Have you passed over this area before?"

"I go where you go."

Early on, they'd searched, skimming back and forth across whole continents. Deserts and seas had come later, for they were all that remained. Much later, Hisoka had sought out hidden places—enclaves that were the homes of isolationists and the tattered remains of ancient groves. All for Nemi. All for naught.

By the time the thrum of engines finally changed, Hisoka had already pulled a vanishing act. On the grounds of a disagreement over the unwarranted application of sigilcraft to his person, Spokesperson Twineshaft politely bowed out. He offered no excuses and begged off any future guest lists, citing his status in the feline registries as "abstaining." Within the hour, all that remained was his packed bag upon the bed, labeled for return, care of Yulwen Dimityblest in Keishi, Japan.

Any would assume he'd taken to the sky, bound for home.

In actuality, he'd taken truest form and hidden under the bed.

No small feat, normally. However, Argent, Michael, and Timur had worked out the necessary sigilcraft. They'd pooled their knowledge to cover Hisoka from head to toe in a variation on a dragon technique for healing sigils, which was anchored to a stone now secreted on Hisoka's person. Michael had traced on the sigilcraft himself. Indeed, Hisoka would have trusted no other to bind him so completely.

The restraints amounted to advantages. He could fade from notice. He had an early warning ward that would trigger at a dragon's approach. An elaborate sigil array on his belly was meant to allow Argent to reach him in dreams. And a dampening effect allowed him to maintain a much smaller size than would normally have been possible.

At a glance, if any managed one, they'd see an ordinary shipboard cat slipping into the shadows.

Leaping to a hideaway tucked between two chimney stacks, Hisoka pointed his nose into the wind, whiskers quivering. There was no sign of land in any direction, but when the engines cut,

Hisoka's hackles went up. With no other warning, the ship glided through a barrier. It tore at him, thrusting him onto his belly, and he growled as he accessed his personal wards, finessing their settings to gain more freedom of movement.

An island appeared, and the ship slowed further as a port came into view.

Hisoka looked back, sifting through his impressions. This barrier's sigilcraft was a potent blend of old and new. Many of the patterns suggested a dragon's workmanship, but the outermost illusions definitely felt foxy, which confirmed growing suspicions that the Rogue had help.

They had no proof it was the Hightip sisters, but Argent believed that Nona and Senna were working against the interests of the Amaranthine Council.

Hisoka had hoped his friend was wrong.

Foxes could be such trouble.

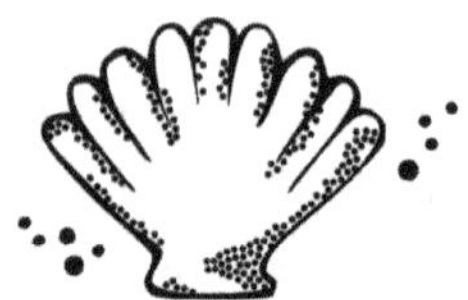

Hisoka smelled a combination of flowers he hadn't encountered in too many years, which might have been nostalgic. But he could no longer hear Novi, and that put a twitch in his tail. The sooner they could dismantle this wretched barrier, the better.

From his perch, Hisoka watched the other conscripted toms disembark. It seemed Pim Moonprowl had a preference for whites, silvers, and grays. Blue eyes were also predominant. Hardly surprising. Her own fur was white, and most lady mistresses fostered the hope that they'd bear a daughter who resembled them.

He wished her well.

His path lay elsewhere.

Dropping to the deck on light paws, he slunk down the gangway, darted into the first available alley, and made for the jungle beyond.

Now that he'd infiltrated the island, Hisoka's next task was to stay out of sight until Inti contacted him. Or until Jacques arrived. Both were needed before they could proceed with Argent's plan.

Hisoka saw no reason not to explore in the meantime. This island would become his hunting ground. Yes, he was trapped, but neither could his prey escape. A pleasing balance.

The barrier's influence was less oppressive the farther inland he moved. He picked up his pace, all springs and bounds. But even through his personal wards, he could feel the limiter. This was a flightless zone? How like a dragon to be jealous for the sky.

He worked his way past another barrier. Aiming for higher ground, Hisoka paused cautiously. Somewhere under the scents of damp earth and overripe fruit, he was catching an odor that gave him pause. Reports had been scarce and scanty, but surely if Inti had known ...!

Hisoka dropped to his belly and eased through the undergrowth.

The hum of insects grew louder. Rotting fruit littered the ground. He sniffed lightly at some of the clutter and confirmed his suspicions. Spoor. So there were other predators in this jungle. And not the usual sort.

He could increase in size, which might dissuade their interest. But he was more inclined to operate beneath it. If he was careful ... ah.

Rounding a particularly large tree, he found himself nose-to-nose with a small child, who stretched out a pudgy clawed hand and grabbed him by the whiskers.

Hisoka immediately took speaking form.

"And hello to you," he said softly.

The boy-child, surely only a toddler, babbled something incomprehensible.

"What language do you speak?" Hisoka inquired. But he was already reassessing his question and posed another. "Do you *have* words, little one?"

The child grumbled around a fistful of rotting fruit, showing no distaste for his scavenged meal.

Hisoka settled himself on the ground and tried to make sense of his discovery. The little one had the mix of characteristics that was common in crossers. But this child didn't carry the scent of humanity, which normally would have suggested he was Kith-kin.

Some of his features were decidedly mouselike—rounded ears, slender tail, and eyes that showed no white. They were thick-lashed and liquid black. Very mouse. Except for the pronged antlers budding above his brow. And the color of his hair, which was resolutely green. Useful for camouflage, certainly. But mystifying when it came to identification.

"Where are your parents?" And because he was curious, Hisoka added, "*What* are your parents?"

The child blinked up at him ... and offered his fruit.

"No, thank you," he murmured, testing the air.

Not only was this small person well-camouflaged, his scent

was unusually subtle. Easily lost amidst the stronger odors that surrounded them.

"Pardon me." Lifting the child, Hisoka proceeded to—as Ever was wont to say—*sniffen* him.

Delighted giggles and nuzzling kisses were the little one's response. Perfectly natural. Entirely trusting. Hisoka felt sure that the child was simply young. He'd grow into his words, given time and someone to teach him.

Warnings buzzed through Hisoka's sigils. Argent's foresight was even more useful than anticipated. "There are dragons here, little one. Wild ones. Did you know the world believes them extinct?"

The boy craned his neck, looking in the correct direction. With a soft chitter, he dropped his fruit and tugged at Hisoka's tunic, trying to burrow underneath. The antlers rather got in his way.

"I agree. You're safer with me. At least until I can locate your kin."

Tucking the sticky child into the crook of one arm, Hisoka held his ground until the crash of foliage would cover the noise of his escape. But he was curious. He leapt into the tree at his back and crouched on a broad limb, wanting a look at the threat.

The warning buzz in Hisoka's sigilcraft fell still, as if Argent's array understood the need for silence. Below, a dragon exploded into view, scales rippling in the sunlight. A whiskered muzzle nosed at the place where Hisoka had been, then lifted to sniff the air. The beast wound its way sinuously around the tree, then charged away in the direction of the port.

"Did you notice his coloring?" Hisoka studied his small passenger, who blinked silently up at him. "Purple scales. Pale underbelly. I couldn't confirm any sort of speckling, but the eyes were definitely red. Do you know what that means, little one?"

The child nestled against him and peeped.

"Yes. I am always where I need to be." Hisoka dropped from the tree and continued on his uphill course. "Now, then. What do you think? Was I here because I needed to see him? Or because you needed an ally?"

A small hand fisted into his tunic, and he burbled more nonsense.

"I'll have to agree. It's usually both."

10

GOING ALL IN

oon lay on his surfboard, low in the water as he stroked back in Inti's direction. He'd tucked the final crystal for Lupe's array snug against his breastbone. It was the biggest of the lot, a pale green that was potent enough to anchor an island. Had one of the local enclaves sacrificed it? Good of them, really. Isolationists weren't famous for lending a helping hand.

Then again, Juuyu was from just such an island.

The defensive sigil set onto Boon's board still hummed with Juuyu's power and personality. Steadfast as the starch in his shirts, keen as the thrill he found in any chase. And then there was Suuzu—same island, same nest. What a softie, especially where Akira was concerned. But plenty of grit, which would give him the polish he needed.

With a grunt, Boon pushed up and sat cross-legged on his board. No sign of land. No sign of ships. Still a while to go before he knocked into that damnable barrier. And on top of everything else, he was missing his crew and feeling guilty about Akira. Suuzu, too, poor kid.

Flopping back into paddling position, Boon muttered, "I'll take my licks if they land."

Juuyu might well be pissed, and Suuzu was probably heartsick. But Inti's tension was real, and the trail had led Boon here. This was a tough choice, but the right choice. Hisoka and Argent had both gone all in.

He paddled onward.

Huh. Was the sun playing tricks on him?

Boon narrowed his eyes, catching some serious glare off the water. Squinting into the blue, he backpedaled to a stop and stared. "Well, now," he called. "This is either a real honor or an unforeseen problem."

Boon had always figured wild imps weren't completely relegated to history, but he hadn't had the pleasure of a personal encounter. Until now.

This guy had serious shine.

And a possible case of skittish.

"Since you're not saying *hey*, I'm guessing you're not a moonbeam. Rumor has it, they can be real chatty." Hopping to his feet, Boon kept the chunk of green clamped between his ankles as he extended a hand. "Star, yeah?"

The imp dipped close enough for fingertips to brush.

"Go on. Grab hold," Boon invited. "You looking for me?"

"Boonmar-fen Elderbough."

"You're not wrong." This was confirming a pile of suspicions. "Any friend of Posy's is a friend of mine."

The imp's eyes widened.

"I never once caught sight of you, but I've always suspected you were somewhere nearby." Boon tapped his nose. "It's nice to finally have some context for a lingering scent."

"I am his secret."

"Fine by me. I don't make a habit of betraying confidences."

"Thank you."

"So … what'll it be? Is this an honor or a problem?"

The imp slid his hand into alignment, so that their palms pressed. *"I can no longer reach Hisoka."*

"Made it through, did he? That's good news." Boon looked off in the direction of the barrier. "That got you worried?"

"He is missing."

Definitely worried, with a side of petulant. Which broke a few impish stereotypes. Kind of killed any chance of summoning up some awe, too. But it was nice to know that stars were people, too. Boon liked people.

"Aaand you're missing him. Understandable. I'm in a similar place. Not used to going solo." Boon nodded to the north. "Any sign of the other guys?"

"They approach. Two days will bring them to this boundary."

"Everything's coming together." And yet he had a star by the hand. "Is there something I need to know?"

The star's grip shifted, and gleaming fingers clung to Boon's wrist. *"There is something I do not know."*

"Okay." Boon wagged his tail for encouragement. "Let's start there. What don't you know?"

"How to press through without falling." The star grimly said, *"I*

do not wish to descend."

"Are you saying there's a way through that barrier?"

"*There is.*" Tension reverberated through his frame. "*I have been warned. There is a trap.*"

"What's anyone expecting to trap way out here?"

"*Impressions. There is a lure. Many have succumbed.*"

He glanced around. "Are there really that many imps around?"

"*Sunbeams, moonbeams, sundry winds, and rainbows.*"

"And stars?"

"*Yes. A star has fallen in this place.*"

"Hey, now." Boon firmed his grip. "Are you in danger?"

"*Not at the moment.*"

"Promise me you'll keep your distance. For Posy's sake."

"*I will try.*"

"Can *I* make it through?"

"*Perhaps.*" The star eased even closer. "*I believe so.*"

"And that's why you came looking for me? You'd like to send me through a little early, check up on Posy for you?"

"*And that star.*"

"Friend of yours?"

"*My twin. My sister.*" Close enough their foreheads touched, the star's voice whispered, "*Nemi.*"

Which mostly confirmed another of Boon's suspicions. "If I can find your Nemi, who should I say sent me?"

"*Novi.*"

"Got it. Just give me a bearing, Novi." Tapping one foot against the green crystal, Boon said, "As soon as I get this guy situated, I'll go on in."

Boon risked some airtime, rising high enough above his board to give his dive extra momentum. Swimming wasn't his favorite pastime. Why flounder about when you could fly? But he cut cleanly into the water, kicking to the spot he'd flagged with a much smaller, less priceless stone, back when Lupe was planning this array.

He gave the remnant a twist, anchoring it somewhat in the sand.

Everything seemed right. There was a slight vibration.

Boon couldn't read sigilcraft like Juuyu or Sinder. Not his thing. He'd always trusted his nose first and foremost. Another reason he wasn't a fan of swimming. Holding his breath felt so ... unnatural.

Sand billowed as he pushed off the bottom, aiming for the oblong of his surfboard. He surfaced and sneezed, holding position long enough to confirm that all was quiet. Whoever lived on the other side of this barrier was clearly confident about its impenetrability. His activities hadn't triggered any kind of alarm, and he had yet to see a patrol.

Sitting in midair, low over the water, he gave his tail a good shake and wrung the water from his long ponytail. He reached over and flipped the pair of jeans draped over his board, in the hopes that they'd dry. Wet denim was no fun. All that chafing.

Boon let his attention turn inward, searching for Inti's voice. But it was a lot earlier than they usually connected. Squinting toward the setting sun, Boon picked out the pinpoint of brightness that was Novi, who was keeping his promise to stay well away.

With no clue what he'd find on the other side, Boon bided his time, not working his way back into his jeans until they were dry. Finally, he rested his palm against the surfboard. "You got me this far, but I can't bring you through. I'll find you after."

Then he rose, trailing his fingers along the barrier's surface as a guide.

Novi hadn't been able to give much detail about the openings Boon was looking for. Only that they were invisible, yet attractive to Impressions and Ephemera alike. There would be sounds, scents, or sensations.

The barrier was already taller than Boon had expected. He was a couple thousand feet above the water's surface. Could be the height was needed to funnel in passing winds or migratory Ephemera. Or maybe the island on the other side was like many he'd seen in these parts, topped by the peak of the volcano that had formed it.

He slowed when a faint scent hit his nose. "Flowers?"

It was no problem to track the scent to its source, especially since he wasn't the only one looking for it. Ephemera flickered in and out of sight as they congregated around ... something. Boon braced his knees against the barrier's slope and waved a hand at the place, immediately jerking back.

"Guess this counts as the right kind of weird."

He reached again, more slowly this time.

Invisible petals brushed his palm, and tiny tendrils wrapped around his fingers. The sweet scent he was picking up definitely made it seem like this was a flower. But Boon could tell it was just a crazy construct, probably advanced sigilcraft, and that the tickle of pollen in the air was coming from inside the barrier.

While he watched, a midivar struggled against invisible coils that dragged it backward. It vanished, presumably inside and presumably unharmed.

"How big's your appetite?" he asked, pushing his arm deeper into the thing, which he decided was less like a flower and more like an anemone. Slender tentacles tickled their way past his elbow, pulling him down.

With his other hand, he tried to see if the opening would be wide enough, and that arm was swiftly wrapped. The entrance dilated, and he didn't resist, only muttered, "Mind the tail."

The thing was clearly intended for live capture, because it pulled him through gently enough. But Boon wasn't ready for the beat-down waiting on the other side. Power buffeted his senses, stealing half his breath and most of his strength. Gravity took hold, and he was dropping. With a startled snarl, he tried to correct his position, to slow his descent, but he couldn't control anything.

And then he hit the water. Hard.

11

BOYS CLUB

Akira pushed the remains of a frittata around on his plate and missed his phone. Normally, he would have spent a solitary breakfast swapping texts with everyone back home. But they were onto the next phase of their journey now, and all technology was banned.

While the big cruise ship anchored at one of their Hawaiian ports-of-call, he and Uncle Jackie had discreetly changed boats. This vessel was much smaller, but it felt newer and way more expensive. Some parts were familiar, like this dining room with its chef-staffed buffet. But the new venues where passengers lingered were pretty far outside Akira's realm of experience. Lounges with live music and liquor. A gambling hall with tuxedo-clad dealers. Smoking rooms and what Jacques called a *salon*, where people gathered to talk on various topics.

The clientele was also a far cry from the big cruise ship, where honeymooners and family reunions had rubbed elbows with shuffleboard playing grannies and first-time travelers like him. As far as Akira could tell, every single passenger on *this* ship was male, and they all carried themselves with an air of careless privilege.

Jacques fit in pretty well. He embodied posh when he wanted to.

All in all, they were an intimidating group, and Akira hadn't tried to make friends. These passengers had to be going to the same exclusive resort they were. What little Akira had overheard—and could translate—seemed to point toward an upcoming auction.

Just then, Jacques sauntered into the dining room. Kind of surprising. He wasn't a morning person, so Akira had expected him to laze about in their cabin for longer. Yet he was trading pleasantries with one of the chefs. Probably ordering some of the fancy coffee he preferred.

Akira felt caught.

He'd been stealing out for an early breakfast almost from the first *bon voyage*, just to sit and stare out the windows and sort things out. Maybe Jacques had been giving him space? But with each passing day, the space between them was narrowing.

"Good morning." Jacques gently gripped Akira's shoulder as he passed, circling to the chair opposite. He'd acquired three chocolate croissants and what looked like a bowl of milky coffee. Favoring him with a sleepy smile, he murmured, "You really shouldn't be allowed to dress yourself. You're almost slovenly."

Akira glanced down at the mélange of pastels that he'd thrown on. "You chose everything I have to wear."

"The elements are poorly combined." Jacques studied him over the brim of his cup, and there was so much *warmth* in that gaze.

Akira had no idea how he managed it, but it was impossible to ignore. "Do you have to do that?"

"What have I done?"

Akira further mangled his frittata. "It's the way you look at me."

"Steady on." Jacques slid one of the croissants onto Akira's plate. "Did you use the face cream I set out last night?"

"No."

"And the hair wax …?"

Akira shook his head. "I just grabbed a shower."

Jacques took another long, slow sip of his coffee, then pushed his feet up under Akira's so he was using Jacques' crossed ankles as a footrest. It was one of the things Jacques did now. Just a small thing. If anyone else in the dining room happened to be looking, they'd see the way their legs were entwined and gain the desired impression.

"I see no trace of gloss." Jacques twirled a finger in the vicinity of Akira's lips. "Gloss is part of your look."

"Maybe you kissed it off," he muttered.

Jacques beamed at him. "That's the spirit."

Akira figured this kind of affectionate harassment was probably exactly the sort of conversation Jacques would have with the person he loved. Because it was so like him. So honest. And Akira didn't think he deserved any of it.

He wasn't Jacques' true love.

This was a sham for the mission.

But it was a convincing one.

Maybe it bothered Akira because it was impossible not to compare. He knew without a shred of doubt that Suuzu loved him.

It was a subtle, restrained love, but it was *there*, and now that Akira had noticed, he wasn't sure how he'd missed it.

Under his careful guard, Suuzu was so … so *sure*.

Yeah, the phoenix was young by Amaranthine standards, but he'd asserted himself, insisting that the years were enough for this attainment. He'd convinced Juuyu to teach him some kind of courting dance. And the moment Akira had given his best friend reason to hope, Suuzu had all but demanded to confirm it.

A kiss.

Suuzu hadn't shied away from it or found it embarrassing. It hadn't been a courteous gesture, and it hadn't been given in gratitude. That kiss had been *taken*.

Akira hated to admit that it had been a relief that everyone was waiting to go and they'd had a boat to catch. Yes, he'd kind of, sort of run away from the intensity of that kiss. But Akira hadn't gone away without promising to return. Because Akira knew without a shred of doubt that he loved Suuzu, too.

But he was so, so unsure how to do that.

"Teach me, *s'il vous plait*."

Akira's head jerked up. It was such an Uncle Jackie thing to say.

"I need lessons in Akira," he said, his gaze sympathetic for once. "Teach me to please you."

"I don't know how to do this. I *told* you I'd be terrible at it."

Jacques' lips quirked. "And I told you that I can make up the difference. Let me."

Maybe Akira wasn't cut out for romance. Maybe the whole problem here was *him*. He couldn't figure out how to shift from friend—or nephew—to paramour. Or boyfriend. Or boy-toy. Or bondmate. Or whatever label someone wanted to stick on him.

How was he supposed to know what to do with a Jacques in love? Because Akira really did love his uncle, and he wanted the man to be happy. But right now, it really felt like the only thing that made Jacques happy was Akira.

"Teach me, *s'il vous plait* ...?" he echoed quietly.

Jacques spread his hands wide. "Ask anything. I'm in the mood to be generous."

"Now that you've had your coffee?"

"You know me so well!"

Akira reached for the croissant, tore it in half, and nibbled at it. This was probably going to be really, *really* embarrassing. But in a way that would undoubtedly work into Uncle Jackie's vacation plans. And maybe even please Suuzu. Eventually. So Akira searched that warm, waiting gaze and asked, "Could you teach me to dance?"

12

SKINSHIP

im stroked Elara's cheek and called her name. She was so out of it. With a strong suspicion as to the cause, Pim bypassed her room and marched straight to the nurse's station, which Elara had pointed out during their tour.

The mare who answered her rap had the telltale coloring of a zebra clan. "What's this? What's happened? Give her to me!"

"You shall not have her!" Pim snapped, though she did try for a polite posture. "She's been pollinated, and I want her brought back to her senses."

"Let me *look*, at least." The mare beckoned for her to come through the half-door, into a room decked out in clinical whites.

Pim spared the short row of beds a glance but kept her hold on Elara.

The mare simply worked around her and quickly agreed with Pim's assessment. "I'll brew the usual tea, and you may use our facilities.

The baths are through here, and they're empty at this hour."

"Show me."

A heavy door led to a room paved in smooth stones. Individual pools were set into alcoves, which allowed a modicum of privacy, yet ease of monitoring for the mare.

"Medicinal baths are one of the many healthful activities clients are encouraged to try."

Pim liked a long soak, but she wasn't familiar with this practice. "Would you recommend it for Elara?"

"Yes. I'll begin the herb sachet and oils."

"Can you ensure our privacy?"

The mare drew herself up and stamped one foot. "I'll guard the door myself."

In fairly short order, there was a pot of tea steeping on a tray and a steaming pool that smelled of minerals.

"Tea first," advised the mare. "Drink it all down, Elara."

Pim checked on her proclaimed sister, whose head lolled against her shoulder. Those big brown eyes gazed at her with weariness, not worry. Still Pim asked, "Do you want me or the mare?"

"No stallions hanging about?" she asked wanly.

"All girls." Pim touched Elara's cheek. "How do you feel?"

"Confused. Cared for." She cleared her throat. "Is there a little girls room?"

The mare pointed the way, and Elara escaped.

"You know her?" Pim asked softly.

"Everyone does. She's a good friend to all who work here."

Yet they let something like this happen to her? Pim's tail lashed, and she rather wished there was something—or someone—on which she could take out her frustrations. But not this good mare. "If she's more at ease with you than me, I'll guard the door."

The mare snorted. "Elara may turn us both out."

"The choice is hers."

Pim firmed her posture just as Elara returned.

She'd abandoned the sheet in which she'd been wrapped, and her robe was neatly tied. Her cheeks were pink from washing away the smeared makeup. "I'm a mess," she murmured.

"Mistress Moonprowl ordered a healing bath for you," announced the mare. "I suggest sharing it. You both need calming."

Elara glanced between the sunken pool and Pim. "We do?"

"Only if you agree," said Pim. "It will help clear your head."

"All right," she said slowly.

"Together?" Pim checked.

Elara simply nodded.

"I will leave you to your lady mistress's care," said the mare, already retreating. "Call for me if you need any item replenished."

The door clicked shut.

"My lady mistress, are you?"

Pim shrugged. "People do like to assume. Tea first."

Elara sniffed at the cup Pim proffered, then sipped and made a face. "Why am I here?"

"I found you and didn't like the look of the situation, so I took you out of it."

Her brow furrowed. "I don't recall …? Where was I?"

"Dr. Kodoku's office."

"My appointment?" Elara glanced around the windowless room.

"What time is it?"

"Morning. First thing." Pim couldn't keep the twitch out of her tail. "You had been crying."

Elara choked down the rest of the cup and poured herself a second. "I hate this stuff, but it works. Meera is good."

"Meera?"

She pointed to the door. "The angel of mercy who manages this corner of paradise. Why did she say *you* need calming?"

"I don't trust that doctor. Did you know he's a dragon?"

Elara blinked. "That … rings a bell. Maybe? If I did know, I must have forgotten."

Which was going to be a recurring problem if Pim wasn't careful. "Where do you want me?"

"Close."

Pim simply began to undress.

Elara sort of … squeaked.

"Am I making you uncomfortable again?"

"God, yes." But Elara's smile showed signs of returning. "Not a bit shy, are you?"

"All in the upbringing." She smiled as she stepped down into the bath. That was something cats and wolves had in common— being comfortable in their skin.

"Close your eyes?" Elara whispered.

Pim turned her back. She heard the slip of silk as it hit the floor and the soft *plash* as Elara joined her.

"Is this part of your grand scheme to seduce me?"

"It can be." Pim glanced over her shoulder at Elara, who'd huddled down so the water covered her up to her shoulders. It looked wretchedly uncomfortable. "But we're beginning as friends. Yes?"

"Please."

Pim settled on the other end of the tub, stretching out before beckoning with a twirled finger. "Let me support you. In case you get dizzy."

Elara crawled closer, turned, and sat, leaning back into Pim's waiting embrace.

"Good girl," she purred. "Trust yourself to me, and I will see you safe."

"You think I'm *not* safe?"

Pim growled.

Elara turned enough to stare. "Do that again?"

"No. No more grumbling. We are safe here, and you deserve to be purred over." Pim let a very different rumble build between them.

"Oh, god. You purr."

Pim pulled her more firmly against her and nuzzled her hair.

"Are you flirting again?" asked Elara. "Because it's lovely."

"Maybe a little, but you need to find your balance. Pollination is similar to inebriation."

"So … you're being a gentleman?"

Pim chuckled. "I've never been mistaken for one."

Tension finally bled from Elara's frame, and she leaned back, trusting her full weight to Pim's greater strength.

Again, Pim praised, "Good girl."

Elara closed her eyes and hummed. "So if I claimed to be in love, it's just the pollination speaking?"

"Let's call it a compatibility of souls. You didn't mention you're a reaver."

"Barely. An ancestry check shows reavers in the bloodline, but it's so far back, it hardly counts. There *is* a speck, though. And I'm glad. For some reason, it was a job requirement."

Which reminded Pim. "I wasn't aware that you're a doctor."

"It's hardly a secret." Elara kept her eyes shut as she spoke. "I'm a scientist with some pretty impressive credentials, if I do say so myself. I was a university professor. Still am, since I'm technically on sabbatical. But I was obliquely encouraged to explore my options, and those options led me here."

"You were pushed out?"

"On my cute little ass."

The growl was back.

Elara patted Pim's arm. "I'm over it and them. And look where I ended up, with a gentlemanly cat who treats me like a lady."

"Wolf."

"Hmm?"

Now that Pim had admitted to the truth, she didn't want to go back to pretending. "I have the heart of a wolf. I identify as a wolf."

Elara half-turned again, eyes wide. "I'm so sorry! We were talking about cat rumors and customs, and I assumed ...! No, wait. *I* asked *you* about consorts. But your file says ...."

"It's not public knowledge."

"Oh, god. Are you coming out to me?"

Pim hummed an affirmative. "A sworn sister should know the truth."

Elara tilted her head. "Wolves are sexy as hell. Do you ever dress the part? Off-screen, I mean. I wonder if the shops here have anything appropriate?"

That was a thought! Pim wasn't going back to the fur miniskirt that had become iconic on the series. Real wolves wore fur that had been collected from packmates or from the one wolf who cherished them. But other basics of the wolvish wardrobe were within her reach. And it would give her a project while she waited for the clinic staff to … oh. Wait. Did she even want to work with Dr. Kodoku any further?

No. No way.

Pim stared at the rising steam, which had been working to clear her head. She wanted to leave, but not alone. And not before she unraveled the case that Linlu and Inti had presented. Not before she found all the caged Impressions and set them free.

"Elara, I may have put you in danger."

"Hmm? I thought you rescued me."

Leaning forward to hook her chin over Elara's shoulder, Pim said, "Something sketchy is happening, and I'm going to investigate."

"A case?" Elara's sparkle was back in full force. "Can I be your partner?"

That would probably be safer for her, so Pim said, "Yes. Although it's not just us. We're assembling a team."

"Really, now! Who else is on it?"

A sudden *creak* and scrape drew their attention to a grate set high on the wall. It popped from its frame and Inti leaned out of the exposed duct. "Here is Pim. Pim is here. Inti needs Pim."

13

BEACHED

Inti!" exclaimed Pim. The monkey had found a way past their guard.

"Inti?" Elara called, almost at the same time, her hands crossed over her chest. "You're still here? But … you're supposed to have …! At least, I *thought* …. Someone said you went away."

"Dr. Perrine was told to *never mind*. Dr. Perrine forgot Inti."

Pim asked, "Is Inti a patient?"

Elara shook her head, then nodded. "I met him at the lab, but that was a long while back … I think?"

"Yes, yes, yes." Inti dropped to the floor and leaned the grate against the wall. "Good, good. Dr. Perrine remembers enough. Remembers Inti. Good."

Pim sternly asked, "Is this *really* the place for a reunion? You're making Elara uncomfortable."

Inti raised both hands and averted his face. "Inti needs Pim."

"*Now?*"

He didn't budge. "Boon is hurt. Boon is hunted."

"Boon?" Pim could taste his urgency, even over the fragrant steam. "Is that your wolf friend?"

"Yes." He pointed to the vent. "Hurry, hurry, come with Inti."

"Where?"

"Out, out, outside."

Pim left the water. "Fine. But we can't go out the way you came in. There's a mare standing guard for us, and I won't leave her hanging."

Inti hugged his tail. "Stars sing warning songs."

She slung a robe around her body and knotted its ties. "I'll help, but I'm taking Elara to my room first. I'll leave the window open. Does that work for you?"

"Yes, yes." Snatching up the grate, he nimbly scaled the wall and slid into the duct. Poking his head back out, he quietly added, "Thank you."

The covering slid into place over the vent.

Elara exhaled.

Pim asked, "Keeping up?"

"Am I right to assume I just met a member of your gathering forces?"

"Yes." Holding out a matching robe, Pim asked, "Coming?"

With only the barest hesitation, Elara sloshed up and let Pim cover her. "Do you think this will be dangerous?"

"I think it will." Pim rubbed their cheeks together and assured, "I will be between you and any threat that might arise."

On their way out, Elara promised Meera to meet for tea sometime soon. Pim chose a quicker expedient, kissing Meera's cheek. In her experience, mares understood the complexities of sisterhood and welcomed many into their affections.

Meera laughed and assured, "I will await the good pleasure of your company."

As they hurried along halls in the residential wing, Pim wondered at herself. She claimed to be a wolf, but she had such cattish tendencies. It wasn't as if she could overwrite everything in her past, nor did she want to. She was who she was *because* of those years. They'd led her here, to the choices that would lead her forward.

"Should I go get my things?" Elara asked.

"No." Pim firmly ushered the woman through her own door, then crossed to open the window. "Pick something of mine. There's plenty."

"Oh! Oh, god." Elara waved inarticulately at the pile of luggage.

"I haven't had time to unpack yet." Pim clicked latches and threw open lids. "Really. Just help yourself."

"Why is there so much?"

"Even if I were to see immediate results, I'm contractually bound to remain on the island for the duration of my pregnancy." Pim wasn't sure how much Elara knew. "That's a minimum of three years. And I like variety."

Elara held up some lacy underthings, a fluttery top, and a pair of loose yoga pants. "These?" she whispered, pleading with her eyes.

"They'll suit you."

She scooted into the bathroom to dress.

Pim called, "What size shoe do you wear?"

Elara leaned around the corner and breathlessly held up fingers. "Are you a shoe person?"

Pointing to a couple of enormous cases, Pim smiled. "You're in luck."

"Can I help you unpack? Maybe ... drop by from time to time, to visit your closet?"

"You should move in. It'll be safer."

Inti hurtled through the window. "Ready to come? Ready to go?"

Pim showed her palms. "Where is he?"

"Three beaches over." Inti shot a significant look in Elara's direction. "Past the fence."

Elara stiffened. "There are wild things out there. It isn't safe."

Inti sidled up to her and gently said, "*We* are wild."

"Well, I'm not. Should I stay back?"

"Come, come, come. There are wild things here, too." Inti took her hand and drew her toward the window. "Dr. Perrine is a doctor. Dr. Perrine knows our secrets. Dr. Perrine will take a leap?"

"Just ... jump? This is the second floor."

"Inti will carry you." He went up on tiptoe. "You *know* Inti is stronger than he looks."

"Yes," she said softly, even sadly. "I know how strong you are."

"Good, good, good doctor." Sweeping Elara off her feet, he turned to Pim. "Follow?"

Pim nodded. "Go!"

Elara only screamed a little.

Inti chittered soothingly and didn't slow down.

Three beaches over was apparently a long way from the clinic. Pim wasn't finished being furious, and that always made her restless, so the run felt good. However, the island was full of unfamiliar scents and sounds, and they were making her jumpy.

Catching up to Inti on a stretch of sundrenched sand, Pim kept pace with him. "What am I smelling?" she asked.

His answer was straightforward for once. "Dragons."

"As in wild ones? Aren't they extinct?"

"Ask your nose." Inti's smile was none too happy. "Watch my back, wolf-friend. I'll be watching yours."

When they reached the correct cove, someone sprawled on the verge between land and sea, but he wasn't alone. Two figures in short robes hovered nearby, standing sentinel. One faced the jungle. The other faced the water. Pim had to wonder what sorts of threats lurked in either direction.

As they drew closer, the pair spied them, then took off running for the jungle, bare legs flashing. Pim would have sworn they vanished before entering the treeline. "Who were they?"

"Friends," said Inti.

Elara asked, "How did Try and Twosies manage to leave the enclosure?"

But Inti only let Elara down and hurried to the marooned wolf, wrestling Boon over onto his back. He sniffed at his face, listened to his chest, then struggled to pull him into a sitting position.

Recalling the need for caution, Pim scanned the dense foliage before escorting Elara closer.

Inti thumped the sagging wolf's back. "Boon is safe. Inti is here."

No response.

Grimacing, the crosser delivered a sharp smack to the wolf's cheek. That earned him a growl that turned into a groan.

Boon was all wolf, built large and well-muscled. Sand clung to brown skin, and bedraggled hair was drying to a lighter hue. Clan was impossible to guess since he wasn't displaying a crest. In fact, the only clothes he wore were a pair of old jeans—sun-bleached, salt-stained, and fraying—and a bandana.

Inti delivered another quick slap, but it wasn't having much of an effect. He scowled out over the water. "Too close, too close, too much."

"Do you mean the barrier?" Pim asked. He'd mentioned she'd be able to feel it if she was on the shore. "Why isn't it affecting us?"

"Pim is tuned." He nodded significantly. "Did you *never mind* your bracelet?"

She checked both wrists. To her surprise, she wore a snug band of plastic with a barcode on it. She couldn't remember who'd affixed it, and she didn't like the addition. So tacky. "In that case, would the sigil you gave me help him?"

"Some, some, yes."

Pim transformed on the spot.

"Oh, look at you," breathed Elara. "Either way, you're gorgeous."

Inti awkwardly reclaimed the sigil, using his tail to brace Boon upright. Pim switched back and crouched at Boon's other side to fasten the necklace. Almost at once, she was treated to a hazy glare from a pair of yellow eyes.

"No females," he growled.

Inti grabbed Boon's face, forcing him to meet his gaze. "Boon is safe. Boon is here. Boon is *early*."

"Don't try to change the subject. Inti, you know I don't work with females."

His words slurred, his eyes kept drifting out of focus. The symptoms were laughably familiar. Pim asked, "How long since you slept?"

"A while. Too long." Adding some growl for emphasis, Boon said, "Go away."

"You know, *I* don't normally mingle with males, but I'm making an exception. If you need to blame someone, look to the stars."

He squinted at her. "A cat? Yeah, there were supposed to be cats. Inti, isn't Posy here?"

"Yes, yes, cats, cats, cats."

"Get me to him," Boon ordered.

Inti chittered softly and turned to Pim. "Take him. Hide him. Hurry. *Heavy*."

"Me?" she asked incredulously.

"Watch over his sleep. Be his safety."

Pim muttered, "He doesn't want me. Can't *you* do it?"

"Inti cannot hold still that long." His eyes pleaded with her. "He-wolf, she-wolf, safe wolf."

"Where am I supposed to put him?"

"Bed ...?"

"You expect me to smuggle him into my bed?"

Inti sighed. "I can ward your room. Nobody will notice."

That *was* appealing. If her suite was warded, she could keep Elara safe, too. "Done. *If* you'll help me get him settled."

"Done, done, done." Inti promised, "Help is coming. Help is here. Hisoka is here."

He gave the name weight. It made Pim wonder. "Hisoka ... as in Hisoka *Twineshaft*?"

"Hush, hush, shush. Secrets must stay secret."

Resolved to uphold her end of this deal, Pim slapped Boon herself. "On your feet, Kindred. Inti has arranged a fine den for you."

The wolf shot her a disgruntled look that seemed to ask, *why are you still here?* But he was definitely more coherent. Inti's charm must be working.

Elara stole up behind Pim and whispered, "What's wrong with him?"

"Sleep deprivation."

Inti got under the wolf's arm and tried to help him upright.

Boon asked, "Why do I feel so heavy?"

"You are *big*."

To Pim's surprise, the wolf lapsed into an easy grin. "Are you sure that's the trouble? I have plenty of brothers bigger. And a sister or two, as well."

Inti dug his heels in the sand and leaned back.

Pim grabbed Boon's other arm and heaved.

His brows drew down, and he grumbled, "No females."

"You don't have many options."

He lifted his chin toward Elara. "What about this guy?"

14

IDIOT WOLF

Pim dropped Boon's arm, lest she give in to the temptation to bite. Stepping back, she placed herself between him and Elara, ready to defend her against more thoughtless words. But Inti jumped into the awkward moment, talking fast.

"Yes, yes, yes. Dr. Perrine is good. Inti trusts Dr. Perrine. Trust Dr. Perrine."

"A doctor, huh?" Boon angled his head to the side, trying to catch Elara's eye. "You willing to stand watch?"

She cautiously answered, "If you're sure."

Pim hissed in frustration, but she could see what little choice Inti had. Rude or not, this wolf was a big part of the crosser's plan. Cooperation often meant ignoring insults, much as Aloora Longstride had done for the first three seasons of *Pure Instinct*.

She selected an appropriately patronizing tone. "Get moving, or I'll have to carry you."

Boon snorted. Pointing at Pim, he said, "Don't let her touch me, and I'll be satisfied."

"Okay …?" Elara's voice steadied. "I can do that."

And they were off.

Inti and Boon walked ahead, conferring in undertones.

Pim pulled Elara into her side. "Idiot wolf. I'm so sorry."

"Don't worry about it," Elara murmured. "It hasn't happened in years, but it's not like it hasn't happened."

"He's *blind*."

"He's also half-drowned and barely clinging to consciousness. I doubt he can see straight, let alone see me."

Despite the distance they put between the wolf and the barrier, his condition was quickly deteriorating. Steps dragged, and he caromed off trees. But somehow, Boon stayed on his feet. Pim guessed it was a combination of momentum and stubbornness. If they stopped now, even for a moment, he'd be down for the count.

Pim guessed she should be blunt. "Wolves will trust their noses over their eyes."

"Oh." Elara managed a weak laugh. "I live to confuse."

"He'll be sorry later. I'll make sure of it."

Her smile was grateful, but her voice was small. "You knew, too."

"You knew I did." Pim took Elara's hand and declared, "And I know my sister has the heart of a maiden."

"That's nice to hear." Still noticeably withdrawn, she asked, "Do you think he'll hate me when he realizes …?"

"No. No, I don't think he could." Pim needed to soothe away Elara's qualms, both for her sake and Boon's. "For a wolf, sleep is an act of trust. He'll be helpless, totally reliant on you to keep him safe while he's dead to the world. When he wakes, he'll have to acknowledge you. From what I've heard, you could even be considered an honorary packmate."

"How can it be trust when I'm lying to him?"

"You haven't lied. He assumed." Pim squeezed her hand and softly suggested, "You can trade apologies when he wakes up. He doesn't seem like a *bad* guy."

"Yeah." Her jaw worked. "Oh, god. I hope I can keep it together."

Pim whispered, "You don't want to?"

Elara rolled her eyes. "Have you forgotten my attitude toward wolves?"

"Sexy as hell?"

"*That.* Exactly that." She whined softly. "And he'll *know.*"

Pim thought it best—for the sake of the team—that she prepare Elara for the next several days. "You know about Amaranthine sleep cycles."

"Yes."

"Have you received any training with regards to tending."

"Nooo ...?" Elara's brow furrowed. "I was supposed to have lessons on the basics, but Naoki-san kept canceling our appointments for one reason or another."

"Ever been assessed?"

"Dr. Kodoku probably looked into the matter." She shook her head. "I've always assumed that I'm nothing special."

"May I confirm that?"

Elara looked surprised. "Are you qualified to give an independent assessment?"

Pim wondered what she'd been told. "Any of us could. I'm actually concerned because he might inadvertently impose. Many Amaranthine arrange for tending when the time comes to go deep. It can be difficult to relax our hold on wakefulness."

"I can't tend."

"Perhaps not, but he could still take." Concerned enough to press, Pim asked, "Will you let me look?"

"Sure." She smiled faintly. "Who am I to argue with a wolf's protective streak?"

They returned through Pim's open window, and she immediately regretted it. By the time Inti wrestled a barely-coherent Boon into her tub, there was sand everywhere.

"Do you need anything from your room? You'll be with me for days."

Elara nodded. "Vitamins. Meds. Books. Basics."

"I'll escort you."

"I'm only a few doors past the first turning."

"Together," Pim insisted. And while they piled together the makings of a prolonged sleepover, she rattled off last-minute advice. "There will be sniffing. There may be growling. Closeness is a given. Oh, and your mood will affect his rest. Be kinder to him than he's been to you."

"I can do that." She took a deep breath and exhaled on a smile. "I should probably be honored."

"It *is* an honor," Pim assured. A high one. One for which she'd been summarily rejected.

As they stole along the empty hallway to Pim's room, Elara seemed to have bounced back entirely. Until she spotted the nude wolf draped face-down across Pim's bed.

"Oh, god." She dropped her things and covered her eyes. But then she was peeking between her fingers.

Pim blandly said, "Yes, quite godlike. And we're going to offer you up to him. Inti, why didn't you cover him?"

The monkey crosser appeared in the bathroom door, dripping denim in his hands. "Fall, falling, fell. At least he had a soft landing."

Rolling her eyes, Pim moved to make Boon more comfortable, but she was six feet from her bed when the growling started. She stepped back. The growl tapered off. She stepped forward. The rumble resumed.

"You two will have to move him."

Elara took a cautious step closer to the bed, then another when she didn't trigger the wolf's warning system. "Is this going to bite me in the ass later?" she whispered.

"Do you want it to?" Pim teased.

With a pleading look, Elara pointed out, "How's he going to react when he wakes up naked in bed with a woman?"

Taking a soothing tone, Pim pointed out, "There's ample evidence that the natural state may be *his* natural state. Note the complete lack of tan lines."

Elara hung her head. "You're *not* helping."

"He won't *let* me help, but you need some." Pim raised her voice. "Inti? Can you wrestle the magnificent beast *under* covers?"

"Ask, ask, ask nicely," he grumbled. But he exited the bath, drying his hands on his shirt and stopping before Elara. Reaching up to touch her face, Inti gently said, "Boon is good. Boon is gentle. Boon is confused. *Sorry*, Elara."

"You are the good and gentle one, Inti. I was sad we lost you. But … we *didn't*, did we?"

"Not lost." And changing the subject, he ordered, "Come, come, come. Inti will tuck you in."

"Turnabout is fair play?"

Pim had to ask, "You used to tuck him in?"

Elara said, "I was assigned to his ward for a while. Over at the hospital."

"Nice word for bad place," muttered Inti.

"Was it terrible?" asked Elara.

"*You* were not terrible." Inti patted her cheek again, saying, "Bright spot in dark place."

She lowered her gaze. "I did try to … lighten the mood."

"Same here. Same now." And with surprising strength, Inti lifted the limp wolf, allowing Elara to pull free the covers. He eased Boon into a more natural position, and urged, "You, you, your turn."

Elara grabbed a book, stacked a couple of pillows, and slid gingerly onto her side of the wide bed, settling in to read. Pim folded her arms and began a mental count. She'd only made it to four when the wolf slid a hand across the gap between him and Elara.

She startled.

He grabbed hold and pulled. Elara struggled for a moment, finally getting herself up on her elbows, but Boon had her by the waist, cheek pressed to her hip, nose firmly planted in intimate territory.

"Oh, god," Elara squeaked. "Is this normal?"

Boon snuffled and nuzzled and hauled her even closer, one arm under her shoulders, the other around her waist. By the time he finished adjusting, Boon had an ear pressed to her ribcage, probably seeking her heartbeat, and he'd draped his tail across her thighs.

Pim softly urged, "It's all right. He's reassuring himself. He's accepted you."

Inti tossed a sheet over them. "Bright, bright, beauty."

Which reminded Pim. "Elara's reserves must be small. What if he tries to replenish himself?"

"Fine, fine. Shift, shift." Inti returned Pim's clay necklace, then began tracing sigils on the door.

Returning to speaking form Pim quietly protested, "He could do her harm. Inadvertently."

Inti half-turned to look at her. "Worried?"

"Of course!"

"No need." With a sad smile, he added, "No one is safe here. Not me. Not her. Not you."

Pim hurried to his side and lowered her voice. "Has she been harmed?"

"*Improved*," Inti corrected, with a faint sneer. "Dragon doctor dabbles, even with other doctors."

She turned to the bed, where Elara was tentatively patting Boon's head.

What was Pim missing?

"Look, look, look," urged Inti, who returned to warding the walls.

So Pim did, pushing against boundaries in a manner that wasn't entirely polite. She gasped at what she found. "But …

Elara said she was nominal! Barely considered a reaver!"

"*Was* is not *is*."

"But …!" Pim couldn't keep the incredulity from her voice, though she did try to keep it down. Elara was well-warded, possibly even sealed, and for good reason. "She's *exquisite*. Nearly beacon quality, surely."

"Yes, yes, yes," agreed Inti. "Not every experiment fails."

"Are you saying she was *made* into … into what she's become?"

"Made, yes. Maybe used for making." His fingers slashed through more sigilcraft, turning walls into barriers. "A beacon is good for breeding."

15

PITTER PATTER

Hisoka focused on keeping his breathing slow and his step light as he pushed through the thick undergrowth surrounding the lower slopes of the island's second highest peak. There were four in all, and this was the northernmost. The previous spire, the one closest to the resort's dock, had boasted an overlook, from which he'd been able to confirm that much. But down on the ground, visibility was reduced to whatever was right in front of his whiskers.

He'd worked out a few things.

Fences penned the island's interior, presumably to keep the presence of dragons under wraps. Those dragons, which gave every appearance of being wild beasts—not Kith—had cleared this jungle of all but birds. This made Hisoka wonder what they found to eat. And shed light on the avid interest the creatures had shown in tracking down possible prey. Namely, him.

Dragons were dangerous enough. Hungry dragons? Terrifying.

Barriers reinforced the fences, and Hisoka had already located several of the wardstones that anchored them. But these upheld isolated boundaries, having little to do with the monumental barrier that kept this island off every map.

Finding *that* barrier's wardstones was his top priority. But Hisoka was keenly aware that he was rarely in any one place for only one reason.

A faint rustle and patter came from behind, and Hisoka gave in to a pint-sized inevitability. Finding a bit of breathing room at the base of a tree, he shifted into speaking form. Moments later, the little crosser who'd been trailing him scampered forward on all fours, then stood and lifted his arms.

"I suppose you count as a complication," Hisoka said. "I shouldn't have picked you up. Yet I don't think I was wrong to do so."

The boy butted his hand, as affectionate as a kitten.

"Do you have a name?" Hisoka inquired lightly. "Most of my friends call me *Sensei*. Can you manage that?"

Dark eyes blinked. This child listened closely, but so far, his verbalizations were limited to nonsensical babbling and the odd peep.

"Let me think."

He'd been putting off giving him any kind of name, even a temporary one. It would forge a bond, something he generally avoided. But Hisoka didn't need a star to tell him that a choice had already been made, and the consequences were his.

"You'll have to make do with a nickname for now."

The child slouched into the crook of his arm, gaze fixed on his face, waiting.

"Since you've been pattering along behind me since yesterday, you shall be Patter. What do you say? Will you answer to that?"

He tapped the little one's nose and chanted his new name.

Tickling led to a gurgling, purring sort of laughter. And a startlingly clear answer. "Sen. Sennn!"

Hisoka's heart warmed. "That's right. *Sensei.*"

Patter snuggled right in.

"I suppose I'll be sponsoring your application to Stately House. I wonder what my friends will make of you?"

Harmonious, for one, was always delighted by anything new, especially scents he couldn't account for. With that in mind, Hisoka breathed deeply and searched his memory. Patter didn't fall in line with any of the clans, and Hisoka had made a point of acquainting himself with *all* of them prior to the Emergence. Nor was Patter an imp of any variety Hisoka knew from lore. If anything, Patter looked like a child-sized pitterhind, sans wings.

His stomach dropped.

"Surely not," he whispered.

Hisoka made an even more careful inspection. There were no signs of the wings that distinguished a variety of Ephemera that looked like small, green mice with antlers. But there was no rhyme or reason to a crosser's nod to their Amaranthine parent's characteristics.

"If it was even *possible* for you to be part Ephemera, who is your other parent?"

Patter wriggled happily. "Sen!"

"Yes, I'm Sensei. And *you* were very likely engineered, which is concerning." He caressed green hair and mused, "But as our friends in the horse clans would say, you are not a bad outcome."

Hisoka wasn't entirely lost. Via Boon, Inti had relayed a succinct description of the island's layout, so there were no surprises with the most basic of basics. But their young insider hadn't bothered to mention certain details that Hisoka would have considered pertinent. Like the presence of dragons. And the pervasive scent of Amaranthine trees.

The more information Hisoka could uncover, the happier Argent would be. Assuming Jacques was successful with his smuggling. Forces were gathering. Coordinating them was their next challenge.

"I miss Novi's perspective," he confided.

Patter peeped sympathetically.

"And I wish I could confer with Argent." From his current vantage, he was able to see enough of the barrier to raise a troubling detail into focus. "The markers are the same as the seal that used to bind him."

These similarities stirred his curiosity.

"I wonder what any of this has to do with Joe Reaverson." Hisoka tapped Patter's nose. "By all accounts, his seal was similar enough to suggest a connection."

Hisoka fixed his gaze on the facility in the valley below. This must be the lab Inti had infiltrated a few years ago. No attempt had been made to ornament the building, yet Hisoka found it fascinating. The place had an unnatural allure. Familiar, since he knew the near-constant companionship of an Impression. But compounded in such a dizzying way, Hisoka had to wonder how many imps were on this island. It felt like scores.

"This many could be dangerous."

Hisoka was still tweaking his personal wards when a sudden rustle of leaves gave him enough warning to push Patter behind him. Then a monkey-boy flung himself out of the jungle, and Hisoka jumped up to catch him. Swinging Inti around to slow his momentum, he laughed when a voice rang through his mind.

Found you! Found you! Found you!

"Here I am," assured Hisoka.

He was quickly tangled. Arms, legs, and tail wrapped so tightly, he grunted in protest. But he hugged their lost boy back.

"Sensei?" Inti whispered.

"I'm here."

"Glad," he sighed. "Glad, glad, glad."

"Come, now. Ease off a little. We should compare notes." When Inti didn't budge, Hisoka added, "I'm not going anywhere. We're trapped together, now."

"Another minute," Inti begged.

Hisoka gave him three before pressing for information. "When will you be in contact with Boon again?"

"Days. He's sleeping." Inti almost sounded exasperated. "Pushed through, dropped far, washed up, tucked in."

"He's here? So there *is* a way in."

"High, high, too high." Pointing confidently, he added, "No flight, no escape."

"Have you located the barrier's wardstones?"

"Yes, yes, no." Inti eased back and offered an apologetic grimace. "The array was easy, but I don't know where the anchor is. Or what it is. Or … who?"

Inti was talking sense, and Hisoka wondered if that was a bad sign.

"What do I need to know?"

The crosser raised a finger. "Boon is safe. Boon is sleeping."

"Where?"

"Trulore."

"Which is …?"

"The fertility clinic." Inti raised another finger. "Linlu is hopeful. Linlu is helpful."

Hisoka needed a moment to process this new detail. "Linlu *Dimityblest*?"

"Yes."

"Not willingly," Hisoka asserted. He couldn't bring himself to think of the moth clansman in league with the Rogue.

"No." With a sad smile, Inti whispered, "Linlu is bound. Linlu is Broken."

"We'll get him the care he needs."

Inti nodded and raised a third finger. "Pim needs help. Pim needs you."

Hisoka hesitated. "Pim Moonprowl."

"Yes, yes, yes." From a pocket Inti produced a fold of glossy paper. "Pim does not know. Pim is not safe."

It was a promotional flier for an auction. And though it was tastefully worded, the intent was criminal. In three days, the bidding would begin for the bedding of Miss Moonprowl. Felines might be sensualists, but they were consenting sensualists.

"You are her spokesperson."

"I am." Deep down, Hisoka would really rather not have to deal with a lady of the feline courts. Especially one who was supposedly assembling consorts. "Where is she?"

"Trulore."

"The same place Boon is?"

Inti patted Hisoka's head. "Pim helped rescue Boon. She's hiding him."

It should have been welcome news. Another ally. But Hisoka was easily as wary as Boon about entanglements with females. Instincts rebelled, but Inti was right. Hisoka spoke for the cat clans. In a very real sense, Pim Moonprowl's concerns were his.

Just then, a small *peep* sounded from behind.

Inti leaned way to the side, his tail thrown in the opposite direction as he tried to see what was behind Hisoka. All this while, Patter had been still and silent, but with a string of nonsense babble, the little guy lifted his arms.

With a gasp, Inti abandoned Hisoka in order to scoop up Patter. "You have Seela's child?"

"You know him?"

"He is Seela's child!" Inti nuzzled the toddler's cheek, then climbed back into Hisoka's arms. With a proud air, Inti announced, "You are a very good cat."

"Why, thank you. I take it you know his mother?"

Inti slowly shook his head. "I've never spoken with her. Seela can't speak. She can't wake. Seela is lost in dreams."

16
POINT OF NO RETURN

Jacques wasn't overly worried about his part in Argent's plan. He'd even made light of it by buying himself a sassy pair of mules as an homage to his primary role in the affair.

"Do you remember how to set up the array?"

"I could do it in my sleep," Jacques assured. "Shall I demonstrate? Since this technically qualifies."

"I will have to leave it to you." Argent came to sit with him on the bench. "Do you have any questions?"

"*Non.* Although, if you insist, I could *pretend* to need hand-holding."

"These meetings may no longer be possible."

Jacques crossed his legs. "You warned me weeks ago. I haven't forgotten."

Before leaving Stately House, Argent and Michael had schemed to boost the potency of the sigilcraft on Jacques' person. Blood had been involved in establishing new layers of protection. Semi-permanent sigilcraft had been layered over older tattoos, all in the hope that *this* connection would endure past the oncoming barrier.

Argent stood and began to pace. "Hisoka arrived ahead of you, and my point of contact with him was immediately severed."

"So it won't work."

"I think not."

"That's always been the most probable outcome," reminded Jacques. "It's why you need that exquisite little array I'm packing."

"I know."

Jacques surveyed the conservatory that was Argent's dreamscape of choice. It was perfect in every detail, and he really did feel as if he were back home. Stately House was the only place he really wanted to be. "We've been past the point of no return ever since boarding this ship."

"I *know*." Argent was sounding especially testy.

"Do you want me to pass along any messages to your brother-in-law?"

The fox's gaze sharpened. "How are things going between the two of you?"

"I'm hardly the sort to kiss and tell!"

"*Tsk.*"

Jacques relented a little. "As promised, I'm devoting myself to him."

The flourish of Argent's many tails puffed. "Wholeheartedly?"

"Jealous?"

"Concerned." Argent frowned. "Suuzu is here at Stately House."

"That's unusual. Doesn't Spokesperson Farroost have work to do?"

"Juuyu wants him to remain with us until everything is properly settled."

He was choosing his words with too much care. Jacques could always tell. "What aren't you mentioning?"

"Quite a bit, but it will keep. *You* are my priority."

"And Akira is mine. He'll be fine. I'll see to it."

Argent sighed. "Do not take unnecessary risks."

"I shall be the soul of indolence." And because there really was nothing else to say, Jacques asked, "How much longer?"

"Soon." Argent sat and reached for Jacques' hand. "I would rest easier if we could maintain this link."

"My duties are few and light. This is a lark compared to what the others must do." Jacques gently chided, "Surely you can trust me this far."

Argent swore, "I will come for you both."

"And we'll await your arrival. Quite possibly at poolside. We brought fundoshi, just to be cheeky."

"*Tsk.* Are you taking any of this seriously?"

"Every bit." But the dreamscape vanished even as the words left his mouth. The dreaded boundary had been crossed, and he and Akira were on their own.

Jacques opened his eyes. The engine noise had changed, so they had to be nearing their port. Still, there was no rush to make ready. A thin line of pearly light showed where the curtain hadn't been pulled all the way shut. Dawn was a while off, and breakfast would be served before they were escorted to their suite on the island.

He eased onto his side and slid an arm around Akira. With one tug, the man came into his embrace without fully waking. Suuzu had him nicely trained. Then Akira was rubbing his nose against Jacques' chest.

Jacques quietly checked, "You know where you are?"

"Mm-hmm. You're more ticklish than he is."

"Your bird boy is typical of his people, and I'm typical of mine. Overflowing with masculinity."

Akira hummed again. "I'd noticed. Been a member of your swim club for years."

Jacques was just a tiny bit pleased. "You checked me out?"

"You're … grandiose. I watch to see what you'll do next. Noticing other stuff was sort of incidental." Akira opened his eyes and smiled sleepily. "If you count his tail, Ginkgo's shaggier. And Nonny has you beat, hands down."

"Ah, ah, ah!" Jacques traced a finger over Akira's lips. A gentle reminder that he needed to watch his words. Akira winced, apology in his gaze, but Jacques still claimed his penalty, kissing him softly.

"Sorry," Akira whispered.

"Show me how much," Jacques ordered.

Akira wriggled upward enough to kiss his jaw in doggish contrition.

It was all for show. Or would be. They'd talked things through, and they were playing by their own rules, most of which had been borrowed from the Amaranthine. Common courtesies would look like overtures, but these familiar boundaries had done wonders for Akira's comfort level.

Jacques wrapped Akira in his arms and murmured, "Are you thinking of your comely phoenix?"

"Yes." Honesty was their first rule, and Akira was unstintingly candid. "Mostly."

He surprised Jacques by bumping a second kiss to his jawline.

The apology had changed to a plea.

Although it was more difficult to adopt a receptive posture while lying in bed, Jacques angled his head in the avian fashion and waited to see what Akira wanted.

With a determined gaze, Akira brushed his lips across Jacques'.

So *grim*. Jacques couldn't help smiling. Stealing kisses was one thing, but Akira was steeling himself for them.

Angling his head, Jacques invited more. Mostly because it was nice that Akira was taking some initiative. Jacques would feel slightly less tortured over his role if Akira could meet him partway.

The next kiss landed on his stubbled cheek.

Arching his brows, Jacques mirrored the action. Then went one better, sliding his lips down Akira's throat.

"Uncle Jackie," he complained.

Which incurred another penalty kiss. Jacques let it linger, then tucked Akira under his chin. "You don't need to, you know. I'll work in the occasional romantic gesture. One a day should suffice to establish the depths of my *tendré*."

"I can handle it." Akira sighed gustily. "But I'm *not* leaving this all up to you. People will think ... wrong things."

"Scandal is rather the point."

To his surprise, Akira kissed his collarbone. "If I'm shy about this stuff, people will think you're taking advantage of me. If *I* work in the occasional romantic gesture, they'll know I love you, too. One a day should suffice, yeah?"

"Ah, me," Jacques sighed. "This is going to break me."

"What?" Akira propped himself up on an elbow, eyes wide with concern. "Why? Everyone's been saying this mission isn't risky. Not for us."

"I'm not talking about our stay on the island. I fully expect to be lazing in the lap of luxury for the foreseeable future." He tried for a brave smile. "It's only my heart that'll break."

Akira sat up, crossing his legs. "I'm confused."

"About?"

"You."

Jacques reached for his hand. "I'm hardly being coy."

"Huh. I thought so before. Now, I think I was right." With obvious confusion, he said, "You're not pretending."

"Marvelous actor, remember?"

Akira shook his head. "You're *not* acting."

Clever boy. Ah, well. Honesty should reign. "I'm *protecting* you."

"I'm not in danger."

"You might be." Jacques patiently asked, "What if words aren't enough? A canine could smell a sham, and a feline would divine one. The same goes for most clans. Nobody can spot a lie if there isn't one."

"You can't just fall in love with me."

"Can't I?" Jacques shrugged. "You underestimate your appeal. And the shocking amount of unattached affection rattling around in my soul."

• • •

Akira had the good grace to believe him. "Look … I don't want to hurt you."

"Lord. So *tragic*. Stop, or I might try to kiss it better."

"Uncle Jackie!"

"*…isn't* here. But he'll be back, by and by. And he'll step aside like the gentleman he is. In the meantime, my devotion is yours."

"This isn't fair to you," Akira grumbled.

"Nor to Suuzu. Yet here we are, neatly embroiled."

Akira reached over to lightly tap his lips, but Jacques didn't apologize for speaking forbidden words. He merely kissed Akira's fingertips.

"After I return you to your beloved, pastels will bring a tear to my eye for years to come."

Akira smiled a little and kept hold of Jacques' hand, brushing his fingertips across the dark hairs that grew there, then the glass ring Suuzu had chosen for him. Finally, he said, "I do love you, Uncle Jackie."

"By any chance, do you *enjoy* our little penalty game?"

Akira didn't rise to the bait. Neither did he blush. He only nodded to himself and said, "I'll do my very best to consider your feelings and … and be respectful. I can be a gentleman, too."

"Dare I hope this means you're beginning to see me as a man?"

"Yeah." Akira's gaze turned thoughtful. "Jacques seems like a pretty amazing guy. I probably wouldn't have met him, if not for this trip."

"Certainly not. Terribly inappropriate." Jacques trailed a finger up Akira's arm and tapped his shoulder. "*Tell me* if I take things too far."

"No problem." Akira's smile was reassuringly warm. "I get the feeling that I'll love Jacques, too. I probably already do, in a friendly way."

Jacques escaped the bed and tossed a chartreuse dressing gown around his shoulders. "Friends to lovers works for me."

Akira tossed a pillow after him. "That's not what I meant!"

"*And* you owe me a penalty," he called in a teasing sing-song before shutting the bathroom door behind him. Leaning against it, he sighed toward the ceiling.

He could do this.

Live in the moment.

Love a man who belonged to another.

Let him go in the end.

Jacques had promised to escort Akira home unscathed. And he'd bloody well do it, even if he was thoroughly scathed in the process.

17

LEGWORK

In an effort to respect Boon's wishes, Pim kept her distance from the bed, even after Boon was sleeping deeply enough to lose track of the waking world. "I think I'll take a walk. Do a little reconnaissance," she announced.

Elara's gaze drifted to the window. "Weren't you going to wait for Inti to get back?"

"He didn't exactly leave us with an itinerary." Pim wished her tail was more cooperative. She was twitching when she was fairly sure tucking would have been more wolf-like. With an apologetic smile, she admitted, "I don't like being confined. A prowl would be ... mood-enhancing. Can I bring you back something?"

"Dinner?"

Pim brightened. That meant she'd have the whole day. "Any requests?"

Elara, who had taken to idly stroking Boon's hair while she read, lowered her book. "How about … something with a story to it?"

The notion sent Pim's tail into an upward arch.

"Am I allowed to find that cute?" Elara asked, eyes sparkling.

"Shush. I can't always help it." She shrugged. "You're interesting. I'm interested."

"Good."

Pim hesitated at the door. "One thing."

"Hmm?"

"If I wanted to find that moth clansman again, where would I look?"

"Linlu?" Elara frowned. "He's usually only at the clinic when Dr. Kodoku brings him along. His office is at that hospital I mentioned."

"Is it nearby?"

"It has to be." Elara hesitated. "I mean, I worked there, too. It's … umm … huh! Why can't I remember?"

Pim raised a hand. "Don't worry. I'll figure it out. It's more important that you stay calm for our sleeper."

"*Calm* might be a stretch. He makes me giddy."

"Am I allowed to find that cute?"

Elara chuckled. "I can't help it. All interesting and interested clauses apply."

Pim didn't have a badge to flash around or a partner to explain the nature of their inquiries, but she'd been mingling with people for centuries. By choice. Because she enjoyed slipping into a role. People intrigued her, and she liked catching their interest, as well.

Some of it was the attention. Elara had been right. People did tend to fall for her.

Some of it was escape. After her second miscarriage, Pim had found placements for her consorts and abandoned her hearth. She'd been mingling with humanity ever since, transitioning effortlessly from one role to the next.

When Denny Woodacre brought the casting call for *Pure Instinct* to her attention, she hadn't hesitated over stepping out. Her debut was touted as groundbreaking. Her openness made her a media darling. And Pim had certainly thrived in the limelight. Television suited her.

Some of it was the attention. Pim really did enjoy being the center of attention.

Some of it was escape. Because she took comfort and courage from her place among the packs. Even if that spot was honorary and she was self-taught.

Pim began her questioning in the shopping area, and though Elara wasn't with her, she was Pim's key. At the coffee shop, she asked what Elara's favorite drink was, so she could bring her a treat. The barista was abundantly helpful, even going so far as to point out a lantern-decked restaurant whose bao were one of Elara's current addictions.

One shop led to another, and along the way, Pim learned more new things about her friend, all of them good. And while she chatted, Pim steered the conversations to suit her needs. Her casual interrogations dredged up some puzzling details.

Former clients.

Extended holidays.

Hazy memories.

Jungle boundaries.

Climatic phenomena.

Wanting an Amaranthine perspective, she presented herself at the nurse's station. "Meera, my dear, is there any way for me to connect with ... oh, say, my manager?"

The mare seemed surprised. "Most people come here to get away from it all."

"So there's no mail? In or out?"

"We have a mailroom, but we're off the beaten path. Deliveries are delayed or go astray. Guests usually wait until their vacation ends."

"What about those who live here permanently?" Pim turned the question around. "Are you in contact with your herd? When did you last attend its Song Circle?"

Meera hesitated. "I wonder. It seems a long time."

Pim simply nodded. Others' answers had been similarly vague. It was time to focus on something more concrete. "Would you happen to know where I can find Linlu Dimityblest? He was aboard ship with me, and I want to clarify some things with him."

"I see him occasionally. Scheduling and paperwork. But his office isn't in this section."

"This section?" Pim pounced. "There's more than one section?"

"Y-yes." Meera's tone briefly swerved into the vagueness that seemed to plague many of the clinic's employees. "It's not anything we publicize, but there are other facilities. Each is autonomous, having its own staff.”

“But Linlu comes and goes?”

“He often attends Dr. Kodoku.”

“Which means ... he’s not here right now, since Linlu is also gone?” Pim wasn’t sure her question would get through the haze, but Meera stamped her foot and rallied.

“The resort. I sent them three cases of the massage oils I make for them. That always means a large group, and he’ll be on hand. The good doctor likes to greet high profile guests *personally*.”

The tip of Pim’s tail developed a twitch. “A resort sounds *lovely*! Is it far?”

“I’m not sure I’d call it far. Simply ... inconvenient.” Which wouldn’t have been informative if the mare hadn’t pointed decisively toward the northeast.

Pim had her bearing. It was better than nothing.

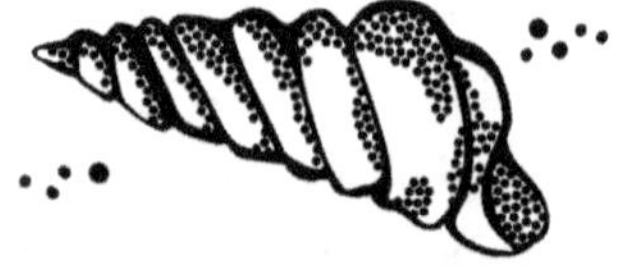

Taking the path to the beach, where a short row of umbrellas shaded empty lounge chairs, Pim stood for a moment considering blue-green waters. The little cove was eerily peaceful, and it took her a moment to figure out why. Oceans were always in motion, yet the water here was still. Bathwater lapped more. There was a breathless calm to the air, as well.

Nature felt unnatural, and it put her teeth on edge.

Pim found a discreet fence and followed it until she located a tree with a leapable branch. Sharpening her claws on its bark, she tasted the air and twitched her proverbial whiskers. She *wanted* to be a wolf on the trail, a tracker after prey, but she knew she surmounted the obstacle with feline grace.

Easing forward, Pim remained alert and on edge. Several yards from the fence, she was brought up short by a barrier, and her wariness multiplied. This was a lot of precaution for a fertility clinic. Or a resort, assuming that's what was on the other side.

Then suddenly, the smell was back, and her tail puffed double.

Inti had said it was dragons.

Baring her teeth, she exhaled on a soft hiss. What had the locals said about the jungle? Strange sounds. Wild beasts. Restless gods. Bad juju.

Taking to the trees again, she found a young branch that bowed past the obstacle. Only then did it occur to her that the sigilcraft might not be intended to keep her out ... but to keep something in.

Should she take a leap? Eight years on an elite taskforce demanded she wait for backup.

Pim dropped back to earth and moved a little further along the enforced boundary, until she hit a patch where the new scent was thick, hot, and fresh as an exhale. Peering fixedly through the barrier, she caught a movement. The dull shine of something purple. Scales.

Maker bless. It really was a dragon.

She slowed her breathing, taking her time sizing up her prey.

No. She didn't want this prey. Nor to become prey.

Pivoting to retreat, she nearly slashed out at the person who'd stolen up behind her.

"Do not strike me," said the female from Dr. Kodoku's office.

Pim had already checked the impulse. "Sorry. No harm intended. I'm jumpy, and you surprised me."

Futari's gaze slanted toward the creature on the other side of the barrier. "Understandable."

"I followed an unfamiliar scent." It wasn't much of an excuse. She'd been using it since her kitten days.

"Foolish. These dragons are not tame, and they are always hungry."

"I wouldn't have crossed over." She glanced back and eased a little closer to Futari. "I'm not even sure I could."

"You have no skill with sigilcraft?"

"None." At least, not with forming it. Pim was pretty good at spotting it.

"So it was not you." Futari eyed her critically. "Who else is out here?"

"I haven't seen anyone."

"*Why* are you out here?"

"I was looking for Linlu." Pim hadn't meant to say so, but what was the harm? She lamely added, "You can call me foolish again. I know this isn't the sort of place he'd be."

"It is not." She looked away, looked back. "Are you going to be trouble?"

"Yes." Pim was shocked at herself and tried to play it off. Slipping closer, she asked, "Am I in trouble with you?"

"Me? I am not the one you should be worried about." With a heavy sigh, Futari asked, "Why is your room warded?"

"Privacy."

"Where is Dr. Perrine?"

"In my bed."

Simple answers could be the most evasive. With the right intonation, they could even be misleading. *Pure Instinct*'s writers had been so good at stymieing Aloora Longstride's teammates, making her much-touted sense of smell invaluable.

Futari blinked, mercifully distracted by this tidbit. "That one?"

"We've been taking advantage of the extra privacy." Pim turned on the charm. "We don't want anyone gossiping about the nature of our friendship."

Arguably true. But inflected to titillate.

"You and Dr. Perrine have become ... close?"

"I would definitely call us *intimate* friends." Pim cupped Futari's elbow and inquired, "Do *you* want to be friends?"

She frowned. "Do not toy with me."

"I'm not teasing." This was true, although Pim *did* have an ulterior motive. Who better to inform her about Dr. Kodoku than his own daughter? But something was bothering her. "Are you happy in this paradise your father created?"

Futari's expression went stark, her gaze unseeing. "Do I seem happy?"

"No. Far from it." Pim wondered what exactly she'd uncovered here. "Are you in need of help, Kindred?"

Red eyes flashed warnings.

Pim chose to ignore them. "Are you his secretary?"

"That is Linlu's sad fate."

"A nurse, then? You were with him when I ...." Pim trailed off, memory fuzzing.

Futari bitterly announced, "I am back-up. If a patient stops listening to him, I can usually keep them *cooperative* for a little longer."

This was good. Disgruntled souls could be the best informants, happy to talk once they found someone to listen. Pim eased an arm around Futari's waist. "What can I do?"

"For me? Nothing. For yourself?" Her smile twisted. "Also nothing. You are lost."

"I know the way back to …!"

"Be quiet."

Pim bit her lip.

Futari's former disdain had returned. "Hold me."

Drawing her into a gentle embrace, Pim kneaded and purred, trying to get the other female to relax. The prickly ones could be surprisingly devoted, especially in ways that mattered most.

"Comfort me," demanded Futari.

"I thought I was." Pim rubbed their cheeks together. "What do you need?"

Pain wracked her answer. "A sister."

"Sisterhood can flourish wherever there is trust." More softly, Pim asked, "Can I trust you, Futari?"

"No." She stiffly countered, "Can I trust you?"

"No." Pim winced and added, "Not entirely."

"I have heard tales of feline treachery."

"I'm a wolf."

"Why would you contradict nature? Why not accept what you have?" Futari's voice quavered with fury. "Why does he never leave well enough alone?"

Pim whispered, "What has he done?"

"Ask his chronicler." She huffed and ordered, "Ask *me* what you really want to know."

Before she could hold it back, Pim blurted, "Did your father rape me?"

"No."

Relief flooded her, and she hugged Futari tighter.

"He does not indulge in carnal acts with his *specimens*. Father will not be satisfied with anything less than his due. His desire is for the winds, four to stir his blood and secure a fitting dynasty."

"So he's a Beckonthrall wannabe?"

"That is *not* a name you should bandy about in his hearing." Futari huddled close, as if trying to hide from his displeasure. "This island is desolate, barren of the one thing he desires most, for the winds have abandoned us."

"Not so much as a breeze."

"Not for centuries," Futari confirmed. "But his little schemes sometimes entrap other imps. He plies them with sway and toys with their lives, often engendering new lives. Like mine. Like my sister's. We are born in captivity, and he idles through his days, indulging his abominable curiosity."

Pim pounced on the heart of the diatribe. "So you *do* have a sister?"

The dragoness pressed closer, fluting miserably. "Not anymore."

18

SMUGGLE BUDDIES

Jacques knew he wasn't meant to pay a speck of attention to staff. Beneath notice and all that. But if his instincts were on point, this resort employed an unusual number of felines. Pretty boys, all. And with an instinct for attention, because the two fellows assigned as their escorts definitely noticed that he was noticing them.

Before any of the enticing possibilities could go to his head, Jacques pulled Akira to his side.

His startled glance melted into simple happiness. "Excited?"

"Quite stimulated."

"Will there be time to explore?"

"To your heart's content," Jacques promised.

Their Amaranthine escorts looked on with indulgent smiles, very much in keeping with feline consorts. One had even begun purring in a hopeful way. His gaze promised every kind of attentiveness, should the invitation be extended.

"I could get a little lost here," Akira remarked.

"*Impossible*. Since I will not let you go from my side." Jacques adjusted his hold and waltzed Akira along the hall. "We are in this together, *non*?"

"I'm entirely in your hands," Akira agreed, cheerful in his formality.

The younger man had been applying himself to their dance lessons. So much so, Akira was already at the point that he didn't have to think so much about what his feet were doing. He fit nicely against Jacques' larger frame, and he responded beautifully to the subtle push and pull of guidance.

"Lord. I'm of half a mind to keep you."

Akira rolled his eyes. "Since when do you do anything half-heartedly?"

"I seem to recall bidding my brother a half-hearted goodbye when I left my homeland."

"You have a brother?"

"*Mon dieu*. Have you never heard me talk about Bon-Bon? I shall regale you with tales of his exploits over dinner this evening. He's deliciously obnoxious."

Their feline attendants opened a door and bowed them through. The suite of rooms was appropriately grand, and their baggage was already waiting in the bed chamber. After a surprisingly haphazard highlight of a few of the amenities, one of the felines—a silver that brought Chiilu of Evernhold to mind— said, "Call for us if you want company."

Jacques beckoned. "Akira, these good clansmen flatter us.

Feline grooming sessions are exquisite, and they're offering."

With an artless smile, Akira said, "Thanks. That would be nice."

"Thank them *properly*," Jacques urged.

There was much rubbing of cheeks and rumbling purrs. Jacques watched carefully, wanting to make sure the white-haired one didn't manhandle Akira, but he was favored with the gentlest of embraces and respectful kisses. Despite their reputation, cats understood restraint, and these had fine manners.

Akira wanted to know their names.

The silver, whose eyes were vividly blue, introduced himself as Anjou. The white, whose eyes were a calm green, gave the name Eiji. Jacques suspected that they'd been assigned because both were fluent in Japanese, which made things easier on Akira.

"Have you worked together long?" Jacques asked.

Eiji hesitantly searched Anjou's face. "I … I suppose that must be so."

The silver touched fingertips with him. "You *do* seem familiar …?"

Neither sounded sure.

However, they were quite capable of a coordinated effort. While Eiji offered to show Akira the view from their balcony, Anjou hastily applied to Jacques.

"Call for us," he begged. "Any time. Every time."

Jacques was frankly baffled by the fellow's neediness. "I'm not lacking for companionship. Neither are you, if your counterpart is amenable. Why not indulge each other?"

He pouted vaguely. "We're not allowed."

"Doesn't that make it all the more delicious?"

"Usually?" Anjou plucked unhappily at his uniform. "Something's strange, but I can't recall *what*. Except that catering to guests is essential, and you are ours. So … please?"

Jacques suspected that these clansmen were in trouble. But inviting them in might invite scrutiny. He casually asked, "*Exclusively* ours?"

"If you insisted. Please, *do* insist."

"My hearth is necessarily narrow, but a cat's balance is uncanny. Will you look to me and only me if I shelter you here?"

"I'd give any vow. Something's wrong here, but you feel right."

Anjou grasped Jacques' hand in both of his and bowed until his forehead touched it. The gesture was heartbreakingly familiar, and Jacques was undone.

He said, "Thank you for your trust. It seems we will be in each other's care."

The silver flew to his partner, and they clung to each other.

Jacques couldn't bring himself to regret his decision. "Akira, these good cats wish to stay with us, and I haven't the heart to turn them away."

"Is that so?" With a small shrug, Akira pointed out, "There's plenty of room."

"And you're not opposed to taking on a couple of consorts?"

Akira shot him a disbelieving look. "Consorts? Not *really*."

"No, not really," Jacques conceded. "But Anjou and Eiji asked for sanctuary. We'll have to find ways to keep them busy."

His young man looked to the felines and softly said, "I think I know what's wrong. This is all very … *touch my nose*."

Jacques obligingly dropped a kiss on his nose. "Nothing changes. And two chaperones will not save you from my wiles."

"I'm not the one who needs saving."

"You say that now." Jacques patted his cheek and suggested, "Help me unpack?"

Akira hesitated. "Everything?"

"I'll feel more at home." Jacques angled his head toward their servants. "And it might just clear the air."

Jacques began with a cursory inspection of the walk-in closet and set the two felines to work arranging Akira's things, with the understanding that if they proved capable, he'd let them handle his own clothes.

Then he knelt before the enormous steamer trunk emblazoned with Smythe heraldry. Randolla had worked with Ginkgo to create a false bottom that was sigiled out of memory, then freshly lined the trunk with gold silk. Jacques opened the hidey-hole and lifted out the first of six tuned crystals.

"In order," Jacques murmured. "Set this one on that dresser over there."

"Sure." Akira peered over Jacques' shoulder. "Wait. Aren't these supposed to be … umm … y'know …?"

Argent had worked some of his foxiest magic on these remnant stones, so at first glance, they looked like ordinary things. The atomizer appeared to be made from green glass, with detailing that ensured it matched Jacques' own brush set. All part of a gentleman's toilette.

"Have a care. It's heavier than it looks."

Akira's face registered surprise, then understanding. He placed it and returned for the next piece of the array.

Jacques handed off what looked like a small vase with graceful curves. "Windowsill," he directed. "It will look well with the light shining through."

Each item was warded to dissuade notice, and all were ornamented or accented in a range of the spritely green that was Jacques' favorite color. He had Akira place the decanter next. Then a hand mirror and a fussy timepiece.

"You thought of everything," Akira said softly.

"Not I. Though a certain someone had me in mind." It was a shame Jacques couldn't keep the items. Each was perfectly suited to his tastes. They were the sorts of gifts he'd have cherished. Tasteful. Personal. He offered the final item with the faintest of smirks. "Bedside table."

Akira took the bottle of oil without comment, but he flushed.

So he wasn't *totally* oblivious.

Jacques moved about the room, carefully adjusting placements.

"Is it working?" Akira whispered.

"No way for us to know. Inti's meant to check on us. He'll be able to tell."

Akira perched on the edge of the bed. "So … we wait."

"We do." With a glance toward the closet, Jacques joined Akira. "How familiar are you with the foibles of the feline clans?"

"I mean … I know Sensei. And Deece."

"Then you know nothing." Jacques took Akira's hand and fit their fingers together. "Hisoka and Deece are the most reserved hearthcats on the planet. Our new friends will likely be excessively attentive. Highly receptive. Eager to please."

"How do *you* know about cats?"

Jacques supposed Akira hadn't been in a position to know.

"Deece treats me like a brother, which led to my meeting some of his brothers. They're much more ... *more*. And his fathers have been *extremely* hospitable."

Akira took a moment to respond, but all he asked was, "You've met Deece's parents?"

"More than met." Jacques gently squeezed his hand. "Do try to read between the lines."

"I ... don't like to assume."

Jacques sighed. "Unlike *certain* people of our acquaintance, I have no desire to remain celibate. I'm quite sure that Argent and Hisoka conspired to provide me with occasional companionship. It's not everything I want, but I have no complaints."

Akira asked, "What *do* you want?"

"Something like this." Jacques shrugged. "Someone like you."

"Or maybe someone like *you*." Akira squeezed his hand back. "Devotion for Devotion."

"More to the point, if you rebuff Anjou and Eiji politely, they'll turn to each other for solace. Don't be too terribly shocked if you walk in on them *in flagrante*."

"What about you?"

"*Moi*? I don't shock easily."

"I meant ... will *you* rebuff them?"

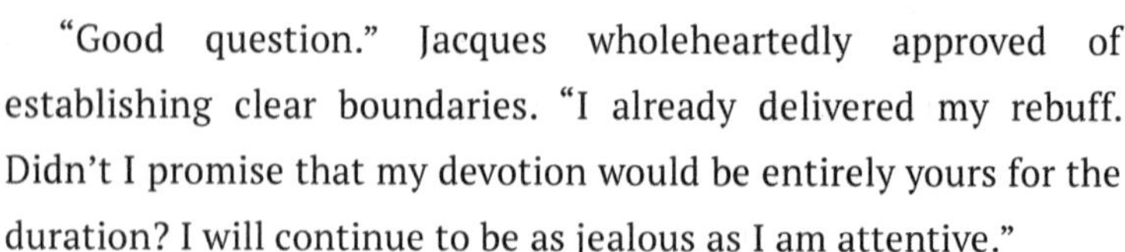

"Good question." Jacques wholeheartedly approved of establishing clear boundaries. "I already delivered my rebuff. Didn't I promise that my devotion would be entirely yours for the duration? I will continue to be as jealous as I am attentive."

Akira leaned into him. "Okay, then."

"You sound relieved. Are you actually relieved?"

"Yeah. Is that selfish of me?" Akira's brows pinched together. "I mean, what if the person you're meant to meet is here somewhere?"

"In the highly unlikely event that my destined partner has been knocking about in these tropics, then they'll have to wait for me a bit longer. Lord knows, I've been waiting on them long enough."

"That's a nice idea."

"Here's another. I've been keeping track. Guess how many penalties you owe me?"

"Err ... didn't the unpacking mean it's safe to talk?"

"Couldn't say. Which means there are things you *shouldn't* have said." Jacques tapped Akira's lips and grumbled, "Anjou and Eiji kissed away all your gloss."

"They seem scared."

"Like kittens when a typhoon is threatening."

Akira frowned a little and nodded a little and eventually said, "You're a good man, Jacques."

"Slanderous brat," Jacques murmured, not at all put out. "Well. I suppose I could be good if I set my mind to it. I did promise to be good to you."

"*Good* as in ... letting me off easy where penalties are concerned?"

"More along the lines of ... good enough to cover your eyes if our new flatmates get frisky."

Akira grinned, all friendly camaraderie.

Jacques let himself bask.

19

FLYING BLIND

uuyu was as sure of his bearing as anyone could be, but there was nothing in view but boundless sea. They were nearing their destination, so he angled his wings, slowing into a spiraling glide and waiting for some clue what to do next.

"Hello, friend phoenix," came a voice, clear as Kindred.

He answered in kind. *"I am here. We are here."*

"Give our wards a moment to let you through. I'm Lupe, by the way."

"First of Reaches," he acknowledged. *"We are six."*

"Yes, that's how many we were told to expect. All right. You should be able to see a little of our beach now. It probably looks strange, but it counts as our front step. You and your team may land."

Juuyu sang out a greeting and swerved toward a slim crescent of sand that shimmered into existence below. He remained in truest form until the last moment, shifting into speaking form in time for his shoes to lightly touch pale sand. Straightening his tie, he stepped toward the lone figure awaiting them and presented his palms. "You must be Priska Runefarer."

"And I know who you all are," she returned in a tone that suggested they were here under protest.

He turned as the rest glided lower. A white wolf and a red dog—Moon and Merit—were followed by a powerful horse with two riders. Colt had insisted that Sinder and Hallow conserve their strength by riding.

"My team," he offered, since he doubted this lady wanted a full and formal introduction.

Priska, whose pale blue hair was messy enough to be distracting, pointed at him accusingly. "This was not mentioned."

Juuyu touched his forehead. "My bondmate is tree-kin."

"Hmm." Her attitude shifted somewhat. "That may work in your favor. Our people will be less suspicious of someone blessed by a tree."

"Nobody mentioned more trees," called Sinder, who was taking shelter behind Colt's considerable bulk. "Are there trees here, too?"

Colt lipped his hair and nickered.

Sinder rolled his eyes. "It's not my fault every tree I meet is fascinated by dragons."

"You will find ours more wary." Priska's lip curled. "Dragons do not have a good reputation in the Eldermost Islands."

"What kind of reputation do we have?"

"Pilferers and pillagers. You strip whole islands of their wild-life, people, livestock, and crops." Her eyes narrowed accusingly.

"Every unprotected island in the general vicinity stands empty."

"You shouldn't hold *me* accountable," protested Sinder. "I'm one of the good guys."

Priska's hum was unimpressed.

Moon stepped forward, concern plain on his face. "How long has this area been at risk?"

She favored the wolf with a flat look. "Places like this have *always* been at risk. Your presence puts us at greater risk."

The entire taskforce shifted into some variation on a receptive stance. But none of them apologized.

"Why?" asked Sinder, who'd come to Juuyu's side. "Why would anyone steal from neighboring islands?"

"You seem a very modern dragon. Young. You would not remember." With a sigh, Priska said, "They are likely hungry. It is an old-fashioned way of life."

"Is she saying they eat islanders?" Sinder asked softly.

Juuyu patted his partner's back and asked, "Who do we speak to about Boon?"

"There is no *we*. And you go no further. Except the dragon." Priska grimly pointed toward a sandbar that was just visible and probably served as a breakwater for this lagoon.

"Seriously? Fine, fine." Sinder held up his hands in surrender. "I don't mind waiting in the water. I like to swim."

Priska nodded stiffly. "Thank you for understanding."

Just then, a man hurried onto the beach from seemingly nowhere. Priska turned and hissed. "Makani, you should not be here."

"Lupe sent me to help greet our guests." The man was tall and broad and bronzed, with long black hair knotted atop his head and decorated by clusters of pink flowers. He presented his palms to the group and offered an almost bashful, "Hello."

Juuyu stepped forward to touch hands and had to look up. Makani's gaze was curious and his smile awkward. To put him at ease, Juuyu went through abbreviated introductions, presenting each of his teammates, before asking, "You are tree-kin?"

"Yes."

Priska hissed.

"We can hardly hide it from another who is favored." Makani tapped his own forehead and shyly added, "My Lupe's mark shines here, for my sister adores her."

Juuyu tried to steer the conversation back to business. "Can you tell me anything about the array Boon is meant to be setting up?"

"Me? Uhh … no."

Priska cut in. "The array is priceless. Yielding it meant removing a layer of our protections in the scant hope it might boost the range of your unregistered reach."

"Did it work?" called Sinder, who still loitered in the shallows, listening in.

"We do not know."

Juuyu asked, "Is the array incomplete?"

"It is finished."

"Does it function?" Juuyu was beginning to be concerned. Had something gone wrong?

Priska stiffly said, "Lupe has been preoccupied."

Merit stepped forward. "Where is Boon?"

"Gone."

"Gone *where*?" growled Merit, who was understandably

protective of Boon, his childhood friend.

Makani made a helpless gesture.

Priska said, "He never returned from his last trek to that uncharted island of yours."

"Two days ago," Makani meekly added.

Merit demanded, "What's been done?"

No answer was forthcoming.

Sinder called, "Which way?"

When Priska pointed, Sinder dove.

While the Runefarer clan had grudgingly permitted Juuyu and his team to rest and regroup on the outermost fringe of their territory, Makani made certain that they were treated well. A small group of smiling men and women brought refreshments. Every one of them was a reaver, and this was their hospitality.

Juuyu and the rest accepted their kindness, though it was frustrating. As yet, they hadn't been allowed to speak with Lupe. And nobody else could tell them about Boon, Inti, or the array. Only Makani knew that the wolf had even been nearby.

A couple of hours passed before Priska stalked back onto the beach. "Your dragon has returned. We are adjusting the barrier to allow him back through."

"Thank you." Juuyu quietly asked, "Will we be allowed to meet with Lupe?"

"Not my decision." Her lip curled. "If it was, the answer would be *no*."

"The situation is urgent."

"Your urgency is not my priority."

Juuyu had no idea why she was being so cagey. "What *is* your priority?"

Priska's jaw worked, but she offered no answer. Only watched Sinder slosh onto the beach, Boon's surfboard under his arm.

He passed it to Merit, patted the dog clansman's shoulder, and addressed Juuyu. "Boon did pretty good. I tweaked the array. It's working at full strength, now." To Priska, he added, "Those are some of the finest remnants I ever saw. Thank you for trusting him with them."

"Not my decision," she repeated.

"Yeah. You know, I've been thinking. I'd like to thank Lupe in person." Hints of sway began seeping into his tone, but he made no actual demands. "I'm one of the dragons who sang for Tzefira's descent. In some circles—especially our kind of Circles—that makes me a friend of the family."

Juuyu made a subtle gesture, calling for caution.

Sinder calmly waved him off. "I know the array's working because Lupe told me so. She and I worked out a compromise. Juuyu and I are expected."

Priska looked away, looked back, and said, "I see."

She fished in her pocket and tossed them each a blue marble. They weren't especially potent, but they were tuned to the barrier. Following Priska, they stepped past it.

Juuyu caught Sinder's elbow and arched his brows in silent inquiry.

"I didn't use sway," he grumbled.

"Yet you negotiated terms," Juuyu countered. "Where is the *compromise* you mentioned?"

"I might have volunteered us for something in order to guarantee an in-person meeting."

Juuyu sighed.

"It's a small thing," Sinder promised, looking embarrassed. "Very traditional. But it was the only thing I could think of, and Makani's twin loved the idea."

"What do I need to do?"

"First, I'd appreciate it if you stayed between me and Makani's sister."

"Certainly." Juuyu knew how awkward Sinder was with the overtures of trees, especially the ones who manifested as females. "And ...?"

"I might need a barrier." With a sidelong look, he added, "I'm going to sing. Well ... we'll make it a duet. Doubly auspicious, that way."

Auspicious. And powerful.

Juuyu's attention was snagged by the small village that came into view. Round, whitewashed houses with shingled peaks were scattered through a grove. Chimes hung in open windows, each spinning musically in playful breezes. Every house belonged to a tree. Or perhaps it was the other way around, since the trees had no doubt been planted beside their twin's front step.

Pink flowers filled the air with subtle sweetness, and Juuyu inhaled deeply before murmuring, "I could sing here."

"*And* ..." Sinder added, easing a little behind Juuyu. "*You* get to hold the baby we're blessing."

20

ORIENTATION

Akira had no particular reason to worry as Anjou and Eiji led the way along hushed hallways toward a vast lobby, then into a spacious dining room. Guest orientation was to take place between the courses of their evening meal.

Although this was a public space, with room for dozens of other guests, tables were discreetly tucked behind woven screens or ornate panels. Akira could hear muted conversations, the clink of cutlery on plates, and even the pop of a cork. It sounded as busy as a popular restaurant, but guests were receiving personal attention and privacy.

Eiji pulled aside a heavy velvet curtain, bowing Akira and Jacques into a cozy nook where a table awaited. The whole setting screamed romantic dinner for two. Jacques made a circuit of the table, then pulled Akira over to a sideboard, exclaiming over the painting hanging above it.

"First rule upon entering a room," he said with a sidelong look. "Make it your own."

Akira couldn't help smiling. "Is that your secret?"

"Hardly a secret." With a thoughtful pout, Jacques said, "It's more of an attitude, really. Every detail is here for our enjoyment. Every courtesy is meant for our comfort. So relax. This promises to be a lovely evening."

"Please *do* relax," urged Eiji. "It is our pleasure to wait upon your every need."

Anjou indicated a menu beside Jacques' place setting. "We will alert the kitchen to your preferences."

Akira only felt a little awkward when Eiji held his chair. It was far more flustering when the feline next pulled out a tuffet from under the sideboard in order to sit beside him. "What are you doing?" Akira whispered.

"Making myself available."

"For *what* ...?"

Eiji opened the menu and showed it to him. The entire thing was in French.

"Oh. Right. Thanks." Really. Akira had been spending too much time with Jacques. Everything was beginning to sound like propositions and entendre.

They chatted for a while about specialties, but Akira was at a loss. "Jacques. Choose for me?"

It was the right thing to ask.

Jacques was in his element. He sent Anjou and Eiji scurrying, and within minutes, they were visited by both a sommelier and a barkeep, and then a chef arrived in order to confer. Akira wasn't sure if this meant the resort staff was extremely accommodating ... or if Jacques really was *that* important.

"What's he asking for?" whispered Akira, when Eiji returned to his tuffet.

"A beautiful meal for his beautiful boy," he purred.

"Oh. Okay, yeah. That actually sounds like something he'd say. But I was sort of curious about ... you know, like, what kind of soup?"

With a coy shake of his head, Eiji said, "I would not dream of spoiling the surprise. This meal is his gift to you."

Which was kind of silly, but also kind of cool. Akira caught Jacques' eye and quietly admitted, "He's been my guide all along the way."

"Trust him," Eiji urged. "He loves you."

Jacques had been right to be cautious. And honest about his feelings. Akira couldn't think of an appropriate response, so he held his tongue.

But Amaranthine didn't necessarily rely on words to draw conclusions. Eiji said, "You long for his happiness. You feel safe in his arms."

"You noticed that already? Guess I can't hide much."

"You can make him happy. Blissfully so." The cat coaxed, "I could show you how."

Time for that rebuff.

"Thanks for the support, but no." Akira looked up and found Jacques watching closely. "I've trusted Jacques this far. He'll take care of the rest."

From across the table, the man blew him a kiss.

Akira ducked his head to keep from laughing.

Eiji was purring when he slipped away to help Anjou set out the first course.

They were five courses into the most interesting meal Akira had ever shared with anyone. The food came on small plates, just a taste, really. Artfully arranged. Interesting to try. Never enough. Akira had never been teased by a meal before. It gave a restless undercurrent to their conversation, which also drew him in, because Jacques spun out stories of his childhood.

"To this day, Bon-Bon considers hedgehogs an unholy horror."

Akira caught his breath and dabbed at his eyes with his napkin. "You're *awful*."

"My brother is awful. *I* am generosity itself. For instance, I found pajamas with wee ickle hedgehogs printed on them. Pure silk. Entirely decadent. So I sent them to dear Bon-Bon last Christmas."

Akira could *see* it, and he slouched in his chair, taken with a fresh fit of giggles.

"Posture," Jacques scolded, even as he slid his feet under Akira's in their usual way.

It was cozy. Akira was completely relaxed. Maybe he'd needed to laugh. Maybe it was the star wine.

Anjou collected their plates and whisked away imaginary crumbs in preparation for another course, but instead, they received a guest.

"Good evening, good sirs. My name is Linlu Dimityblest, and it is my responsibility to familiarize you with our facilities and amenities."

Oh. It was orientation time.

Akira had entirely forgotten.

The newcomer lightly clapped his hands. "How are you finding things thus far?"

Jacques casually lifted a hand so it was palm-up over his shoulder. To Akira's surprise, Anjou immediately took a position behind Jacques' chair and rested his fingertips upon that palm.

Jacques said, "Your staff is unusually affectionate."

"Ah. A group of felines was recently brought in to tempt another of our guests. We have a lady mistress on the island." With a flutter of fingers Linlu added, "Newcomers are especially susceptible to the pollen. They find it ... *invigorating*."

"Lord. They've been pollinated?"

"Everyone on the island is, to some degree." Linlu's smile was bland. "Our particular combination favors couples."

"*Oui*. I'm quite stirred up. But should you be talking about such things openly?"

"You are Jacques Smythe, near constant companion of Argent Mettlebright. Most believe you keep his confidences, so it stands to reason that you are privy to delicate matters such as this."

Jacques arched his brows. "Shocking what people will assume in the absence of actual facts."

"Are you claiming ignorance?" Linlu asked smilingly.

"I am embracing discretion."

"Laudable." Nodding toward the felines, Linlu asked, "Are you dissatisfied with the arrangement?"

"Far from it." Jacques threaded his fingers with Anjou's. "He and Eiji will be staying in our suite for the duration of our stay. I demand it."

"Also laudable."

"*Non.* I am a hedonist at heart."

With a light laugh, Linlu changed the subject. "I do apologize for interrupting your courses and your conversation. I will keep necessary information to a minimum, and after you have finished your meal, I will guide you through a leisurely tour of the facilities."

Jacques stood and murmured something to Anjou, who slipped away. He beckoned to Eiji, who moved Jacques' chair around the table, setting it beside Akira's. The tuffet was stowed to make room for three more chairs. Jacques even offered to have new place settings brought so they could share the remainder of the meal together.

"That would be inappropriate," warned Linlu.

"Who will quibble? As a guest, my preferences should be indulged."

Hand pressed to his heart, Linlu murmured, "Maker bless, you are magnificent."

Jacques dropped into his chair and claimed Akira's hand. "Good of you to notice."

"However … I must caution you against drawing more attention than you already have."

The moth clansman's hands moved in ways Akira found familiar. He was working sigilcraft. Actually, if Akira tipped his head and squinted, he thought he could see a faint sparkle. Like dust motes in formation. He rubbed at the tattoo on his shoulder. Was this a lingering effect of Suuzu's fiddling with the sigil during the few days before they'd parted?

Jacques watched Linlu with what passed for polite interest. Unless you knew him. Which Akira did. At times, especially important occasions, Jacques could be a little scary. It occurred to Akira that being Lord Mettlebright's near-constant companion had provided Jacques with impressive mentors. Sometimes, he was as keen-eyed as Argent, and at others, he exuded the same diplomatic poise for which Hisoka-sensei was famous.

"There now. Better?" Linlu inquired.

"Has something changed?" Jacques asked.

"Perhaps. Shall we see?" Presenting his palms, their liaison said, "My name is Linlu Dimityblest."

"You mentioned that earlier," Jacques said blandly. Then blinked. "Wait a tick! If I remember correctly …?"

"I am certain you do. Now."

"Lord. Why are *you* here?"

Linlu made a helpless gesture. "Why is anyone here?"

Akira squeezed Jacques' hand and whispered, "What is it? Who is he?"

"Lord," he repeated faintly. "Akira, this is one of the original founders of Wardenclave, missing for what … three centuries?"

"The years have been long." Linlu's smile was thin and tired. "I ran afoul of a couple of vixens."

20

REPUTATION PRECEDES

Pim came to herself in a lounge chair beside the pool, but this time, the only thing she couldn't recall was how she'd gotten there. Her conversation with Futari was clear in her memory. There hadn't been a lot of information, and little of it was useful in the grand scheme of things. But the events Futari hinted at had been life-rending.

The dragoness was certainly allied to her father, but Pim believed self-preservation was at the heart of her compliance. And ... hatred.

Had she been able to comfort Futari even a little? Or did being dumped poolside amount to a rejection of her offer of friendship?

Rubbing at her forehead, Pim decided it was a good sign that she retained any memories at all. Unlike Dr. Kodoku, Futari hadn't forced her to *never mind*.

"Pim?"

She turned her head. And gaped. Hisoka Twineshaft crouched a short distance away.

"Are you Pim Moonprowl?" he inquired.

"Yes."

"Come with me."

"Yes."

Pim thought they were both a little surprised by her immediate compliance. They didn't go far. Only to a place that hid them from view. Even though it wasn't really necessary, she found herself asking, "Spokesperson Twineshaft?"

"Yes."

"What are you …?" She trailed off, at a loss. Not so much because he was here. Inti had spilled that little secret. Pim was trying to make sense of the child who rode on his shoulders, clinging to his hair. "Who …?"

"I call him Patter."

The child rested one chubby cheek against pewter hair … and peeped.

"He has antlers," she whispered.

"I had noticed." Hisoka patiently inquired, "Where is Boon?"

"My bed." The guy actually flinched, so she clarified. "Inti warded my suite. It's the best we could do, under the circumstances. Boon was able to go deep."

"Alone?"

"My friend Elara is watching over his rest."

Hisoka's flared brows drew together. "Boon would not have accepted a female companion."

"That's debatable." Waving off his bafflement, Pim said, "His preferences drove me from the den. I've been conducting my own investigation ever since."

He slowly—perhaps reluctantly—eased into a receptive posture. "What have you learned?"

Pim was ready. She'd been mentally organizing a list all along. "This facility was built with the comfort of human guests in mind. There are signs of multiple renovations in order to modernize the amenities to appeal to wealthy clients."

"Clients," he echoed. "Like yourself?"

"Yes. And I'm not the first Amaranthine desperate enough to pay Dr. Kodoku's fee."

"What does he promise?"

"Children."

Hisoka lifted a hand to pat the child he carried. "Adoption?"

"Procreation," she corrected. "He claims to have found an answer to the Waning."

"So he *is* trying to appeal to the clans." His gaze finally met hers. "Or … to certain individuals."

"Probably. Linlu would know. But there's something else that's strange." She summed up the findings from her interviews. "Many of the people here have been residents of the island for as long as they can remember. They came for one reason or another, and they stayed on. And because they're effectively cut off from the outside world, they don't know me."

"I take it you are unaccustomed to anonymity."

Pim's tail twitched. "I'd wager they're equally clueless about *your* identity. Elara is the only person I've met so far who's aware that the Emergence happened."

Hisoka took his time answering. "Why is she different?"

"She hasn't been here as long. A relatively recent hire." Pim bared her teeth. "Futari says she's becoming less susceptible to Dr. Kodoku's words. Maybe because she used to be staff?"

"May I meet this woman?" He smoothed his hair. Or tried.

Patter interfered with further rumpling. Pim had never seen Spokesperson Twineshaft looking quite so disheveled. It was charming.

"Do you mind if I make a stop first?" She was already backing away. "I promised to bring Elara dinner."

Pim was a little shocked at herself. This was *the* Hisoka Twineshaft, arguably the most influential Amaranthine in the world.

He seemed equally unsettled to have been preempted. But his manners were excellent.

"Yes, Mistress Moonprowl." Inclining his head, he murmured, "I will be waiting here."

Pim burst through her suite door, laden with bags of steamed buns and a carrier of drinks, which included a bottle of milk for Patter. While she hastily unburdened herself, dumping everything on the table, she said, "He's here."

"Who? Inti?" Elara put down her book. A different one than she'd been reading earlier.

Her bedside reading light was the suite's only illumination, so Pim flipped a couple of switches.

"Guess again." Pim hurried to the window. Twilight was amazingly brief in this part of the world, so it was already dark. But starlight was enough for her to see by.

Hisoka waited in the shrubbery below, talking softly to the antlered child. He glanced up, pointed her out, then changed his grip. "Catch?"

Pim immediately leaned over the sill, arms open.

Bless his little heart, Patter mimicked her. And Hisoka tossed the baby up.

"Elara, look!" she softly exclaimed. "Isn't he precious?"

Her friend was dumbstruck.

Pim turned to see Hisoka Twineshaft crouched in front of the window. "Inti *did* mention ...?"

Elara softly asked, "Will there be any *other* Most Eligible Bachelors joining us?"

"Most of my people don't make headlines." Hisoka straightened, ran a hand over his hair, and indicated the bed. "May I check on Boon?"

"Go ahead. Reassure yourself." Pim dragged her attention from Patter's soft gaze to ask, "Elara, do you need a break?"

She simply shook her head, eyes wide.

Hisoka hesitated. "May I approach?"

"It's fine." Elara guiltily snatched her hand from Boon's hair. "He's fine."

"So I see." Kneeling beside the bed, he reached across Elara to rest his palm against the sleeping wolf's cheek.

Boon's breathing changed. He turned his face into Hisoka's palm, inhaling.

"How long has he been deep?" Hisoka asked.

"Day before yesterday," said Pim, who was watching closely. She'd purposefully not told him anything about Elara. His reaction to her would define her opinion of him.

"Thank you for seeing to his comfort." Another pause. A proffered palm. "My name is Hisoka Twineshaft."

"I *know*."

"I suppose many do. And you are?"

"Elara."

Pim crisply interjected, "Dr. Elara Perrine."

Hisoka inclined his head. "I understand you were formerly a member of the staff?"

"Glorified lab assistant, really. Naoki-san handles all the really important work. At least, the stuff Dr. Kodoku doesn't do himself." She seemed to lose her train of thought. "But that was before. Now, I'm a regular client. Like Pim."

"And you're a reaver," he said, both hands now cradling hers.

"Not especially."

"Not so." Hisoka looked toward Pim. "She's bright as stars. You would agree?"

There it was.

With the drop of the appropriate pronoun, Pim's tension faded, and her tail settled around her ankles. "She is."

While Spokesperson Twineshaft continued to question Elara, Pim plunked Patter on the table and rummaged through her bag of takeout. The boy chittered and cooed over the bao she gave him, which was cute, but she was more focused on Hisoka's voice. It was familiar, but ... different. Softer and warmer than the tone he took when addressing nations.

And he was so unassuming. Almost like he didn't want her to take notice. It made her wonder.

In most episodes of *Pure Instinct*, the criminal seemed above suspicion at first glimpse. Too ordinary. Even helpful. Not that she thought Hisoka Twineshaft was actually some kind of criminal mastermind. But by trying to fade into the background, he'd piqued the interest of the wolf in her.

Patter was also watching Hisoka. Holding his half-eaten bun toward him, he called, "Sen, Sen, Sen!"

Hisoka turned, and his lips quirked. "Yes?"

"He wants to share." Pim unpacked the food. "There's plenty."

"Sen?" asked Elara.

"My friends call me Sensei." Rising, he offered a hand to help Elara up.

"Oh ... umm ... no. He doesn't like it when I leave." She shifted demonstrably, and Boon's arms tightened as he nosed at her hip, rubbing his cheek against the silk of her borrowed chemise. Elara pet the wolf's hair and quietly admitted, "It's nice to feel wanted."

"You have been generous with him. I'm sure he'll return courtesy for courtesy." Hisoka knelt again. "Do you know? I have a favorite companion when the time comes for sleep. Most do, since we must trust ourselves completely into another's keeping."

"That's a confession for the ages! You're famously *un*attached."

Hisoka shook his head. "I remain so, in part because I chose a partner with whom I cannot accidentally bond-build. Boon has similar priorities, since he's a lone wolf."

Pim thought she understood. "Has he been bond-building with Elara?"

"There are signs."

"Did I do something wrong?" asked Elara.

"Peace," soothed Hisoka. "If I understand the circumstances correctly, you aren't at fault."

"He mistook me ... umm," Elara whispered, shooting a pleading look in Pim's direction.

"I wondered." Hisoka cleared his throat. "With apologies for the personal nature of my inquiry, is it possible that you ladies sometimes share garments?"

Pim nodded.

Elara explained, "We're basically the same size, and it's easier than moving a bunch of things from my room."

"Ah." Hisoka quietly asked, "Am I right in my guess that your current garment belongs to Pim?"

"Yes. Gorgeous color," said Elara. "I couldn't resist."

He hummed and cast a worried look Pim's way. "That would explain the mingled scents."

Pim covered her mouth.

Hisoka sighed. "We won't know for certain until he wakes. In the meantime, Inti has encouraged me to remove you from this place. Will you come with me?"

Leave Elara? Instincts rebelled. But rather than answer, Pim raised a question of her own. "Where *is* Inti?"

Hisoka hummed vaguely. "Several details need to come together. He's seeing to another one."

He may as well have said, *none of your business*. Which wasn't

any way for a team to operate. But maybe the illustrious spokes
-person didn't understand that she could be useful. "You can trust
me, you know."

"It isn't that I *don't* trust you."

Another rebuff? Pim had no trouble at all tucking her tail. "Inti
wanted me *removed*? I'm capable of defending myself."

"Against dragon sway?"

Pim wavered. "No."

Hisoka stood, withdrawing a paper from an inner pocket.
"While I don't like to be the bearer of bad news, Inti brought this
to my attention."

She scanned the flier, paled, and slowed to read it more carefully.

"I'm assuming this was put together without your consent?"

"What is it?" Elara called.

Pim shuddered.

With a sigh, Hisoka pulled her into his arms before speaking on
her behalf. "Kodoku is the leader of this place? Founder, owner, or
whatever he calls himself?"

"Yes," said Elara.

"And he is a dragon, having purple hair and red eyes?"

"Is he?" Elara asked.

Pim nodded.

"It would seem he has undertaken a money-making venture,
and Pim is at the heart of it." A growl slipped into his next words.
"Resort guests will be bidding for the chance to bed her."

"Nightly," spat Pim, though her voice was muffled against
Twineshaft's tunic.

Elara urgently begged, "You have to get away!"

"Not if it leaves you vulnerable," she argued.

"I can add to Inti's wards. Elara will be safe until Boon wakes, and then she will be even safer." Hisoka tucked Pim under his chin. "Come away with me, Mistress Moonprowl. You can help me survey the island. I must locate the wardstones that anchor its barrier."

Pim could practically feel this cat's years, and they were weighty with power. Right at this moment, she couldn't imagine trying to rule over him in the manner of mistresses. She only wanted to shelter for a little longer. Just until she found the courage to lash back at the damnable dragon she'd been fool enough to trust.

Almost, he made her wish she was still a cat. But Pim shook her head.

"I'm a good tracker," she offered, easing out of his arms and adopting a receptive attitude. "I understand teamwork."

Hisoka scooped up Patter and stepped back. "Thank you, Mistress Moonprowl."

"Pim, sir," she corrected. "Call me Pim."

Taking an assertive stance, Hisoka searched her face and seemed to come to a decision. Including both women, he asked, "Didn't I mention that my friends call me Sensei? I'm sure I did."

22
CHECK BOXES

During their after-dinner tour, Jacques walked ahead with Linlu, deep in conversation. They were talking low and fast in English, and Akira gave up trying to follow. His steps lagged, as well, which forced Anjou and Eiji to separate. The former prowled along behind Jacques, and the latter remained at Akira's side.

"Are you well?" Eiji asked.

"Fine." With a shrug, he said, "I usually just follow Jacques around, so I don't need to know every little thing."

"Do you want to return to the suite?"

"This is fine. Really."

Eiji hummed. He sounded skeptical.

It made Akira curious. "Am I behaving strangely?"

"I'm not sure. The customs of my clan color my perceptions."

Intrigued, he asked, "How do I seem to you?"

Their steps slowed, and Eiji's gaze flitted briefly to Jacques. "You want him close, yet you're not jealous. You wait for his gaze, yet his attention confuses you. You go willingly into his embrace, yet you're not intimate."

Akira rubbed the back of his neck. "It's come to my attention that I'm kind of a late-bloomer."

Eiji's gaze softened. "Pelts come in every pattern."

"What a nice way to put it." Akira shyly added, "I'm still figuring things out, but I do love Jacques."

"That is well. You're the only one he sees."

"Umm … yeah. I figured that out, too."

Up ahead, Jacques turned to watch him and Eiji. Akira waved, wanting to set his mind at ease. Then Linlu said something that seemed to startle Jacques … and pulled his attention away from his dawdling paramour. They passed through a set of sliding doors, Anjou close on their heels, leaving him and Eiji in a sudden hush.

And Akira was blindsided.

He staggered under the sudden onslaught, except Akira wasn't really being attacked. He was used to the enthusiastic affections of the crossers back home, so he was hugging this one back even before he recognized the gingery hair and chanting voice.

"Found you, found you, found you," Inti sighed, hiding his face against Akira's shoulder.

"Wait, Eiji!" Akira gasped.

Eiji snarled, but he held back the strike he'd readied.

"He's my friend." And to Inti, "I was hoping we'd meet. But you shouldn't have startled us like that. What if Eiji accidentally hurt you?"

"Sorry, sorry." Inti eased from Akira's arms and reached up to pat Eiji's head. "Good, good, good kitty. Protect Akira. Now, hold this for Inti."

The monkey crosser pressed something into Eiji's hand.

He held it up, so Akira could see that it was a disk of hardened clay into which a sigil had been inscribed. They'd worked with something similar back in high school. Clay sigils had been a specialty of Goh-sensei's.

"What's it for?" Akira asked.

Inti simply raised a finger, his attention fixed on Eiji's face.

Akira watched as well, and little by little, the feline clansman's expression changed.

"Your name?" Inti asked, presenting his palms.

"Eiji."

"Do you remember your full name?"

"I'm Eiji Woodhearth."

Akira was startled to realize that up until now, Eiji *hadn't* remembered. What had this island's dragon done to him?

"Good, good." And in that coaxing tone again, "Do you remember why you're here?"

"A consort call …? My coloring fit the lady mistress's preferences. It seemed a good opportunity."

Eiji's attention swung back to Akira.

Unsure what to expect, he asked, "Do you remember me?"

"Akira. Of course." He cast a wary glance along the halls and stepped closer. "Stay close. I don't think this place is at all safe."

"Inti, what did your sigil do?"

The crosser's eyes sparkled. "It worked."

"This. Can I have one for Anjou?"

"Yes, yes, yes. But first, take me to Jacques' room."

Eiji frowned. "What for?"

"Reasons."

Akira laughed. "It's fine. He really is a friend. Let's go."

Along the way, Inti chattered at Eiji in an odd mix of sense and nonsense. Mostly about the usefulness of hiding items in truest form and the dangers of dragon sway. But also about strange pollens, caged lorefolk, and the kinds of tricks that foxes can play. Akira couldn't help but feel that Eiji was being briefed.

"Do you have skills?" Inti held up a hand and amended, "The kinds needed *outside* a lady's chambers."

"Sigilcraft."

"You're good with wards? Barriers?" Tail curling around Eiji's arm, Inti asked, "Are you a crystal adept?"

Eiji nodded.

Inti clambered into his arms and kissed both his cheeks. "Good, good, *good* kitty."

The feline accepted both the compliments and affection with an easy smile. And once Inti climbed further, to perch on Eiji's shoulders, the cat took Akira by the hand and led him down the hall. With a dangerous light in his eyes, Eiji grimly said, "Let's secure our hearth."

Jacques was mildly disgruntled, and his reasons were beyond pitiful.

He should be delighted that Inti was safe. Coming home to find him curled up with Akira on the bed had ticked off another item on their mission checklist. Argent would be pleased that his apprentice had come through this ordeal with such flourish.

Their tricksy crosser had not only finessed the array into perfect alignment, he'd unfogged Anjou and Eiji.

Free of sway, the felines proved to be more than pretty faces. Eiji had been part of an enclave, apprenticed alongside other sigilcrafters. And Anjou was a tribute from the Bonhomie clan, which meant he had insider knowledge about Impressions, *and* he knew how to handle several weapons.

Strategic alliances.

Unforeseen assets.

Yet Jacques was feeling more and more inclined to sulk.

"Jacques? You okay?" Akira asked softly.

Honest answers only. He sighed. "I was looking forward to a nice, private seduction. You've gone and turned it into a cuddle orgy."

Akira glanced down at the monkey-boy huddled against his chest. "He was exhausted. Way overdue for sleep."

"I know."

"Umm ... did you want to hold him? I'm pretty sure he only picked me to tease you."

Completely possible, but Jacques thought that was beside the point. "I don't care about his *reasons*. It's the results I don't like."

Ever the peacemaker, Akira asked, "You want to trade?"

"I do. Stay."

Jacques threw back the duvet and stalked around, sliding in on Akira's side of the bed. When he was done rearranging, he pressed against Akira from behind, with the younger man's head pillowed on his arm. Sliding a hand along Akira's thigh, Jacques haughtily said, "*He* is not the one I wanted to hold."

"So … this is better?"

"The improvement is so miniscule, I refuse to credit it."

Akira turned his head just a little. "Did something happen?"

"Dinner was an exquisite affair."

"It was."

"And there was star wine."

"Your favorite."

Akira really was the personification of patience. At times like this, Jacques found a resemblance to Tsumiko. He sighed. "And … I was enjoying your company."

"Same." No trace of hesitation. Not a bit of guile.

Jacques grumbled, "Under these circumstances, it would have been entirely appropriate for me to kiss you."

"Oookay, yeah. I can see that. But with this and that, you missed your chance."

"And I come home to find you with another bloke in your arms."

Akira chuckled. "I don't think *this* counts as cheating."

"Say what you will, I feel slighted."

"Be fair." Akira gently released Inti and turned to face Jacques. "The romantic gestures were supposed to be for innocent bystanders. And ours are missing."

"Anjou and Eiji are busy in the closet."

"Oh. Was there more to unpack?"

"If that was a euphemism, then yes. They're unpacking with enthusiasm."

Akira's eyes widened.

Jacques touched his face. "Lord. I'm still amazed that a man of your years can blush."

Ignoring the jibe, Akira asked, "What do you expect me to do?"

"Nothing. I'm in a mood and can be safely ignored."

"I'd never ignore a friend!"

"Sympathy makes you easy prey for rakes and cads alike." He rubbed his cheek against Akira's, feline-style. "Fortunately for you, I am neither."

"Oh, I don't know. This part of you feels a little dangerous."

Jacques guessed Akira *did* have a teensy thread of self-preservation somewhere deep down. "I am somewhat gratified to be acknowledged as a threat to your better instincts."

"Eiji thinks we're a couple, you know. It's just like you planned. He believes you're courting me."

"I told you we could carry this off." Jacques searched Akira's upturned face. "I am enamored enough to be patient, and you're curious enough to be open to seduction."

"What if I kissed you goodnight?"

Jacques missed a beat.

It was more like a few beats.

"As we've already established, it's pointless without an audience."

"I don't want an audience. This whole thing is between you and me and Suuzu."

"The pact, you mean?"

"Yeah. We're pactmates, and that means something to me." Reaching up, Akira tugged at one of Jacques loose curls. "Teach me, *s'il vous plait*. I need lessons in Jacques."

He was touched.

And he wanted to be touched.

But maybe they should start with something that was too serious to sulk over. "Did you know that when I first came to Stately House, I was terrified of dragons?"

"Nope."

"*Terrified*," Jacques repeated.

"I'd never have guessed. You and Lapis are really good friends. And there's Kyrie."

"Before the Emergence, my grandfather would get up the most ridiculous expeditions, chasing rumors of mythical creatures in wild places."

"Amaranthine."

"Yes. He'd gotten this group together, mostly university students. There were rumors of dragons in the north, and they were going to spend a summer searching. I begged to go along."

"You were interested in dragons?"

"Not in the least. I was interested in one of the undergrads. He had just the right amount of smirk in his smile. We would have had fun." Jacques tightened his hold on Akira. "But Grandfather put his foot down. Didn't want me distracting his team. He left me home. I was *livid*."

Akira was listening. Not judging or teasing. Really listening. Jacques had come to think of this as an Amaranthine quality. Having someone's full attention was flattering.

He came to the dreadful crux. "A few weeks later, they sent in another team to … to pick up the pieces. Grandfather's team found their dragon. It was the Rogue."

"He kills the males," Akira murmured sadly.

"And takes the females. Kyrie's mother was among them." Jacques revisited the horror of those days and grimaced. "If I'd gotten my way …! I used to have the most abysmal nightmares."

Akira started preening him, light fingers through his hair.

All Jacques wanted was more. "Suuzu is going to pillage me."

"He wouldn't."

With a sigh, Jacques said, "I didn't get the chance to tell you. Linlu says that the owner of this resort wants to welcome me personally. Tomorrow."

"Time to face the dragon?"

"*Mon dieu.* I don't fancy facing him alone."

"Take me along."

"*Non.* You'll stay right here with Anjou and Eiji." Jacques would do whatever was necessary to keep Akira safe. Even this.

"Uncle Jackie," Akira whispered, sounding worried.

Maybe it was a slip of the tongue. Maybe Akira was giving him an opening. Maybe Jacques should have resisted, but he was furious and frightened and frustrated.

Pent up emotions made for potent kisses.

Jacques eventually drew back and whispered an apology. "There will be pillaging and pillories in my near future."

"I'll talk him out of it."

"I'll be more careful."

"And I'll be right here."

Jacques was probably a little bit of a rake and possibly even a cad. Because kissing Akira had settled his nerves. And holding him made him feel safe from the dragons.

Jacques found himself in a tangle, courtesy of Inti. The monkey crosser had turned during the night, flinging an arm around both him and Akira and curling his tail over Jacques' shoulder. But Inti wasn't the one who'd woken him.

A hand in his hair.

A kiss for his cheek.

"Jacques? There's someone at the door." Anjou knelt beside the bed. "They're asking for you."

23

BOND BUILDING

Boon always skimped on sleep when he was on a trail. Even when pushing his limits, he could get by on a day or two of downtime. So though he wasn't completely rested, his mind stirred, sure there were things he needed to be doing. Eyes closed, body slack, he was already pulling in information about his current disposition.

The barrier had worked him over but good. He remembered hitting the water. The lingering ache in his ribs was probably from that impact.

Tropical humidity and a chorus of crickets. Okay, sure. That jived. His memories were hazy, but he knew he'd found both Inti and the hidden island. But time had passed. It was dim. Maybe even dark. Probably not the same night. How many had passed?

Indoors, in bed, in company. Not too surprising. He'd always

been quick to gain and give trust. But he couldn't recall names or faces.

Replete. As in overfed. And still wallowing in the good stuff. So he'd found a reaver. Boon didn't know this soul, but there was a warmth to its brilliance. Nice. *Needed.*

Fingers combed through his hair. Probably had been doing so for a while. Felt good. Felt safe.

Firming his grip, Boon pushed his nose into his bedmate's belly, breathed deeply, and gruffly asked, "Did we trade names before I faded out? I can't remember."

The hand fled, and there was a dramatic increase in his companion's heartrate.

"Sorry. Did I surprise you?" Boon lifted his head. "Is English good? Because I know … uhh. Huh."

He was holding—and being held by—a human of middling age. And he was getting a whole hell of a lot of mixed messages. Boon tried not to stare at the silky, frilly, strappy parts, but there were definitely breasts involved. That could mean trouble, but he wasn't sure how much. "Uhh. Peace … friend?"

"Hi. Hello," came a somewhat breathless answer. "Good morning. You're awake earlier than they said."

"Light sleeper." Boon scanned the room, mostly to gather his wits. Hell. If his father could see him now, he'd be duly bonded and summarily bound. "Where's this?"

"The residence block inside Trulore Clinic. You're safe. Inti made sure. Sensei made doubly sure."

Boon knew Inti had been here. Posy, too. But the predominant scents were of a different feline. A female. And …

this person. "I don't remember much."

"Inti brought us to the beach where you washed up."

"Who has a share in that *us*?"

"Me and Pim. This is her room." His companion favored him with a humorless smile. "I'll apologize for both of us. 'No females,' you kept saying. But there was nobody else. So when you decided I was fine, Inti made the most of things."

"I *really* don't remember. Mind if we start with introductions? I'm Boonmar-fen Elderbough. Boon's fine."

"Elara Perrine."

A feminine name. Probably not the one she'd been assigned at birth. Hell and damn, he'd blundered bad this time.

"Elara. Got it. I'm clearheaded enough to see my mistake." Tail tucked, eyes averted, Boon asked, "How many ways do I need to apologize, Reaver Perrine?"

"*Doctor* Perrine, actually. I'm not a reaver." She hesitated. "At least, I wasn't. Pim and the rest say otherwise."

An interesting detail, but Boon had never been susceptible to diversion. "Elara," he said quietly. "Don't put me off. I'm trying to apologize."

"It's no big deal. There were extenuating circumstances."

"I'm not the kind of guy to hide behind excuses." He sought her gaze. "My mistake won't go away just because we ignore it. Face me. Correct me. Show me the path that leads to trust."

Elara whispered, "I'm a woman."

"Please, pardon my mistake, Dr. Elara Perrine. And thank you for your companionship while I was catching a few winks."

"Apology accepted." And with a conflicted expression, she asked,

"You're not angry? Or do I not actually count? No, wait! Ignore that last part! It's silly to be disappointed that you're *not* upset."

Boon propped himself up on his elbows. "I get you. If I don't work with females but I'm making an exception for you, it'd mean I don't actually see you as female. You're used to catching people in this sort of lie?"

"Yes."

"Must be tough."

She squirmed and looked away. "You growled like crazy at Pim."

"Feeling left out? I could summon up some indignation if it'd help." He rumbled like he would for any of the young cubs from his pack, playing at a ferocity that he'd only ever use for their protection.

Elara gasped and squirmed.

At first, Boon thought he'd inadvertently frightened her, but ... that wasn't the direction scents were shifting. "Well, now. Guess that's better than skittish."

"Oh, god. Listen. I'm on record as being attracted to hot wolves."

"Thanks for that. But you get that this is platonic, right?"

"Up here?" Elara tapped her forehead. "Clear as glass. But the rest of me is only too happy to veer from a more reasoned approach. Very awkward. So sorry. Also, I'd like some clarification. Why no females? Do you prefer males?"

"Not afraid to barge past boundaries, are you?"

"That seems to be the trend with wolves. Both you and Pim." She touched his shoulder. "It's like you said. This is the path that leads to trust."

"All right. Not a problem. I don't mind." Boon shifted up the bed so he and Elara were sharing a pillow. "For me, it's not one or the other. It's neither."

"You're ... disinclined?"

Boon huffed. "Usually, I'm driven to distraction. Too many matchmakers in the family. And family friends are just as eager to shove prospects into my path. Nobody seems to understand my choices."

"I get it." Elara leaned closer. "I *totally* get it."

"Thanks for that, too."

She promised, "I won't boundary-barge if you tell me where they are. Like ... is this bad?"

His arms were still around her, and he tightened his hold. "Nah. I'm comfy."

"Don't you need to rush off somewhere?"

"Not until I'm sure you're okay."

Elara glanced around. "You mean the wards and things?"

"Them, too, I guess. Though sigilcraft isn't my thing." Boon frowned. "Even so, I wouldn't mind a closer look at your seal."

"I have a seal?"

"You've definitely been sealed. The sigil's on your back. Not sure what I can figure out, but it can't hurt to nose around a bit."

"Do I need to move?"

Boon said, "Nah. I've had access all along. Which I should probably apologize for. How long have I been holding you?"

"Since the day before yesterday."

Plenty long enough to be bond-building. Boon knew the signs because he'd always guarded against them.

Elara asked, "Why would you need to apologize?"

"I've been drawing strength from you. Tapping into your soul without prior consent." Boon grimaced. "*Rude* would be putting it mildly. It's infringement."

"But I never noticed. I feel fine." She shook her head. "If anything, I feel better than ever. Safe. Steady. More whole."

"Hang on a sec. Let me ...." Boon turned all his attention inward, testing his impulses. He wanted to protect this woman, which was fine. But did he feel the need to keep her? Had things gone that far? He should probably get clear before things progressed any further. Except there was *another* instinct niggling for attention. Hell and hellions, he was in so much trouble.

Fingers on his cheek startled him.

Elara asked, "What happened here?"

"Zigged when I should have zagged."

She lightly traced his scars, gaze neutral. "These look like claw marks."

"Yep." He turned his face, let her look. Casually, he asked, "About the female cat who lives here ...?"

"Pim is a wolf."

Boon drew a blank. "I'm getting a really strong scent of a feline."

"That makes sense, but Pim identifies as a wolf."

"Huh. That's ... different." He tried to realign his thinking. Again. He cleared his throat. "I should probably get out of here."

"I understand."

She lowered her gaze, but Boon was way too invested. Her soul-deep longing was right there, and it surprised him on a couple of levels. She was attracted to him, yeah. But what she wanted was a continuation of the connection they'd already forged. And it wasn't the infringing kind of wanting. Elara really did get that this was platonic. And that was nice. Maybe even needed.

When he stayed put, she stole a peek. "Go on. I'm not holding you back."

"Not until I'm sure you're okay." Honestly, Boon was afraid that if he let go now, Elara would break a little. "Listen for a sec, okay?"

She nodded.

"I'm not looking for a bondmate."

Elara smiled. "Relax. There will be no shotgun wedding, Boonmar-fen Elderbough."

He pressed on. "But sleep is a kind of bond."

"Pim said that's how you'd see it."

"She's right. Or part right. Because all my infringing adds up to *another* kind of bond. And it's not the sort of thing I can ignore."

"You sound unhappy." Elara searched his face. "I'm going to be a huge inconvenience, aren't I?"

"I wouldn't say *that*," he protested. Even though that was probably an understatement.

"Only because Amaranthine are so polite."

"Aw, hell. Look, Elara. I want to keep an eye on you, but I have things to do, and I can't be dragging you along."

"Leave me here. It's safe, right?"

"Ohhh, you know how it is. Clear as glass in the old noggin. But instincts rebel." He slowly extricated himself, retreating to the bed's edge. "You have to promise me you won't leave."

Elara frowned. "For how long?"

Boon hesitated. "At least until one of us comes for you. Do you have enough food and whatever for that?"

"I'll manage."

Which would have to be good enough. And really, Boon should have left it at that. But that other niggling instinct wasn't hushing up. So he asked, "About the other one. The … the she-wolf. Where is she?"

"Sensei took her away. They're searching the island together."

Boon leapt from the bed, urgency thrumming through his veins. He stalked to the window and scowled at the distant trees, where birds were beginning to call for dawn. While a wolf's instincts could cause problems on occasion, a cat's were truly troublesome. Hisoka might be in an even bigger pinch than he was. "I need to get to where he is."

A strained giggle came from the direction of the bed.

He turned in time to see Elara cover her eyes. Her scent blew through a mix of emotions made all the more potent by their connection. It was the strangest combination of interest and amusement. Boon glanced down and grunted. "Pants?"

Eyes still covered, she pointed toward the bathroom.

Boon checked his stride. "Sorry to cut and run like this. I'll find you again. That's a promise."

"Because we share a bond?" Elara lowered her hand, but her eyes stayed on his.

He pushed at his loose hair. He wasn't used to having it down. "After things are sorted here, we'll come to terms. If I had a pack, I'd bring you in, but I'm a lone wolf. Would a pact please you?"

"You don't owe me anything."

"Wrong." He plunked onto the edge of the bed, facing her. Snagging a pillow for modesty, he grumbled, "As far as I'm concerned, you're mine. I owe you my thanks, and that comes with my trust and my loyalty. By the same token, I'm yours."

Saying it out loud drove the point home.

For most of his life, he'd fled from every type of entanglement where females were concerned. Yet here was a shining soul that even the Moon might envy.

"Aren't you angry?" Elara asked again. "To have someone forced upon you in your sleep?"

"Amaranthine are definitely vulnerable while we're deep. It's why we're careful to choose a good den and a trustworthy companion."

She eyed him closely. "As a good friend once said to me … don't put me off. I'm trying to understand instincts I don't possess, Boonmar-fen Elderbough. In your place, I might be *furious*."

"What's done is done."

"So you're just going to take your lumps?"

"Don't get me wrong. I'm not a slave to my instincts. Been living contrary to them for most of my life. I *could* fight this." He took her hand and lightly clasped it. "I don't want to."

In a small voice, Elara asked, "You want me?"

Boon's tail switched and settled across her knees. "I *have* you. You're mine. Simple, right?"

"So long as it stays platonic."

He nodded once, then lowered his gaze to the hand in his. "About that she-wolf …?"

"Pim?"

"Right. Pim. Is she going to have a problem with this?"

Elara smiled warmly. "I can't imagine she'll mind that you and

I have become friends."

He may have growled a little.

Radiating concern, Elara whispered, "What's the matter?"

Boon had little choice but to drag the truth into the open. Such was the path to trust. "Long story short, she's mine, too."

24

UNGODLY HOUR

omeone's at the door?" Jacques murmured, disoriented. "Who?"

"I don't know her." Anjou helped him pull free of Inti's tangle.

"Lord, what time is it? I don't *do* early." He shuffled into the bathroom.

"She insisted." The feline helped him into a dressing gown, then plucked at its sleeve. "I don't like her voice."

Jacques looked up sharply. "What did she look like?"

Anjou drew a shaky breath. "Dangerous."

If their unexpected guest was a dragon, that might be the only part he could remember. "Right, then. Bring Eiji and take my spot. Keep the kids safe."

Anjou's grip on his sleeve held him back. "Will you go with her?"

"Wouldn't miss it. Clandestine meetings are deliciously informative."

At the door, Jacques found an Amaranthine female with a severe haircut and a bad case of distaste. Likely for him. In the dim, her eyes raked him from head to toe, and it was so much like one of Maman's disapproving looks, it was almost nostalgic.

"Lord, it's early. Is something amiss?"

Gripping her clipboard like a shield, she answered in words heavy with sway. "Doctor Kodoku will see you now. Follow me."

In any other situation, Jacques would have protested the presumption, the ungodly hour, and his dishabille. But he was meant to be helpless to deny a dragon's bidding, so he tightened the knot holding his dressing gown shut, stepped barefoot into the hallway, and offered his most charming smile. "Lead on, dear lady."

Jacques knew from Papa Socks that this must be Futari, one of the three dragons holed up on this island. He was frankly baffled by her short hair. In his experience, which included visits to both the harems and the heights, dragons would no more crop their colorful tresses than they would skip a mani-pedi. And they tended to waft about, draped in gemstones and an excess of filmy fabrics. Yet this female was stiff and starkly unadorned.

Something about her choices felt religious. Like ascetics who take a vow of poverty.

He'd hardly quibble with someone for their choices, but hers felt all wrong. Unless they weren't hers? Would it be too out of character to strike up a conversation? Bon-Bon certainly spared no thought for the help. But Jacques wasn't his brother.

"I'm no stranger to early meetings. His lordship keeps all hours."

She didn't respond.

"Any chance the good doctor will be serving coffee?"

Her glance had a quelling quality.

"How strict is he? I propose a kitchen bypass. I'll carry the tray if there are fresh pastries in the offing!"

She stopped in her tracks.

"Surely, you must indulge from time to time. What say we do a bit of scavenging?" He further pressed, "What should I call you?"

"You want to know my name?"

"It's the usual way to begin."

"I am not a friend." That felt like a warning.

"You say that now." Presenting his palms, he said, "I'm Jacques."

Though she didn't touch him, she grudgingly answered, "Futari."

"Ah! I know a smattering of Japanese. Futari is two. *Non*, it's used for a couple. Along the lines of … the two of us."

She seemed to struggle with that. Pain pinched delicate features. And then she was reaching. Resting her fingertips lightly over his heart, Futari firmly said, "You need to stop talking, now."

Jacques acquiesced with a smile.

Futari led him through an entrance that required a keycard, then up a curving stairway. An ornate door led into a cross-shaped chamber, which was typical of draconic architecture. Wood paneling lent richness to a room that was carpeted, draped, and dripping in deep reds.

The figure seated at the desk had to be Dr. Kodoku, who

watched him over steepled fingers. Jacques thought to check on the lady dragon. He'd been told often enough how dangerous it was to take your eyes off one. So he saw Futari's expression as she gazed at her boss.

His guesswork realigned itself.

This lady may have taken vows, but they weren't the religious sort. Futari had been wronged by this other dragon. What was that old saying? *Rest, regard, and revenge cannot be rushed.* Jacques was quite sure that she harbored a deep and abiding resentment toward her kinsman. And that her bleak ensemble was either mourning, warning ... or both.

"I will bring coffee," she announced.

Kodoku's eyebrows lifted. "Whatever for?"

"He wanted some."

Jacques waited quietly. She'd told him to stop talking, and that order hadn't been rescinded.

"Since when do you cater to the whims of the wealthy?"

Futari's chin jutted stubbornly. "He asked nicely."

"Never mind." His words held traces of sway. Nothing too pressing, but very likely effective on the average person. "Jacques Smythe, I presume?"

He held his peace.

Kodoku's welcoming smile dimmed. "Futari?" he inquired sweetly.

She winced. "He was talkative."

"Hardly a trait I'd discourage."

Futari hissed softly and tucked hair behind the point of one ear. The light was better in here, and Jacques could tell its hue. She had the same deep purple hair as Kyrie. And yes, the eyes lifted to his were the correct vintage. Once upon a time, he'd been given permission to swoon at the sight. Strange to think how much had changed since then.

She said, "Doctor Kodoku will see you now. You may converse freely."

Catching her hand, he bowed over it. "Thank you, Futari."

With a small shake of her head, she muttered, "You will not thank me, Mr. Smythe."

The door shut behind her, and Kodoku cheerfully ordered, "Never mind about her. My daughter is a moody thing and not to your usual tastes. Or is she?"

"I wasn't aware that my tastes were on file."

He smiled thinly. "Answer my questions, Mr. Smythe."

"Ask away!"

"Are you interested in my daughter?"

"Futari intrigues me, but not every meeting leads straight into the boudoir." Jacques took a chair across from the desk and crossed his legs, exposing most of his thigh. "To be fair, not every meeting *doesn't*. And I seem to be dressed for one. Yours, mayhap?"

Kodoku laughed that off. "Let us keep things professional, Mr. Smythe."

"I'll meet you at whatever level you wish, though I prefer not to stoop."

The dragon hesitated. Lord, Jacques loved a good riposte.

"Oh, never mind. Never mind all of that." He scrutinized Jacques over the top of his glasses. "Tell me about yourself, Mr. Smythe."

"Oh, do call me Jacques. And I'm nobody of consequence."

Turning it around, he said, "Thank you for providing a sumptuous hideaway where my indulgences won't be questioned or remarked upon."

Kodoku's eyes narrowed, and his next words were thick with sway. "You will satisfy my curiosity."

Jacques uncrossed and recrossed his legs. "About …?"

"Stately House." Coming around his desk, he composed himself, one hip perched against its edge. "Tell me about Stately House."

"An old family estate. Bit of an architectural mongrel, given all its additions, but it's a charming mélange, very East meets West. Lovely views. Terribly remote, which most of us prefer, though it's next to impossible to slip away for dinner and a show."

"I am more interested in the children who live there. Where do you get your crossers?"

Jacques supposed subtlety went out the window when you could essentially erase whole conversations from memory. He aimed for a candid tone but kept it brief. "Some enroll in the school. Others qualify as foundlings."

"Do they ever leave?"

"Even less often than I do." He glibly confided, "This is my first proper holiday in more than a decade."

"Do you interact directly with the crossers?"

"*Naturellement.* I am an honorary uncle."

Kodoku hummed. "What security measures are in place?"

This line of questioning wasn't entirely unexpected. Argent had considered many motives, including this one. Jacques waved a hand vaguely. "Oh, the usual sorts of things, I imagine. Barriers and a bodyguard. He's a personal favorite. I'm in his bed nearly as often as I'm in my own."

The dragon blinked.

Jacques recrossed his legs again.

"Could you lead a crosser out past the barriers?"

"Lord, do you know how long a walk that would entail? I'm not much of an outdoorsman."

"*Could* you?"

"Theoretically. But not without a follower or two checking to see if anything was amiss." He couldn't quite keep the edge out of his tone. "Why do you ask?"

"Do not worry over that." Kodoku drummed his fingers. "Could you bring a guest in?"

"Not without permission."

"Are you aware of any crossers living in the public sector?"

"Certainly." And when prompted, Jacques breezily expanded. "There are a handful of crossers at New Saga. And some of our students have siblings back home."

"Can you provide a list?"

"Alas, I could only speculate." Jacques tried for self-deprecation. "Argent only trusts me so far."

Kodoku considered that for a moment. "How much does Mettlebright value you?"

"I have my uses, but I'm only human. That makes me replaceable."

"Uses? What is your role?"

"I'm Lord Mettlebright's man. My duties include—but are not limited to—managing phone calls, answering correspondence, moderating press conferences, and curating his lordship's wardrobe."

Jacques watched the dragon dismiss his entire way of life with a roll of his eyes.

"You like them young?"

"Is that an accusation?"

"Observation. Your companion is certainly … fresh-faced."

"Never underestimate the glow that can be achieved with proper skin care."

Kodoku snorted. "He's a boy. You like boys?"

Jacques hated the leading tone, but he recognized the opportunity it might represent. "Children love me."

"If I provided a crosser or two for your enjoyment, would it improve your attitude toward me?"

He put up token resistance. "I wouldn't want to upset my partner."

"A second suite. With my compliments." Kodoku pushed off the desk and prowled closer. "I could give you a shining boy. Or one whose blooms intoxicate. Perhaps you like the caress of fur or scales? A fluffy tail?"

Jacques hoped his marvelous acting was enough to hide the shrivel of revulsion. "Crossers, you say?"

"Unique ones. Unlike anything else in the world."

"I must confess myself curious." That much was true.

"Arrangements shall be made."

Kodoku loomed closer, and his eyes caught the light.

"*Mon dieu*. You have amazing eyes."

He lowered the frames, allowing Jacques to see him plainly. "You favor red eyes? Most find them unsettling. Dangerous."

"Dragons are beautiful," he whispered.

Then Jacques had to quickly rearrange his limbs, for Kodoku

straddled him. Seated there, he cupped Jacques' face between his palms. Jacques couldn't stop his heart from hammering, but his response seemed to please the dragon. Total sadist.

"You like this sort of thing?" inquired Kodoku.

"That all depends on which part of *this* you mean." Jacques was feeling more threatened than seduced. "Where I come from, we ask before we touch."

"You will let me do as I please."

"As you say." And because it seemed appropriate, he asked, "May I touch?"

"No."

Jacques kept his hands on the arms of his chair and murmured, "Yes, doctor."

Kodoku searched his face, prodded a few glands, sniffed lightly. "No diseases."

"I am in good health."

"*Not* a reaver."

"Very not."

"And yet ...!" Kodoku kneaded the back of Jacques' neck. "Something here?"

"A tattoo."

"More than that." An unpalatable coolness entered his tone, and his grip tightened. "I'm quite sensitive to sigilcraft, you know."

Jacques' heart sank. "Do tell."

The dragon slid a hand down his side and circled a spot near Jacques' hipbone. "This one's older, too. An early attempt? It failed, didn't it?"

"Nonsense. That whorl has been complimented by many a ...."

"But what's this?" Kodoku caught his chin and crooned, "Say *ah.*" Jacques opened.

"The one on the roof of your mouth to obscure the one on your tongue ... hmm. But where ...? My, my! Your lord and master keeps you on a tight leash."

"I'm a fortunate fellow."

"As am I." Kodoku tugged at the single knot keeping Jacques' questionable modesty intact. "Foxish puzzles have become a specialty of mine, and unraveling their workmanship is an exquisite pleasure."

Jacques was still trying to frame a protest when a soft clatter and rattle preceded Futari into the room. She spared them a glance, set a laden tray on a side table, and announced, "Coffee."

Kodoku dismounted.

Jacques retied his dressing gown.

"Make a note, Futari. I want this one back. Tomorrow morning will do." The doctor's gaze slithered over Jacques from head to toe. "Reserve a room."

"Near his current suite?" she asked, her tone flat.

"No, not here. He'll be getting a tour of the lab."

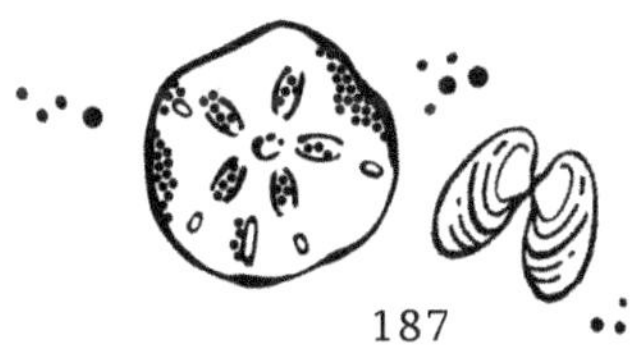

25

TAKE ONE FOR THE TEAM

Pim had no trouble keeping up with Hisoka as he led her deeper into the jungle. Exhilaration thrummed as his course forced her to focus, to push her usual limits. There were only the three of them, but she was sure this was what running with a pack must be like.

Not until he stopped for water did she break the silence. "Tell me about yourself?"

"Most of what anyone needs to know about me is a matter of public record."

It was a mild rebuff. She tried again. "Maybe I don't keep up with the news like I should."

"There are other sorts of headlines."

"I also avoid tabloids, if that's what you mean. They're no kinder to me than they are to anyone." With a soft sigh, she added, "And my name has been removed from the rotation of gossip circulars from the feline courts. You probably knew that."

"I *did* look you up before embarking."

That surprised her. "You can't have known I was here."

"On the contrary, I am here by your invitation." Hisoka's tone remained calm, but his hand was in his hair. "Your call for consorts made a convenient cover."

She hadn't known about the arrangement, but she nodded slowly. "That's one good thing, then. I'm glad it helped."

Hisoka kept his attention on Patter, who wasn't drinking so much as playing in the water.

"Could you tell me some things that *aren't* a matter of public record … but are also true?"

He blandly obliged. "Hisoka Twineshaft is a native of Keishi, Japan. He is universally pleasant, perpetually patient, eerily punctual, and notoriously difficult to reach."

Pim chuckled.

Hisoka relaxed. A little.

"Sensei, you forgot about Patter. He's not a matter of public record."

"True. And he'll very likely always be a secret. Along with much of what's happening on this island."

"It's a regular hotbed of sensationalism. But at this point, I don't think I regret coming."

"May I indulge my curiosity?"

Pim crooked her fingers. "I'm used to questions."

"What happened to your former consorts?"

"Oh. Them …."

Before any more could be said, there was a rush and rattle in the foliage. Pim dropped into a wary crouch, and then Boon was simply *there*.

A dominant stance, full of warnings. Like she was trouble. Or maybe even dangerous. Wildness rippled off him, and his tail bristled low. Pure wolf. But when he spoke, his tone was casual, even cheerful. "You okay, Posy?"

Hisoka circled the wolf and placed Patter in his hands. "What do you make of him, Boon? I've been wanting your opinion."

Every speck of menace disappeared so fast, Pim's ears were left ringing.

"You okay?" the wolf pressed.

"We're managing." Hisoka gestured for peace. "Shall we keep introductions brief? Pim, this is Boon. Boon, this is Pim. Now ... about Patter ...?"

The wolf swept his tail to one side and lowered himself to a seat on the ground, all in one smooth motion. Very graceful. Pim tried sweeping her own tail to the side and found it difficult to get the arc right. Too much curl to the motion.

Yellow eyes flashed her way—cautious, curious.

She stiffly asked, "Elara?"

"Behind enough wards to keep her safe for the time being."

Pim noted the pronoun.

And Boon noticed her noticing. "We talked it all out, and we're good. You good? Or do I owe you an apology, too?"

"You don't owe me anything."

"Not so sure about that. Thanks for the save."

Pim shifted into a neutrally polite posture to let him off the hook. "It's fine."

The only problem was, he didn't look fine. She'd swear he was fronting. It probably had something to do with the whole *no females* thing. Should she give him more space? Pim glanced Hisoka's way, hoping for guidance, but that put a puff in Boon's tail.

What on earth?

Patter peeped and reached for one of the many necklaces Boon wore. "*Hey* to you, too, runt. Where'd this guy rummage you up from?"

"Sen. Sen. Sen."

"That's him. I'm Boon. And you must be Patter." The wolf brought him up and nuzzled his cheeks. "Never woulda thought it possible, but who am I to argue? You're here. And darn cute."

"What do you think?" asked Hisoka.

"Little guy's something new. Kind of *has* to be part pitterhind." Boon tweaked an antler. "That's practically a gimme."

"And the other parent?"

Boon didn't even hesitate. "Moonbeam."

"You're sure?"

"I'm a wolf, Posy. I'm sure."

Pim whispered, "Then Seela ...?"

Boon's head came up.

Hisoka filled him in. "Inti knew this child. Patter came from the same lab. All Inti could say, though, was that this is Seela's child."

"And that Seela isn't awake," supplied Pim. Any detail could be important. "Seela is lost in dreams."

Boon hesitated. "No kidding? Hey, does the array work?"

Hisoka shook his head. "We'll need to get to Jacques to find out."

"Point the way."

Pim did, and Boon stood. But he didn't move. "What do you think, Posy? We have a top-down priority list?"

"Disassembling the island's barrier is most important. We need to find its anchor." Hisoka asked, "Why do you want our communication array?"

"To get a message to Penny. If possible."

With a glance to bring Pim more into the loop, Hisoka asked, "What does Merit Starmark have to do with pitterhinds?"

"Nothing, far as I know. But he told me once, a while back, to keep an ear cocked for the name Seela. I guess she's been missing for quite some time. Friend of a friend of the family, or something."

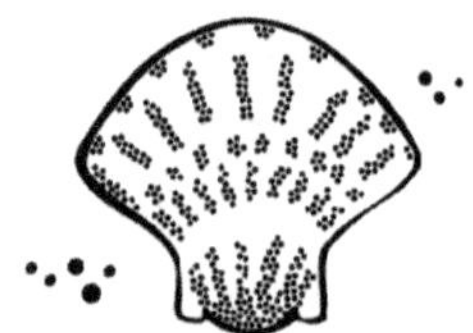

Boon knew he needed to talk to Pim, but like the Boss said, there were higher priorities. This mission had a timeline, and his downtime had already cancelled out his early arrival. The lady wasn't going away anytime soon. Not that he'd let her.

Hell and hellions, that last bit had asserted itself way too easily.

So she was his. Fine. Done deal. But his … *how*?

It didn't have to be awkward. What if he just went with it? How would he treat Pim if she was one of his packmates? Elara had said she wanted to be a wolf. No, wait. He needed to keep this straight. Elara said Pim *identified* as a wolf. So … wolf. Another done deal.

Boon slowed his breathing and tried to align this information with what his senses were picking up. Might take a little time. Her tail was *really* throwing him off.

Actually, that was as good a place as any to start. How had Elara put it? Barging past boundaries.

"Tail troubles?" he asked.

Pim's puffed and curled around her ankles. Totally a kitty move, and she definitely knew it.

He raised a hand. "Your roomie made sure I didn't make the same mistake with you that I did with her. So I'm asking as a friend. One wolf to another."

"Really?" She sounded suspicious.

Not enough trust to be getting personal.

Boon backed up a little. "Will you get burrs in your bushel if I'm less polite than diplomacy types like Posy here? I'm used to saying it like I see it. You okay with blunt?"

Hisoka gazed off into the trees, a little smile on his face, leaving the wolves to sort out their own differences.

"I can appreciate honesty." And she slid into a receptive posture, easy as you please.

Right to it, then. "Your tail's a nice touch, but the nuances are off. You don't spend much time with wolves?"

"No. Between work and the whole awkwardness of …. Well. I don't know who or how to ask."

"Stick close to me, if you want. I can explain stuff, show you things."

"Like a mentor," posed Hisoka, butting in and making it oh-so official.

"Well, yeah. I mean, it's not like you and Isla. The packs are more informal. But I'm plenty used to fielding the kinds of questions whelps gotta ask."

Pim's eyes flashed with interest. "Isla?"

Hisoka's smile was bland. "Isla Ward's apprenticeship is a

matter of public record. She's part of my office's diplomatic division."

"Any other females in your cortege?" Pim asked, the tip of her tail twitching.

"No."

"Why the exception?"

"That's the way of things. Mentors and apprentices work in tandem." Holding out his hands for Patter, he smoothly added, "Trust yourself to Boon, and you'll undoubtedly find a firmer footing on your chosen path."

And he strolled off, neatly excising himself from the proceedings.

For once, Boon was willing to take one for the team. He was already invested.

"You okay if we start with kid stuff?"

"So long as you don't patronize."

"Nah. Beads and knots count as fun for all ages. Good place to begin, and plenty of scope. There's a whole language to it." He brushed his fingers across the collection of necklaces he wore. "It's not a big secret or anything. People tend to find out if they're a friend of the packs or ... well, if there's a documentary about it, I guess. Reaver kids even learn some of the basics at summer camps."

"I know *about* wolvish accessories," she said slowly. "All part of the look. It's really a language?"

"Sure. Different types of knots carry meaning. Combinations of knots spell out bigger ideas. Throw in special materials, and one little bracelet can get downright gossipy."

She'd been edging closer, and Boon was letting it happen.

He teased open a knot and shook out a slim cord that had been wrapped three times around his wrist. "Nice and slow," he murmured, demonstrating the most basic knot. "The tricky part is spacing them evenly."

Two more knots, and he passed the cord to her. "Have at it. Keep your row tidy, and there's a prize."

Her tail quivered, and her focus narrowed. She had the knack down by her fifth knot, so he stopped paying close attention to her hands. Boon was more worried about taking in her scent and sifting through his instinctual responses to it.

Familiar. Not a problem.

Friendly. Ditto.

Female. He was curbing the need to bristle over that. Too used to fending them off.

Feline. Which he was supposed to disregard. But … the disparity intrigued him.

One of the reasons he was hell-bent on keeping females at bay was the pull they had on his instincts. Even if he didn't want a bondmate, he was very aware of she-wolves. So he steered clear. But Pim's scent was at odds with her chosen identity. Which begged the question: *could* he be attracted to her? He'd never heard of Amaranthine from different clans intermingling.

Did they?

Could they?

Maybe Pim was … safe. No sparks. No heat. No pull. He wasn't feeling the urge to initiate a chase or ready a den. Pim felt neutral. And that could mean there was nothing to fend off. He could kick back, relax, and be himself. Or be her mentor, anyhow.

26

TANDEM

Eventually, she asked, "Is this right?"

"Let's have a look." Boon scooted closer and reached for the cord.

Pim tensed.

"Nice and easy," he soothed. "Like Posy said, mentors and apprentices work in tandem. Both of us are going to have to build toward trust."

"I know," she said stiffly.

"No rush. No worries. And no keeping quiet when something needs saying."

Pim softly said, "Less closeness, please."

"Can do." Her uneasiness confused him, but he didn't have to understand to be courteous. Boon simply put more space between them. "Now, let's see. This is solid work. A good first effort. If a cub brought this to me, I'd yield that prize I mentioned earlier."

She didn't *quite* hide her smile.

This one liked compliments, which was a total kitty quality. Except she didn't want to be a cat … and wouldn't thank him for bringing up clan stereotypes. Hell, this was hard. Boon was still having some trouble shoving her into the wolf category. But maybe that was okay. He could just give Pim her own category. Yeah. That should work.

"So, with wolves. We earn our beads. And this is good for a few."

Her gaze flicked to his modest collection of necklaces. "All your beads are earned?"

"Well, no. They all have significance, though. Some were gifts. Some were prizes. Some are mementos. There're all sorts of traditions about the giving and exchanging of beads."

He fiddled with ties and removed three round beads from a bracelet at his wrist.

"Aren't those yours?" Pim asked cautiously.

Boon sorted through and found another length of cord, this time from his ankle. "Adults always carry spares. Gotta be prepared. There's always some whelp hoping to make an impression."

With that eager light in her eyes, she was just as excited as any cub.

He was kind of enjoying himself. She made it easy.

"Okay. May I suggest something that might come off as … intrusive?" He held up a hand. "It's to help. It's just sorta personal."

Pim waved between them. "Go ahead and assume I'll always hear you out."

Boon kept it simple. "I want you to try tying this at the end of your tail."

Her brows arched.

"The weight might tame it a little. Make you think twice about how you move." Boon brushed at his shoulder, not wanting her to think he was criticizing. "Most cubs pick up the lingo of posture and tail position way early. It's as much a part of our language as words. Maybe more so. If you want, we can cover some basics ...? Get you up to speed."

Pim was already nodding. And knotting the beaded strand into her luxuriant white tail. "Yes. Start at the very beginning. I'd be grateful."

Boon stood, bounced on the balls of his feet, then took a neutral posture. He beckoned for her to do the same, and they faced each other.

"When you're in a good mood, just doing your thing, it feels right to keep up a low sway. Doesn't need to be much. Sorta depends on your personality, I guess. Some folks are more enthusiastic about life. Others take it easy. Your tail broadcasts that, just like facial expressions or tone of voice."

He demonstrated.

She approximated. And frowned.

"How's it feel?"

"Odd. I'm resisting the urge to shake it off. But ... this really might help."

She twisted, peering over her shoulder, like having a tail was new and novel. Boon was catching a whiff of something. She was almost scowling in concentration, but her scent was all kinds of upbeat and optimistic. Nice.

Boon continued. "Let's say a friend strolls up. Elara, for

instance. You're happy to see her, which adds a little lift to your mood … and your tail. Give a bit more wag. It lets someone know they're welcome."

Her sway … wasn't.

He circled her, trying to figure out what to suggest. While Boon didn't spend a ton of time with felines, he recalled a good deal of tail movement—lashing and arching and switching and flicking. Any time the tip of a tail quivered, it'd always reminded him of a rattlesnake. Coiled to strike. Dangerous.

Right now, Pim's tail was puffed in obvious irritation.

"Try mirroring me." Boon squared off with her again.

She obeyed, but it was pretty clear she needed practice. Her tail was seriously flexible, all lift and curl.

"If it's not working for you …."

Pim's posture shifted into something more dominant. "I want to keep trying."

"Not a problem." He kept up his own pendulum sway and asked, "You mentioned work?"

"Yes." She went all wary again. "You've … never heard of me?"

"Nope." He hesitated. The question implied he should have. "What's your gig?"

"I'm an actress. American television."

"Oh. Huh. I'm not one to sit still, and I never really liked television. No warmth. No soul-sense. No scents. Very confusing."

Pim considered him with those big blue eyes of hers. "I hadn't thought of that."

"Wolves are terrible actors, you know." Boon tugged at his ponytail. "If we're happy, you know it. If we're annoyed, it's obvious. Only real way to hide anything is to hold your tail reeeally still. But a limp tail usually leads to wariness because we're used to total honesty. With our noses, our tails, and our songs, we hide nothing from each other."

Her own tail went still. "I played a wolf on television."

Boon huffed. And immediately felt like a jerk. "Ah… sorry."

Pim narrowed her eyes, but not at him. She seemed to be thinking. "I have a feeling I botched my portrayal, and I'm about to find out how badly."

"It's probably little stuff. We're different—one clan to the next— but not *that* different. And on the upside, other wolves probably also don't watch television. No one to criticize."

She softly said, "Someone always criticizes, but I think I did some good. Americans liked Aloora, and their attitude toward wolves improved."

"Good of you to step up, since wolves can't act."

Pim's smile was grateful, but her tone was so dry. "I did what I could. Earned some acclaim. Even received a thank you from Adoona-soh Elderbough."

"Huh. Small world."

She arched her brows, which seemed to be Pim-code for *nice try*. Possibly with a side of *try harder*. He should probably explain. It was kind of funny, really. She didn't know about him any more than he knew about her.

But first.

"You don't want me too close. Do I need to know why?" At her expression, he raised both hands. "Just trying to get the awkward stuff out of the way right off. With wolves, there's usually a fair amount of full-contact sniffing. All part of getting to know someone.”

Pim eased right back into a receptive stance. “I don’t know what that means. I mean, I could guess, but … no. You’ll have to *explain* full-contact sniffing.”

“Easier to demonstrate.”

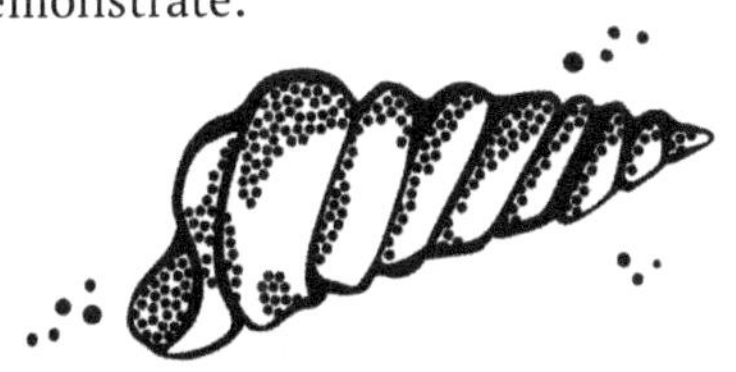

“I suppose.” Pim’s tail came around to wrap her ankles, the beads thunking softly against her foot in chastisement.

Boon stayed right where he was. “You’re wary of me … why?”

“Probably for the same reason you’re wary of me.” She stepped into his personal space and stubbornly held his gaze. “I’ll trust you this far. I need to know. Just show me, already.”

“You got it. Nice and easy.”

He had to crouch. Wolves were pretty imposing, but this one was keeping most of his wild side under wraps. If she’d been in the mood to split hairs, she’d have called him a good actor. At least he didn’t patronize.

Boon said, “Closer means clearer. And contact brings even more stuff into focus.”

“Stuff,” she said flatly. What did that even mean? She preferred more precise direction.

“Gimme a sec. Just trying to … sort you out.” His nose grazed her jaw. “It’s even more effective in truest form.”

“I know.”

"Guessing you wouldn't want to try that."

"No. But I'll … defer to your judgment, since you have the years."

"I do. But we're good. I don't want to make you any more uncomfortable than you already are."

"I'm not."

He eased back to meet her gaze. "Pim, even if you're a stellar actress, my nose isn't going to be fooled at this range. What's standing between us and peace?"

Pim sighed. "You're very … male."

Boon stilled. His posture slowly shifted into apology, and he tucked his hands behind his back. "Am I imposing? Hells, Pim. Were you … mishandled?"

Her nose worked, too. And as he said, at this distance, scents were clear. His concern was genuine, and he looked ready to leap to her defense. Pim closed her eyes and breathed deeply, trying to center herself. "Not mishandled. I … miscarried. Twice. And I don't want to *ever* go through that again."

Silence.

And then softly, "*Pim.*"

She risked a glance. He looked heartbroken.

"May I touch?"

Pim quavered under his gaze, wanting what he was offering, even though she didn't want him. One nod.

With a sigh, he enfolded her, practically curling around her.

He didn't say a word, but he made little sounds—groans and huffs and sighs. Gradually, she relaxed into the comfort he was offering, glad it didn't come with platitudes and apologies. Boon held her with all he was, and she was picking up on all sorts of … *stuff.*

The guy was older than he seemed. He didn't just have years on her. It was more like millennia. And he radiated all kinds of dominance and confidence, which she was used to countering in kind. Grateful as she was, Pim couldn't figure out why he was suddenly embracing wolvish stereotypes—protective and possessive.

She pushed, and he immediately released her.

His lashes were damp. Of all things. She felt increasingly sure that she didn't understand wolves at all.

He grimaced. "Can I ask a personal question, just to get *all* the awkwardness out of the way?"

She sighed. "Go on."

"Elara is … attracted to me," Boon began.

Pim thought that was putting it mildly.

"Are … you?" he asked gruffly.

That took her aback. "No. Not at all."

With a relieved sigh, he muttered, "Same. You think it's because of uhh … our different …."

"Family backgrounds? No, I don't think that's it. At least, not for me. Ever since …. Well. I prefer females."

Boon blinked. "Guess that's … convenient."

Pim didn't bother hiding her annoyance.

His hands settled into a position that begged for peace. "One of my Elderbough cousins is similarly inclined. She runs with another she-wolf. They're bondmates, even if theirs isn't a traditional den."

She backed up a step. "Elderbough?"

"Oh, that's right. Guess you were shortchanged on the intro." He offered a wan smile. "Boonmar-fen Elderbough."

"Does that mean you *know* Adoonah-soh?"

"Mom? Sure." His tail swung higher. "We were especially close when I was tiny. Am I sensing some hard-core admiration here?"

"I ... suppose," she admitted.

"Not gonna lie. My mom's pretty epic. Once we clear this mission, I'll introduce you."

Pim took a neutral stance. "I wouldn't want to impose ...."

"It's no big deal. Kind of need to, anyhow." He fiddled with a bracelet, eyes averted. "There's something I need to say. Last of the awkward, I swear."

And she knew. Hadn't Hisoka warned her?

Dazedly, she took a receptive stance.

"Yeah," he said gruffly, acknowledging her. Boon knew she knew, but he still spelled it out. "I went deep in your den. Woke up with my nose in Elara's ... well. Come to find she's a beacon, and I'd been awash for days. Plenty long enough. It's just about the fastest way to go about bond-building."

Boon rubbed the back of his neck.

"Your instincts," she said, offering a way forward.

"She's mine."

"And me?"

"You're kind of lumped in. Somehow. Not sure how I'm going to explain to my parents, especially Dad. Going from swearing off females to claiming two at once? It's not very wolvish."

"You'd actually claim me?"

"Already did." Boon's gaze was solemn. "You're mine."

27
CULMINATING SONG

Sinder really hated being off the grid, but some missions did take them into parts of the world where technology wasn't a priority. Hallow had chosen a nearish island, and they'd made it their base of operations. Which was good. Priska had wanted them gone, and Sinder wasn't eager to find out how badly.

Their new haven was tiny, and exploration hadn't taken long. Sinder only had to catch fish for meals and patrol the array. So ... swimming. Until go-time, his only real job was swimming.

"Anything?" he asked the empty beach.

"Nothing yet. I've been checking. Fernanda fussed all night."

"Need another lullaby?"

"We'd take you up on that in a heartbeat, but I doubt Priska would approve."

"Definitely not." And because he was restless, he asked, "How close do they have to get before you'll know we've got incoming?"

No answer.

Sinder tapped the green crystal that allowed the link-up. "Lupe?"

"Sorry. Just a sec. Spit up."

"Better out than in, I guess." And he was definitely guessing. He didn't usually deal with kids. Not unless it was in-game. Some of those puny hotshots had serious skills. Although … come to think of it, Timur's little guy had been okay in small doses. Gregor.

Lupe still hadn't answered.

Sinder probably shouldn't be plaguing the new mother just because he was bored. Waiting was all part of the job. Once things went down, there'd be nothing but crazy, so it was important to eat, rest, and make sure all the moving pieces were in readiness.

Humming the lullaby he and Juuyu had sung over Fernanda, Sinder rearranged yellow seashells into a ring on the sand. Maybe he should hunt for more. They could be souvenirs. Well, probably not the tiny ones, since they'd be a choking hazard. He should take another swim, hunt up bigger ones. They'd give him an excuse to drop by Stately House.

According to his file, Timur had moved there permanently.

Something moved in his periphery, and Sinder turned to look. Dunce and double dunce. He really shouldn't hum. Several Ephemera drifted closer, attracted by his voice. And he hadn't even been trying.

They were harmless. And amusing.

Sinder hummed with a little more intent, glad for the distraction. That's when a juvenile wind dragon glided into the open. Without a second thought, he switched to words and sang coaxingly. With a *tootle-peep*, the little thing rushed him, draping its length around his shoulders and nuzzling his cheek.

"Hello, you." Sinder stroked a crest of pale green fur. "I'm pretty sure you *don't* belong here. Are you a rebel spirit? Or lost and lonesome?"

Dainty claws reached to touch the green crystal.

He held it closer. "So it *wasn't* me you were after? I'm wounded."

The critter, who was easily three times the size Rifflet had been at summer's end, wriggled around to look him in the eye. *"Sing more?"*

Sinder's impressions formed effortlessly—a child with an adventurous streak, happy to see him, and female. "Hello, again. I'm Sinder Stonecairn of the Icelandic Reach."

She looked up at him with eyes that were a soft coral, a match for the splotch of color at the base of her throat.

"Do you have a name?"

"Not yet."

Which seemed an odd answer. "Is there some kind of hold-up with the application?"

Sleek scales wound more snugly around his shoulders. The wicked spike at the end of her tail swung like a pendant over his heart. *"The song is ... is cul-min-a-ting."*

"That's a big word for a little wind dragon. Where'd you hear that?"

"The stars."

Sinder glanced at the endless blue of the sky. "You made friends with the loftiest of impressions, huh?"

"Cadmiel."

"Whoa-kay. That's some *serious* name-dropping. Does he come here often?"

She crooned some notes.

He hummed them back.

She *tootle-peep*ed in a pleased way.

Not entirely distracted, Sinder asked, "So you belong to the stars?"

"No. The boy."

"What boy?"

"The promised boy." She rubbed her narrow muzzle under his jaw. *"I will belong to the boy. Bring me?"*

Sinder was intrigued. "Cadmiel told you to hitch a ride with me?"

"No. Auriel did."

"Oh, well of course. Naturally." He warily scanned the sky again. "You can't hardly start anything without Auriel of the Dawning putting in a good word."

His sarcasm was lost on her.

She trilled agreement.

"So ... the boy? Which boy?"

"The promised boy."

Her insistence wasn't really clarifying matters. Sinder pointed out, "There are a lot of boys in this world."

"He was here. In your thoughts." She tugged at his hair. *"While you sang."*

Sinder had been humming that lullaby for Fernanda. Oh. Okay, yeah. He hadn't been singing it with Lupe's baby in mind. "Gregor?"

She warbled hopefully and repeated, *"Bring me?"*

"You want to go to Gregor," he checked. Because angels or no, this was too crazy to believe.

"Yes."

"Do you know how far from here he is?"

"No."

Sinder guessed he now had two excuses to show up on Timur's doorstep. How hard could it be to smuggle a wind-dragon out of the tropics? Juuyu was probably going to quote all the laws this would break.

Another idea rose to the surface, and he tried Lupe again. "Do you have wind dragons here?"

"I really couldn't say." Her tone was laughing.

"Would Priska give us access?"

"You know the answer to that question, too." She changed the subject on him. *"I was about call out to you. Two people just passed our outermost array."*

"That's good news. Unless it isn't."

He could think of one or two problems that usually came in pairs.

Within the hour, Juuyu was welcoming the newcomers and apologizing for the scant amenities offered by their speck of an island. Sinder had guessed wrong about who'd arrived, but he was glad to be wrong. At least, he was pretty sure he was wrong. You never could tell with foxes.

He'd feel a whole lot better if someone—*anyone*—knew where the Hightip sisters were right now.

People-ing was usually his job, but he hung back in order to observe. Maybe he was being overly cautious, but … so were Moon and Hallow. There was no harm in making sure that they were dealing with allies, not infiltrators.

But then his passenger *tootle-peep*ed, and Tenma Subaru turned, spotted him, and waved.

Busted. Sinder waved back, and the man left Goh's side in order to present his palms.

Matching them, Sinder said, "You came."

"How could we not? We're Inti's tribe." Tenma quietly added, "And there might be people here who need me."

"Who told you where to find us?"

Presenting the tips of his fingers to the little wind dragon, Tenma said, "Argent did."

It figured. The fox probably had the largest stake in what went down here. "I half expected Lord Mettlebright to show up personally."

"I doubt he'll be far behind."

Sinder brightened. It was good to be right once in a while. "On his way, then. Not alone …?"

"No. He was arranging for more help. Mostly for the captives, I think. At least, that's what I was told. With Argent, it's best to assume you know as much as you need to know."

"I trust him." Sinder cautiously asked, "Any chance he's bringing Kyrie?"

Tenma shook his head. "Can you imagine him bringing his son into this kind of danger?"

"No." Even if that was the very thing they might need. "No,

he never would."

All of the sudden, Lupe's voice carried. *"Sinder, I have news."*

Lifting a finger and turning his back, Sinder strolled away from Tenma. "They're here, if that's what you mean."

"No. It's Inti. He was asleep. Gone deep. But he's awake now, and the array works. I can reach him."

"That's welcome news."

"He ... wanted me to pass something along."

"Oh? Is he being cryptic again?" Sinder had been helpless to unravel some of the messages Inti had relayed to Boon. They were either coded or out of context. Or entirely literal, if Auriel and Cadmiel were loitering about.

"This one's straightforward enough, but it doesn't make any sense to me. 'Seela is here.'"

"That's it?"

"That's it. Just that."

"Seela is here," he echoed, but it didn't ring any bells. "Who's Seela?"

A millisecond later, Sinder was nose-to-chest with a tense wall of wide-eyed Starmark.

"Sinder." Merit had him by the shoulders. "Did you say ... *Seela?*"

28

WHAT KIND OF MONSTER

he knock came far too early, but Jacques had only slept in fits and starts. He was up and dressed and properly caffeinated. If only he'd also been prepared to find Dr. Kodoku at the door.

"To what do I owe the honor?" he managed.

"It occurred to me that I've not met your boy." With a genial dose of sway, he ordered, "Bring him out."

"Won't be a moment," Jacques promised, indicating the bedroom door. "Maybe two. I'll make certain he's presentable."

And he closed the door in the dragon's face.

Would Kodoku have noticed the sigilcraft in their room? Possibly. No, more like *probably*. He'd bragged about having a gift for it.

Hustling into the bedroom, he was startled to find Inti sitting up, pulling sigils from midair. "The dragon wants a look at Akira,"

Jacques announced.

"Look, look, look," Inti murmured. "But do not let him touch."

"Right. Shake a leg, Akira. I need you looking properly debauched."

"Huh? Oh. Sure."

As he rolled out of bed, Jacques softly called, "Anjou, Eiji, a little help?"

The closet door slid open, and the two felines slunk into the open, looking rumpled and relaxed and enviably sated. Indicating Akira, he said, "Dragon at the door. I need camouflage. Rub up against him. If Dr. Creeper takes a whiff, he needs to think *orgy*, not monkey."

Eyes bright, they set to work.

Jacques retreated to the bathroom long enough to snatch up a couple of essentials. When he returned, his paramour had his hands in the air while Eiji stole his pajama pants and Anjou buttoned him into one of Jacques shirts. From behind. While nibbling at the side of his neck.

"Guys, is this really…?" whispered Akira.

"Boyfriend shirt. A classic." Jacques cleared his throat. "Lose the briefs?"

"Agreed. I apologize, Akira," murmured Eiji.

Curling toes and flushed cheeks were the man's only actual protest. He managed to retain a receptive posture. This was trust, and it warmed the cockles of Jacques' heart. Among other things.

"Well done, gentlemen."

Akira stood there, rattled and flushed and ever so slightly desperate.

Jacques inspected the fresh love bite, added a sloppy smear of tinted gloss to Akira's lips, then kissed him lightly. "Now. Before the effects wear off."

As he pulled Akira toward the door, the younger man whispered, "This is … drafty. And you have gloss on your …."

"Rather the point. I'll try to stay between you."

And then they stepped into the hall, where an impatient dragon awaited. "How long does it take …?" he demanded peevishly.

Jacques shrugged eloquently. "Extenuating circumstances."

"I can hardly examine him if he's huddled behind you." Applying sway, Dr. Kodoku said, "Bring him out where I can see."

He complied, because he had to, but Jacques kept a hand clamped firmly at the back of Akira's neck. It wasn't much in the way of protection, but a little posturing couldn't hurt.

The dragon noticed his hand. And the fresh love bite. Reaching for the flapping tails of Akira's over-large shirt, he lifted for a look.

Akira squeaked, grabbed, and tugged the fabric back, softly stammering, "D-don't!"

"Not pre-pubescent," remarked the doctor.

"Now you've met." Jacques smiled thinly. "May I send him back to bed?"

Kodoku's nose wrinkled. "Have you been sharing him with those felines?"

"All very consensual." And raising his voice slightly, he called, "Eiji? Come fetch Akira."

Jacques could have kissed the feline, who emerged naked, bussed Jacques' cheek, and gathered Akira inside.

The door clicked firmly shut, and Jacques breathed a little easier. Even though it meant facing the dragon alone.

"No reavers in his bloodline?" asked Dr. Kodoku.

"I hardly chose him for his pedigree," Jacques murmured, his gaze fixed on the passing scenery, which was one big tropical thicket. Quite monotonous, really.

"Why, then?"

Hardly the most clinical of questions. Was he actually curious?

"Tell me why," he demanded silkily.

"Love."

His interest fell off, which suited Jacques fine.

Dr. Kodoku sighed. "Unsuitable for paternity, but there are other ways to contribute. Never mind that, though. More importantly, do you have access to the Amaranthine Council?"

"Argent maintains close ties with the other members of the original Five. They are regular guests at Stately House."

"And they know you?"

"They know *of* me." It wasn't a lie. But he'd hardly dish about certain members' sleep habits.

"Do you have access to the beacon?"

"Lord Mettlebright is exceedingly protective of what's his." No need to mention that all of them were his. Or that Tsumiko considered Jacques family.

Dr. Kodoku changed tack. "Have any of your crossers reached breeding age?"

Jacques strove for even tones. "There's Ginkgo, I suppose. We specialize in children."

"So do I. Fortunately for you." And with a sly smile, the dragon added, "Nearly there."

Which was both off-putting and ominous, all things considered.

The inquisition continued throughout the drive, but finally, Futari pulled to a stop in front of a building that had all the charm of a prison.

"My lab is inside. And housing. A room's been provided." Again, that glitteringly indulgent gaze. "I have a few preparations to make before your tour. I will send for you later, after you have had time to rest and recreate. Futari?"

She grimly said, "This way."

Jacques murmured vague courtesies and followed. Once they were through the first door—which required a key card—he quietly asked, "What's he hinting at?"

"I believe Father is trying to woo you."

"Dare I ask about his methods?"

She paused to search his face. "I will be very disappointed if you live up to his expectations. I did what I could. He speaks English."

"Oh, good lord. Did he actually procure a boy for me?"

They turned onto a bare hall and stopped before a stark door. Futari handed him a key card.

Jacques used it, and a soft *click* welcomed him inside.

A spare kitchenette. A water closet. A bedroom door. Jacques couldn't decide if the color scheme was *meant* to be depressing or if it was an unhappy accident. The tepid clash of beiges and grays certainly dampened his spirits.

"He is in there." Futari pointed to the bedroom.

Jacques' fists balled tightly enough to hurt. "What does your father expect me to do?"

"I shudder to think."

"What about the boy?"

"He did not believe me when I told him you would be kind." Futari dully added, "There are precedents."

"How old?"

"Ten."

Jacques winced. "What kind of monster does Kodoku think I am?"

Futari's gaze flicked to the door. "This kind."

"Stay with me, please?"

She inclined her head.

Dearly hoping he wouldn't find a child tied to his bed, Jacques opened the door.

This room was similarly dismal, and in the farthest corner, under a barred window, a boy sat hugging his knees. He was ramrod straight, and there was a rebellious glint in his eyes. In that moment, he reminded Jacques of Nonny, but only in attitude.

"Lord, you look just like him."

And he did.

Except he didn't.

Purple hair fell in soft waves to square shoulders. And Jacques wasn't imagining the tail that curved across the floor. His complexion wasn't quite so pale as Kyrie's, but the scales and freckling were much the same. As was the burgeoning coronet of pale horns.

"Do you have a name?" Jacques asked.

The boy's gaze darted to Futari, then back. "Nine."

"Your name is … Nine?"

"It's more of a number. It's what he calls me."

The accent was American. East Coast. Jacques asked, "Do you like it?"

"Would you?"

"*Non*. I'd be incensed."

The boy's eyes narrowed. "What's that mean?"

"Angry. Furious. Outraged."

He nodded. "That's a good word. I'm incensed."

"I'm Jacques. I won't hurt you." And because that might not be clear enough, he promised, "I won't lay a hand on you."

With another glance at Futari, the boy said, "That's not how it usually goes."

Jacques quietly seethed. "Have you been offered to guests before?"

"This is *my* first time. Not many people like red eyes." His scaled tail smacked the low pile carpeting. "You have strange tastes."

"That's slanderous. He was *incorrect*."

"He thought I should be … how'd he put it … *prepared for my ordeal*. That's another good word. Ordeal."

"I'm not an ordeal. I'm your *uncle*."

The boy went right on, as if Jacques' claim meant nothing. "He also told me not to kill you, even if things get … uncomfortable."

Jacques needed to sit. He perched on the edge of the bed that dominated the room.

Almost gleefully, the boy went on, as if his words meant little. "Submit. Pretend. Please him. He gives a lot of orders, you know?

He thinks I have to listen. He's wrong."

"You're no longer susceptible to dragon sway," Jacques surmised. "Or you never were."

"Give yourself a hand," the boy ordered, his tone heavy with sway.

Jacques didn't.

Smirking, the boy said, "Neither are you. Interesting, isn't it, Futari?"

She leaned against the wall, arms folded, gaze thoughtful. "There are a lot of interesting people on the island at the moment. Things are happening."

"Culminating," agreed the boy. And to Jacques, "That's another good word."

Jacques sighed and asked, "May I know your name? Your real name?"

His tail slapped the floor again. "Sibley."

"And ... you're American."

"I guess. Been here for a while, though."

"Your mother?"

Sibley shook his head. "Died when I was born. Me, I got snatched out of an enclave."

Jacques glanced Futari's way. "You steal children?"

"Not me," she said grimly.

"Your father?" Jacques guessed.

She rolled her eyes.

"I was pretty little. I didn't know better, and they tricked me." Sibley clenched his jaw and looked away. "It was foxes."

Futari left, called away, and Sibley retreated into a wary silence. Jacques sighed and stretched out on the bed, letting himself go limp. He'd found one of the children Argent was desperate to reach, but Sibley felt unreachable. At least while the boy was in this dismal room, he was safe. Maybe that's all Jacques could offer.

He'd dozed off when a finger traced his eyebrow.

Jacques opened his eyes and searched Sibley's face.

"You looked sad," the boy said.

"Must have been a dream," Jacques murmured.

"Why did you say you're my uncle?"

"Because my nephew is your half-brother."

Sibley didn't seem surprised. "Another one, huh?"

"There are more of you?" Jacques ventured hopefully.

"Why do you care?"

"Because there's somebody who loves you very much. She's an amazing lady, and a bunch of us are trying to make sure her prayers are answered."

"You answer prayers?"

"*Non.* But I have a part to play in a daring plan. And if all goes well, I can bring that lady all the things she's been hoping for."

"What sort of things?"

"You for one. And others like you. Or unlike you, since Dr. Creeper bragged about his unique selection." Jacques had no way of knowing if this room was secure, but it was too late to call back anything he'd already said. "Would you like to be rescued, Sibley?"

The boy shook his head. "It's no good. You're done for. This is the lab. He's got you."

Jacques needed him to be wrong. "I'm not alone. Help is on the way."

"I don't believe you."

"That won't stop them."

Sibley carefully laid his hand across Jacques' throat.

"My turn for an ordeal?" he asked softly.

The boy asked, "What are you gonna do?"

Jacques smiled and let his eyes drift shut. "I'm going to trust you."

"You're being stupid."

"If I'm behaving foolishly, it's only because I'm happy."

There was some discreet sniffing, which made Jacques smile.

"What?" demanded Sibley. "What're you happy about?"

Jacques opened his eyes and held the boy's gaze. "I'm very happy to learn that my newest nephew is good and smart and brave. Well done, Sibley. Leave the rest to us."

His hand slowly retreated, and the boy tentatively asked, "What'd you say your name was?"

"Jacques. But you may call me Uncle Jackie."

Jacques woke when Futari returned, possibly because one or another of Argent's sigils pulsed in warning. She stood over the bed, incredulity on her face. Sibley was curled against his side, clinging to Jacques' shirt, sound asleep.

She indicated the door.

He eased out of bed, taking the time to tuck a blanket around Sibley. Having never been one to abandon a bedmate without a word, he patted his pockets and came up with a monogrammed handkerchief. Running it over his skin, Jacques carefully refolded it and slipped it into the boy's hand.

A reminder. A promise.

"I'll come back for you," he murmured, then followed Futari out the door.

Once the door clicked shut, she demanded, "What did you do?"

"I hardly know. But it always works." As he walked with her along bleak halls, Jacques said, "As an ordinary human, I pose no threat to anyone of Amaranthine heritage. We've speculated that it makes me seem safe. But who can say for certain? Could be I'm universally charming. Care to weigh in?"

"No."

"So … time for the grand tour?"

Futari simply said, "Dr. Kodoku is ready to see you."

"Make sure Sibley stays safe until I get back?"

She shook her head. "That is a promise I cannot keep."

Jacques stopped. "He's not being passed along to some other guest, is he?"

Futari tilted her head. "Not him. You. I cannot promise you are coming back."

29

SHAKY CONNECTION

octor Kodoku went through the motions of guiding a tour, though he didn't divulge any information about the rooms they passed through. Every workstation was empty. Jacques was beginning to suspect that the dragon had spent the last few hours dismissing his employees. All very ominous.

After many locked doors, they came to one plastered in warning labels. "Here is where I do most of my private work. Pet projects, if you will. I am curious if your own people are doing similar things at Stately House."

"There's no lab," Jacques said. "Just the mares and their remedies."

Kodoku pressed, "What do you do with the crossers you collect?"

"We adopt them."

"Yes, yes. I have no interest in quibbling terms. In a sense, I adopt crossers, as well. Though most are born here. And all of them contribute toward the future in one form or another." He happily explained, "This is a top tier research facility. We apply ancient knowledge to all sorts of problems—old and new."

Meaningless words.

Empty boasts.

Jacques had experienced enough to ignore this dragon's rhetoric and quietly despise him.

"I am sure we can find *some* way for you to contribute." Dr. Kodoku seized Jacques' elbow and steered him toward a wide door at the opposite end of the room. "This is where you will begin. All part of my security measures. Surely, you understand the need for caution."

"Wasn't this meant to be a tour?"

"Yes, yes. Plenty to see, but they are secrets, and you have far too much sigilcraft lacing your person."

"Gifts from my lord," he murmured.

"They must be removed before we can proceed."

Jacques balked. "These are permanent. Tattoos."

"Not all," Kodoku said smilingly. "You are probably not even aware of all the ways you are warded. Layer upon layer. It should prove a lavish feast."

He flicked and tapped and inserted a different sort of key into the box beside the door, which unlocked with a shrill whistling. Jacques dug in his heels. This had an air of finality about it, and he was feeling more and more the coward.

"There he is," Dr. Kodoku said with a dramatic wave of an arm. "Amazing, yes?"

Jacques quailed inwardly as a figure unfolded from a bulky huddle on the floor in the corner.

He had a blocky build and was large enough to be daunting. That and he seemed to be made of stone. Dark gray and rough-looking below the waist, all along his arms, and atop his head. But here and there, through gaps in the gray, luminous color showed. Face, shoulders, and torso were fully exposed, and the sight was striking, as if someone had carved him from chartreuse crystal.

"You've heard of remnant stone, surely?" the dragon inquired.

"I have," Jacques said faintly.

"He is the fullness. The last of his kind left upon the earth." The dragon preened. "Cadmiel abandoned him, but I have given him purpose. Exquisite, is he not?"

From where he stood unmoving, the creature settled his hands into a plea for peace.

Jacques found the nerve to brazen through. "Do you mean to say he's from one of the lost clans?"

"Mountain clan. Obviously." Dr. Kodoku casually applied sway. "Go to him, Mr. Smythe. He is undoubtedly hungry."

That was worrisome enough that Jacques forgot to keep up the pretense of susceptibility. Holding his ground, he asked, "What does he eat?"

"Sigils." And with a clang of finality, the dragon locked him in with the rock imp.

"Hello." Jacques matched the other's peaceful stance. "I'm Jacques. May I know your name?"

It was interesting trying to read facial expressions on someone whose countenance was partially translucent.

Taking the—admittedly shaky—initiative, Jacques stepped forward. Once. "I've met a scant few Impressions, and I understand you're one of their number. A few need physical contact in order to communicate. Assuming you *can* communicate with an ordinary fellow like me …? Not a reaver, you see."

Jacques stepped again.

"Lord, you're a big one. Stars are dainty by comparison."

The rock-man shifted his feet and licked his lips.

That looked strange. And reminded Jacques that Dr. Creeper had said the imp was hungry. His next step was much harder to take.

"Language could also be a problem. My Old Amaranthine is embarrassingly limited."

Jacques was close enough to tell that *this* stone—unlike remnant stones—glowed with a life that didn't need to be sparked by a crystal adept. It was as if nebula and stars were captured within his body, slowly wheeling and pulsating. It was captivating.

"May I touch?" Jacques peered up into a craggy face. "This is probably incredibly rude, but I want to know what you feel like."

His lips parted, and he held out a hand.

Jacques immediately reached back.

The hand was slightly rough, like stone, but the imp was also warm and pliant. His fingers were long and dexterous, and he wove theirs together. "Brave one, I will not hurt you." The voice rattled like gravel.

"Oh! Well! Right, then. That makes things more convenient." Jacques tried again. "May I know your name?"

"Dayith."

"Charmed." He settled the fingertips of his free hand against the imp's bare chest. Here, he was all smooth planes and silken facets. "Do you know something? You're my favorite color."

The imp smiled faintly. "I am sorry."

"For being gorgeous? Nonsense."

"I will not hurt you," Dayith promised again.

Jacques wondered if he should have kept his distance. "What are you going to do?"

Drawing him closer by their connected hands, Dayith pushed up the sleeve of Jacques' linen coat, then the cuff of his shirt. "Here is one," he murmured, pressing his lips to Jacques' wrist.

"Is there a sigil there? Wouldn't surprise me."

Dayith held his gaze and licked.

Something indefinable tugged. It was unlike any sensation Jacques had experienced, a prickling, tingling, and peeling. It was also hot and wet. Like … well, like anyone's tongue would be. "What are you doing?" Jacques whispered.

"Surviving." The imp's eyes slid shut, and he stole another taste. "He does not feed me often."

Jacques tried to pull away.

Dayith didn't let him go. "I must."

"Can you get by with one or two? Some of these have great personal significance."

"If I do not take them all, Kodoku will take your life." Again, he promised, "I will not hurt you."

Jacques knew he was helpless, but he still protested. "Argent marked me. These sigils mean I'm his. I don't want to lose my connection to him."

The imp tugged him nearer. "Close your eyes and keep that connection foremost in your mind."

"Why?"

"Trust me." Glancing down, Dayith added, "And remove any clothing that obscures your sigils."

Jacques' eyes widened. "I have sigils absolutely everywhere."

"I know." Faceted green eyes searched his, and trembling fingers touched his cheek. "I am sorry."

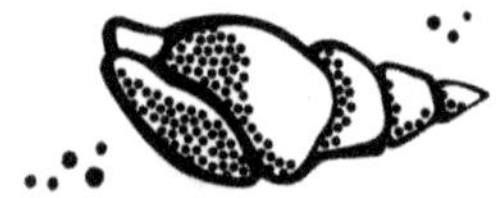

Argent Mettlebright was arguing with Andor when the first niggling touch of a mind drew him up short. Without any further warning, he was dragged into a dream he hadn't created.

"Is it really you?" asked a breathless voice.

He swung around. Jacques stood there, tears on his cheeks. Storming over, he demanded, "What is the meaning of this?"

"Survival … I suppose. And a certain amount of trust."

Argent's tails were out and flailing, but he managed a steady tone. "Perhaps you should tell me what is happening?"

"Specifically?"

"If you would be so good."

"Dayith is licking me."

Argent was incredulous. "Perhaps you should confine yourself to *pertinent* details?"

Jacques laughed weakly. "Did you know that rock imps eat sigils?"

"No."

"Dayith is confined in Kodoku's lab, and it's feeding time. I'm breakfast." His lip trembled. "I'm apparently covered in them. Didn't know. Can't tell. Have you been sneaking in extras? Or was it Kyrie? Lord, your sigilcraft must be of high quality. He's ... ah. Let's go with *pleased*. Lots of very pleased sounds."

"We tattooed you."

"Hardly an obstacle. He has to work a little harder, but they lift away like the rest. Ink and all. It ... tingles."

"*Pertinent* details," Argent grumbled. "Are you in danger?"

"Probably." Jacques shivered. "Dr. Creeper moved me to his lab, and it's universally agreed that this is beyond the pale."

"Immediate danger?"

"Of embarrassing myself, certainly. But nothing more."

"What about Akira?"

"They split us up, but he's with Inti."

Argent hummed. "Do they know?"

"They know I'm not a pedophile." He swallowed hard. "Kodoku left a boy in my room like a mint on the pillow. Brave lad. Tell Kyrie he's got a little brother named Sibley."

"I will." And grudgingly, "Why are you squirming."

Jacques sucked in a breath. "Remember that third tattoo? Somewhat regretting the placement right now."

Argent firmly sidestepped that. "You are using my sigil. Am I right in assuming this imp initiated contact?"

"Yes."

"Why?"

"I can guess." With a soulful gaze, he admitted, "This might be *goodbye*."

"May I speak to him? What was his name?"

"Dayith." Jacques cleared his throat. "He's very focused on the task at hand. Not many sigils left, actually."

Thinking fast, Argent asked, "Is there anything he wants from us?"

Jacques looked away, looked back. "Send the winds. Th-they've abandoned this place."

Progress. Argent said, "We can do that. Ask him to keep you safe for me."

Surprise registered, and Jacques nodded. "He promises."

"I have promises to keep, as well."

He could see Jacques' brave face slipping. "Tell Suuzu ...."

"You will tell him yourself," commanded Argent. "And until you return to my side, your duty is to Akira."

"I'll try." His expression grew mournful, his eyes pleading without words.

"Jackie," Argent groaned. "You need to understand ...."

But the sigil linking them was swiftly dismantled—consumed— and their connection was gone.

Argent opened his eyes and winced at the wattage being put out by Stately House's secret star. "I am fine. Jacques is less so. You may put me down, Andor."

The bear was cradling him close and grumbling unhappily.

"Well, Eri?" Argent posed to Andor's longtime companion. "Do you have anything to contribute?"

They wrung their hands, then cupped Argent's face, and their voice settled into the fox's soul. *"Who can summon storms? Who can call the winds and give them direction?"*

"Dragons," Argent mused aloud. "They can woo the wind to

their side. We are on good terms with Beckonthrall ...."

"Bethiel shepherded the skies with the help of four winds." Eri grabbed his hands and squeezed.

"I know the tale. They were called the Changing Winds."

"She is one of them. She can help."

"Can you be more specific? Where am I meant to find one of Bethiel's fabled winds?"

Eri looked skyward, looked back, and smiled. *"Wardenclave."*

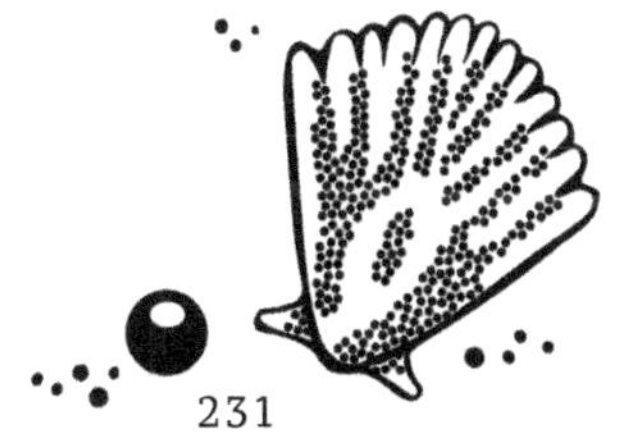

30

CAUSING TROUBLE

Elara wasn't good at isolation. Staying put had been easy when she could run her fingers through a hot wolf's hair. Go figure. But books were beginning to pall, and she alternated between worrying about Pim, Inti, and the rest ... and feeling left out. But what good could she do?

Which turned out to be an excellent question.

So she was actively pursuing answers.

Because memories were slowly surfacing. Half-forgotten glimpses of the lab. Fuzzy snatches of conversations. Situations that had broken her heart until Dr. Kodoku had told her to disregard them. But they only seemed to come to Elara when she wasn't trying to remember, which was exceptionally frustrating.

An orderly approach was required.

Elara distracted herself with the luxuries Pim had left behind, giving herself a proper pampering. Full-on spa treatment. And while she relaxed, she let her mind drift. And calmly took notes. Which she organized and fleshed out with as much tenacity as she'd applied to her thesis.

When Pim and Boon came back for her, Elara intended to be ready.

A tiny tap stirred Elara from her meditation. Another drew her attention to the window. Hurrying over, she peered cautiously down and immediately relaxed into a smile. Inti stood below, juggling pebbles.

He gestured for her to open the window. She quickly complied, and he sprang toward the nearest tree, pushed off, gaining enough height to reach the decorative ledge above the window below. With no pause, tail swinging, he jumped high enough to get a hand onto her window ledge.

Elara leaned down, reaching for Inti's other hand, and he grasped her arm without a moment's hesitation. She pulled, leaning back, and in one scramble, he tumbled into the room. Seated on the floor, he peered around worriedly.

"Boon?" he asked softly.

"Woke yesterday. He told me to wait here since I would have slowed him down."

"Pim?"

She knelt beside him. "Left with Hisoka Twineshaft."

Inti's tail looped around her shoulders. "You're with me, then, Dr. Perrine."

Without much dignity, she pulled him into a hug.

He tutted and patted and called her courageous. And she supposed she'd need to be and firmed her resolve.

"Next, next, next. Inti will bring you to Akira."

"A friend of yours?"

"Good, good, good friend. A good man."

She nodded, clung a little tighter, then let go, sitting back on her heels.

Inti tapped her nose. "I need you to pack. Anything you might need. Running shoes. Emergency rations. Maybe camping."

Elara wasn't accustomed to Inti sounding quite so sensible. "Is this the real you?"

He pinched her cheek and slipped back into something more familiar. "Inti is Inti, and Inti is your friend." Studying her closely, he accused, "You are hungry."

"Couldn't be helped. Confined to quarters. I'm down to my last packet of cashews."

Inti pulled two oranges out of interior pockets in the short vest he wore over his tunic. "Eat. Pack. I'll find more food."

As he leapt to the sill, she could only beg, "Be careful."

But he was already gone.

Elara thought it beyond brassy to just walk out the front doors of Trulore Clinic, but they didn't turn any heads. "Are you doing something?" she whispered.

"Wards for you, wards for me." Inti's glance held a puckish gleam. "Inti is tricky like a fox."

"Are there foxes here?"

"No, nope, none." He gave her hand a squeeze and pulled her toward a stand of palms in the landscaping. "Senna and Nona are away."

"The redheads from security."

"Tricky, tricky vixens." Inti paused behind the screening leaves and tapped her nose, then his own. "If Dr. Perrine sees a red fox, she must run away from her. If Dr. Perrine sees a silver fox, she must run to him."

"Another friend?"

"Mentor," he said proudly. "Now *we* must run. Inti will carry."

Elara hugged her bulging bag of supplies. "I've got this."

"Good, good, fine," Inti readily agreed. "And I've got you."

Without further ado, he hauled her into the cradle of his arms and took off.

"Oh, god. Why is the princess treatment so undignified?"

He snickered.

"Where are we going?"

"Akira's at the resort. That's where he started."

Inti explained a little more, about a man named Jacques and an array of crystals, about forces gathering beyond the island's barrier and the importance of finding its anchor. She appreciated the context. And the distraction from the monkey-crosser's springing gait.

"It would have to be in the lab. He keeps all his favorite things there."

"You remember more than before ...?"

Elara said, "Thanks to you."

He grimaced. "I wish the memories you lost were kinder."

"They aren't. But I can be."

Inti hustled Elara along empty halls, then pushed her ahead of him into a suite, calling, "Dr. Perrine is American. Only English." And to Elara, "Here is Akira."

An Asian boy perched on a bar stool, clad in a silk dressing gown while an Amaranthine male did his makeup. A second male sidled up to flank him, lips parting as he inhaled. Testing her scent, no doubt.

She tried not to let it bother her. "Going out on the town?" she asked lightly.

"We finished packing, and we were bored," Akira said in careful English. "Grooming calms everyone down, and I don't mind. It washes off."

He moved to slip from his seat, but a hand at his shoulder prevented him. Akira looked up, clearly puzzled, and the Amaranthine eased around, firmly blocking Elara's view. The other one's gaze seemed to be begging Inti for an explanation.

Akira didn't wait for one.

Pushing between the two males, he smiled up at Elara, palms offered in the Amaranthine style. "I'm Akira. How do you want to be called?"

"Elara." She matched his greeting.

"Got it. I should probably go clean up." But he hesitated. "Eiji? Anjou? Aren't you going to say *hello*?"

She stepped back. "It's fine. We can cover the niceties later."

Inti backed her up. "Go, go, groom. Get ready to run."

"I'll hurry." And to Elara, "I'm going after Jacques."

"Your partner."

Akira fiddled with the ties of his dressing gown. "Yeah. He and I were supposed to stay out of trouble, but that dragon took him. So we'll go find him first."

Elara looked to Inti. "Dr. Kodoku took him?"

"To the lab," he confirmed. "Do you remember that part?"

"I'm afraid so." She gently caressed Akira's hair. "When someone goes into the lab, they don't usually leave again."

"We can rescue him. And anyone else who's there."

"I'll help," she promised, caressing the boy's cheek. "You can count on me."

Inti poked his head between them, checking Elara's face, then Akira's. "Dr. Perrine comforts many children. Dr. Perrine *loves* children. But Akira is no longer a child."

"It's probably the makeup. Well ... and I *am* short."

He switched to Japanese to scold, but the monkey crosser only snickered. Inti petted Akira's hair and pecked his cheek. "Inti and Akira both play tricks."

Elara was almost afraid to ask.

Akira didn't make her. With a sheepish smile, he volunteered, "I'm twenty-six, but I'm supposed to seem younger. To be scandalous."

"Oh, god," she whispered. "I'm so sorry."

He waved his hands. "I don't usually look like this. Not that I have a choice. Jacques packed for me, and everything is for his boy-toy."

She laughed. "You're usually more manly?"

"Just ordinary." He pointed toward the bath. "I'll change."

One of the Amaranthine followed him in, the other stayed back to offer his palms. "Eiji Woodhearth. Cat clan."

She met his palms and waited to see if he'd question her.

But he only rubbed his cheek against hers and whispered, "Peace, lady. We only want peace."

"Thanks, cutie pie." And because she *did* understand now, she added, "Sorry if I confused you."

He nuzzled her other cheek and sighed, "Stunning."

Suddenly, the other one was there, pulling his friend away. "Apologies, lady. Your personal wards are no match for your brilliance." And to Eiji, "What were you thinking?"

"Mmm ... I was thinking, just a little ...?" He offered a wistfully apologetic smile. "And then ... just a little more?"

"More *wards*," grumbled his companion, who herded Eiji into the bathroom.

Moments later, Eiji leaned out long enough to ask, "May I adapt one of the crystals in the array to anchor her wards?"

Inti clucked his tongue. "I will do it, *cutie pie*. Go, go, groom."

He cast a longing look in her direction, but he went.

"I thought I was sealed."

"Was, was, were." Inti favored her with a long look and sighed, "Wolves."

"I'm causing trouble," Elara murmured.

The crosser patted her hand and quietly said, "Inti is counting on it. And Kodoku is not."

When Akira and the two felines finished their grooming session, Elara nodded approvingly. Honestly, she didn't think Akira looked any older; his maturity had a boyish quality, all innocence and optimism and good humor. She especially admired his easy acceptance of his friends' affectionate touches. Enough so that she asked, "Do humans get hugs, too?"

He laughed and walked into her arms. "Friends?"

"Definitely." She confided, "I don't like to be alone."

"Same for me." He leaned back, searching her face. "Should I call you Elara-onee-san—older sister—or maybe Elara-sensei? Since you're a doctor."

She whispered, "Sister, please."

"Sure thing."

Inti horned in on the hug and announced, "Dr. Perrine used to work in the lab where Jacques was taken. She can help find Jacques."

Elara eased free and crossed to her bag. "I've been piecing this together. I'm not sure how much good it will do."

Her map of the lab building was as precise to scale as she could manage.

"Map, mapping, mapped," Inti muttered, trailing his fingers over her grid. "Anjou, Eiji, come memorize the layout."

Akira crowded close, too. "Where will Jacques be?"

"That depends on how much trouble he's in." Elara touched the front entrance, then indicated a long corridor. "The rich and famous get to admire the trees and get drunk on pollen. It loosens their purse strings, as it were. But there's a security office just here."

Inti growled softly.

Elara could sympathize. "At first, I thought it was pretty cool of Dr. Kodoku to put women in charge of security, but they're real bitches. And not just toward me."

"*Two* women?" Akira asked. "What do they look like?"

"Petite. Perky. Redheads."

"Not bitches, then. It's them, isn't it?" He was looking worriedly at Inti. "You found those two vixens."

"Oh, god," Elara whispered. "You were being *literal* earlier?"

"Foxy, foxy foxes," the crosser confirmed. "It's good they're not here."

Elara tapped the central lab. "If Jacques is in as much trouble as you think, he's probably here. My workstation wasn't far from a door. The details are hazy, but anyone who was suspected of making trouble for Dr. Kodoku always went inside for ... for questioning, I guess?"

There was an empty space in the middle of her careful map. An unaccounted-for block.

Akira asked, "What's inside?"

"I don't know. Or it's possible I don't remember."

"He's a dragon, so yeah." Akira asked, "What about Linlu Dimityblest?"

She touched an office near the entrance. "All paperwork and deliveries go through Linlu. He's a little like a secretary, though it's Futari that Dr. Kodoku keeps closest. She's his daughter, but he treats her like a lackey. Futari assists him with his ... private projects."

"That's two dragons." Akira frowned. "Isn't there another one?"

"Not that I recall." Elara gently touched a long row of small boxes. "Although some of the children who come here 'for treatment' show signs of draconic heritage."

"Crossers." Akira touched the cages she'd mapped. "Are you talking about the Rogue's children?"

She could only shake her head. She didn't know what he meant.

Inti answered with grim confidence. "The kidnapped ones, yes. The ones born here, no. They're the results of Kodoku's *private projects*."

"So the Rogue's not here?" Akira checked.

"No, *nyet*, and *non*," Inti said in wry tones. "But not never."

"Partial success, huh?" Akira sought Elara's gaze and asked, "By any chance, is there a scientist here called Naoki?"

Both Elara and Inti touched the central lab again, their fingers bumping together over one of the largest workstations.

"He's here?" Akira asked softly. "He really is? I wasn't positive, but ... he's actually here. That's good."

She thought he was blinking back tears. "Dr. Naoki Hajime.

You know him?"

Akira's expression couldn't have been more vulnerable. "He's my dad."

Inti chittered softly to himself and muttered things in what sounded like Japanese. "Pen, pen, pencil?" he demanded.

Elara withdrew a case from her bag and offered it.

Choosing a red one, he paused with the nib nearly touching her map. "May I?"

She nodded.

He made several neat amendments, talking as he went. "Naoki has a greenhouse. Here are the trees. Here is the room where Seela is sleeping. Foxes put stolen children here. And *this*." He carefully outlined the room Elara had singled out earlier. "You do not know what's in this room?" Inti checked. "Do not remember?"

"No idea," she confirmed.

"Then this is where we must go. No matter what."

"Why?" asked Akira.

"This is the only room Inti could not get into. This room is the only place left to look."

Akira poked the monkey-crosser's shoulder. "Tell us, already. What do you think we'll find inside?"

"The anchor."

31
THE RIGHT KIND OF CLEAR

isoka came to a standstill before a plinth on which a pale blue stone sang with a bright note.

Boon's tail bristled. "How many of the wardstones have you already located?"

He inclined his head toward Pim. "We confirmed the locations of two. This is the third. Inti reported that there are four of these. However, their anchor has yet to be found."

"And they're all like this one?"

"So far."

"Kind of straightforward, isn't it? I mean, we're meant to be dealing with dragons, foxes, or both. They don't do plain and simple. Not if they can figure out a way to complicate it." The wolf crouched, sniffed, and scowled. "This isn't convoluted. It's not even trying to confuse me. I'm not buying it."

"You have a point." Hisoka turned Patter loose and cautiously circled the plinth. "I'm wise to the ways of foxes, but that doesn't mean I can't be tricked."

Boon grunted. "You're better with sigilcraft than I am, so I'll trust your say-so, but this is a little too …."

"Staged," said Pim. "This has been staged."

"I think so, too," said Boon.

"Search for something more subtle," suggested Hisoka, who was really missing Novi right then. "The resonance feels authentic, so the actual stone must be close."

Pim said, "Inti's a trickster himself. He had to have found the real thing. Would he have marked it somehow … for us?"

"I like how you think," said Boon. "Posy, take the high road?"

Hisoka wasted no time scaling the nearest tree. Naturally, Patter was quick to clamber after him, not stopping until he was settled on Hisoka's shoulders. So there were small hands firmly clamped in his hair when he turned his attention to their surroundings.

Pim was already leaning out from a nearby palm. She called, "Those pebbles on the path make an arrow. Maybe."

"No kidding?" Boon strolled that way.

"Or he could have been marking a trap," warned Hisoka.

"A little sooner, next time?" grumbled Boon, who yanked at his ponytail. He'd stopped short.

Pim asked, "Did you spot something?"

"Found something." And turning so he could see Hisoka, he glumly added, "Can't move."

"On my way," Hisoka called, waving for Pim to keep her vantage. It still intrigued him that they were getting on so well. Boon kept adult females at bay with a combination of polite avoidance, strict ground rules, and warning growls.

The packs generally respected his preferences, especially since there seemed to be vows involved. Harmonious sometimes slipped into matchmaking mode—which was amusingly hypocritical of him—but Boon always rebuffed his efforts to bring him into the family.

Maybe Boon was at ease because Pim had no designs on him?

But something else had occurred to Hisoka. Boon repeatedly made a point of positioning himself between Hisoka and Pim. Not exactly warning her off, but definitely providing a buffer. Hisoka could only be grateful, since he was similarly strict where females were concerned. Instincts weren't absolute, but they could rear up at inconvenient times. Boon was protecting him.

By the time Hisoka reached the trapped wolf, his tail had developed a tick, so Hisoka pressed a hand to his shoulder. Patter immediately took it for a bridge and scurried across.

Boon snorted. "C'mere, runt. Least I can do is free up his hands so he can free me."

Hisoka remarked, "He's not shy of us."

"Ever tame a pitterhind?"

"Can't say I have."

Boon's tail settled into an easy sway. "It's about this easy, so long as you're gentle. And moonbeams are devoted, once you win them over."

Hisoka's curiosity stirred. "Ever tame a moonbeam?"

The wolf's gaze was neutral, but his tone was easy. "I've met a few. They're sometimes bonded into the packs."

"No … unaffiliated ones?" Hisoka pressed.

"Why? You needing *another* imp?" Boon arched his brows, but breezily went on, "We're several turnings away from the next maiden-tempting moon."

Another imp? That look in Boon's eyes. He knew.

Dropping to one knee, Hisoka fumbled longer than he should have with the simple trap.

When it released, Boon huffed and offered a hand up. "Your star was worried. And not just about you. When were you gonna mention that this is personal?"

"How much did Novi say?"

"Next to nothing." Boon's gaze briefly darted to Pim, who'd made the leap to another tree. "You have a thing for his sister?"

Hisoka blinked. "No."

Boon sighed. And waited.

The whole truth was neither simple nor easy to part with; Hisoka kept his words few. "My sister had a thing for his sister."

"Huh. And where's *she* in all this?"

Ancient history still hurt. "Dead."

Boon had never seen Posy be anything but calm. He wasn't exactly cozy with the feline, but they were plenty acquainted. And this whole deal was clashing heavily with Boon's previous assessment of his boss.

Posy wasn't the sort of guy kids clung to. But Patter.

Posy wasn't one to spend time with females. But Pim.

And by all accounts, Posy wasn't one to get his hands dirty. Yet here was the illustrious Hisoka Twineshaft—damp, disheveled, and looking increasingly riled. Boon didn't like the dragon's chances if things got messy.

One thing did make sense to Boon. "This Nemi. You consider her kin?"

"A childhood friend," he quietly confessed. "As close as a sister."

"Okay, then. We'll get to her," promised Boon.

Hisoka's gaze pleaded with him. "I *must*. I vowed it."

"That's the right kind of clear. I like simple goals." He added a rumble of authority. "First thing I need you to do is ferret out this stone. Whisker up if you need to."

But Pim called out then. "I think I found something. It doesn't *look* like anything, but ... I'd swear it's here."

Boon moved in with more caution this time, and Hisoka circled around, taking a slightly different approach. While weaving sigils.

"Those." Boon narrowed his eyes. "I've seen something like them before. Ginkgo was messing with them."

They were tiny things. Hardly noticeable. Spinning outward, they clung to whatever they struck, marking both the seen and the unseen.

"I had Kyrie teach me." Hisoka smiled faintly. "Did you know Sinder thinks the boy's an ambuscade?"

"That's a term I haven't heard in a long while." Boon eased closer to the illusion that Pim had pinpointed. "This feels pretty basic. Either of you picking up on any extra nonsense?"

Pim seemed surprised to be asked. And surprised all over again that Hisoka waited for her to speak first. She simply said, "I sense an illusion. Nothing more."

"Agreed," said Hisoka. "The wardstone's presence has been masked."

With the glimmer of tiny trackers to guide him, Boon reached out, grunting in satisfaction when his fingertips met the silken facets of a crystal. It was bigger than he'd expected, and it keened softly at his touch. "That's not right," he muttered. "Posy, can you scuttle the illusion?"

"What is it?" Pim asked.

Boon beckoned her closer. "See what you make of this."

She knelt and reached past the wardstone's defenses. "Definitely a remnant stone. It sings." Her brow furrowed, and her tail slowly puffed. "Is it talking?"

"Sure sounded that way to me." Boon sat where he was, waiting for Hisoka to weigh in.

He reached, and his brows slowly rose. "This is new. Or ... perhaps very old."

"It's certainly my first talking rock."

"Give me a moment," Hisoka murmured.

Pim quietly asked, "It has to be a remnant stone. Right?"

"Doesn't feel like any remnant I've ever handled," said Boon. "Similar, but not the same."

Hisoka finished disassembling the sigils that obscured their view, and Pim gasped. Boon grunted his agreement. A luminous green crystal had been propped upright by a circle of local rock, which was near to black. The contrast was striking.

Boon flicked it with his claw. Pim shot him a chiding look and smoothed her hand protectively over its surface. Which was interesting. His immediate impulse was also to shelter the wardstone, and he was used to trusting his instincts.

Patter toddled up and wrapped his arms around it, nuzzling and crooning. Danged if the rock didn't match the runt's note and sing along.

"Oh, my." Hisoka sank to a seat and rubbed distractedly at his hair.

Pim quietly asked, "Is it just me, or is this crystal alive ... and aware?"

"Gotta be," agreed Boon, who looked to Hisoka. "You know what we're looking at?"

"I may have seen something similar. Once." Meeting Boon's gaze, he echoed his earlier remark. "Similar, but not the same."

"Any threat involved?"

"No! None," Hisoka assured.

So Boon lifted the stone from its setting. The shape piqued his interest. Roughly oblong, flatter on one side than the other. The ends tapered, and there were broken edges.

Hisoka said, "Impressions reproduce in unique ways. Under the right circumstances, there can be something like a chrysalis."

Pim edged closer to Boon, nose twitching. "This is a child?"

"I believe so."

She moved to take the stone, and Boon loosened his hold, but instead of taking it away, Pim realigned the crystal, pressing the flat side into Boon's abdomen. "Like this," she murmured.

Boon cradled it to his gut in mute disbelief.

"Yes." Hisoka gestured between them. "If the carrier is male ... yes."

"And this kid's being used as a wardstone?"

"So it would seem."

Boon offered the crystal to Pim, who immediately cradled it to her belly while she explored the shattered edges. Though she frowned, Boon could feel her purr.

He gruffly asked, "Whose kid is it?"

"I can only speculate." Hisoka gestured at Patter. "There may have been tampering."

"Mountain clan, though," said Boon. "Gotta be. Not that I've ever heard tell of rock imps. Just the remnants."

Pim spoke up. "There are more wardstones—at least three more—and they're linked. I think that's who this one is talking to. Their siblings."

Hisoka held out his hands, and Pim surrendered the stone to him. He held it to his heart, expression thoughtful.

Boon cautiously asked, "Could it be part ... star?"

"I don't know." With a fragile expression, he said, "I don't want to leave them behind."

"Oh, we're bringing the kid along." Boon pointed between them. "Three of us. Three more wardstones. Let's grab them and meet back up. Reunion time."

32
SPLIT UP

Pim had to wonder what would have happened to her if Inti hadn't barged in and destroyed her ignorant bliss. She'd wanted a child, and Dr. Kodoku had promised her one. But nothing in the literature had specified that her newborn would be entirely typical ... or even entirely hers.

What if she'd submitted to his miracle cure for the Waning, only to find herself carrying a rock imp or an Ephemeral crosser? Her babe might have been sired by a moonbeam or a star or a tree or a storm, assuming all the lore she'd ever heard was true.

Honestly, that part didn't bother her so much. Not really. Her child would still be hers. How could she not love them? Except *here* was evidence that suggested that children may have been forcibly taken from their parent. Carrying a child wasn't the same as keeping them.

How many young lives had Dr. Kodoku stolen?

And put to use like … like things.

Pim tried not to show how agitated she was. And in this, she took some small comfort. Because here, too, was evidence that she didn't need to carry a child herself in order to love them. Patter was adorable, and the stone chrysalis in Hisoka's hands stirred her instincts.

Fostering had never been an option in the feline courts. She'd given up a traditional hearth to pursue her career. There were no consorts to run her household, and she didn't want them. Pim had *planned* to raise the child as a single mother. Only she suspected that was also no longer an option. Both she and Elara had to sort out the nature of their bond with Boon.

"Why the long face? Second thoughts about going solo?"

She shook her head. "I'm quite capable of doing my part."

"That's my girl," he said easily. But then he blinked and shot sheepish glances between Hisoka and Pim.

Hisoka calmly said, "Have a care. Such endearments could be considered patronizing. If Isla were here, you would have triggered a lecture."

Boon's tail actually tucked. "No offense, Pim. It just … makes it easier to think of you as pack if I refer to you like I would kin."

"I see the compliment," she stiffly assured.

He sniffed lightly.

He searched her face.

He checked her tail.

"Well, what do you know?" Boon's posture firmed. "You actually mean that."

Pim simply nodded.

"Hold up," he murmured, working through his collection of necklaces. Finding the one he wanted, he freed it. "Most of these hold significance to more than me. Gifts from mentors or friends. That sorta thing. But this one's all mine. Made it myself."

Without further explanation, he dropped it over her head.

There were three stones, with a pair of blunt fangs for spacers. The knots were simple, identical to the ones she'd just learned. As far as she could tell, there wasn't any message. Easing into a receptive posture, she ventured, "This has *no* significance?"

"Just the personal kind." Slowly reaching out, he hooked its cord with a claw and lifted. "I lost my milk teeth in truest form. I used to think they made me look like a fierce hunter."

Pim could picture it, and she smiled.

"So this is a slight?" She was only teasing. Or fishing for a compliment, since she was sure this was another one. "Are you saying my abilities are on par with a weanling's?"

Boon snorted. "I told you. You're earning beads. They're never an insult."

"But these aren't spares. They're yours."

"And by wearing them, you're acknowledging the bond between us." He placed a hand over his necklaces. "That's how it is for wolves."

Pim was prouder of her new necklace than any of the acclaim *Pure Instinct* had netted her.

Boon turned to Hisoka. "Work with me here, because I'm hazy on the finer points. Will stealing the wardstones be enough to wreck the island's barrier?"

"That's very unlikely. Only removing the anchor from the array would accomplish that. However, there should be a shift in resonance, which may introduce weak points. If your team notices, they could exploit them."

"Can you contact them?" Pim asked, since it was the sort of thing that came up a lot on the series. "Coordinate our efforts?"

"Inti could," said Hisoka, who peered up. "It's too soon to tell if we'll be able to regain the sky ... or hear its songs."

Boon asked, "You think Juuyu could dismantle the barrier from the outside?"

Hisoka hummed. "Not alone. But he won't be."

"Who's here?"

If anything, Hisoka seemed flustered. "I lost contact when I passed through the barrier. Unless Inti reaches out to one of us, we'll have to trust the plan."

"Which is?" Boon prompted, bouncing on the balls of his feet, as if eager to get on with things.

"We'll meet at the lab. That's where there are captives in need of rescue. And that's where Akira will go, given half a chance." He explained, "His father might be there."

"That's a hell of a twist."

Hisoka smoothed his hand over the wardstone and said, "Hardly the first. Probably not the last."

"Got it." Boon beckoned for the crystal with both hands. "If I rig something, I can take the runt. You've got your hands full with Patter."

Pim stepped forward, already unbuttoning her overshirt. "Here. You can use this."

"Whoa, now," protested Boon, gaze averted.

"Oh, stop. I'm still wearing more than you are," she snapped.

He risked a peek at her snug sheath, which she'd chosen because it was so similar to the style adopted by she-wolves. Despite her words, Hisoka maintained the downcast posture of a consort, which really didn't suit him.

With a quick fold and twist, she enclosed the wardstone in a sling, then held it in place between Boon's shoulder blades while he knotted the shirtsleeves, cross-bag style.

"Secure?" she checked.

He crouched, twisted, and even did a backflip. Rolling his shoulders, he peered over his shoulder … and sniffed the fabric. He caught himself and cleared his throat. "Solid. Ready, Posy?"

"Certainly." Hisoka pivoted to face the peak he'd be scaling.

To Pim, Boon said, "Stay safe."

And they were gone.

Pim was grateful that they hadn't hesitated over leaving her alone. That would have been the worst sort of insult. But she was suddenly, keenly aware that she was the only one with empty arms.

Aiming for the southern peak, Pim paused in the topmost branches of a tree that swayed under her weight. A faint sound stirred her curiosity. Water?

She worked her way to the ground and immediately regretted it. The foliage was so dense, she could barely move. Crouching, she shifted into the smallest version of truest form she could manage and cocked her ears. Belly to the ground, she pushed past thick stalks and razor-edged fronds, whiskers quivering with caution.

Yes, she was stealthy. Silent on dainty cat's paws.

But a dragon's camouflage was the stuff of legends.

The risk had her so on edge, she was looking for enough space to shift back when she put a paw into running water. Sluggish enough to be almost entirely silent, it slipped away through the undergrowth. Pim lapped some and wrinkled her nose. Tepid. Murky.

Leaves rattled off to one side.

Pim didn't hesitate. Scuttling to the nearest tree, she streaked up and around its trunk and shifted back into speaking form. So high above the jungle floor, she couldn't see them, but she could hear them.

Two of the wild dragons had abandoned subterfuge in order to squabble. Probably for the right to get to her first. Their fluting and snapping sent birds winging away.

In another direction, Ephemera spiraled upward, betraying the slinking approach of another dragon. Pim held her position, waiting to see if any others would turn up. How many hunted in this thicket? Distant trills suggested at least two more.

Fine. She'd deal with them.

Because if they were hot on *her* trail, Sensei and Boon wouldn't have wild dragons nipping at their heels. Testing the springiness of the limb on which she perched, Pim gazed toward the jutting peak that was her destination ... and chose a path based on likely looking trees. It would be a dangerous game, but that only increased its appeal.

Clucking her tongue to entice her pursuers, Pim made her first leap, leading the chase.

They were fast, these dragons. But Pim fell into a rhythm, using the bowing of each tree to fling herself further along. Birds scattered before her, and the jungle began to thin. She was nearing the shoreline beneath her designated peak, and she planned to take to the beach, where an uninterrupted stretch of sand would allow her to ditch her stalkers at speed.

She was certain now that she wasn't dealing with Kith. Quick to quarrel, these dragons wasted a lot of their time trying to fend off their competition, undermining any hope of success. If they'd cooperated, they might have been able to corner her. Maybe.

As it was, Pim had been able to confirm that eight beasts were tailing her. They were all of a kind, with deep purple scales and freckled lavender underbellies. Red eyes supported her suspicion that these dragons were directly tied to Dr. Kodoku's clan.

Pim didn't know enough about the dragon clans to guess which they hailed from.

She knew a Starsweep model with similar freckling, but their scales were of a plummier hue. The only other dragons she'd met with red eyes were Deeptroves, but their scales were pure gold.

Were Dr. Kodoku and his daughter outcasts? If so, what had happened to Futari's mother? And to her sister, for that matter. The dragoness had clammed up pretty quickly after that small admission. Pim wouldn't be the least little bit surprised if it turned out that Kodoku had experimented on his own child.

Specimens, Futari had called them. To him, they were nothing more than lab animals.

Pim reached a narrow strip of beach. Leaping down, she backed toward the water's edge, waiting for her pursuers to break cover.

They didn't.

That was strange.

A scuffle ensued, and she watched in growing mystification as purple scales twisted and gleamed just beyond the jungle's edge. Suddenly, a scrawny beast tumbled onto the sand, as if he'd been forced out by the others.

He was a pitiful thing, really. Lacking in luster, with a ragged mane and scars all along his body. Properly tamed and shepherded, he might have been a beauty, for this was the right of all dragons. But these beasts were feral. A shame really. Wild dragons were widely believed extinct, even among the clans. In a way, Pim was glad to know that some had survived, though barely.

Clearly, Kodoku was neglecting his duty to them, and in this state, they could only be a menace to humanity.

Could another clan be brought in to manage these stragglers?

The outed dragon flailed to its feet and tried to return to the shelter of the trees. As if all interest in her and the hunt was gone. As if it feared the sand, which didn't jive with what little Pim did know. In her experience, dragons adored sun-bathing and swimming.

Why avoid such a simple pleasure?

A slosh and patter of water droplets sounded behind Pim, and she whirled. Slowly, she backed away from the water's edge, even though that brought her closer to the scrabbling, keening dragons.

They weren't avoiding the sand.

Nor the water … at least, not exactly.

Pim hissed at her foolish mistake. In toying with her prey, she'd trapped herself between eight hungry dragons and a … well, she wasn't sure *what* it was. Sea monster pretty much covered it.

33

FINDING SOLACE

Jacques was certain Argent had been about to say something important. But the connection fell apart, plunging him into a stark—and surreal—reality. He was naked, spent, and held close by his co-captive. Fantasy fodder, if given just the right spin, but Jacques suspected that this experience would fuel a whole new round of nightmares. Provided he lived to dream again.

"Did I hurt you?"

How to answer. Jacques was intact, but he'd been robbed of something precious. Was this how it had been for Kyoko, missing and mishandled for months, caught and kept by the Rogue? Would he share her bitterness and fury once the numbness faded?

He hoped not.

"Did I hurt you?" repeated the stone imp.

"*Non*. But they're gone, and I'm sticky." And to his embarrassment, tears welled up.

"I am sorry for your losses." Dayith awkwardly added, "They were beautiful. Full of love."

Tears quickly turned to ugly sobbing.

Jacques had known there would be risks, but this ...? It was so personal. So intrusive. He hadn't even realized such a thing could be stolen from him. All his years of wishing to be like reavers, only to have his first inkling of kinship be a sort of rape.

And just to confuse the matter, the one who'd laid him bare was cradling him so carefully, offering clumsy comfort.

All Jacques wanted was for his lord and master to come sweeping in and ... wait. No. *No.* He didn't want Argent to see him. Not like this. Heaving deeper breaths, Jacques worked to calm himself. And when he pushed away, Dayith let him go.

Jacques tottered to the rumpled mess of his cast-off clothes and rummaged for his handkerchief. Gone. Right. Sibley had it. Clearing his nose on his undershirt, he slowly dressed in the rest of his ensemble, which was considerably worse for wear.

Hating the silence, he quietly spoke. "I probably can't see Ephemera any longer."

Somehow, Jacques couldn't bring himself to look at his companion. Lord, he felt dirty. This had all the awkwardness of a morning after in a stranger's flat. His skin was raw where the tattoos had been, which made his clothing uncomfortable. But they were the only armor left to him.

"Jacques Smythe."

He glanced up. The imp knew his name? Had Kodoku mentioned it? Possibly.

"Can there be peace between us?" asked Dayith.

So many sarcastic remarks begged to be hurled, but Jacques tamped them down.

"I have wronged you."

"You have." Leaning heavily on all his diplomatic training, Jacques wearily asked, "Did you have a choice?"

"No."

Jacques buttoned his cuffs. "I know where the blame lies, and it isn't with you."

Dayith lifted a hand between them, palm up. "Can you trust me?"

"You ... you let me see Argent again, and that was good of you." He straightened his tie, pushed back the disarray of his hair, and put away his battered feelings. For now. Placing his hand in the imp's, he announced, "I'm meant to be helping free you and whatever other imps are being held on the premises. Not that there's much I can do."

"Jacques Smythe." The stone-rough hand gently closed around his. "I made you cry."

"I've stopped now." This didn't seem to satisfy Dayith, so Jacques added, "I was sad."

"I am sorry."

"Lord. Stop apologizing. I believe you."

"You fed me." There was wonderment in his tone. "It was promised, and it was good."

Jacques couldn't bring himself to be happy about that part.

Dayith went on. "This was to be the sign by which I would know you."

"Sign? That's a very starry turn of phrase." And because

he really was passingly acquainted with Impressions, Jacques ventured, "Are you saying I was foretold?"

A big knuckle brushed at his cheek. "We have been waiting for you, Jacques Smythe."

"Is that a royal *we*? Or is there someone else hanging about?"

Dayith made the sign for secrecy, then softly called, "Solace? Now, please."

And then they were three.

An imp with some kind of glittering shrubbery atop his head crowded close in order to look into Jacques' face. "Is he the one?"

"He is the one."

Tree. *Had* to be a tree. That was all right. Papa Socks had mentioned other trees, and Jacques had been the one to vow that they'd find and rescue those locked away here.

"How do you do. I'm ...."

But the tree didn't wait for niceties. Arms flung around his neck, pulling him down into a questing sort of kiss. Inexpert but enthusiastic. And sweet as nectar. Somewhere in the middle of it, the prison cell vanished.

Daylight and the lazy slap of waves. A soft tinkling like chimes. The scent of flowers. Jacques pushed away and peered around. They'd carried him to a tiny cove created by a niche in black rock. Overhanging jungle foliage hid the sky. Partway up the steep rock wall, a gnarled tree grew. Its roots twisted and clung, and its bark was a rough gray that looked like stone.

Jacques turned to look at Dayith, whose crystalline facets glittered all the more brilliantly in natural light. "You can get out?"

"Not on my own."

"I can go wherever I want," boasted the other imp. "Mmm…almost."

The tree was manifesting as male, and he was bare except for a simple loincloth, much like Dayith wore. His features were pert, which gave him a youthful air. But his complexion was decidedly gray. Jacques had never seen the like, but even more striking was the cascade of foliage that decorated his long, black hair. He was crowned by gemlike leaves, all in the same peridot hues as Dayith's crystal.

Startled, Jacques glanced back at the tree and allowed that he was impressed. Its entire canopy, every leaf, looked to be shaped from the same kind of stone. An absolute work of art. Luminous and living. And the source of the faint musical chiming he'd first noticed.

"You're a tree?"

"Half," said the imp, who reached up to pet his cheek. To Dayith, he reported, "He is very soft."

"Be gentle." And meeting Jacques' gaze, he added, "This is Solace. He is my son."

Half tree, half rock? That explained this new imp's faceted eyes. They were just like his father's. "Do I want to know how that works?" Jacques ventured.

"Dayith is my parent," Solace cheerfully confirmed. "I was sprigged. Or … spliced? Both. Or neither. Mmm … it does not matter. I am here, and so are you!"

"You are safe, Jacques Smythe. Just as I promised your fox," said Dayith. "Shelter here, with us, until the end."

Solace seemed fascinated by Jacques' clothes. Leaving the tree to his exploration of pockets and buttons, Jacques took a longer, more careful look around.

The sand was unusual—black streaked with green. A steady stream of water splashed over stone, coming from somewhere above, collecting in a rocky basin. Jacques was thirsty enough to check if it was potable. "Is it safe to drink?"

"Only for trees." Solace shot a pleading look in his father's direction. "I will be careful …?"

"Quickly and quietly," Dayith urged.

Jacques barely registered that the tree-crosser was gone when he was back, offering a chilled bottle of sparkling water.

"This?" Solace asked hopefully.

"That will do nicely," Jacques assured. "I don't suppose you can procure a bath with the same ease?"

Dayith waved at the sea. His son pointed to the freshwater pool.

Stifling a sigh, Jacques said, "It will do. Provided you don't mind my sloshing about in your drinking water."

"I will share." And to Dayith, a blissful, "I get to share."

"You don't often get company?" Jacques inquired as he peeled out of his shirt.

"No. I am a secret." And with a soft gasp, Solace trailed fingers through Jacques' chest hair before pressing his palm against his belly. "So, so soft."

Jacques tried not to be put out. Life at Stately House kept him on the move. He cut a fine figure in his fundoshi.

But Solace's only basis for comparison was a literal rock. "Compared to your sire, I suppose."

"And you are ours." He looked to his father for confirmation. "He is ours?"

"Until he goes."

Solace's fingers hesitated in their petting. "He will go?"

"Far from here," confirmed Dayith.

"Is that good?"

"Very good. He is the answer we have been waiting for."

The tree gazed up at him with faceted green eyes. "I will be so good to you!"

Not that long ago, Jacques had made the very same promise to Akira. It was a little eerie, almost like a sign. And all at once it occurred to Jacques that this tree-crosser resembled Akira—slim and young and smiling. The beginnings of an idea blossomed into startled certainty. "Dayith, who is his other parent?"

"A tree."

Which wasn't nearly specific enough. "Was he sprigged by Hajime?"

The stone imp's eyes widened.

Jacques laughed and contemplated the resemblances. Tweaking the point of Solace's elfin ear, he said, "You look a little like your brother, who is very dear to me."

"Which brother?"

"You have many?"

"Many, many, many. But they do not know about me." Solace repeated, "Which brother?"

"His name is Akira, and he's entirely human."

The tree crosser traced a finger over Jacques' lips. "My human brother makes you smile?"

"*Naturellement.* I love him."

"Will you love me, too?"

Jacques promised, "I will make an effort, for his sake. Now let me wash."

"I will help. Since you are mine," said Solace.

That gave Jacques pause. The meaning of such a phrase could vary widely, depending on the clan of the claimant. Who knew *what* it signified for Impressions? "Yours ... how? Perhaps you should tell me what was foretold."

"You are my future." Solace stroked his arm. "I know what to do. I think. Mmm ... I will try. Is there time to try?"

Both of them looked to Dayith for answers.

"He is only human. We must prepare him first."

Jacques' immediate thought was swiftly dismissed. Surely not. All that earlier licking had left him wary of further incursions. It became suddenly important to retain his pants. "Shall we talk it through?" he ventured.

Solace tried for another kiss.

Leaning back, Jacques quietly asked, "What's this about? Trees don't take lovers."

"*Half* tree," he corrected.

"Right. And do imps of your father's sort ... ah. Shall we say ... co-mingle with members of the clans? In the procreative sense. Or recreative, I suppose."

Again, they both looked to Dayith.

He finally said, "Not always by choice."

Jacques immediately felt bad for his suspicions.

Solace flickered away and returned, a single flower in his hand. Plucking a petal, he held it to Jacques' lips. "Taste."

Gently catching the tree-crosser's wrist, he asked, "What for? Because I am a longstanding proponent of *informed* consent."

Dayith took a peaceable posture. "Solace blooms for you. Take in his scent, taste his pollen, eat his petals. They will prepare a place within and make you ready. You will carry my remnant song."

"I'm not a stone," Jacques managed.

"No. You are soft. But your soul is silent." Solace softly added, "It would be better if we could sing together."

"Are you talking about …?" Jacques' heart began a heavier beat. "Do you mean to say you could turn me into a reaver?"

"I stole your sigils," said Dayith. "They filled me, and so my song brims. Let it spill over into you."

While that wasn't a nice, solid *yes*, Jacques figured it was close enough. Maybe this was a little like what had happened to Mikoto Reaver … or to Lord Beckonthrall. Mingling with imps had worked wonders before, so Jacques took a receptive stance and said, "Right then. Have your way with me."

Solace playfully twirled the flower under Jacques' nose. Pollen tickled and clung to his lips. He touched them with his tongue and found a subtle sweetness, reminiscent of that first kiss Solace had thrust upon him. Quite pleasant. Possibly addictive.

This time, when Solace held up a flower petal, Jacques parted his lips.

Relief showed on the tree-crosser's face. "Is it good?" he whispered.

"Lovely," he assured.

Another petal touched his lower lip, and he took it. And the next. When the first flower was spent—all seven petals, by his count—Solace kissed him lightly, vanished briefly, and returned with a small bouquet.

"How many am I meant to eat?" he asked.

Dayith peered into his face and asked, "How do you feel?"

"Rather foolish, but no matter. Carry on."

By the third flower, Jacques may have been slightly tipsy, and Solace's attentions took on a euphoric quality. Somewhere into the second bouquet, Jacques realized that he was reclining in Dayith's arms, and he touched the rock imp's face. "You really are my favorite color," he murmured.

"Can you see the Ephemera yet?"

Jacques gazed upward, into boughs of gleaming crystal. "Not sure I'm focusing on anything at the moment."

Then Solace was back, and there was pollen on his lips, and Jacques obligingly kissed it away. Probably poor form, snogging a fellow in front of his father. Wait. *That* wasn't the issue here. His conscience stung, and it was as if all of them felt it.

"What?" gasped Solace. "What was that?"

Dayith rumbled in a pleased way. "It is working."

But the tree-crosser worriedly asked, "Why are you sad?"

"Akira," he managed weakly. "I'm meant to be kissing Akira. Or ... the other way around. I think if you were kissing Akira, it would make Suuzu happy. Well, he'd pillory the lot of us, but ... this should be for Akira."

"Nooo," Solace said gently. "*You* are mine. You were foretold."

"But he … he loves him, and it's lovely."

"As lovely as me?" The tree imp seemed to be pouting.

"Even more so, but only because I've cared longer." Jacques let himself wallow in good memories. "I wish we could all go home together. Papa Socks would love you, and Tsumiko would love you, and … and I would plant you in Ginkgo's garden, and you would shine like a cathedral."

"Oh," Solace said softly. "Oh. I felt *that*, too. What is that?"

"His thoughts linger in a far-off place."

"Is our future there, shining and beloved?"

"Yes. In that good place." Dayith sounded so sure, and he even smiled a little. "Can you hear us? Listen for the song."

Jacques closed his eyes and waited to see if a dream would snatch him up. But no. This was something entirely different. Like trading tepid tap water for a flute of star wine. He could hear the songs of stones and the descant of fallen stars and the whisper of ephemeral wings.

Light was seeping in, encouraged along by soft words and sweet kisses.

He was awash, might even be drowning, but he knew what this was from all of Michael's lectures and from Lapis's near-worshipful descriptions. They made more sense now. Firsthand bliss was uniquely compelling. And nothing compared.

Jacques embraced trust and left himself wide open to the light that he hoped would forever mark his soul … clung to the one who was putting it there … and begged him not to stop.

34

REACHING FOR ANSWERS

Elara let Inti herd her into the suite's bedroom, where she was immediately drawn to a vase on the window-sill. Before she could touch it, the monkey-crosser caught her arm. "Not yet. Inti needs the array."

She pivoted, scanning the room, which was dominated by a bed that could fit a crowd ... and probably had. Now that she was looking for them, Elara could see that Akira and his partner had forgotten other personal effects. "Tell me what I'm looking at."

"Fox illusions. Crystal array." Inti pulled her onto the bed after him. "For communication."

"With whom?"

"Not sure. Inti will reach. Someone will reach back." He settled himself against the pillows and patted the place at his side. "You stay here. No kissing kitties."

"What kind of girl do you think I am?"

"Smart. Kind. Brave." And with a glance toward the door, Inti quietly added, "Lonely."

She supposed he was right. "My tastes have been running to wolves."

"For now …?" he challenged.

"From now on."

"Good, good, good." He beckoned her closer. "Come by Inti."

Elara chose a pillow and settled alongside him. "Why do you do that? Why play the fool?"

"Nobody minds a silly monkey. They do not fear what they find cute." With a small shrug, he added, "Inti gets lonely, too."

Taking his hand, she asked, "Did I ever do anything to hurt you?"

"Good Elara. Gentle Elara." He patted her head, but he didn't really answer.

She whispered an apology.

"Lend me your light?"

"I thought you were going to lock it away. You told Eiji you'd ward me."

"Yes, yes, yes. But first … trust Inti. I'll only borrow a little."

"Whatever you need."

He snickered softly, which made her wonder, but from Elara's perspective, the only thing Inti needed was a nap. Maybe it was a meditative state? Totally relaxed, he seemed worlds away, and it really was lonely. But she pulled his hand into her own and tried to trust him just a little bit harder.

The better part of an hour passed before his eyes opened.

Thin lips quirked, and he pulled her close, so that her head was over his heart. "Inti is glad for Elara. Inti has never reached so far.

Farther, farthest, Farroost."

"You seem pleased." She hugged him back, smiling when the weight of his tail draped her waist. "I'd ask you to explain, but maybe if you just tell me the parts I need to know …?"

"Does Dr. Perrine believe in telepathy?"

She hesitated over that, then chuckled. "Let's say I do."

"Inti is a reach." And shedding nonsense, he said, "I've spoken with as many as I could find. Our help is near, and they are ready. If we can topple the anchor, all will be well."

"Who did you talk to?" Elara's mind raced. "Pim? Boon? Hisoka-sensei?"

"Yes, Boon. They are stealing wardstones. But also Sinder, who is a peaceable dragon, and Juuyu, who hunts dragons. Argent is scary-mad. And … Goh-sensei is here."

His voice changed, and Elara asked, "Is Goh-sensei special?"

"Inti had no family. But Inti has Goh. He is monkey clan."

"So he's family. And he came for you?" She searched his flushed face. "I'm glad you have people who care about you."

"Inti does." He patted her head. "You, too."

"Not the back-home sort. But I might be stringing along a couple of wolves. Does that count?"

"Count, counted, counting on it." Another laugh bubbled up. "You could end up with a couple of kitties, too, if my wards are sloppy. Should I be sloppy?"

"*Tempting,* but no. I have a good feeling about my wolves."

A rap sounded on the door, and Akira leaned through. "I heard voices. Are you done?"

Inti scrambled to his feet and bounced on the bed. "Ready to run?"

"Sure. We're all packed. Just waiting on you two." He glanced between them. "Everything go okay?"

"Better." To Elara's amusement, Inti wrapped himself around Akira and rocked from side to side. "Inti found Linlu. He needs us. And ... he will try to keep Dr. Naoki with him until we arrive."

"Did you tell him about me?"

"Nope." Inti lifted Akira right off his feet and did a little dance. "Surprise is the best tactic."

Elara found herself flanked by Eiji and Anjou and smiled gratefully at this show of acceptance. They nudged closer, and she suspected that they were testing her boundaries. Which Inti hadn't added yet.

Eiji swayed into her, eyes half-lidded, and Anjou grumbled something in French.

Inti gently set Akira on his feet before coming to her rescue. He was all smiles, which was a good look for him, and it gave Elara hope that things would work out.

The instant she opened the door to their suite, alarms blared.

"Is that for us?" asked Akira. "Did we do that?"

"No," said Elara. "This is one of the general alarms, warning guests to keep to their rooms and wait for further instruction."

Inti waved for them to follow, and they hurried along the hall.

"General alarm?" Akira asked, his free hand over one ear.

She had to raise her voice to be heard. "Could be a weather-related incident. Could be a breach in the fencing somewhere. Once it was … intruders."

Akira was incredulous. "How are intruders supposed to find an uncharted island hidden behind a barrier?"

They jogged through the lobby, right out the front doors, and Inti led them along a gravel road. Insistent blaring quickly faded into the distance. Now that it was less noisy, it was easier to think back. Actually, Elara suspected that Inti's newly-applied sigilcraft was the reason her memory was clearing.

"Last time …." She was answering Akira, but the whole group stopped to listen. "Last time Dr. Kodoku raised the general alarm, it was because one of the children escaped from their cage. He ordered a hunt. And when he didn't get his specimen back intact, he was livid. The others suffered."

Akira looked stunned.

Inti grimly handed down orders. "We won't risk the jungle. This road leads to the lab. Eiji carries Akira. Anjou carries Elara. Fast, fast, faster."

Immediately, Anjou was offering his palms. "Are you all right with me?"

Matching his greeting, she said, "I'm sorry to impose."

He lifted her without a hint of effort and spared her a smile. "This is no trouble."

"I can be all kinds of trouble," she assured.

"And I would have enjoyed finding out how much." Anjou strode after the others. Eyes on them, he quietly added, "I am as smitten as Eiji, if not more so."

She was touched.

He promised, "I will do all I can to protect you."

"And I'm as grateful as I can be." Elara found his accent adorable, so she asked, "Where are you from?"

"The Bonhomie clan is part of a cooperative in rural France. We are makers of fine cheese, and the others dabble in honey, wine, and chocolates."

"Sounds idyllic. Why would you want to leave?"

"I answered a consort call. My mother thought I might find a good place, and I wasn't opposed to offering myself."

Elara should have realized sooner. "You're here for Pim?"

"You can never tell what might appeal to a lady mistress." Anjou was running fast now, but he wasn't the least bit winded. "I hoped that travel would bring new things."

"Do you regret leaving home?"

"*Non.*" He dimpled prettily. "I have found adventure aplenty, and I am where I am needed. Perhaps I will even meet Spokesperson Twineshaft."

"Devotee of his?"

"I admire him greatly," Anjou staunchly declared.

They chatted amiably enough, which was a nice distraction from the potential dangers ahead ... and on all sides.

When his step faltered, her imagination leapt from one dire possibility to the next, but it wasn't anything terrible.

"What ... is that?" Anjou muttered to himself.

"Not *what*," Elara chided. "*Who.* I know them, and so does Inti. See?"

Two children were hugging the monkey-crosser, who'd wrapped his tail around both of them while patting their heads.

"Tree child is Seventh Try. Or just Try. Star child is Two-hundred Twenty-two." Inti rumpled golden curls. "Twosies for short."

Eiji put Akira down, and the young man was quickly on his knees in front of the children. "Hey, there. Can you understand me? My English isn't the best."

"I understand," said Twosies primly. "I *always* understand!"

To Elara's surprise, Twosies switched to fluent Japanese. At least, it sounded authentic to her, and Akira was beaming. "I didn't know he was bilingual," she murmured to her companion.

Anjou set her down with traces of reluctance and kept her arm tucked through his. "According to our lore, stars speak *every* language."

"Do you know what they're saying?"

"Akira wants to be called *uncle*. And he is asking after Jacques."

With a sheepish look Elara's way, Akira switched back to English. "Jacques is tallish, and his hair is brown with soft curls. He likes nice clothes, and he's fancy in lots of little ways. He always smells good, and he has fine manners."

The more he rambled, the worse Elara felt for him. Akira's concern was so clear. "He loves this Jacques?"

Anjou hesitated, but then he nodded. "Their affection is mutual, but also—shall we say—chaste ...? Theirs is an exquisitely slow seduction."

Akira had continued during their aside. "He usually speaks English, and he would have introduced himself as Uncle Jackie. Does that ... sound familiar?"

"He is not in the garden," said Try, whose tree branch antlers scattered pale pink flowers.

"He is not," said Twosies. "We know, because we are looking for him, too."

Try hurried to Elara and her skinny arms wrapped around her legs. "I want to live."

Akira protested, "Why would you *not* live?"

"If we do not bring Jacques to Dr. Kodoku, he will put us out."

Twosies hugged himself. "I do not want to be food for his pets."

Try shakily reported, "He already took Sibley."

Elara could easily believe the outspoken young crosser had mouthed off again. Sibley was supposedly here for treatment, but he'd tried to tell her over and over that he'd been kidnapped. A detail she'd always managed to forget moments later. "Maybe he tried to run away again?"

"Dayith will know," said Try.

"Dayith *would* know," agreed Twosies.

Inti looked to Elara, his eyebrows high. "Who is Dayith?"

She had to admit, "I have no idea."

35

BARGE

Somewhat to Sinder's annoyance, Juuyu spotted them first.

"They are here," the phoenix quietly announced, gaze fixed on several flecks in the hazy distance. "Do you know what that is?"

Sinder squinted, then swore softly. "I wonder how long those things have been in mothballs. The polite term is *windship*, but we call them barges behind the lords' backs. Way back when, they were a sign of prestige. Kind of like a limo. Pack up the harem and a picnic lunch, and take the equivalent of a Sunday afternoon drive."

The first of three windships came near enough that Sinder could make out polished wood, fluttering banners, and the stout perches that allowed a team of dragons to grab hold and carry the barge aloft. He was trying to pinpoint clan colors and crests when Juuyu warbled softly.

"Not all of them are pleasure crafts."

Sinder swore again and with a bit more vehemence. The last windship in the formation looked more like a whaling vessel, hung with nets and bristling with weapons. Admittedly, there were blue pennants peacefully fluttering from every blest harpoon, but he held little doubt their edges were sharp. A circle of blue flowers marked that windship's side, confirming Sinder's suspicions.

"The Order of Spomenka," he said, rattled in spite of himself. "They brought dragon slayers?"

"Hmm," agreed Juuyu. "The dragon lords want the Rogue stopped as much as, if not more than, all of us."

With a low glide and impressive precision, the two dragons carrying the first windship backwinged in tandem and deposited it on the beach without so much as a bump.

"You think any of the Junzi are on board?" Sinder asked.

Juuyu shot him a warning look. "Unlikely. They are all under Argent's protection."

"Fine by me. Those things are seriously scary."

The little green wind dragon darted to Sinder, nearly throttling him before shoving her head into the top of his tunic. As the windship's doors flung wide and dragon lords began emerging, Sinder took pity and loosened his laces so she could slip out of sight. She hugged his midriff tightly, and he absently patted her through the fabric.

"Okay, wow. They didn't send just anyone. The coral is Lord Shywind, and the gold is Lord Deeptrove. Aaaand ... that's Lord Beckonthrall himself. Oh, shit." Sinder hid behind Juuyu and did his best to be unnoticeable.

"What?" Juuyu softly inquired.

"Lord Yonkeep's here."

"So?"

"He's my afir. Err … grandfather. Sagacity Yonkeep beget most of the greens in the northern hemisphere. My mom's his daughter."

"Why are you hiding from him?"

Sinder was still trying to figure out how to answer when the Spomenka ship settled in the shallows, and its gangway dropped. Several battlers debarked, and they moved to confer with Moon, who never seemed to mind longwinded greetings.

That's when a familiar figure strode down the gangway, a sleek black panther close on his heels. Sinder lost his train of thought and strangled back an awkward trill.

Juuyu's glance held concern. "What now?"

"Timur's here."

"Hmm?" Without any fuss, Juuyu signaled to the man, who changed course.

Sinder fidgeted for a moment, torn four ways and flighty as winds. He'd just about made up his mind to break cover when Timur leaned around Juuyu, all easy grin and teasing tones. "Is this how you greet an old friend?"

"Hey … Timur. Long time no … whoa!"

Hands slid under his armpits and the big lout lifted him up, studying him at arm's length. "Have you been taking care of yourself? No new injuries, I hope?"

And then Sinder was being half-crushed in a bear hug. He probably should have protested the handling, but strong fingers began kneading at vertebrae, and he warbled weakly and went limp.

"What did you do?" inquired Juuyu.

"Oh, you know. Tricks of the trade," Timur said. "Any word from our people on the inside?"

"Inti contacted us earlier ...."

While Juuyu offered an abridged report, Sinder reacquainted himself with the cheery rumble of Timur's voice. He'd missed this man, who'd patched him up and held him together during last summer's training camp. Timur had known just what to do, even guiding him through the rite of passage when Sinder gained the sky.

Juuyu trailed off, then quietly asked, "Truly. What did you do?"

Timur's grip shifted, gathering Sinder into a cradling embrace. He sounded cautious when he said, "I suppose we made an impression on each other. I'm glad." And close to Sinder's ear, Timur added, "And here I thought you were glad to be shed of me."

"Don't ply me with your Spomenka skills and pretend to be surprised they work," Sinder grumbled.

A low growl began at close quarters, and Sinder flinched. Fend had reared up on his hind legs behind Timur, his forepaws on his partner's shoulders. Orange eyes narrowed as the big cat bared his fangs.

"Well, hey, Fend. It's been a while." And because he still had scars from the last time, he lamely added, "Please, don't bite."

"Not worth my time. Or his. I thought we were finally rid of you."

A haughty voice, silky with disdain. And definitely coming from Fend.

Sinder gaped.

Fend's eyes narrowed.

That's when Sinder's passenger wriggled partway free of his tunic in order to deliver a sharp series of peeps. *"I will not let him bite you!"*

"Thanks for that, pipsqueak. I need all the help I can get when Fend's around." Sinder avoided eye contact like a coward. He shouldn't be able to hear Kith. Not unless they were dragons.

Timur cheerfully drawled, "And hello to you! May I beg an introduction?"

"She's ... uhh. She and I found each other earlier. I guess you could say she booked passage, so I'd been planning to smuggle her off the island." He stroked the crest atop her head, trying to calm her down. "I might be off the hook, though. Since you turned up."

With a questioning look, Timur asked, "What's her name?"

"No name. Didn't want one." Sinder risked a peek at Fend, whose unblinking gaze was making him increasingly uneasy. "She wants her boy to give her one. Short story shorter, she's got her heart set on Gregor."

Fend's attention finally veered away, straight to the wind dragon.

"Do you, now?" Timur inquired of the little one. "And how did you learn of my wee lad?"

Sinder reeled a hand. "It's not like she came with a letter of introduction, but she's been dropping names like Auriel and Cadmiel."

"And Soriel and Bethiel," she interjected smugly.

"No kidding?" Sinder asked, darting another look at the clear, blue sky. "You weren't kidding when you said culminating."

"Is she saying something?" Timur asked. "Lilya talks to Rifflet all the time. Leaves the rest of us out of the loop."

"This little one has a lot to say, for sure. And I'm not surprised about Lilya, since she's a fellow. Very similar to reaches." He tapped his chest. "Always hearing things."

Fend's whiskers were suddenly quivering much too close for comfort. Timur gave the big cat's chin a casual shove. "I think I'm missing something important. Nobody's ever mentioned your being a reach. Isn't that a reaver classification?"

Sinder cast a sheepish look in Juuyu's direction.

His partner sighed. "You would not have heard of it because it is *meant* to be a secret, albeit an open secret. Sinder is our team's communications specialist for good reason."

"How many times have you heard me introduce myself?" Sinder asked.

Timur shrugged. "Countless times."

"And what do I *always* say?"

"Sinder Stonecairn of the Icelandic ... Reach." Timur beamed at him as if he'd done something clever. "I thought it was a *place*."

"More of an agency. We're specialists, and before the Emergence, guys like us were the hub of the dragon lords' communication network. We're more reliable than heralds. Well ... a reliable reach is more reliable than a herald."

"Are you an *un*reliable reach?" Timur inquired lightly.

"I would sometimes say more than I should." Sinder could feel the tips of his ears burning. "Hisoka's never complained."

Juuyu blandly added, "One of the greater mysteries surrounding our illustrious leader."

"So you're a mind-reader," said Timur.

"Nooo. Terms and conditions definitely apply. Back home, we relied a lot on potent crystals and favorable winds. Nowadays, the dragon lords swap selfies and nail art inspiration on a discreet server. Reaches are mostly obsolete."

Juuyu offered more context. "Sinder helped to train Inti, who is also a reach. Their connection was unique."

"Until it wasn't. I still want to know how he managed to ignore terms and conditions and touch base with you directly." Sinder shook his head. "Crossers have uniquely scary levels of untapped potential. Hope that Kodoku guy hasn't realized it."

"I understand there are a lot of dragon crossers here." Timur's expression had gone all fond. "Will you be helping them find that potential?"

"Me?" Sinder fidgeted. "Not me. Lapis is the one who'll cuddle and dote."

Timur laughed.

"You unlocked Kyrie's potential. You uncovered Lilya's gift."

"I just happened to be in the right place at the right time. Anybody could … have …." Sinder trailed off when he noticed that Juuyu and Timur were giving him odd looks.

Fend began to purr.

Sinder cautiously offered his hand.

The big panther dipped closer, but he didn't sniff or lick or butt his head against Sinder's open hand. He closed his jaws over it. While he didn't bite down, there were teeth in play. Sinder could feel them dimpling his wrist, and he didn't dare move.

"What did I ever do to you?" he asked softly.

"You can do nothing. You will say nothing."

Sinder didn't speak his protest aloud. Didn't need to. *"I can keep a secret."*

Mocking eyes. Mocking tones. *"No. You can't. I wonder how*

many I can steal."

"Fend!" Timur intervened, sounding more exasperated than worried. "Where are your manners? That was an offer of peace."

"*It was surrender.*"

Sinder was pretty sure dragons were supposed to be bigger and badder than cats, any day of the week. But Fend left him feeling outclassed.

Juuyu hummed. "You know how some clans are about dragons. Maybe Fend is flirting?"

Which was absolute bullshit, but Fend let go so fast, it was almost funny.

"Show me," said Juuyu, who carefully inspected Sinder's hand for injury. The big cat hadn't broken skin. Just left a little kitty spit.

Timur gave his partner a hard look and shrugged him off. "He's probably just teasing. Shall I insist on an apology?"

"From a cat?" he asked weakly.

Timur chuckled and hauled him higher so he could bump a kiss to Sinder's cheek. "I apologize, Zolottse. Fend's jealous. He knows how dedicated I am to dragons."

Sinder really wanted more of this man's attention, but he could *feel* a basso rumble that promised pain. "Dunce and double dunce, Michaelson. Are you *trying* to get me killed?"

36

BATTLE CRY

Juuyu watched Sinder carefully, ready to intervene if his partner needed him, but the more he studied the pair, the less he worried. Sinder was clearly content to remain in Timur's grasp, and Timur showed no sign of relinquishing his hold.

The man's fingers expertly sought pressure points that Juuyu was familiar with from his own training. A sharp nip at the right juncture could render a dragon insensate for hours. Yet Sinder was limp and blissful.

Interesting. It would seem that members of the Order of Spomenka learned more than dragon slaying.

Juuyu was beginning to wonder if he'd been inadvertently neglecting Sinder when Timur invited them to come and meet his Uncle Sergei. At this point, he finally set Sinder down, but he kept a hand on the dragon's shoulder … much to Fend's annoyance.

The Kith's behavior puzzled Juuyu. He was unusually assertive. Some of his posturing could even be interpreted as dominant, and Timur treated him as an equal. Not all partnered reavers gave equal footing to their Kith companions.

Somewhere high overhead, a dragon fluted, and attention swerved to the sky.

One by one, the dragon lords lifted into the air. Something was happening.

Sinder double-timed it back to him and jerked a thumb. "I want a look, too. Coming?"

They pushed off together, and as soon as they were high enough, they could see what the promontory of their small island had been blocking from view. On the northern horizon, ominous clouds were spiraling and piling in an unusual display. The sea had changed moods in that direction, choppy as it tried to flee. But most impressive by far, though small in comparison, was the silver fox running before the storm, his full flourish flying.

"He brings the wind," Juuyu murmured.

Sinder whistled a few choice notes before countering, "Argent's pulling one seriously pissed-off storm."

Juuyu was already catching resonance shifts when Inti's voice broke through for a second time. Sinder had been cornered by his grandfather, who was all aflutter over the little wind dragon now decorating Timur's shoulders, but Sinder excused himself with a curt, "She's spoken for, and I don't have a spare."

"How is it that I can hear him?" Juuyu murmured, once they were away.

"It's not like Inti *explained*," Sinder grumbled. "But from what I gather, he's befriended a beacon, and she's adding oomph to his range."

"There are reavers on the island?" Juuyu frowned over this development. "Kodoku has colluders within the In-between?"

"You know as much as I do on that score. How about we go find out?"

"Ahead of the rest?"

Sinder rolled his eyes. "Kind of our job. We're frontliners this time, so let's get in there."

"Agreed."

Inti's message had been short and mostly to the point. *"Close, closer, closing in. Check for gaps!"*

"Can you swim?" Sinder asked.

Juuyu was mildly surprised that it had never come up before. "Not in truest form, but yes. I learned to swim in speaking form."

"Guess you did grow up in a beach community, more or less." Sinder's pace quickened as he aimed for the sheltered lagoon on their island's opposite side. "If we want to keep a low profile, it's best to swim. So ... want a ride?" he shyly offered.

"Thank you."

Juuyu rolled up his shirtsleeves and checked his weapons and personal wards one last time before wading into the water. Cutting a shallow dive, he found Sinder waiting in truest form, and they surfaced together.

"*Upsy daisy,*" the dragon cheerfully ordered.

But Juuyu could feel the underlying edge. "You are angry?"

"*Not personally. At least, not exactly.*" Sinder glided out, staying low in the water. "*Reaches catch a different kind of resonance than crystal adepts and sigilcrafters. We don't just read the room, we catch moods. Inti's not in a calm place, right now.*"

"He is angry?"

"*Angry, sure. And furious with himself. And desperate.*"

"Why?" asked Juuyu, as Sinder picked up speed.

"*Wish I knew. But it's probably not good, since he called for backup.*"

Sinder circled the barrier, giving Juuyu time to make his own assessment.

"It was not visible before?" Juuyu checked.

His words had no trouble reaching his partner. "*Totally invisible. Bashed into it the first time I swam out here.*"

Thin lines and runes wavered over the water. "Definitely warped. There should be weak points."

"*I wish Kyrie was here. He's practically immune to wards. Walks through barriers without noticing.*"

"Hmm. A useful trait for infiltration missions."

Sinder arched his slender neck to look Juuyu in the eye. "*Want to recruit him?*"

"Perhaps. In time."

With a small shake of his mane, Sinder asked, "*How's it look to you?*"

"Complex," he admitted. "And increasingly convoluted."

"Definitely in flux. I'm going to go under. Boon said that he got a better connection under water, so the barrier might be weakened there."

"I will wait here." Juuyu sat a little above the surface of the water and narrowed his focus. Multiple layers made it difficult to study. Unmaking something on this scale would be next to impossible, but he could interpret enough to tell that the outermost markers were vulpine. All the things they'd expected to find in California had been here. It was a wonder Boon had tracked this down on his own.

Sinder eventually surfaced. *"Found our way in. I'll get you through, then follow. Might be a bit of a squeeze, but I can shift underwater if I've got to."*

So Juuyu trusted himself into his partner's keeping. A deep breath. A long dive. By the time the bubbles cleared, Sinder was already thrusting his tail past a weak point in the barrier. Sand stirred as he wrestled at it with claws, then thrust his muzzle through.

"On three," Sinder ground out. *"One ... two ... go!"*

Releasing Juuyu, he got his other forefoot in play, and the gap widened enough for Juuyu to glide through. He pushed toward the surface but turned in the water to watch Sinder try to squirm after him. The ungainly struggle ended when Sinder shifted into speaking form. Despite sodden clothes and billowing hair, the dragon was a strong swimmer, yet Juuyu could tell something was badly off.

They surfaced together, and Sinder floundered, choking.

Juuyu hooked his arm and held him up.

"What's *wrong* with this place?" he complained. "I don't feel so good."

"Dampeners." Juuyu eased Sinder onto his back and began pulling him toward shore. "Let me. I have protections you do not."

Sinder eyed the mark on his forehead, lay back in the water, and let himself be towed.

They didn't get far before Juuyu felt something pass beneath his feet.

Sinder had noticed, too, and he flipped onto his belly and ducked his head under. When he popped back up, his eyes were wide. "We should get out of the water quickly. Or ... actually, let me swap to truest form."

Juuyu quickly found himself astride Sinder, who propelled them around a rocky promontory, bringing a thin length of beach into view. And the female who appeared to be defending it from a dripping, hulking creature.

The rattling call of a wild dragon sent Juuyu into immediate action. Or an abortive attempt, since the dampeners prohibited flight. "Pardon me," he said, planting his feet between Sinder's ridges. "I need to fly."

With a leap that pushed his partner under, Juuyu shifted into truest form with a flash of vivid feathers, the heavy beat of wings, and an ancient battle cry.

A tuneful call put Pim's back up, and she swiveled to find more creatures coming up out of the sea. Quickly assessing these new opponents, she wondered if she should be more worried about the dragon in the shallows or the enormous bird whose heavy wingbeats were scattering sand.

But the pale dragon started frantically signaling peace with his dexterous claws, and the phoenix swerved upward, gaze fixed on the forest. So Pim turned her attention back to her pitiful attacker. It was a mangled cross between a reptile and a mammal. Red eyes were the only thing that suggested dragon. Well, that and its teeth.

It moaned and lunged, dragging seaweed as it pulled itself across the sand.

She danced out of the way, trying not to let her disgust show. The thing reeked and snapped and grunted, yet she couldn't bring herself to hurt it. This misshapen beast probably wasn't much different from Patter or from any of the other crossers that Kodoku had manufactured. Ugly or no, this creature couldn't help being ... whatever it was.

"You okay, miss?" called the dragon, who'd shifted. Giving her bulky attacker a wide berth, he reached her side and did a doubletake. "You're Pim Moonprowl!"

"Here for an autograph?"

"Uhh ... maybe later. I'm Sinder. He's Juuyu, and we're here for Hisoka. Seen him? Unassuming fellow. A pewter tom. Shy of girls. About yay tall." He held up a hand, accurately marking Spokesperson Twineshaft's height, all the while casting a worried look at the jungle behind them. "Why are we still here? Running along beaches is supposed to be good for exercise. And for clean getaways."

Pim grudgingly admitted, "I was trying to reason with it. To see if they have a voice. Because ... they might."

"Whoa-kay, let me give it a try." And stepping in front of her, Sinder called, "Hey, you. Listen to me, okay. Time for a quick chat."

"I'm listening," Pim grumbled. Wasn't she right here? What else *could* she do?

Sinder shot her a startled look. "Not you. Aw, shit. Pim, I need you to cover your ears and hum for a couple of minutes."

So she did. Though she kept a close eye on Sinder as he gesticulated at the sea monster. Then led it into the water.

The opening theme of *Pure Instinct* was catchy, and she'd almost made it through twice before Sinder was back in her face, gently removing her hands from her ears.

"That's enough. You can stop humming. Sorry about that."

"You used sway," she said dully.

"Uhh. Yeah. I totally did, and I'm really sorry. I swear, my partner will lecture me later." He winced as something crashed in the trees behind them, and a dragon's squealing cries suddenly cut off. "He's kinda busy at the moment. So … Hisoka?"

"What did you do to the … crosser …?" she asked.

Sinder glanced toward the trail of bubbles that remained where the creature had submerged. "Your instincts were good. I don't think the poor guy can form words, but he can understand them. Not sure what his pedigree looks like, but there was dragon in the mix. I think on some level he's been trying to connect with his kindred. Of course, on another level, he might have been trying to eat them."

"What'll happen to him?"

"Preservationists, probably." With a wheeling of one hand, he added, "Best thing for him—beings as you're *worried* and all—is to get Hisoka Twineshaft on his side. Or Argent. But I *know* where Lord Mettlebright is."

"Sensei was headed there," she said, pointing in the general direction. "We split up to collect wardstones. Me, Sensei, and

Boon. We're supposed to regroup at the lab. I'm probably late."

"Well, I can see how you might have been distracted." Sinder winced when the phoenix reappeared over the trees, a pair of limp dragons dangling from his talons, to drop them on the beach. "Mind if I ask you something?"

"Go ahead."

His gaze was sharp, and his tone was careful. "Why are you wearing Boon's beads?"

With pride, she said, "He's my mentor."

"You taking up tracking as your next career?"

"I'm a wolf." It was getting a little easier to say it.

He didn't really react to that. Just waited for more.

"I have a lot to learn, and he offered to teach me."

Sinder's eyes narrowed. "*Boon* offered? Big fella. Trebellaire pelt. Rocking some facial scars. *Also* girl shy."

"It's a long story, and it involves a monkey, a beacon, a lesbian, a hyacinth camisole, and some accidental bond-building. Want to guess which one of those things is me?"

"I'm guessing that wasn't my cue to laugh." Sinder offered his palms in belated greeting. "I never wear hyacinth myself. Much more into yellows. Hey, are you okay?"

"No." She met his palms and quietly added, "But also yes. Does your friend need help?"

"I'm really no good in a fight. Usually talk my way out of them. And dragons are *his* specialty. Natural predator, killer instincts, immune to sway, yadda, yadda, yadda."

"So you're with Boon."

"Yep! There's six of us. One big happy taskforce." As another pair of drooping dragons hit the sand, Sinder strolled over and rolled the nearest one into a recovery position. Stroking the speckled underside of the dragon's muzzle, he remarked, "Juuyu's just a little too good at this, you know?"

"They're alive!" Pim exclaimed, hurrying to help Sinder rearrange the unconscious beasts.

"Well, sure. Just because he *can* kill them doesn't mean he's gonna. Endangered species and all that." Sinder warbled in dismay over jutting ribs and scarred scales. "I hear Lord Shywind is into the rehabilitation of ferals. Bet he'll offer sanctuary."

The phoenix lowered another two dragons to the sand, this time shifting into speaking form once he was low enough. Even so, he stumbled to one knee. The barrier was definitely affecting both of them.

Pim said, "Without tuning, it's worse the closer you are to the water. Inti gave me a sigil, so I don't notice so much."

"May I see?" inquired the phoenix, extending a hand.

"I need to shift. I'm collared."

Juuyu stepped back to give her room, and Sinder combed through her fur to locate the clay disk.

"A few moments," begged Juuyu, whose hands moved as he studied the item. "Hmm. I see. That will do."

Pim returned to speaking form while the phoenix wove a sigil, swift and sure. He pressed the first to Sinder's back, then began another for himself. "Better?"

"Much."

"Hmm." And to Pim, "Where is the need most urgent?"

"I have to collect the wardstone from that nearer peak."

Juuyu rested his hand over his heart, applying his sigil, then inclined his head. "You two go. I will deal with these six and the two who fled. As well as any stragglers who might cause trouble."

Sinder raised his hand.

Juuyu's head did this funny little avian tilt.

"Oh, come on," coaxed his partner. "After that display, I want some reassurance that you're still on my side."

With a low warble that almost sounded worried, Juuyu pressed their palms together.

"I was going for a high five, but that's close enough." And Sinder took off running.

Pim gently clapped her hand to Juuyu's, just in case he needed the demo. But his faint smile suggested that the phoenix liked toying with all dragons. Especially Sinder. As she jogged after him, Pim tried to give her tail the same kind of friendly swing that Boon would have.

When she caught up to Sinder, he said, "I really am sorry about the sway."

"Thank you."

"Do I ... make you nervous?"

She didn't feel compelled to answer, but she faced the question squarely. A wolf was always honest. "I had an unpleasant experience with Dr. Kodoku. It seems I'm entirely susceptible to dragon sway."

"Most people are. Want me to help with that?"

"Is there a cure?"

"It's more like building up a resistance." He stopped in the path. "Can you trust me?"

Pim's impressions were all good. Her decision was easy. "Sure. I trust you."

Sinder beamed at her. "Touch my nose."

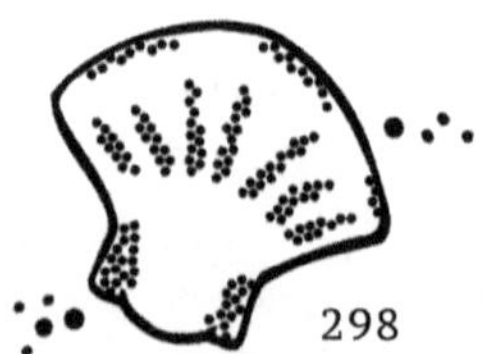

37

NOT IN A CALM PLACE

ervous didn't begin to describe how Akira was feeling. There were so many people he wanted to find, and there were just as many people he wanted to keep safe. Plus, this was supposed to be the part where he'd find his dad.

It's why Suuzu had let him go.

These people were the reason for the risk.

Kids in cages. Captive souls. Stolen lives.

Akira could be brave for a bit more, so long as it meant getting Jacques back and bringing Naoki home.

"Check, checkers, checking," Inti muttered. Pointing to the righthand side of the hall, he urged, "Eiji and Akira, this side. Elara and Inti, left. Anjou, see if you can find a weapon."

From Elara's map, Akira knew they were in the hallway that would lead to the room where Kodoku kept the crossers caged. But what if someone had been isolated in one of these other labs? Akira soon lagged a little behind the others. Part of it was that he couldn't spring from door to door in a single bound like Inti, and part of it was worry. He wanted to be *sure* nobody got left behind. How awful would it be if he missed someone who needed to be found?

The rooms along this hall were filled with microscopes and bulky machines that did who-knew-what. Exam tables with heavy straps and sealed packets of surgical instruments. Vials and jars and beakers and flasks. It was all so stark, and it made Akira sad. And angry.

How many of the people who worked here thought that experimenting on crossers was justifiable? Were they all under dragon sway? Or were there actually people in the In-between who thought this was okay?

Quickly and quietly, he stepped far enough into each room to make extra certain it was empty.

Had the people here heard the alarms earlier? Is that why nobody was around? Had the children been frightened by the noise? Most of the crossers Akira knew had sensitive ears. Loud noises *hurt*.

Elara and Inti reached the end of the hall and disappeared around the corner. Eiji had leapt ahead, so Akira only had a few more doors to check. The first was another empty exam room, but the next was different. It was longer, and the light was different. Akira's attention was drawn to the skylights high above. This was a little like Goh-sensei's room back at New Saga High School—long, high, and filled with the scent of earth and plants. And flowers.

Without really meaning to, Akira stepped further into the room, letting the door go. It clicked shut behind him, so he reached for the handle, but … oh, that wasn't good. No handle.

Maybe there was another door?

The answer stalked in from the opposite direction. Dr. Kodoku drew up short and snapped, "You there! You're not one of my … oh, wait. You're that one from earlier."

"I'm … yeah. Hi?"

Kodoku strode over and twirled a finger at him. "You look different without all the … shimmery bits. But why are you *here*? More importantly, where is your lover?"

"Umm … Jacques?"

"Tell me where your lover is." The dragon's words were heavy with sway.

"I don't know, sir."

"How did you get in here?"

"The door wasn't locked …?" He gestured helplessly. "I got separated from my … cats."

"Useless." Then he turned and called, "Get over here! Someone's strayed in, and I need you to get rid of him."

A bespectacled man hurried into view, and Akira's breath caught. He looked Japanese, and he wasn't very tall. And the way he frowned with concern was so much like Tsumiko. Before he could stop himself, Akira whispered, "Dad?"

Dr. Kodoku pivoted. "What did you say?"

Akira shook his head.

"Naoki, do you recognize this boy?"

"He is not one of our patients."

"I know that! His lover is one of our guests at the resort. He was whoring with cats even before the sun was up."

Akira blushed. He didn't like for his father to get the wrong idea about him.

"Should I return him to the resort?" Naoki casually offered.

Kodoku lifted a finger. "Why did you come?" More sway.

"To find Jacques."

"Yes, well ... he is missing. Ran off with my most priceless resource." His gaze narrowed. "Tell me, chattel. Would he come back for you?"

"He ... might ...?" With Kodoku prowling closer, Akira knew he shouldn't attempt a lie. "I hope so. I love him."

"We could *try* bait, I suppose." A finger touched Akira's chin, lifting his face. "Tell me, boy. Did you recognize Naoki?"

"No. I must have been mistaken."

Kodoku angled his head. "Were you now?"

"Yes, sir."

Akira held very still when Kodoku bent to sniff at his throat. Dragons might not be as good with scents as wolves, but they weren't nose-blind. And his ties to Naoki couldn't have been closer. This man had carried him. Somehow.

"Naoki, this boy is kin to you!" His tongue dragged up Akira's throat. "A son? Did you know?"

"I am ... astonished."

"His mother?" Kodoku inquired sweetly.

Something sparked in Naoki's eyes. "I would hardly endanger her by bringing her to your attention."

The dragon began running his hands over Akira, kneading at glands while humming to himself. "You never had any inclination toward females before. It's always limited your usefulness."

"I have my work," Naoki said stiffly. "I was not looking for companionship."

"You had Hajime." The dragon peered at Akira's father over the top of his glasses. "You still pine for him."

"My friend is long gone."

"But not as long as I was led to believe." The dragon's voice dripped with sway. "Tell me, boy. How old are you?"

Akira stuck to his cover story. "Eighteen. Almost."

"Impossible. Your father has been here for … hmm …. It's been nearly twenty-four years since your return, hasn't it, Naoki?"

His dad's jaw worked. "I do not mark the anniversary of my recapture."

Kodoku turned back to Akira, still pointlessly using sway. "Who is your mother?"

"I don't know. Nobody will tell me."

Suddenly, there were claws at Akira's throat. Pain bloomed, as did blood. Calmly, coolly, Dr. Kodoku asked, "I wonder. Do *you* mark the anniversary of this boy's birth, Naoki?"

"Don't do that. If your poison were to …!"

Kodoku released Akira and moved away, rummaging for a wipe and cleaning his claws. "How old, Naoki?" he asked in a hard voice.

"Akira is twenty-six."

"Was there a mother?"

Naoki shook his head once.

"Did you get Hajime to sprig you?"

The man stood silent.

Dr. Kodoku went right on. "He's wandered rather far afield to be tree-kin. What became of his seed?" When Naoki refused to answer, the dragon turned to Akira. "Where is the seed? You were born with a golden seed."

"I wasn't. There's no seed."

Naoki quickly interjected, "It's true. He wasn't born with a seed in his hand."

"Really? Now that *is* interesting." Kodoku's eyes took on a shine. "Golden seeds do not simply vanish. One of you has it."

"I don't know what you mean," Naoki said.

Akira nodded. "If I'd had a seed, that would have meant … good things. But I don't."

Kodoku fluttered his fingers dismissively. "There are aberrations. Little defects. One of you has it, and I would wager it is the boy. I would have noticed if Naoki was harboring, and you are ridiculously well-warded."

"I don't have one," Akira repeated. But he shot a look at his father and tentatively asked, "Do I?"

Naoki looked heartbroken. "There was no seed. That is the truth."

"That is your version of the truth," countered Kodoku with a superior smile. "And I know better. How long do you think he was in my care? Unique beyond compare. Utterly priceless."

"Hajime is not a collector's item."

"Not anymore. Not since you." Kodoku glanced Akira's way. "Do you know how many years your father has? Even now, parted from his partner, he endures. Fascinating, is it not?"

Akira didn't think his dad looked terribly old. Thirty-ish, maybe. Then again, Akira was nearing thirty. He wanted to ask, but it seemed wiser to cling to some semblance of ignorance.

The dragon hadn't wanted an answer. He probably just liked having an audience.

Kodoku said, "It took years for him to stabilize. Centuries to mature. And even then, he showed no sign of bearing fruit until … you."

Naoki's lips compressed into a thin line.

"You stole him from me," Kodoku accused silkily. "And so I stole you from him."

"He is gone," Naoki insisted dully. "He is free."

"Do not doubt the hold you have over him. He will come for you, but it would seem that I no longer have to wait." Waving at Akira, he purred, "Here is the means to sprig Nemi again. Her defiance is at an end."

Kodoku grabbed Akira's arm with enough strength to bruise and pulled him along. While he didn't resist, it was difficult to keep up. Amaranthine didn't know their own speed.

"Wait!" Naoki scrambled to match Kodoku's pace. "Where are you taking him?"

"My lab. I need to perform a thorough examination, and once I find the seed, I will extract it."

That sounded bad. And yet ….

Akira had to ask, "I have a seed?"

"Undoubtedly. It has happened once or twice. Was it before your time, Naoki?" Kodoku slowed somewhat for the sake of his audience. "Every so often, the seed doesn't find its way into the infant's hand. It might be dropped. Or become lodged."

They passed through two more doors, and Akira found himself in a windowless room with a row of low tables. There were straps on some, and there were chains on others. Akira found the floor especially unsettling. The entire room had been tiled in red, and there were drains set at intervals.

"You are a defective twin," Kodoku cheerfully announced. "In such cases, during the natural course of things, only after your death—assuming you were buried intact—would your body serve as fodder for your twin's sprigging. This is how many an orphan tree takes root. Can you imagine what would have happened, had you lived out your pittance of days, only to be cremated? That *would* have been a great loss."

This was news to Akira. Big news. Good news. His voice shook, "My twin's here? Safe?"

Pulling Akira to one of the tables, Kodoku said, "Up."

He grudgingly eased onto the bare, cold surface, warily eyeing the doctor.

Kodoku studied him narrowly for a few moments, then sighed. "Down. Undress. Then up. I'll have to deal with some of the sigils first. Where is Futari?"

Naoki ventured, "Overseeing the staff's evacuation. On your orders."

Muttering to himself, Kodoku stalked toward the door. "I will find her. Prep him."

The door slammed shut, and in the silence that followed, Akira heard the faint snick of the lock. "What do you think he's going to do?"

"I dread to think." Naoki looked pale. "If he cannot immediately find what he wants … vivisection?"

Akira winced, then thrust out a hand. "Let's stick to the good news, then. I was hoping to find you here when I agreed to help. Well, no. Actually, when I agreed to help, I was just doing a favor for Boon, since I owed him one for getting started on Suuzu's nest. But once I found out about you from Tabi-oji, I was kind of counting on this being the right place. I promised him that I'd bring you home, so this is great."

"Dear boy, this is the farthest thing from great. Do you understand where you are?"

"Yeah. I'm with my dad for the first time. I mean, I know you were around when I was tiny. Tsumiko's told me some stuff, but I don't actually remember you. Only the way home smells, and I guess that's more because of Tabi-otosan than you."

Naoki took a step closer, lowering his voice. "Are you talking about Hajime?"

He looked so bewildered.

"Yeah," Akira said, trying to pack in as many words as he could while they were alone. "He introduced himself as Tabigarasu, but Tabi-oji was friendlier. And then when everything came out, it was Tabi-otosan. Did you know he was trying to gather the Junzi in order to come after you?"

"Oh … oh, no."

Akira smiled. "He had the whole In-between running around in circles, trying to figure out who'd stolen them. But in the middle of one of his heists, he met me. Turns out I'm not as forgetful as most people are when it comes to little red flowers."

Naoki cautiously reached for him, touching his shoulder, then his hair. "Akira ...."

"Yeah. It's me."

Fingers gently probed the fresh wound on his neck. "You are in a great deal of danger."

"No more than anyone else that's on this island. And don't worry. Help is on the way." Edging closer, he promised, "You can trust us."

The door swung open, and Kodoku shot them an impatient look. "Strip him and strap him down."

His dad looked paralyzed, so Akira simply started to undress, passing along each article of clothing as he did so. He kept his focus on Naoki, memorizing his face, ignoring the dragon.

The table felt cold against bare skin. Naoki whispered apologies as the straps anchored Akira to it. Kodoku's gaze swept him without really seeing him. And finally, Akira owned that he was afraid. Whatever happened next, he couldn't stop it.

"Normally, I would rid you of all that sigilcraft before proceeding with anything invasive, but your lover has robbed me of my usual methods." Looming closer, Kodoku demanded, "Tell me how he did it."

Akira could feel the insistent tug of sway. "I don't know. So ... you're a dragon?"

"Telling tales, Naoki?" Kodoku's gaze was cool. "I thought you had learned your lesson."

"He didn't have to tell me anything. I knew right away. So ... are there other dragons living on this island?"

Kodoku frowned. "Why are you questioning me?"

"Because I think you know the answers."

"Oh, hush. Just stop."

Akira did, but only long enough to frame his next question. "Do you have kids?"

"And how would I manage that, hmm? Dragons of my sort are not favored with brides."

"Having a wife isn't the only way to have a kid. Look at me."

"I *am* looking at you. Entirely human. Unendowed. Rubbish."

"That kind of hate speech can get you into a lot of trouble with the Amaranthine Council and its many tribunals." Akira sternly recited, "All persons, no matter their race, species, heritage, or clan, is protected under the peace accord. You're behind the times."

Kodoku frowned. "You will be quiet."

Akira intended to prove he didn't have to.

"Resistant, are you? Well, then. I shall rephrase. You will be quiet, or I will render you incapable of speech."

Naoki came to stand on the other side of the table. His hand was trembling when he placed his fingers against Akira's lips. A small headshake begged for silence.

Kodoku launched into a topic more to his liking. "Hajime survived culling, but grafts were less successful. After various tests, all I had left were a handful of hybrid seedlings. Halves and quarters. Also rubbish. Until Naoki. Ah, the harvest you inspired! And shall again."

"Hajime's gifts were never meant for you," Naoki whispered.

"Amaranthine trees are marvelously potent. I had long hypothesized that their fruit would become the answer to the Waning. A golden seed does not merely find fertile ground, it makes the ground in which it's sown fertile."

Surgical implements began putting in an appearance off to one side, and Akira shot his father a worried look. Naoki looked close to tears.

Caught up in his recitation, Kodoku went on. "When Naoki vanished, taking Hajime with him, they were thorough. Every sample gone or destroyed. Barely a trace remained. Indeed, most forgot he was ever here, but that's how it is with his variety of tree." A grim stare. "And they took with them the last pure seed. *Your* seed, no doubt."

Which couldn't be right. Because there was Tsumiko to consider. But Akira wasn't about to mention his sister.

Hands began tracing over Akira's skin, and he tugged at his bonds.

"Oh, do stop the virginal squirming. Just considering the sigilcraft. You've been thoroughly foxed. And you can hardly mind me after cavorting with felines all night." Kodoku hesitated, sniffed, prodded, and huffed. "Or so you implied. The toys brought here by guests generally get more use."

"Jacques is patient. He'd never take what's not his," Akira fiercely insisted. "He'd never hurt someone he loves."

"And he loves you?"

"So?"

"He left you behind, and now he has lost you. Or himself, should he return for you. I wonder if this could be considered a family trait? The inspiration of devotion. It bears studying. I shall need blood. Perhaps some other fluids. A tissue sample. A sprigging might even be in order. Would you like to be a grandfather, Naoki?"

The roving fingers dug into the soft place low on Akira's belly where Suuzu had first found the subtle glow of something extra.

"Don't!" Akira exclaimed. And when that inspired a knowing smile, he lamely added, "Th-that tickles."

"One last pure seed," the dragon crooned. "Where is Futari when I need her? Naoki, you will assist. Cooperate, and I might even let you use a topical anesthetic."

Naoki snapped, "Akira is my son. At least let me do it!"

"No. I will not risk your damaging the seed to thwart me." Rolling his eyes, Kodoku said, "By all the winds, an extraction will not kill him. I will do it with my bare claws if you insist."

Akira said, "I have a request."

"You are hardly in a position to negotiate."

Ignoring Kodoku entirely, Akira sought his father's gaze and asked, "Please, Dad? Will you hold my hand?"

38

LOTUS EATER

Jacques lolled across Dayith's lap, gazing around with an increasing sense of wonderment. "What's all this, then? Lord. Have these been here all along?"

Solace gave the vicinity a quizzical assessment. "Yes? Nothing has changed."

"He has changed," said Dayith.

"I do believe I have." Jacques peered into the stone imp's face. "Can you do that to just any bloke?"

"You are the only one here."

Solace tipped his head to one side. "You were the only one foretold."

"But ... hypothetically. If I brought you Akira. *There's* a thought. Could you pop over to the resort and collect Akira? He needs this."

"Resort?"

"Fancy hotel on the eastern shoreline ...? Akira's there. I can give you the number of our suite ...?"

Solace looked to Dayith. "*Could* I bring someone?"

Eager to sway matters in their favor, Jacques explained, "He's a fine young man. At the moment, he's *my* young man. Genial fellow. Trusting to a fault. Undoubtedly arrayed in pastels. Probably forgetting to use the wax and gloss, which only goes to show how much he needs me. Oh, and his waltz is passable ... provided you're willing to lead."

Two pairs of faceted green eyes blinked.

Jacques attempted to simplify. "He's short, Asian, and ... precious to me."

"I am sorry," said Dayith.

"Too far?" Jacques asked. "I could go find him. Bring him around."

Solace looked so sad. "Father, can you help? Akira is my human brother. Should we try?"

"I am sorry," repeated the stone imp.

And Jacques could feel his regret, for it washed up against him in an invisible wave. So many losses. So much pain. There was real sorrow in his sorry.

Dayith's suffering reminded Jacques of Argent, and so he didn't want to add to it. "Right, then. I would like to explore my options."

"You must stay," Dayith warned.

"I want to explore ... here." Jacques gestured around. "Es -pecially those."

"What?" Solace asked, trying to follow his gaze.

With a little help, Jacques made it to his feet and tottered a few steps, reaching up. He carefully closed his hands around a tiny, jellyfish-like bubble that had been twirling lazily through the air.

"This, for example." The creature was translucent, yet it

had substance. Tiny tentacles wrapped around his fingers, and faceted eyes sought his gaze, blinking innocently. "No sting. That's good of you."

"They will not harm you," Solace said wisely. "They never harm anyone."

"Am I hurting it?"

"Nooo. You are soft. And gentle."

Jacques asked, "Why can it fly when my feline companions complained they could not?"

Solace ventured, "Did they descend?"

"*Non*. Descent is for imps from the sky clans. My friends are Amaranthine." Jacques ventured, "Ephemera seem to be exempt."

"Many find our haven and remain," said Dayith. "Kodoku cannot explain them, and so he toys with them as he does the rest of us."

Jacques found three more creatures that had to be Ephemera, then followed a fourth straight to Solace's trunk. "I've been known to climb trees. Mostly in self-defense. May I?"

Solace appeared in the limbs above, beckoning. "Come up! Come see!"

He shed his shoes. The branches were crooked and rough enough to provide good footing. "You really are part rock," he remarked.

"Half. Not all." Solace perched on a limb and swung his feet. "I am ... myself?"

"That's how it is for crossers. Some of ours need to sort through all their inheritances. Something tells me I'll be doing the same." He reached for an Ephemera he knew by name. Perhaps midivar were native to the tropics? The gemlike snake briefly alighted on his forearm, then darted higher with a buzz of iridescent wings.

"You have inheritances?"

"My father has all sorts of pedigree, and my mother saw to the social graces. And now I have an inheritance from Dayith."

"And me. I have something for you, too."

"Is that so?" The scent of flowers was stronger here, up amid the branches. It made Jacques feel hazy and happy.

Solace produced a flower, only this one wasn't all soft petals, and he didn't press it to Jacques' lips. Faceted crystal sparkled at the end of a tapering rod, and Solace tucked that stem-end into Jacques' shirt pocket. The piece reminded Jacques of the hair ornaments that Tsumiko would wear while in traditional attire.

"Something to remember you by?" he inquired lightly. "And in my signature color. Did you make this?"

"Cadmiel did. Do you like it?"

"I do. Very much." Jacques hesitated, for something about that statement seemed important. "Did you say Cadmiel? As in ... *Cadmiel* Cadmiel?"

"That is the name he gave."

"Kodoku has an angel trapped in here?"

"No," said Dayith, watching placidly from below. "We were visited long ago, when the barrier was less of an obstacle."

"When you were foretold," added Solace.

Jacques asked, "How long ago?"

"Long, long ago," Dayith replied vaguely.

Which probably went straight past centuries and on into millennia, all things considered. Jacques bowed his head. "I left you waiting that long? Very rude of me, I'm sure."

"Could you have come sooner?" asked Solace.

"*Non*. The circumstances surrounding this little holiday are … well, suffice to say they're complicated. But what's a minor miracle between friends? Especially when there are angels involved."

"You are here, and I am glad." The tree lightly touched Jacques' hair. "Is that not enough?"

Curious, Jacques indicted the glittering crown in Solace's hair. "Would it hurt if I touched your leaves?"

"No, no. They loosen and fall, and new ones form. That is how I am." He pointed to the beach below. "That is how it has always been."

The fine sand below shimmered green in the sunlight. Was it all from these leaves? Jacques reached for one on the nearest branch. He barely bumped it, and it came away in his hand. To his astonishment, it immediately crumbled in his palm, dusting his skin like glitter.

"I can't decide if this is tidy or a huge mess," Jacques remarked. "What do you do on windy days?"

"There is no wind."

Dayith concurred. "The winds have abandoned this place."

"A sort of boycott?" Jacques began a cautious descent. "Dr. Creeper has been misbehaving with imps, so the winds want nothing to do with him?"

"That is part," said Dayith.

Jacques was used to verbal gymnastics. "What's the rest?"

Neither imp answered. And their matching smiles were so … wistful.

That's when Jacques remembered. "Earlier! With Argent! You asked him to bring the winds. *Why?*"

"Because he can do what we cannot."

Jacques leapt the final distance to the sand. "But if there's so much as a breeze …!"

Dayith calmly countered, "There will be a storm."

He peered up into the fragile canopy. "What will happen?"

"You know."

Solace quietly confirmed, "I will be ravaged."

"Surely not!" Jacques' mind raced. "The others wouldn't want that. None of my friends would want that!"

"They will not mind," Dayith assured.

"Because they will not know." Solace patted the crystal flower showing above Jacques' pocket. "No one knows about me."

"*I* know!" Jacques needed to fix this. "I could get word to Argent. And … wards! If we can get you warded in time … barriers within barriers, and all that."

"You will need it more," said Solace. "There might be slivers and shards and there will be so much sand, and you are so soft."

Dayith promised, "You will be safe. Help will arrive in time."

"Soon," agreed Solace.

"How soon?" Jacques snapped. There was no view of the sky here, so he strode out into the water. The green sands were silken underfoot, and their little cove was shallow.

Dayith followed him out past the rocks, warning, "Not too far. There are creatures in the water."

But Jacques wasn't looking down. He peered toward the horizon, turning in place. Clear. Quite clear. And …. "*Mon dieu,*" he whispered.

Around the curve of the island, he could just see strange clouds racing toward them. They looked like silvery serpents in the sky, swirling and twining as they scudded nearer.

All that furor made the stillness all around them strange. There should be a leading wind and choppy waves. Yet the island was as stifling and stagnant as ever.

Jacques sloshed back to Solace, who was too calm, too resigned. "We only have minutes! We need to do something!"

"Yes. We are doing what must be done." The tree took his hand and petted it. "This is not death, Jacques Smythe. I will sleep. Father and I will sleep and sleep and sleep."

"That is the way with stone," said Dayith.

"You'll be safe?"

"Untouched," he promised. "Together."

The quality of the air changed, and Jacques felt his hair raise. Had the winds already reached the barrier? Then clouds swallowed the sun, and he was sure. "You should hurry. You should go to safety."

"Not yet," said Dayith. "One thing remains."

Solace went up on tiptoe. "Did you know that an imp's kiss can bestow a blessing?"

"I ... actually, yes. I was aware." Jacques' gaze darted from father to son. "Are you going to mark me?"

"Twice," said Dayith. "If you will permit it."

Mustering a touch of formality, he said, "I understand the compliment. I can only be honored."

Dayith carefully pushed aside Jacques' hair, pressing a kiss to his nape. The whole thing was so solemn, full of portent.

Solace went up on tiptoe to whisper in his ear. "I hope I will dream of you, Jacques Smythe."

Then he offered his own parting kiss.
Jacques hated that it meant goodbye.

39
REAL DEAL

Boon crouched at the base of a tree alongside the road, trying to calm down the voice in his head. "That's real frustrating, I'll admit. But just because he's on the wrong side of a door doesn't mean he's in mortal peril."

"He is, he is, he is! Inti knows!" Inti's voice cracked. *"The stars are crying."*

Whether it was because they were both on the same side of the barrier or because Inti had gotten ahold of one hell of an amplifier, Boon was reading him loud and clear. Not typical. He could only surmise that Inti's reaver half was involved in making the reach possible.

"Calm down. I'm on my way, and I'll have Pim and Posy with me."

"And Sinder."

"No kidding? Better and better. Keep trying, and we'll track you down."

The connection faded, and Boon resisted the urge to pace. He was a big part of the reason Akira was in this mess, and he intended to get the kid out.

"Should have asked about Jacques." Boon caressed the facets of the second wardstone, which fit neatly into the crook of his arm. It responded with a note that harmonized with the song of the wardstone on his back. They seemed happy to be back together.

The ring of a third note was his first warning that one of the others had reached him.

Boon stood as Hisoka slipped into the open.

Almost immediately, a fourth note joined the chord. Pim and Sinder broke cover not far from him and swung their way. But Juuyu took the cake, gliding in low over the trees, fiery feathers dusting the ground as necessity drove him to use the road for a landing strip.

First thing, Boon offloaded his wardstones on Juuyu, whose weak warble was hard to interpret. "You got any lore to go with these little guys?"

"Enough to tremble for their safety. And there are four?" Juuyu rested his cheek against the glittering surface and crooned one of his lullabies.

Sinder tossed off a casual wave as he brought forward another wardstone, and Boon patted his shoulder in passing, but he was intent on reaching Pim, who stood back, looking scuffed and frazzled. But her tail lifted, and he could tell she was trying to give it just the right swing.

He grabbed her shoulders and searched her face. "Trouble?"

"I invited some." Her chin tipped to a haughty angle. "Hungry dragons are easily lured."

Boon snorted. "Where'd you run into my guys?"

"They washed up on the beach where I was … embroiled."

Sinder interjected, "Pim didn't need our help. We butted in!"

She rolled her eyes. "Their timing couldn't have been better. Juuyu made quick work of the ferals."

"Okay if I express my relief?"

Her brows knit, then arched. "Only if Sensei gets the same treatment."

"Deal." And before it could get awkward, he pulled her into a snug embrace. "Just reassuring myself. You look a mess, and that's messing with me."

"I'm *fine*."

"Yep. Definitely. But you've gotta know about a wolf's protective streak. Comes standard."

"Don't you dare coddle me."

"Wouldn't dream of it. Trust me, it could be worse. My dad, for instance. He's the last word in overprotectiveness." He set her at arm's length and asked, "My team gawking?"

"Completely agog."

"Expect more of that in the near future. Lots more." Boon grabbed her hand and dropped three beads into her palm. Then spun on his heel to keep his word. "C'mere, Posy!"

Pim slowly and carefully added the new acquisitions to her bracelet. It gave her the chance to watch Boon interact with his actual team.

Sinder, the one with the latest tech.

Juuyu, the one with a killer instinct.

Boon, the elite tracker. And leader.

She was intensely curious who else might be in a group assembled by Hisoka Twineshaft. Thanks to Sinder, she had names, but he'd been a little more focused on coaching her through the basics of resisting dragon sway.

Something about the way Boon singled her out and held her ... well, it shouldn't have surprised her. Wolves were as honest as they came, so it wouldn't even occur to him to hide their connection from others. Pim supposed she was still uneasy with his claim on her, but he showed no hesitation.

Like she wasn't imposing.

Like Pim was his to mentor, his to protect ... his.

And somehow, Boon was handling all this in a way that didn't put her back up. She liked him. She trusted him. And she could already tell that she'd end up loving him with all the ferocity for which felines were famous. Except that she could now consider it wolvish loyalty.

Boonmar-fen Elderbough was hers to respect, hers to challenge ... hers.

He turned slightly from the group, tail lifting a little higher as he beckoned for her with a casual jerk of his chin.

Hisoka was saying, "I agree with Juuyu. Entrust these wardstones to the tributes for transport. Shall we secure them at

Stately House? I'd like Michael to have a look."

"We got enough tributes to go around?" Boon asked.

"Plenty," assured Sinder. "You can even have your pick of dexes if you want, so you can keep tabs on everyone."

"That'd do nicely." Turning to Pim, Boon said, "Inti chimed in a bit ago. You catch any of that?"

"No. Tell me." She hadn't meant to make it sound like an order.

"Yes'm." A smile briefly creased the corners of his eyes. "Akira got separated from the group. At least, that's the *latest* hitch."

Sinder raised a hand. "Jacques is missing. And there are imps and crossers to rescue."

Hisoka calmly pointed up. "Did anyone else notice the sky?"

The sun vanished as if on cue, and Pim hissed softly. Clouds writhed around the barrier, churning into little whirlwinds that brought tentacles to mind. They seemed to be grappling with the barrier, which bowed and buckled.

Sinder whistled. "Okay, if that doesn't evoke doomsday, I don't know what would."

"Wind imps," Pim murmured. "Futari said the winds had abandoned this place."

"Yeah, well … they're back," said Sinder. "And they're pissed."

Boon asked, "Anchor still first on our priority list?"

Juuyu hummed. "It is easier to track the known than the unknown."

Everyone looked to Hisoka, who simply stood there, stroking Patter's hair.

When he didn't contribute further, Boon took charge again. "Juuyu and Sinder, take the wardstones. We think they're tuned to the anchor, so maybe they'll lead you to it. I need to get to Akira.

My fault the kid's here. Say, Posy ... want to see if you can track down Jacques? And Pim ... what's your priority?"

"Elara," she blurted. "I want to find Elara. Next. *Now*."

"You know ...? Same. Pim and I will look for Akira, then see if we can connect with Inti, Elara, and ... seems like there's a couple of felines with them. Males. Anybody know what's up with that?"

"I got nothing." Sinder took the remaining wardstone from Hisoka, and without another word, the partners disappeared into the jungle.

Boon offered Pim her shirt back, and she buttoned into it. To Hisoka, he said, "We're going on ahead."

She kept pace with him, running along the road. "Did he seem out of it to you?"

"A bit. But I wouldn't worry. Posy has a gift for showing up in the right place at the right time."

Pim believed it.

"Mind if we run? As in ... hard?" Boon indicated the road. "I want to catch up to our people before they get themselves cornered or caught."

"Go," she urged.

She kept up. Barely.

But then Boon drew up short. "Quick lesson for running with wolves."

Did they really have time for this?

Even if they didn't, he went right on.

"Don't follow directly behind. Shoot for a little back and a little to one side or the other. Range a little." His hand described a weaving motion. "Keep your senses keen for side trails or details that reveal more about our quarry. If your leader's head is down because their nose is to the trail, keep your head up. Because it's easy to get … well, it's sort of like tunnel vision, but with scent. So we run together, and each position has a role to play. The more wolves in the party, the more specific their roles."

"There are only two of us."

"That means I'm offense, and you're defense. I run straight on, and you make certain I don't blunder into an ambush or miss a double-back."

"I can do that."

Boon took her word for it and ran on.

Pim followed, this time with purpose.

Someone had left the laboratory door propped. As they eased through the empty reception area, Pim quietly asked, "If this is where the dragon's going to be, why didn't Juuyu come with us?"

"His first obligation really is to those wardstones. Tributes operate under their own set of rules, and I'm pretty sure imps get the highest priority. And … he trusts me to deal with the dragon."

"Are you impervious to sway?"

"I am." He tapped his scarred cheek. "And thanks to this, I'm probably also immune to Kodoku's poison. Do me a favor and use me as a shield if he gets testy. Or … you know … put him down in a way that keeps his claws immobilized."

"I can do that."

Boon murmured, "That's my girl."

Like he'd expected no less.

She decided that Adoona-soh had raised him right.

While he prowled the perimeter, she slipped into investigator mode. "These are business hours. Why is this building empty?"

"A lot of people left in a hurry." Boon circled back to the entrance, then raised a hand. "Stay put. Ten seconds."

He left her there.

She'd counted to eight when he skidded back to her side.

"Employee housing is right around the bend. They're all on lockdown until someone gives them the all clear. Just as well, given the storm that's looking for a way in." Boon bared his teeth and drew in air, growled, then sighed. "Elara went *this* way with Inti, Akira, and the felines. But ... Jacques went *that* way. And he was alone. With a dragon."

"Didn't you say that Akira is your responsibility?"

"Yeah. But he and Jacques are both here because of me."

Pim asked, "Are they like ... packmates?"

"Not in any official way, but we have a bunch of people in common." Gazing off in the direction he'd indicated, Boon said, "Jacques is ... huh. It's beyond my abilities to explain Jacques to anyone, but I will say this. I trust the guy. And so does Argent Mettlebright, or he wouldn't be here."

Pim asked, "What is it you're not saying?"

"Jacques was nervous, and that makes me nervous."

She took a receptive posture.

With a grateful glance, Boon took off in Jacques' direction.

She followed, staying a little behind and a little to one side. Between Akira's descriptions and Boon's decisions, Pim's curiosity with regards to Jacques Smythe continued to increase.

Gradually, Boon shed caution. There really wasn't anyone in this part of the building, so they walked at an easy pace through shabbily sterile halls.

"It doesn't feel like a trap," she murmured.

"Nope."

"I hope he's all right."

"Same."

"Elara, too."

"No doubt."

She asked, "What if something's happened?"

"Then we'll turn the tables." Boon sounded completely relaxed. "And it's only been a day, more or less. How much trouble could she get into?"

"Is that a challenge? Because it sounds like a challenge I'd take."

"Contrary sort, are you? That'll keep things interesting."

Pim had to ask. "You don't mind?"

"That you have a personality? Most folks do." He took a turning without any hesitation.

"I mean … you don't regret the bond?"

"Why bother? Not my style to look back and wonder." Boon paused and gave her a searching look. "Are *you* regretting the bond?"

She shook her head. "You're good at reassuring me that everything will work out."

He gave her a funny look. "Did I say something like that?"

"It's more along the lines of your attitude, your outlook."

"I'm just doing the best I can with what I've got."

Pim asked, "Do you think it's … fate?"

"Could be. If you're looking for fancy labels, I know a guy who'd call this 'a confluence of destinies.'" He strolled on, checked his stride, backtracked a few steps, and jerked a thumb at what looked like an ordinary apartment door.

Both of them listened intently.

They traded a look, and Boon shrugged, then knocked.

To Pim's surprise, she caught the sound of light steps, and a tentative voice asked, "Who's there?"

"The name's Boon. Is Jacques Smythe with you?"

The door opened a crack, and red eyes peered through, sizing them up.

"Hey, there, kid," said Boon. "Any chance you recently met your Uncle Jackie?"

"I mighta."

"He here?"

The boy let the door swing farther open. "He was gone when I woke up."

Pim took in details. Dragon crosser. Could be Kodoku's or even Futari's child, based on coloring, except this boy's accent was pure Boston. What was an American kid doing in the tropics? The handkerchief he clutched in one hand was embroidered with two ginkgo leaves and the initials **JS**. And when he eased into the open, she tallied up signs of malnutrition and neglect.

Boon crouched before him, palms on offer, and that's when the kid sized up Pim.

"Aren't you that detective lady?" he demanded.

"Yes." She couldn't help smiling. "You watch *Pure Instinct*?"

"Used to, yeah. We had a TV at the enclave." He looked between them. "You're wolves, aren'tcha?"

"We are. You got a name, kid?"

"Sibley."

"Any idea where Jacques is?"

The boy hesitated. "Are you the rescuers he talked about?"

"Sure are. Well, more like the advance team. I'm a tracker."

The boy hummed in a skeptical way.

Pim offered her hand. "Sibley, will you come with us? We can keep you safe, and you can help us find your uncle."

He reached for her, then twitched his hand back. "You maybe better not touch me. Poison claws. Sometimes I can't help it."

"You're all mine, then." And Boon pivoted, offering his back. "Climb on. Thanks to a confluence of destinies, I've been inoculated against your sort of dangerous."

"What's confluence?"

"Kinda like when two paths cross. Makes for meeting someone new."

"That's a good world. Hey. You think I'm dangerous?" This seemed to please the boy.

"Sure. How about me? Do I seem dangerous?"

"Kinda, I guess." Sibley set one small hand against Boon's broad back. "You're really here to help us?"

"Yep."

"Then ... I'll go with you. On one condition."

40

BROKEN SILENCE

Hisoka didn't know what to do.

Well, yes, he knew he was meant to be searching for Jacques. But only because Boon had assigned the task to him. The wolf was no doubt aware that Jacques was Hisoka's preferred companion whenever he retreated to Stately House for sleep. And to a wolf's way of thinking, sleep was sacred. And binding. So of course Hisoka would want to locate Jacques.

In all of Hisoka's long experience, his relationship with Jacques Smythe was unusual in that it was entirely one-sided. Jacques gained nothing from his long days abed, watching over Hisoka. The man expected nothing more than a continuation of their little routine. It had intrigued Hisoka at first. Now, he relied upon it.

Jacques was the perfect balance of unflappable, irreverent, and indulgent. There were no pedestals, no liberties, and no questions. They weren't exactly friends. When asked, Jacques had settled on a term that suited them nicely: intimate acquaintances. Or simply … *intimates.*

Hisoka should go to him.

He *would* go to him.

But just now, when everyone had looked to Hisoka for direction, he hadn't known what to do. And in that moment, Hisoka had realized something terrifyingly important. He'd always had a little extra insight thanks to Novi. Their shared vow had influenced Hisoka's choices, which had in turn changed the world. But Nemi was here. And once Novi took her back, their vow would be fulfilled. His star would be gone for good, taking all his prompts and insights into the distant skies, leaving Hisoka to lead the clans alone.

And he didn't know what to do.

"Are you listening? Can you hear?"

Novi's voice was such a welcome surprise, Hisoka nearly shouted. "I hear you!"

Patter gave a concerned peep.

"Have you found her?"

"Not yet, no. But we will." Heart heavy, he added, "I have cause to fear that she's been mishandled. The dragon here has been crossbreeding impressions."

"I will not think less of her if she has become a mother."

"Me, either." He peered upward. "Are you near?"

"I promised Boonmar-fen Elderbough to remain at a safe distance."

A pang of fear lanced through Hisoka's heart. "Stay back, please. Even if the barrier has weakened enough for us to talk, it's still a trap. All within its bounds cannot fly."

"I do not wish to descend."

"I'd be happier if you were able carry your sister aloft."

"May it be soon." And after a few beats, he confessed, *"The wait grows both shorter and longer."*

"It does." And all at once, Hisoka knew what to do. Well, he didn't *know,* but the idea seemed good. "Novi, can you get word to Paltry? Discreetly?"

"The dex at Moonglade Tearoom?"

"Yes. He has been searching for a lost moonbeam, and I think she may be here."

"May I bring him?" He cautioned, *"It would mean betraying our secret."*

"Our vow doesn't mean more than his vow. He should be here." Hisoka urged, "Do it swiftly."

"I will not tarry."

And with that, Novi was gone.

Patter ventured, "Sen?"

He smiled for the little crosser. "I shall see you safely into your family's keeping. Now, shall we see if we can be of use to anyone else?"

With half an eye on the barrier, Hisoka stayed on the road.

Reaching up to pat Hisoka's cheek, Patter repeated, "Sen?"

"Would you like to know my secret?" Hisoka had never entrusted it to anyone. Not even Michael. "Will you hear me out?"

The child crooned softly, as if he were picking up on Hisoka's sadness.

Maybe this recitation wouldn't count as breaking his silence, since he doubted Patter would grasp much, let alone repeat it to another soul. But Hisoka wanted to unburden himself. He could bury the secret here, in the place where they'd find Nemi. And maybe … well, maybe both of them would be free.

"Mine is an old story. Not the oldest. I'm not one of the eldermost. But my mother *is*, and she has a part of one of our people's oldest stories. In a small way, so do I."

Patter's gaze was flatteringly rapt.

This time, Hisoka's smile came a little more easily, and he lapsed into the sing-song style of a tale-bringer. "It's not precisely true to say I was born in a grove, but my birthplace became the center of one. My mother was one of the ten who fought and freed themselves from the harem of a tyrant, only to nearly lose her life during their escape. She was one of the ten who met an angel along the way and received a golden seed from Soriel's hand."

Hisoka gave Patter a solemn wink. "Neither of us was conceived in the usual way."

Patter's gaze flitted to the surrounding trees, and Hisoka stopped to listen. When the little crosser offered a small *peep*, Hisoka carried on along the road.

"My twin sister and I were among the first generation of tree-kin, and our birthplace became one of the Eldermost Groves." Hisoka cleared his throat. "I should clarify, since many do misunderstand. When I say *twin*, I do not refer to the golden seed an infant carries into the world. I am referring to a fraternal twin. My sister Hoshiko and I were born together, and according to my mother, she is the one who carried the seed."

This part had always been difficult for him.

"I have no proof, and I have reason to be grateful, but … I have always believed that Mother lied. You see, the lady mistresses have always given preference to their daughters. Hiroki called me

Brother, but it was Hoshiko who planted and tended and shared Hiroki's years. She also shared her fate."

Hisoka's steps slowed. "When the world was younger, and Impressions still visited the clans, humans began to believe that the Old Groves held the secret to everlasting life. There were those who wanted to steal a tree's blessing for themselves. And there were those who wanted to prevent anyone else from laying claim to it. Whole forests were razed and set ablaze."

Patter whimpered.

"Yes, it was a terrible time." Hisoka slipped into the shadows, for the laboratory roof had come into view. "I was away when it happened. Novi and I had gone off together because we wanted to see more of the world. We returned to a scene of utter desolation. My mother railed against me for not being there to defend Hoshiko and Hiroki."

Her bitter words at that time had added weight to Hisoka's suspicions. In her grief, Mother had twisted things around so that Hoshiko's death was his fault.

"My sister died in my place. And during the grove's destruction, Hoshiko's best-loved person, a star who often came to rest in Hiroki's branches, did all she could to save them. Nemi. She was there. Survivors confirmed seeing her. Yet nobody knows what happened to her. Or at the very least, they couldn't recall." He shook his head. "This was during a time when clans kept their own secrets. I never imagined that a dragon might be involved."

Hisoka reached one of the laboratory walls and stood for a while, studying the sigilcraft that laced its walls. All of it looked to be designed to keep things in, rather than out.

In a low voice, Hisoka wearily asked, "During the early days, when I was working to unite the clans in preparation for the Emergence, were Nona and Senna smiling behind their hands, knowing that my sister's beloved was languishing in a trap of their making?"

Patter reached up, wrapping small arms around Hisoka's neck.

"I should have warned you it was a sad story." Bowing his head, he rubbed his cheek against the boy's and sighed. "I'm not even sure we'll have a happy ending. But the waiting and wondering are over, and that's something, I suppose."

"Pardon me."

Hisoka was already crouched, ready to spring away, before he spotted the speaker. With a fresh pang of regret, he hurried forward. "Linlu," he groaned. "What's happened to you?"

With a whispery laugh the moth clansman submitted to a brief inspection and a much longer embrace, which he had to share with Patter. When Hisoka stepped back, Linlu summoned up traces of formality. "Hisoka Twineshaft. This way, please."

He frowned. "Has someone sent for me?"

Linlu's expression gentled. "I was given to understand that you were sent to her."

He was going to where Nemi was. Finally. Hisoka followed Linlu in a state of disarray that was so unlike his usual persona, he barely recognized himself. It wasn't that he was feeling particularly nostalgic or vengeful or destined. Just tired and uncertain and vaguely embarrassed that it had taken him this long to keep one single promise.

Despite popular opinion, Hisoka wasn't all-seeing, all-knowing, or all-powerful. Inspiring so much trust was certainly useful, but he wondered if people would be as quick to follow his lead if they knew that the only reason he showed so little doubt was because he had more experience hiding it.

Humans were especially prone to sweeping assumptions. Most never realized the size of the staff he retained to pull off most of the work they seemed to think he managed singlehandedly.

Right now, he was feeling wretchedly singlehanded.

He wasn't, of course. Even here, without his friends, assistants, and all the ranks of scribes and diplomats who helped him navigate the necessities of his office, he needed Linlu Dimityblest to lead him by the hand.

As if sensing his thoughts, Linlu turned, gaze soft as he showed his palm. It was likely to pull Hisoka past one of the barriers they faced, no doubt the moth clansman's own handiwork, but ... after they were through, neither of them let go.

41

STORMFALL

A security door.

A narrow, windowless hall.

A warded panel.

"She is here," Linlu murmured, pausing outside the door. "Descended, of course. Long since. Senna dropped her on Kodoku's sire's doormat like a cat with a prize to impress his lady mistress. Ah, do pardon the analogy."

"It's fitting," Hisoka conceded.

With a small squeeze, Linlu released his hand, pressed his palms to the sigil-laced panel, and slid it aside. He gestured for Hisoka to precede him.

Stepping through, he could only stand and stare.

The room was small, cramped, and barren of comforts, yet he felt as if he'd entered an ancient treasure room. Filling most of the space was a softly-glowing mass. The sheen brought crystal to mind, yet a scent filled the air—organic, resinous, captivating.

"What is this?"

"She wove for herself a covering. It is a little like a chrysalis," said Linlu. "Sigilcraft and stardust, for her part. Tree sap and green sand, which Dayith smuggled in after … well, after. She has long been as you see her now, and so Kodoku cannot use her for anything else. Not anymore."

Hisoka rested his hand on the formation, which definitely glowed from within. The whole thing was etched with sigilcraft—some draconic, some vulpine.

"Nemi wrested many small victories, this being the finest. Her resistance thwarted Kodoku's plans. This room fouls his mood, so he keeps his door barred." Linlu indicated an armored hatch that looked as if it belonged on a nuclear reactor.

Peering past the chrysalis's uneven surface, Hisoka could make out the softly glowing profile at its heart. She was facing the door. Wait, no. Moving further around the room, he was certain he'd found a second profile, this one tipped toward the ceiling as if searching for the sky. He wasn't seeing double.

"She's not alone?"

"Nemi has a child. They share the same dream." Linlu moved to his side. "She will relinquish that life to no other."

Hisoka swayed where he stood. "Do you mean me?"

"Stars know many things. Nemi knew you would find her."

Again, Hisoka rested his palms against the mass that held her, a star trapped in amber. How was he supposed to get her—and her child—free? He was trying to read the runes, to see if he could unmake them, when the faintest of melodies touched his soul.

"She's singing …!"

"Stars do." Linlu's smile was sad. "She is comforting the children. She is the lullaby they listen for."

Recognition and realization clapped together with the force of a peal of thunder. "Nemi is the anchor."

"She is."

"She sings for the wardstones?"

"Yes. They are Dayith's children. And the others, too, hear her voice in their long days and in their fleeting dreams." Linlu said, "Set her free, and her voice will join the culminating song."

That was the plan.

But … how?

Hisoka tentatively pushed and pulled at the formation. He scratched and hit and even kicked it once. All without response. Looking to Linlu for help, he only received a small headshake. And so Hisoka rested his forehead against the chrysalis and said, "Nemi, I'm here. Novi and I found you. I'm sorry it took us so long."

The encasement shuddered.

Hisoka pressed closer. "Nemi?"

A single, keening note vibrated from within, building strength. He couldn't bring himself to step back. Was she suffering? Was she begging for help? Frustration growled up from his soul, and he pushed harder.

All at once, as if by some trick, the chrysalis crumbled. Beginning at the top, it turned into soft green sand that hissed as it sheeted to the floor. The two people who'd found sanctuary at its center teetered together, then slumped into Hisoka's waiting arms.

Nemi and her child were tangled in so much pale hair, they

were inextricable, so he hefted them both, quick-stepping to the corner and sinking to a seat against the wall.

Linlu remained where he was, knee-deep in glittering sand, looking up at the ceiling. "That did it," he whispered. "Can you hear them?"

While Hisoka wasn't sure what the moth clansman meant, there was plenty to hear. There was a building roar and a wordless shout and the shattering of glass somewhere nearby as the entire building rocked on its foundation.

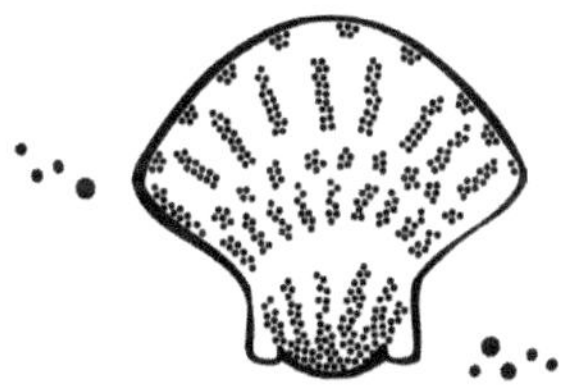

Boon eased into a lope, letting Sibley point the way along empty halls. Scents weren't much help, so he didn't realize they'd reached their destination until he pulled up short in front of a large, square door plastered with black and yellow warning labels.

Pim inspected the keypad by the door.

"What's in here, kid?" asked Boon.

"Home sweet home for the likes of me." Sibley slid from his shoulders and tapped in the code. There was a click and a chirp, and the boy grabbed the handle, leaning back with all his weight.

Pim's nose was twitching when she grabbed hold and helped pull, and the look she cut his way was somewhat dazed.

His own tail puffed. "Aww, hell. They keep you in cages?"

"For our own good," Sibley said, rolling his eyes. He ran down the row, tripping locks.

Pim glided after him, but she was stumped because every cage required a code. So she dropped into a crouch beside the door, her hands tucked behind her back. A pointedly peaceful posture.

Boon remarked, "This place isn't exactly secure if you know all the codes."

"Locks aren't what keep us here. If anyone acts out, Kodoku picks his least favorite, and they suffer." Sibley shot him a surly look. "That's why *I'm* the least favorite."

"You're protecting them," Pim said admiringly.

The boy turned bashful and busied himself organizing the captives. Several were dragon crossers. Others were much harder to pinpoint. Like the little girl with antennae who shone with a light all her own. And a boy whose inheritances included both hooves and scales.

Over and over, Pim offered her name, a smile, and promises of safety.

Turning his way, she asked, "Where do we take them?"

Boon appreciated the trust, but he didn't have any answers.

That's when all hell broke loose and thundered against the building. The lights flickered once and went out. A sound rose, shrill and angry, and with an earsplitting groan, part of the roof lifted, letting in a wind that blew papers into a small tornado and rattled equipment to the floor with a clatter and crash.

Boon wondered if the kids would be safer in their cages, but there was no way he'd ask it. Instead, he shifted into truest form, sheltering them from falling debris by standing over them.

It was confusing, this sudden storm, but the kids didn't make a peep. And that was confusing in its own right. But then, a gust of wind buffeted him and … hell and damn, the thing petted him.

"Wind imps!" exclaimed Pim.

She wasn't wrong. And then she was hovering a handsbreadth from his muzzle. "They've given us back the sky!"

Inti appeared at the ragged gap between roof and wall, holding out both arms. "Quick, quick, quicker! Bring them up. Bring them out. Into the garden. The trees will hide them!"

One of the toms Boon had caught a whiff of earlier dropped through the gap and took a receptive stance. Pim immediately set him to work, helping her ferry the children up to where Inti and the other tom waited. It was all very efficient. Even Juuyu would have approved.

Boon simply stayed where he was, giving shelter to those waiting their turn. But a fresh scent teased at him. From where? He peered around the topsy turvy room. Beyond the double row of cages, on the far wall, a door had buckled in its frame, creating a gap. A wolf's senses were keener in truest form, so the scent he was catching was faint, distant. But it was one he'd been looking for. Boon would have sworn the winds were bringing it to him.

"That's all of them," Pim called.

He hadn't noticed. Shifting back into speaking form, Boon tugged at his ponytail.

She quietly asked, "Why is your tail still?"

"I'm trying not to react," he gruffly admitted. "I smell blood. It's Akira's."

Pim slowly eased into a cooperative stance—neither dominant nor submissive—meaning she wanted an equal share in what was to come. "You get to him. I'll go to Elara."

"That works." An instant later, he was wrenching the warped door from its hinges.

Blood. Boon wasn't imagining it. He stumbled into a run, only to pass the door he needed. Reining himself in, he rattled the handle. Locked. And there was another of those keypads, which made him wish he'd kept Sibley with him.

He drove his fist into the center of the door.

The small dent wasn't worth the smarting in his knuckles.

With a faint click, the door eased open. "A wolf?"

Quickly showing his hands, he declared himself. "Boonmar-fen Elderbough. Is Akira here?"

"I'm afraid so." The door opened further. "I was just patching him up."

He drew a deep breath, trying to figure out why the guy had no scent. Then it clicked. Not no scent. The same scent. Or pretty darn close. "What're you? A brother?"

"His parent. Naoki Hajime."

From inside, Akira's voice carried. "Boon? I'm here. Dad, it's okay. Boon's a friend."

Naoki waved him inside.

Ducking through the door, Boon scanned the crystal-lit operating theater and spied Akira strapped to a table. "What happened here?"

"Kodoku cut into him, and he wasn't terribly gentle." Naoki clenched shaking hands. "It took longer than I like to make sure no lasting harm's been done."

Boon ripped the straps from Akira's ankles and wrists, growling with enough volume to rattle the trays of surgical implements. "Where is he? Is he still here?" Because with a dragon, you were wise to be cautious.

Naoki shook his head. "Futari, his daughter, came and called him away."

Akira added, "He left with her. Said he'd be right back."

"How long ago?"

"Not very long." Naoki gestured toward the ceiling. "Just before all the noise."

Boon found the incision, now stitched shut, and sniffed worriedly. As far as he could tell, there wasn't any poison in the wound. Over the noise of his own growling, he realized that Akira was talking, his voice a steady flow.

"Calm down, Boon. I'm fine. It's all right. I'm okay." A cold hand found his cheek. "Boon, listen to me. Come on … please? I know there was some blood, but my dad stitched me up."

Their gazes locked.

Akira smiled. "Hey. Thanks for finding me."

Needing to collect himself, Boon gathered the man into his arms and sat on the floor. "I'm sorry, kid. I'm so sorry."

"Not your fault," Akira assured, leaning into him.

Boon begged to differ. "This whole mess …!"

"Was the *best* thing that could have happened. This was *necessary*." He tipped his head back, gaze searching. "This man is my dad. Or ... well, my parent. I didn't even know I still had parents!"

Boon shot another look at Naoki, who sighed. "It is a *long* story."

"Let me up," Akira urged.

"You're hurt," he grumbled. "And ... where are your clothes?"

"Here." Naoki hurried to collect a tidy pile of pastels.

"Come on," Akira coaxed, giving Boon a firm push. "It hurts some, but it'll heal. Let me up. There's something important. He left it, didn't he?"

"Yes." Naoki handed Akira a shirt, then explained, "Kodoku found his seed."

"Your what now?" Boon asked, helping him find his feet.

Akira chuckled. "Turns out I'm tree-kin." He tottered over to a counter.

Boon followed and spied it in a little glass dish—a blood-streaked golden seed.

"Where's Suuzu's necklace?" Akira muttered fretfully.

Naoki brought over the very necklace Boon had helped create, the very reason Akira owed him the favor that had brought him here. New items had been added over the intervening years, including a slim metal column.

"Hope it fits," Akira mumbled, fiddling with the reliquary's catch.

"Want help?" offered Boon.

"Yeah. My hands are shaking too much. I might be in shock, but ... look. This is real. I have a seed." With an achingly sweet smile, Akira said, "That horrible dragon found my twin."

Boon located the catch. It was a close fit, but the seed slid into the reliquary. Making sure it was secure, he looped the necklace over Akira's head … and followed it up with the minty green shirt he seemed to have forgotten he was holding. "Tree-kin, huh? Does Suuzu know? Or Juuyu, for that matter. He's close enough to call on."

"They know about *me*. Not this, though. A seed. I can't wait to tell Suuzu." He rested his hand over his treasure. But then his happiness fell away, and he tensely asked, "Is Jacques okay?"

42

FLOURISH FLYING

Argent knew he should attack this problem dispassionately, but there were too many ways this was personal. So Hisoka and the rest were just going to have to settle for a passionate attack.

Spokesperson Mettlebright was away from work without notice. Very rude. He'd crossed several international boundary lines without permission. Couldn't be helped. He'd annoyed Salali Fullstash by letting himself into Wardenclave. Ginkgo would have to smooth that one over. And Argent regretted nothing. So far.

Tails flying, reservoir brimming, he ran at speeds the Amaranthine Council would consider impolite, if not impolitic. Humanity might yet balk if they understood the full extent of the clans' strength. Argent would have to apologize to Hisoka. As soon as this mad dash reunited them.

To some, it might look as if Argent was being pursued by the storm he'd gathered. In truth, he was pulling the winds in his wake, showing them the way, even as it was shown to him.

Eri had told him how it would be.

Help from on high, like answers to prayer.

Even now, guiding stars winked ahead of Argent. Unable to catch them and confirm his suspicions, he'd contented himself with numbering them. According to most lore, there were seven. In a few tales, there were ten. But old stories rarely told the whole story.

Driving ever onward, he wondered what his bondmate would think when he told her he'd seen twelve. As far as he was concerned, she warranted an introduction. Tsumiko believed in them more than most. And trusted them as she trusted the Maker.

In a sense, he was acting on his bondmate's behalf. While she hadn't placed any demands on him, her hopes were transparent, and her faith in his ability to bring them to pass *might* have been daunting … if he were any less capable.

She wished him to succeed, and so he would.

Savior.

Protector.

Patron saint.

Parent.

Granted, there were more pleasurable ways to become a father, but this was satisfying in an entirely different sense. Any child he could rescue from Nona's and Senna's clutches amounted to an act of quiet revenge. Or perhaps recompense? As speaker for the fox clans, he carried a certain amount of responsibility for the Hightip sisters' actions.

Yet Tsumiko had asked him *not* to seek revenge.

Instead, he would seek the children.

Every child of the Rogue, no matter how wretched the circumstances of their begetting, was a precious life. Yet they'd been born bereft. Orphaned. Unwanted. Exploited.

Tsumiko wanted them. And now that Kyrie knew, he was urgently, tenaciously insistent. The boy could not, would not leave them be. They were his kindred. No, Kyrie counted them even dearer. He wanted Argent to find his brothers and sisters. And to bring them home.

Dragons fluted as Argent approached the island where the taskforce was quartered. Two pleasure barges? Lord Beckonthrall had gone above and beyond. And the Order of Spomenka had already arrived. Hallow seemed quite at home dividing and directing the assembled ranks. Argent almost felt bad for the strategist. The oncoming storm represented an unforeseen alliance, but it would also be a monumental distraction.

Welcoming notes changed to sharper alert whistles.

Argent switched to speaking form in order to alight on the sand. He was already beneath notice, for every eye was on Mikoto Reaver and the small allotment of Alpenglow healers stampeding into earshot.

"Raise barriers! Tzefira can only do so much to confine them!" warned Wardenclave's headman.

Wind whipped up, tearing at hair and clothing.

The dragon lords fanned outward, hands weaving, sigils blending with impressive delicacy. Argent had to wonder if their easy synchronization was a matter of long practice or a benefit of their familial bond. Lord Beckonthrall's entourage seemed to be composed entirely of his sons, dragons whose mothers were descended winds.

Trusting them to know what they were about, Argent strolled toward Merit, though his attention remained on the boiling sky. "I take it the island is there?"

"Directly under," confirmed Merit. "I assume this isn't a meteorological event?"

"Impressions."

"So many." He huffed and admitted, "I'm not surprised. I've been seeing stars all morning."

Argent scanned the sky. "Close enough to speak to?"

"No visitations, but I can hear them."

"Are their lyrics worth repeating?"

"Vague celebration about things foretold and things fulfilled." Merit spread his hands helplessly. "Even my grandsire says that a star makes the best sense in hindsight."

Argent put little stock in prophecy, but Tsumiko would want to know. "Take a note of anything that might interest my lady."

Merit favored him with a small smile. "I will. Gladly."

Beyond the dragons' newly formed barrier, the clouds spiraled in a dance that should have been impossible. This wasn't how nature behaved, and on some level, Argent grew wary. Every imp he'd met was gentle, generous, or both. But wasn't that the very same veneer the Amaranthine fostered with regards to humanity? What little he knew suggested that Impressions could be incredibly dangerous. Power on this scale was generally categorized as an act of God.

Argent wished Tsumiko could have seen this for herself. His first impulse was to tell Jacques to try to capture it on video for her. But then he noticed that Tenma Subaru was already doing so. He moved to the man's side. "Is that for Lilya's sake?"

"And Kyrie. And Ever." Tenma offered a small shrug. "I'm under strict orders never to leave any of them out."

Given that Kyrie was sure to show the clip to his mother—he always did—Argent was satisfied. He also added Tenma to the long list of people who mustn't be harmed. He was about to ask after Goh when Inti's excited chatter filled his mind.

"Clatter, batter, shatter!" And more softly, *"Inti can reach you, now."*

So the barrier was down.

A tiny corner of Argent's fury faded. *"So you survived?"*

"As ordered!" came the cheeky retort.

"Anything to prevent me from forcing my way in?"

"No, nyet, *and* non.*"* More wistfully, Inti asked, *"Take me home?"*

"You shall be brought," he vowed. *"The others?"*

Inti's report was highly abridged, and there were too many variables. Argent tried not to let it worry him that Inti hadn't been able to account for either Jacques or Akira.

Argent wanted to hurry things along, but first ... he needed to make certain that his claim was clear. Striding into the midst of the dragon lords, he addressed himself to Lord Beckonthrall. "While I acknowledge your superiority on many of the matters at hand, I will thank you to leave the crossers to me. Stately House claims them. Even and especially the dragon crossers." He stiffly added, "My son wishes to meet his siblings."

Lord Beckonthrall spared him a glance before his attention returned to the sky. "*You* brought this storm."

"Someone on the island requested it. I obliged them."

"Since when do winds answer to you?" There was no accusation in Beckonthrall's tone. He seemed genuinely curious. "Did you use the Junzi?"

"I did not. And they do not answer to me." Argent angled his head toward Mikoto Reaver. "His story is sure to interest you. Ask him for it later."

"So be it. Now. With regards to the crossers, the promises of Lapis Mossberne bind us. Those you seek to save will be safe. We yield to your claim. Yours and your lady's. Our business is with the barrier and with the dragon who cowers behind it."

"Have you sorted out who he is?"

Before Beckonthrall could answer, light streaked across the sky with all the haste of a comet. Argent had only seen it once before, and that had been on the sly. Hisoka never explained the corners he managed to cut during travel, and out of courtesy, Argent never asked. But … he'd managed a glimpse. Enough to suspect impish involvement.

The new arrival certainly wasn't Hisoka, and the star who'd brought him wasn't sticking around. Passengers barely dropped, the imp changed course, flying into the storm.

Merit rushed forward, exclaiming, "Paltry! How …?"

Ah. Argent knew the wolf in a passing sort of way. Jacques was fond of his teahouse, which was situated in the neighborhood below Kikusawa Shrine. He was a dex, and he'd forged ties with a curious companion. Churlish, a descended moonbeam, apparently boasted a skill with pastries that rivaled his own. Or so Jacques claimed.

"Why on earth did you bring Churlish into this muddle?" exclaimed Merit.

Waving aside the question with an impatient flick, Paltry demanded, "Where are they? Which of them is here? Or is it all three? Doku? Kodoku? Shisoku?"

Argent rocked back on his heels. Where had Paltry heard these names? Those who'd had contact with Hajime and his information were few ... and sworn to secrecy. Yet Paltry reeled off the names like one who'd always known them.

The moonbeam pulled at Paltry's sleeve and spoke for himself. "Where is Seela?"

Merit pointed wordlessly to the storm.

Paltry drew his sword, scooped up his moonbeam, and took to the sky. Wonderful. A loose cannon.

Just then, someone lightly inquired, "Have all the players assembled, then?"

Argent flicked a look at the speaker, who hadn't been there a moment before. He was from a dragon clan, though Argent didn't recognize his crest. And unless he missed his guess, he numbered among the Broken.

"Was that Paltry and Churlish, just now?" he pressed.

"Sway doesn't work on me."

"Apologies, Lord Mettlebright. I sometimes forget myself in

my excitement." His smile wasn't anywhere close to apologetic. "Well? Do tell!"

"Yes, they were here." Argent's guard was up. "How did you arrive?"

"In the usual way." Fingers fluttered vaguely at the sky. They were unadorned by jewels, a rarity among dragons. But heavy bangles weighed at his wrists. Confirmation.

"You cannot fly."

"Not unaided." With a small smile, he asked, "Do you find me suspicious?"

"Increasingly so. Why are you here?"

"Shall we call it a confluence of destiny? This epic has taken its sweet time crescendoing. I am certain its finale will prove worthy of ballads."

The pause turned awkward, for Argent was waiting for a *sensible* response.

With a small laugh, the dragon said, "I'm a bard, you see. Maybe you've heard of me?"

"Clearly *not*. However ...."

Something had caught Argent's eye, and he stepped into the dragon's personal space. Yes, there was a faint shimmer, slyly dropped upon the bard's cheek. The sign of an Impression's regard. Recent events had conspired. He was getting very good at spotting even the subtlest of marks.

Argent quietly inquired, "Which of the gathered stars is yours?"

"Clever fox. I do have a friend just there." He swept a hand toward the east, where one of the winking lights shone against the blue. "And if his good opinion doesn't secure yours, then I will mention that Paltry and Churlish *adore* me. And once upon a time, I was a chronicler of the Moon, mentor to a saint, and ... well, lighter on my feet."

"A bard ...?" Argent had only just begun paying attention to such things, since the fairly recent addition of a Song Circle to the estate.

The dragon held out a hand as if hoping Argent would kiss it. "Opulence Windlore, known the world over as Opal the Sage."

43

SUMMONED

Sinder had to jog to keep up with Juuyu's lengthening stride. "What *was* that? Do you know what that was?"

"I can only speculate."

"I'll take it."

"There is no longer a need to locate the anchor. One of the others must have found it."

"Yeah. Barrier's down," Sinder added, scanning the sky. "How worried should I be?"

"You are a dragon," Juuyu reasoned. "Woo the wind long enough for me to deal with this."

"Not sure I want to call that much trouble down on our heads." Hugging the two wardstones he carried, he muttered, "Talk about flirting with disaster."

They'd reached a low stone wall reinforced with sigilcraft. Through the faint shimmer of a fairly standard barrier, Sinder could see a lawn that belonged on a golf course and fussy little houses and gazebos, one under every tree.

Setting down his two wardstones, Juuyu set to work dismantling runes. "I want to secure the trees."

"Let's do that, yeah." It made total sense that Juuyu's first priority would be the trees that'd end up in his keeping. "Tribute shortlist."

"Hmm." The barrier wavered, and Juuyu pushed a hand through. Leaping lightly onto the wall, he remarked, "Flight is restored."

"Oh. Handy." But there was a sound in his head. "Your ears still ringing?"

"No." From the other side of the wall, Juuyu beckoned. "Give me the stones."

Sinder offloaded his own, then reached for the two on the ground. But all the while, he was trying to place the source of the noise he was picking up. Was it the wardstones? The wind? He peered up into the eye of the storm. Gusts puffed against him in little bids for attention, but the storm had bypassed the garden ... and *not* because there was a measly barrier between them and it.

"They're avoiding this place."

"Yes." Juuyu pointed. "These winds have a shepherd."

A pair of horses reeled through the sky, each with a rider. "Isn't that ...?"

But there was a sort of *pop* inside Sinder's mind, and the previous buildup of tension released like pressure on the inner ear. A voice rumbled its way into that space like a gentle avalanche.

"Sinder Stonecairn."

"This is he. Who's calling, please?"

From his side of the wall, Juuyu shot him a quizzical look.

"You are needed. Can you follow my voice?"

Good question. Sinder turned in place. "Which way am I supposed to … oh." There was a definite pull. He'd never experienced the like, but that was happening a lot today. "Yeah. I have a bearing."

"Hurry. He needs you."

"Who does?" Sinder pried. "If I knew who …?"

"Jacques Smythe."

Sinder swore and shoved the last wardstone into Juuyu's hands. "Gotta fly. I've got a line on Jacques."

Juuyu frowned. "Should you risk the sky?"

"It'll be fine. Probably. I mean, like you said, I'm a dragon."

While Sinder didn't want to woo any wind in a permanent sense, he quickly realized that a little help would be welcome. So he sang. Snatches at first, since it was hard to catch his breath. But the winds noticed and adjusted their courses, giving him space, buoying his wings. Because they wanted to hear more.

He sang a nonsense song. One of the silly ones his father had taught him. It was supposed to invite winds closer without binding them. Up until now, Sinder had thought that explanation was nonsense, too. But as his voice gained strength, his companions multiplied.

"Anyone see anything?" he muttered, wheeling when his course took him out over the water. He swung back around, scanning the jungle. How was he supposed to find anything out here?

As soon as he was back over the trees, that inner compass tugged the other way. He'd overshot again. Had there been a boat? Was Jacques in the water? Maybe the shore.

Slipping free of the clinging winds, Sinder dropped into the sea and reoriented himself. Jacques must be stranded on the beach. He surfaced and swam, calling out, "Nearly there."

"We are here."

The cove was tiny, well-hidden, and thick with a scent that had Sinder breathing more deeply. Recognizing the signs, he grumbled, "It *would* have to be a tree."

Green light flashed, and there was a racket like too many windchimes. Then Sinder was sure he was in the right place because he could almost ... sorta ... weirdly *feel* that Jacques was there. Wading to shore, he cast an uneasy look at the jangling tree overhead, but he spied Jacques and hurried forward, only to come up short.

"You ... you're the guy who called?" Sinder ventured.

Jacques was clinging to a ... huh.

Going out on a limb, Sinder ventured, "Mountain clan?"

With a quirk of his lips, the imp eased Jacques away from his body so that Sinder could take him. The man was all flopping limbs and dishevelment. Lowering him to the sand, Sinder patted his cheek. "You okay, Jacques?"

Brown eyes rolled slightly before finding focus. "I know you," he drawled.

"Are you pollinated?" He shot an accusing look at the bizarre tree that jangled overhead.

All at once, there was a young male kneeling beside him, an ashen beauty who glittered like a trove. He touched Jacques' face, then touched Sinder's.

"Totally a tree."

"Half," the imp cheerfully corrected.

"What did you do to Jacques?"

"We waited for him. For a long, long time, we waited." The tree's eyes glittered like faceted gemstones. "He is ours, but he is yours?"

Sinder had no clue what was going on, but he nodded. "I'm a friend."

"We *love* him."

"Yeah … most people do." He glanced between the half-tree and the rock guy. "How are you even here? I mean, the mountain clans left ages ago, after sowing the land with remnants. But you're … you're the real deal. And here I thought that little wind dragon I picked up was crazy for dropping names like Auriel and Cadmiel."

But instead of giving any of the facts that Hisoka would definitely ask for, the rock imp nodded to Jacques and said, "Save him."

"That's the general idea." Sinder waited for more. Nothing was forthcoming. He huffed and asked, "Why are you worried? The barrier's down. Help's on the way."

"Because," rumbled the rock imp, "the wind is changing."

Something did shift then, and a gust shot straight into their little cove. The noise overhead changed. Crystal leaves rattled, shattered, and dropped, and the wind caught the resulting sand, spinning it in a tight little cyclone.

Sinder gathered Jacques close and brought out his wings, folding them to try to create a windbreak. It didn't do much good. Sand was getting everywhere, and it stung.

"Look," Sinder warned, raising his voice over the tumult. "We're going to talk after this is all over. A nice long talk."

"Perhaps. If you are very patient." There was a wry edge to the imp's voice. "As patient as stone."

And the two imps disappeared.

Left alone with Jacques in an escalating grit-storm, Sinder transformed into truest form and worked his coils around to give them both some shelter. Tucking his wings, he deployed a couple of small shield barriers for good measure. Then he rearranged Jacques and tapped a long forefinger against his cheek.

The man shifted a little and opened his eyes. "Lord. You're even prettier than I remember."

Sinder fluted softly. The guy *had* to be pollinated.

Reaching up to stroke Sinder's face, Jacques murmured, "I always did like the feel of dragon scales, and you're a stunner."

Something was different about Jacques, and Sinder was trying to sort out what. With great care, he tapped the man's other hand. Jacques slowly uncurled his fingers, revealing a crystal flower. It glowed the same soft yellow-green as the rock guy. Which was also the same color as the sand that was currently taking a layer off his hide.

"Where are Dayith and Solace?" Jacques asked.

Sinder gave a tiny headshake and burbled a negative.

"The winds came, didn't they?"

It was a rhetorical question. Sinder flicked his tongue to catch the tears that began trickling down Jacques' cheeks.

"I would have liked to do more for them. But what *could* I do? And then they went and ...." His lips trembled, and his eyes pleaded. "Suuzu is going to hate me for this, too."

Sinder made a soft tutting sound, attempting comfort.

"Has anyone made certain that Akira is safe? Or ... there's a boy named Sibley. And two felines called Anjou and Eiji."

Sinder rolled his eyes. *"Give me half a minute, and I can ask, but there's not much use. This isn't my speaking form."*

"Right. Sorry." Jacques fiddled with the crystal flower and murmured, "Place your call or whatever."

"What did you say?"

"Not a thing. I know you don't like to advertise that you're a reach, but ... I'm in the know." Jacques made a locking motion beside his mouth. "Mum's the word."

"Jacques ...?"

"Carry on." He heaved a shaky breath. "I am entirely fraught, and I'd be grateful to know if Akira is safe."

Sinder angled his head, trying to get a better look at Stately House's butler. Their entirely ordinary, completely unendowed butler. But he found a sure, steady brilliance where none had been before. *"Dunce and double dunce. You're a reaver!"*

"Non. I haven't the correct bloodlines to be a reaver. There should be another name for people who are born unendowed but later gain that certain something." Jacques jauntily posed, "Would it be too outré to suggest calling my sort Smythes?"

44

STRONG TIES

Y
ou ... don't know?" Akira looked much too pale. "He was supposed to be here. His scent should be here."

"I was on his trail earlier. I can pick it up again. We can even make that next on my agenda." Boon held out Akira's pants. "One thing at a time, kid. Let's get you dressed."

Naoki hurried forward to help. There was some murmuring and fussing. Bandages were involved, and Boon's nose was briefly overwhelmed by the sharp scent of a disinfectant. But he was more interested in the assortment of glass jars lining a rack above the counter where Akira's seed had been left. Some were slender as test tubes. Others were squat and square. All were marked with symbols Boon couldn't interpret, but ... he knew gold when he saw it.

When Naoki escorted his son to a bathroom off on the other end of the room, Boon plucked one of the glass bottles from the collection. Flicking the stopper free, he gave the contents a cautious sniff. Kinda ... different. He wasn't sure he liked the way it smelled.

He worked his way down the row, searching for something that appealed to him more.

"What are you contemplating, wolf friend?"

Boon flinched and looked into Naoki's upturned face, tail firmly tucked. "These are golden seeds ...?"

"Some are a pure strain. Others are experimental hybrids."

"So ... they'd work?"

Naoki hesitated. "Before I answer that, would you mind answering my first question? What are you contemplating?"

Clearing his throat, Boon went for the short version. "I have two ladies who'll be in my care from now on. Both of them came here hoping for a miracle."

"I see." Naoki asked, "Do you understand what something like this would mean for them?"

"It'd mean the world to them."

The man shook his head. "Issues abound. The need for secrecy cannot be ignored, and that often leads to isolation. Comparative lifespan is a factor, especially if the carrier is human. And then there's the needs of the tree. They long for community. They belong in groves."

"Okay. Got it. Can do."

"Can you expand on that?" Naoki had begun rearranging the vials, but he paused to search Boon's face. "Increase my trust, wolf friend."

"Boonmar-fen Elderbough," he offered belatedly. "My clan has strong ties to Stately House."

"And ...?"

"That's where Akira lives. His sister, too. They have beacons and barriers, an enclave's worth of community, and all the kids here will probably end up there. You, too, since you're kin." He was rambling a little, but he was also warming to the idea. His tail lifted. "I'll speak to Argent about granting us whatever space you think my pack will need."

A smile bloomed on Naoki's face, and he plucked two vials from the collection. "These. I give them freely."

Boon found himself asking, "Are they yours to give?"

"They are. And when all of this is over, I'll gladly tell you how they came to be here."

It was enough. Boon went to pocket the vials but hesitated again. Too obvious, and he wanted to get these to where they belonged without a fuss. So he popped the tops, dumped out the two golden seeds, and eased them into his front pocket, hiding them in the soft creases and folds of old denim.

Akira shuffled back into the room, a hand pressed to his side but a smile on his face. Boon was headed his way, intent on hauling him off his feet, when an unexpected voice rang clear in his mind.

"Boon? You close?"

Startled, Boon answered aloud. "Paltry?"

Akira mostly wanted to protest the coddling, but he wasn't feeling all that great. Maybe it really was shock. He felt cold, and he was shaky on his feet. So when Boon lifted him and led the way down a hall in order to meet up with another wolf, Akira just went with it.

This was safety. Suuzu would want him to be safe. But was Jacques safe? He bit his lip, reasoning that when it came to tracking, two wolves were better than one.

The wolf standing in the lobby was new to Akira, but he knew enough to guess that Paltry was a tribute. They were the only Amaranthine who trained with weapons. A sword rode at Paltry's hip, but more notable ... he *also* had a passenger.

Someone was tucked into the crook of his arm, almost exactly the same as Boon carried Akira. Except that Paltry's companion shone.

He brightened further and pushed at Paltry's arm. "Put me down."

"Is it safe?" Paltry's gaze rested on Akira.

"The halls are empty. Churlish should be safe enough," said Boon. "Akira's injured, or he'd be fending for himself, too."

Naoki, who was puffing a bit as he caught up, exclaimed, "Paltry!"

Shock registered on the wolf's face, and then he was kneeling before Akira's dad. "How are you *here*? When you vanished, Hajime was beside himself, and we searched ...!"

He didn't answer. None was needed. But Naoki beckoned to the shining boy. "She's here, Churlish. I've done what I could."

"Seela?" His voice shook as he peered around. "Why is Seela in a bad place? This is *ugly*."

"It is," Naoki agreed. "She has been brave for a long time. I told her about your search. And about your wolf. I hope you do not mind."

Churlish grabbed Paltry's hand and begged, "Where is she?"

Naoki led the way through halls, but they ran into a mess of debris. Boon needed to set Akira down in order to help Paltry shift obstacles, but he seemed reluctant.

"Give him to me," demanded Churlish.

Paltry chuckled. "You think you can lift him?"

"He can lean on me," corrected Churlish. "*He* is not absurdly tall."

"Forgive this wolf for being so ungainly," Paltry answered, tail swaying.

Boon steadied Akira on his feet, and Churlish slipped under his arm. Akira was delighted to get a closer look. "Are you an Impression?"

"Moonbeam. And that is my wolf. Do you have a wolf, too?" he asked, indicating Boon.

"I have a phoenix," he replied with equal gravity. "And ... I'm tree-kin."

"I did not know! Nobody told me." His pouting perusal ended in a confident statement. "You are mostly happy. So is Paltry. *Finally.*"

Akira looked toward Churlish's wolf, whose tail hadn't stopped wagging. "Yes, your wolf seems happy."

Churlish's tone turned shy. "I think he is pleased because ... this is one of the tasks I set. Finding my sister. He is mine, and I am his ... but there is something uncomfortable about a promise you cannot keep."

His sister. A moonbeam? Akira felt bad for her. "She'll be okay now."

"I will make certain."

"*We* will," corrected Paltry. "Mind your feet. There's broken glass."

They picked their way along a short hall, and Naoki indicated a door, but Paltry was already at it. Akira had to wonder what moonbeams smelled like to a wolf.

The room looked like it belonged in a hospital ward. With the power out, there weren't any lights, but Akira didn't need them to see the figure on the bed. Just like Churlish, she glowed softly.

Naoki crossed to her, picked up her hand, and murmured something as he began a quick checkup.

"I'll be fine if you want to go to her," Akira offered.

But Churlish stayed right where he was. In fact, he'd tucked himself a little behind Akira.

Paltry took charge instead. "Is she drugged?"

"Asleep. She took refuge in dreams sometime before my recapture." He cautiously added, "Kodoku was furious, so he meddled with her. He can be so spiteful."

Akira wondered what he meant by *meddled*. But he was afraid to ask.

Boon groaned, though. "Seela's *child*."

"What?" asked Churlish. "What?"

Naoki cleared his throat. "Kodoku has a fascination for impressions. There are many crossbreeds on this island."

"Am I an uncle? Does he mean I am an uncle?" Churlish's grip on Akira tightened. "That is how it works, is it not?"

"Well ...." Naoki looked uneasy.

But then Boon said, "That's exactly how it works, and I've met the runt who'll call you uncle. Posy found him. He's with Hisoka."

"He is?" Naoki whispered. Patting the sleeping Seela's hand, he asked, "Did you hear, my dear? Your child is safe with Hisoka. Come, now. Wake and greet your brother."

But nothing happened.

Akira gave Churlish a small push. "Talk to her. Let her hear your voice."

"I can do that," he murmured. "I should do that."

Paltry boosted the moonbeam onto the bed, where he knelt beside his sister. "Seela? Seela. It is Char. Only I am not Char anymore. I have a wolf, and my wolf gave me a new name. For balance, I gave him one, too."

Akira eased closer, and Boon noticed. He came over, scooped him up again, and brought him over so he could see. That's why he felt Boon suddenly tense. Akira looked up and softly asked, "What's wrong?"

"A noise. Not far from here. A door, maybe?" Boon looked to Paltry, and the two of them angled their heads toward the hall. "Hold up. This might be good."

Then Akira caught a soft skittering as something swung around the corner and scampered across the floor on all fours. Naoki turned and exclaimed, "Oh! Oh, my. You found your way back? That's very tenacious of you."

A child pulled himself up Naoki's leg.

He had to be a crosser, what with the antlers.

His dad cuddled him close and asked, "Did you have help? Hmm?"

Boon helpfully rumbled, "Seela's child."

"Wh-what?" Churlish exclaimed, reaching out with one hand, then drawing it back. "What?"

Paltry rubbed at the side of his face. "Well, now. He's ... really very cute, don't you think?"

"Part pitterhind," Boon interjected.

"But … but I *love* pitterhind!" Churlish reached with both hands this time. "Will he come to me?"

"The way I heard it, Ephemera fly to imps and reavers alike," said Paltry, all soft and smiling.

Naoki passed the child along, and Akira watched as Churlish did the most sensible thing ever. He fell in love.

They were still crooning and giggling over finding each other when the girl on the bed opened silvery eyes … and smiled at her brother.

45

STAR CROSSED

Hisoka didn't know what to do. Nemi and her child were bound together, and he suddenly wondered if—in the simple act of sitting on the floor—he'd forced her child's descent. Looking to Linlu, he hoped for direction.

The moth clansman turned to the other door, spun a mechanism set into its center, lifted a lever, and pushed. Swinging wide, the door hit the outside wall with a resounding clang. Nemi and her child didn't react.

"This way, please." Linlu beckoned for him to follow. "It will be easier for Novi."

Although it should have been strange for Linlu to know his star's name, Hisoka couldn't bring himself to be surprised. At the moment, he was simply glad there was someone who knew what to do.

"Patter?" Hisoka had lost track of the boy. "*Patter*?"

"Gone on ahead," Linlu soothed. "Come along."

Getting to his feet proved simpler than anticipated. "Flight is possible again," he murmured.

"Yes, yes. Every good thing in its time."

"Have I grounded them?"

"Not at all. That one was not born to the sky. With Dayith for a progenitor, their feet were already firmly planted on the ground, so to speak."

"The father?" Taking care not to knock either imp as he eased through the doorway, Hisoka followed Linlu across yet another hushed hallway. The laboratory opposite was round and high-ceilinged, with tall windows topped by transoms. Orderly rows of plants and cages lined the walls, right up to an open ceiling.

With a start, Hisoka realized that the architecture was eerily similar to that in his private suite. This sort of arrangement fostered communion with the stars. But in this case, it very likely contributed to their descent. "He traps them here."

"Sings them straight into captivity," Linlu confirmed grimly. He moved to one of the counters, rummaged in a drawer, and returned with a slim blade. "A moment. Forgive my haste, dear lady."

He hacked off Nemi's hair at the nape, and with much tugging and loosening, she slid free of the warm, wheat-colored coils that bound her to her child. She was clad in a simple slip. Linlu cradled her as gently as if she were one of his own whisperlings.

Patting her cheek, he said, "Come, now, my dear. Your rescuers have arrived. All is as it should be."

Nemi stirred, and her lashes fluttered, and she opened eyes that perfectly matched her twin's. Hisoka had always liked that the color defied description. It would have felt sacrilegious to call them *beige*, especially since they gleamed like a precious metal.

Starlight usually flashed. It worried Hisoka that Nemi was so dim.

He found his voice. "Hello, Nemi. We're here. Finally."

"Novi?" she murmured aloud.

That was a shock. Nemi no longer had a voice that was meant for the wideness of skies.

"I am here!"

Both of them looked upward, through the circular opening in the ceiling. Novi blazed there, just above the roof.

Linlu called, "It is safe, good star. None will hold you here."

Without any further caution, Novi dropped into the laboratory, coming to hover over Linlu and his sister. He reached down. Nemi reached back.

"We did try," Hisoka murmured.

"I know." She favored him with a wan smile, and her attention fell to the figure in his arms, still wrapped in the lost silk of her hair. "For you."

He wavered there, suddenly feeling encumbered. "I don't understand."

"You will," she promised.

Hisoka edged closer, trying to reunite them. "A child should be with their mother."

Nemi pulled at the short ruff of hair that Linlu's hasty haircut had left her. "I have done all I could. For longer than you realize."

Again, he tried to offer his burden, this time looking to Novi for help. But his oldest friend only collected his sister from

Linlu. Hisoka rose with them. His words felt so clumsy, useless to convey the enormity of the losses that lay between them. "I *am* sorry it took so long."

She still had an impish smile. "Rejoice, for your search has ended."

"Come away," urged Novi, who only had eyes for her. "I will carry you into the sky for one last song."

Last? Hisoka wanted to reach for her and couldn't. She was so dim. Was she going to fade away entirely? "Was I too late?"

"This is the fullness of time."

"But … this one!" he protested, still unable to believe that she'd leave him with her offspring.

Nemi's words took on the ring of portent. "You always held yourself apart, but you were never meant to be alone. Here is an answer none could foretell, yet you found it. Keep this gift close, less for my sake than for your own."

And then Novi's rising sped up, and he soared away, leaving Hisoka in bewilderment. "Have I just been made a father?"

"No, no. I think not." Linlu beckoned him back to the floor. He tutted and crooned as he unwound handfuls of hair. "I keep the records, so I know the truth. Nemi's child attained their first millennia several decades ago, though this is their first breath of wild air. A second birth, perhaps?"

Hisoka snatched at the practical. "I will need your records for the trial."

"You may have my papers, but I wonder if a trial will be possible."

"What would prevent us?" he asked.

With an apologetic smile, Linlu indicated the door, where a

heaving, seething Dr. Kodoku stood glaring.

"What have you done?" he all but shrieked. And gaze settling on Nemi's child, his tone darkened with need. "That! That is *mine*!"

Elara had been trying to calm the garden dwellers when the lab doors burst open, releasing a stream of children. Someone had set them free. She'd turned to tell the good news to Juuyu, the phoenix who'd taken charge and was calmly, quietly greeting every tree, when a streak of silver checked her stride. And then Pim pressed up against her, rubbing their cheeks together and vibrating with a pleased purr.

"Oh, god. Are you clinging to me? That's so cute." She pulled her in and laughed a little. "Does this mean you missed me?"

Pim drew back enough to search her face. "Are you hurt anywhere? Were you afraid? Do you need anything?"

"No. Yes. You. I was so worried!" And when this only served to rile Pim, Elara rolled her eyes. "Don't give me that look. I knew you could handle yourself. It's just ... nothing's holding you here anymore."

If anything, Pim looked even more insulted. "I wasn't done flirting with you."

Elara laughed a little more. "I'll enjoy that. However, I'm out of a job, and I'm definitely tired of the tropics. Maybe we should travel?"

Pim clung more tightly. "I was ready to settle down."

"We aren't going to get the future we were promised, but I

think there's a bright side."

"Are you thinking of a certain sexy wolf?"

"Don't underestimate my ambition," Elara chided. "I'm thinking of *two* sexy wolves. If they'll have me."

Pim's smile seemed sad. "Boon's mind is made up, but I feel bad. We weren't in his plans."

"So you saw him? Is he all right? And is he all right with … everything?"

"I do think we'll be okay. But we can't really make any decisions about the future without his input." Pim shyly added, "Maybe we're a pack, now?"

Elara had given that part some thought already. "Something tells me I'll be needing my new packmates to protect me from here on out. I don't know the first thing about being a beacon. And I don't like my chances if a couple of redheads turn vengeful. Or turn up hungry. My memories of them are hazy … but unpleasant."

"They used to eat our scraps and strays," interjected a cool voice. "If there was even the faintest glimmer to the souls Father tossed out as dragon fodder, the vixens stole their prey."

"Futari," Pim gasped. "I didn't realize you were here."

"That happens more than you might think."

Elara raised her hand. "She wasn't here. That is … she wasn't with us."

Pim let her go and edged between Elara and the dragon. But then she did something strange. Pulling Futari into her arms, Pim gently asked, "What do you want?"

"My sister," she said dully.

"Elara and I are here. Will we do as sisters?"

Red eyes flashed. "It is not the same."

"No. It'll never be the same. But that doesn't mean we couldn't be something good." Pim coaxed, "Let us steal you away from here."

"That is not why I am here." Stepping back and squaring her shoulders, Futari said, "Two moons shall bear witness. Come with me."

"Two … moons?" Pim's head canted to one side.

Futari went on. "Two sisters to understand my fury. Both strong enough to hold me back. Both soft enough to let me have my way."

Elara raised her hand. "What is it you want?"

Her chin angled haughtily. "There can be no recompense, so I will settle for revenge."

"Against your father," Pim murmured.

Raising her voice, Futari called, "Lend me your blade."

This time, Elara could feel the sway in her words and idly patted at pockets. If she'd had a blade—*any* kind of blade—she would have surrendered it. But it was Anjou who stepped up and unsheathed the sword at his hip. He grimaced, though, and Elara thought he was resisting the command.

Juuyu was there in the next moment. He slapped Anjou's shoulder.

The feline immediately leapt back, eyes wide. "Dragon!" he hissed.

"The dragon's daughter," corrected Pim. "We should take Futari into protective custody. She can testify."

"Do you know where Kodoku is?" asked Juuyu.

Futari held out her hand and said, "Give me your sword."

The phoenix didn't budge. But he asked, "Why should I?"

"I am tree-kin. Do you know what that means?"

"My father is tree-kin. I grew up in a tree's heights and in a tree's arms."

Futari's chin quavered. "You know! You *do* know!"

"You were born with a golden seed in your hand?"

"Yes! My twin! My sister!" Her voice was low and dangerous. "He carried us, and so we were his. His to command. His to dissect."

Juuyu warbled a series of notes that clearly communicated dismay.

She took courage and went on. "He took her leaves and nipped her twigs. Then shortened every branch and limb. He peeled back her bark, leached her sap, carved into her heart, and eventually uprooted her. He ignored our screams while he pulped her for paper and feasted upon her last flowers. He tested her slivers, tasted her ash, and searched for her limits. When he found them, Kaneko was no more. And I … I have long been bound to her murderer. Give me my revenge!"

To Elara's amazement, Juuyu drew a blade, flipped it, and presented its hilt to Futari. "Lead, and I will follow."

Pim wavered in place. "You're going to kill him?"

Juuyu inclined his head. "Unless another reaches him first."

"That's … not very …." She looked to Elara for support. "What about a trial?"

"We two will strike. You two will bear witness. Is this not a just balance?"

To Elara's surprise, Pim very slowly, very carefully tucked her tail. "I am lacking in years and in understanding. I don't know."

Juuyu came to stand before them. "I am a tribute of the Farroost clan. My duties are clearly delineated … and further refined by phoenix tradition. You have already seen, so you already know. Dragons are my prey."

"What would Boon say?" she ventured.

Smile lines creased beside Juuyu's eyes. "He will say that I have stolen his quarry."

46

CLANLESS

Linlu beckoned to Boon and quietly announced, "Hisoka has need of your support."

He inhaled deeply, growled softly. "You were with him?"

"Until just recently, yes."

"Where is he?"

"Nearby. I can guide you."

"Is he in trouble?"

Linlu calmly revealed, "A great deal. Two lives hang in the balance. One of those is his own."

Boon was torn. He still carried Akira, who was just as much his responsibility, if not more so. And Paltry had his own pack to consider. In desperation, he flung his thoughts outward. *"Penny! You there?"*

"Near enough you don't need to shout," came Merit's bland response.

"Can you get to where I am? I have Akira."

A beat later, Merit said, *"Argent will reach you first. Are you in the building?"*

"Hang on. Lemme get outdoors." Boon strode out of the lab, along the hall, and to a large square window set with glass blocks. It let in light, but all Boon could see through it was green. "This should do it," he muttered.

"Do what?" Akira asked, sounding worried.

"Oh, you know. Let's call it a shortcut."

"You can't open this kind of …."

Boon reared back, balanced on one foot as he drove his heel against the glass, shoving half a dozen blocks into the courtyard beyond. He kicked and pushed the rest through, where they clanked and cracked against each other on the ground below.

"Oh," Akira said, smiling crookedly. "Yeah. Shortcut."

"Hold tight," Boon warned, shouldering through the gap and—bless whoever wrecked that hellish barrier—leapt skyward. "Should be able to see incoming backup."

He'd barely cleared the roof when an enormous silver fox swerved their way.

Akira waved with his whole arm. "Here! We're here!"

"He knows, kid." Boon squinted. "Really not in the mood for a collision."

Thrusting out both arms, Akira shouted, "Whoa!"

Argent shifted in midair, though he kept his full flourish of tails on display. Coming even with Boon, he held out his arms in silent command.

"Catch up to you later, kid," Boon promised, all but tossing

Akira to Argent before backtracking for Linlu. The moth waited in the courtyard below, pointing urgently.

Orienting himself on that heading, Boon was saved from further guesswork when Hisoka leapt through an opening in a nearby section of roof, his arms full of … something. Someone? As Boon neared them, his nose was having all kinds of trouble sorting the scent. But there were more pressing matters.

From below, an imperious voice commanded, "Get back here! At once!"

Boon crouched at the edge and eyed the lone figure in the lab.

"You!" he snarled. "Wolf! Bring me the star child!"

Deep breaths. More ranting. Finally, Boon turned to Hisoka. "This can't be the Rogue."

"Agreed."

More useless railing. Several threats. Boon muttered, "Is he just going to sling insults?"

"He can't follow. He can't fly."

Boon didn't much like the way this hunt was panning out. "This isn't the end."

"Not for everything, no. But we've done some good … I hope."

"How's this going to go down?" Ignoring the dragon's demands, he looked to Hisoka for answers, only to grunt in surprise. "Hell and hellfire! Here comes comeuppance."

Hisoka's eyes widened.

They both took several steps away from the circular opening and took submissive postures. Juuyu on a tear did that to a guy.

Fiery wings beat, and for a breathless moment, their phoenix seemed suspended, but he tucked and dove with reckless precision.

"Did he have a passenger?" Boon was sure he'd seen a slender figure clinging to Juuyu's leg. Hastening back to the edge, he sucked in a breath, hoping for some hint as to why there was now a three-way standoff below.

Pim and Elara arrived then, as did Goh Impleer, who had Inti on his shoulders. Boon pointed to the monkey-crosser in greeting, and the kid took that as an invitation to switch venues. He leapt and clung, murmuring, "Good, good, good wolf."

Boon ruffled his hair distractedly, most of his attention fixed on the confrontation below. Juuyu spoke with grim authority, and one phrase in particular stuck out. "Two moons? What's he mean?"

"Us," said Pim, whose tail had developed a twitch. "Elara and me. We're supposed to bear witness to … whatever this is."

Paltry arrived, looking entirely at ease with two moonbeams occupying his arms, and Patter occupying theirs in turn. Merit also had a passenger—Linlu Dimityblest. Like most of the Starmarks, he'd grown up in the town that the moth clansman had helped to found, and his expression was thunderous as he alighted and stalked to the verge. Boon scanned their faces and quickly decided that his ladies were too vulnerable to be here. Pim and Elara were susceptible to dragon sway, and Kodoku was laying it on thick. Entirely useless, where most of them were concerned, but one stray command could endanger the lives of his new packmates.

Standing behind them, he wrapped his arms around their shoulders.

They glanced up, as startled by him as he was at himself.

Inti tickled their chins with his tail and quietly warned, "Even this dragon is a dragon."

"Don't take your eyes off of one," Boon advised. And because he never could give up on a trail once started, he pressed, "I see *one* moon. Moonprowl. Where'd you wrangle the second?"

"Though their names for her are seven-score, wolves only see one moon." Inti's voice took on a teasing lilt. "Moon, moon, blind Boon."

Boon snorted. "You can't teach moon lore to a wolf."

Elara touched his arm. "There are other moons, you know."

His gaze skidded briefly to hers. "That so?"

"I should know. I chose my name." With traces of pride, she revealed, "Elara is one of Jupiter's moons."

That there could be multiple moons was a bizarre idea. It almost felt sacrilegious. As unheard of as a wolf taking two females for his own. Yet in that moment, Boon decided that there was some truth to what his father always said about Elderbough trackers. He really *could* taste the beginning of a soul bond. Well, *two* bonds. And an elusive scent he'd encountered before. That whisper of the Maker's meddling that lingered in the wake of miracles.

Having plunged through the circular opening in its ceiling, Juuyu immediately hated the lab into which he'd carried Futari. Information rushed at him from all sides, and piecing it together sickened him. But mostly, he was angry, and that would not do. So he cooled his ire and tried to tighten his focus, even though details begged for his attention, begged for anyone to see.

Plants arrayed the shelves, softening strict lines and freshening the air. But their trailing ends and reaching fronds couldn't completely hide the cages. Or the lingering scent of fear.

In liquid. Under domes. On boards. Specimens had been taken from all sorts of creatures. Some were innocent enough—feathers, eggshells, shed scales. But there was a jar with slender leg bones that had belonged to young. Another held beaks. Another tiny fangs.

There were stretched hides and shed skins and feathered wings, all neatly pinned to boards for study or for display. Chunks of crystal littered most surfaces, always in the same shade of yellowish green. Coiled locks of gleaming silver and gold hair suggested captive moonlight and starlight. There were vials of pollen and dried petals. Strips of bark. And capped beakers of blackened wood and pale ash.

Juuyu tallied up the staggering loss of life this room represented … and willed his churning emotions to settle into steel. Since before he cracked shell, he had been set apart for war—taught and trained and tuned. "Maker mark, and Maker move," he breathed.

Futari quailed, and Juuyu supposed he hadn't fully reined in his fury.

Unsheathing two blades, Juuyu began the rote Hallow had drilled into him. There was much to answer for. "What is your name, Kindred?"

"Go away," snapped Kodoku. "Begone. Can't you hear the winds? They've finally come, and I must sing!"

Futari spoke. "He is Kodoku, and we are clanless."

"Not every clan is recognized. That doesn't diminish our value." The dragon pivoted, and he drew himself up. "And you! You're avian? We don't have any avians. *Yet*. How did you get in here? This is a secure facility!"

Had this person missed the signs of his exposure? The entire island had been laid bare by the winds he was so eager to woo. Juuyu stayed on task. "Are you Kodoku?"

"*Doctor* Kodoku," he returned snippily. "Fetch that back!"

Juuyu turned enough to see where he pointed. Several Amaranthine had gathered around the opening in the ceiling. That was good. Many witnesses.

"Do you know how long I have waited to get my hands on that hybrid? Futari, did you see? Nemi abandoned her child!"

"Is that how you see it?" his daughter asked coolly.

"You. Bird. Bring it to me!" His eager words were heavy with sway. "I bred sky with stone, and it worked. But they hid their child from me. Me! The centuries wasted!"

Juuyu sought Hisoka's gaze, since he was the one clutching a huddled figure to his chest. The cat looked … uncertain. But his hold on the coveted crosser tightened, and his posture shifted into an almost wolvish display of possessiveness. Juuyu inclined his head and returned to his own duty.

"An unrecognized clan?" He pressed for more. "Who sired you? Who carried you?"

Kodoku hadn't yet given up. "You should do as I say!"

"Phoenixes are impervious to dragon sway."

"Nonsense! All the clans bend to our will. We are superior to every other people!"

"If that was your cradle lore, the one who sang it was spinning lies." Juuyu flatly announced, "Dragons are a phoenix's prey. On this day, you are mine."

If anything, Kodoku merely looked annoyed.

"There was a census. Every dragon from the eldermost to the hatchery is accounted for. You are not in those records. Why?"

Kodoku shouted—entirely ineffectually—for one of their onlookers to bring him the child.

Juuyu lost patience. Darting forward, he twisted the dragon's arms behind his back and applied pressure to the appropriate vertebrae. Kodoku yipped and writhed. Juuyu eased the tip of one talon deeper. The dragon went stiff and still as blood beaded up, then trickled down, staining the collar of his fine shirt.

"Where did you crack shell?" Juuyu asked. "Who gave you your name?"

"What do you think you are doing?" Kodoku finally sounded worried.

"Asking questions that require answers." Juuyu cut loose, then, letting this prey get a sense of his vastness.

Some instinct must have kicked in, recognizing the threat Juuyu posed, because Kodoku's pallor changed, and his voice cracked with tension. "Who are you to question me?"

"Your true name?"

"Kodoku." And with a hiss that promised pain, he amended, "Celestoria Kodoku."

"No!"

Juuyu's gaze flew to Hisoka, who was shaking his head in urgent denial.

"There is some doubt to your claim," Juuyu murmured. "Why have you stolen a name that has only ever been ascribed to stars?"

"Stolen?" he sneered. "My brother and I were born to our name as surely as you were to yours. I know who I am. *What* I am. Why I am superior!"

A brother. Was this the other dragon? The Rogue? "Where is your brother?"

"My twin is *dead.*"

Juuyu wanted to back away from this claim. Not just a brother, but a twin? From the earliest days, dragons and phoenixes had this in common. Those who cracked shell were born alone. A twinned birth meant their mother had carried them while in speaking form. "Who carried you?"

"It does not matter. She is gone."

Juuyu warbled a warning note.

With a peevish scowl, he jutted his chin toward the sky. "Celestoria Nemi. That star you stole? *She* is my mother."

47

CELESTORIA

Hisoka couldn't bear to listen any longer.

Backing away from the tableau inside the lab, he took to the air. Maybe it was cowardice, but he didn't want to face this revelation. It was the first time he could recall trying to flee from a secret. But he stalled in midair. Where could he go? The entire facility was hemmed in by rampant air currents.

While he stared up into that distant patch of blue where Novi had taken Nemi, all Hisoka felt was … empty. No ideas. No thoughts. Nothing. He was cognizant enough to know this was probably bad—or at least not good—but he didn't know how to go back.

"Spokesperson Twineshaft," came a vaguely familiar voice. "Hisoka …?"

He turned to find Hannick Alpenglow at his side. Nodding back toward the lab, Hisoka said, "Linlu is there."

"That is welcome news, but *you* are the one who needs me right now."

"I'm uninjured."

Hannick's smile was kind. "I know what I'm about, Kindred. Can you ride?"

Hisoka just stared at him, trying to make sense of the question.

"Never mind. If I may?" Without actually waiting for an answer, the big healer drew him into his arms, rearranging things so that the one Hisoka carried was also secure. "And who do we have here?"

How was he supposed to answer that?

Nemi's child? One of Nemi's children?

Hisoka turned his face away, and Hannick didn't press for more.

They approached the churning mists, yet the storm didn't really touch them. It was as if individual currents slipped by, easing out of the way, allowing them safe passage. One gust seemed to toy with his hair. Another caressed his cheek. When the star-child's hair fluttered, Hisoka pulled them closer. For Nemi's sake. And maybe for Hoshiko's. And Hiroki's.

Swallowing hard, he shut his eyes and left all the thinking and deciding and acting to someone else.

"What is this? What happened?"

Hisoka flinched guiltily and opened his eyes. Argent. How many times would they ask him? He didn't have answers. Not anymore.

"Let me get him inside," Hannick said quietly. "Can we secure a room?"

"I will see to it." And touching Hisoka's shoulder, Argent made it a promise, "I will see to it."

Water stretched below, choppy from the winds, but endlessly blue. And then there was an island. A windship was rising from a beach, carried aloft by fluting dragons. Hisoka recognized enough pelts and coats and crests to know that Argent had planned for every eventuality.

Hannick touched down beside another windship and ducked through the door.

"Here. This one," called Argent.

When Hannick sat upon the curtained bed that dominated the room, he kept Hisoka on his lap. It was probably undignified, but he couldn't bring himself to care.

Argent was back in view, concern creasing his face. "Who is this?"

"A child given into my care."

The fox's brow arched. "And … all this hair?"

"It's Nemi's hair."

Bafflement. Worry. Decision. "I will ward everything. Hannick, get him to take some fluids while I work." Taking Hisoka's face between his hands, Argent promised, "You will have secrecy for this. I can do that much."

Then Hannick moved, settling Hisoka against heaped pillows. He was gone and back, and Hisoka grimaced over a gulp of tonic.

"May I?" The healer indicated the child. "Help me unbundle them."

Hisoka supported the limp figure while Hannick unwound locks of hair. It would have been so much simpler to cut the mess away. Still, the healer acted as if cutting a single strand would cause injury. Slowly, Nemi's child was revealed—slender limbs, jutting bones. They were gangly and undernourished.

"No sign of animal features," Hannick remarked. "This is not an Amaranthine crosser."

"Both parents are Impressions."

"Who is Nemi?" asked Argent.

"The child's mother." With a weary sigh, he averted his face. "It's a long story."

Hannick pulled away the last of the hair, and Argent set it aside.

"Hisoka," the healer murmured. "You need to know that this person is an adult."

"Is that so?" he asked vaguely.

"Up," Hannick ordered. "I want to tuck them in."

The healer took away the child-who-wasn't-a-child, and Hisoka slid from the bed and backed away. Should he go? Could he go? The walls glittered with fresh sigilcraft. Argent's handiwork. Hisoka knew they were safe. He also felt trapped.

"Help me understand what I'm looking at," Hannick said.

He'd settled his patient and drawn the blankets to their shoulders. Kneeling beside the bed, the healer was pulling the child-who-wasn't-a-child's hair into a loose braid. Their hair was the same pale, shining gold as Nemi's. Hisoka edged closer, daring to look. While this person didn't have the same inherent glow of a star, glitter seemed to fleck their pale skin, like thousands of tiny facets that caught the light.

"Were they like this when you found them? Asleep?"

"They were bound together in a chrysalis. He and his mother. I don't think he's ever been outside of it before now."

"Not so hasty." Hannick raised a cautioning hand. "This person is genderless. I have seen it before—with trees, of course—but the principle may apply to any imp. Some manifest as male or female immediately. Others put off choosing. Sometimes forever."

"Is that so?" he managed numbly.

"Do you know their name?"

"Linlu might."

"Should I bring him next?" Hannick asked.

Hisoka dragged his gaze from the floor and shifted into a submissive posture.

"Bring him," Argent directed, ushering the healer out. He made fast the wards, pulled a stool to the bedside, and sat Hisoka upon it. "Tell me what I need to know."

Words came slowly. "This person is my responsibility."

"Then I will make certain no one comes between you."

Hisoka hung his head. "Am I under your protection, then?"

"*Tsk*. Had you never noticed?" he haughtily inquired.

Almost, he smiled. "Argent, I don't know what to do."

"Tell me why." He sounded like he already knew.

"There was a star ...."

"Was?"

"Novi and I, we vowed to find Nemi. His sister. She was captive for so long. He took her away, and ... he's gone. And I don't know what to do."

"Because he was your secret counsel. Your guide."

"You knew?"

"I suspected, but no. You were careful." Argent frowned. "I can *feel* your distress."

Hisoka restated the obvious. "He *left*."

"If it's counsel you're lacking, I have been at your service ever since you rescued me. I may not be a star, but I have connections, as does Sinder. And Isla, for that matter."

He tried not to show his dread.

Argent clicked his tongue, pulled Hisoka's head against his chest, and surrounded him in the full flourish of his fox tails. "If Jacques was here, I would put you into bed together. You need rest."

"I would let you." And a beat later, "Where *is* Jacques?"

"You have not seen him?"

"No." And he was afraid.

"I will deal with my galivanting manservant in due course. But here is a conundrum."

Hisoka looked up.

Argent angled his head toward the bed. "This person has never been without companionship. Do you think it will be worse for them to wake alone or to wake with a stranger?"

The question was impossible. "Tell me what to do …?"

"So be it." And more softly, "Will you trust me?"

Hisoka had shared dreams before. With Hiroki, of course, though that was ancient history. And in recent years, with Argent, who had a knack for drawing dreamers together. Hisoka knew the feel of a fox dream, and he trusted his friend … but he rather wished Argent hadn't sent him in alone.

The setting was a simple circle of trees—dappled sunlight, darting ephemera. And Nemi's child stood a few paces away, back to Hisoka. Now that they were standing, more details came to light. They were too thin, all juts and angles beneath the thin tunic that was Argent's nod to modesty. Somehow, they had more height than Hisoka expected—a little taller than Argent, a little shorter than Michael. And that shining hair rippled to the base of their spine.

Novi had always worn his hair much shorter.

And Nemi was now shorn, thanks to Linlu.

Hisoka wondered what choices this person would make, now that they had many and more. Was he meant to guide those choices?

They turned then, and Hisoka shifted into a peaceable posture. "Hello. My name is ...."

"Hisoka?" they asked.

"Ah. Yes." Showing his hands, he asked, "You know me?"

"Mother foretold you."

He wanted to protest. Diplomacy dictated that he set aside his own feelings and consider those of this person. To make peace. To set them at ease. But his own feelings were getting in the way. Almost, he called for Argent.

They came closer, and Hisoka searched eyes that were a flat gray, like lusterless stone, so out of place on a person whose features seemed to have been sprinkled with stardust. Their eyebrows were little more than dots, and those lifted quizzically.

"I ... knew your mother. Long ago. We were friends."

"I remember." They gesticulated, then seemed to become distracted by the movement of their own hands. "She showed me."

"She went away." Hisoka winced at his own words. Since when did he blunder when delicacy was needed? "Her twin took her to safety. You're safe, as well."

"Mother foretold it," they reminded. "She knew how it would be, and she told me you would come for me. That you would be mine."

Hisoka barely stopped himself from adopting a submissive posture.

Somewhere deep inside, he was afraid of the consequences of Nemi's prophecy. Yes, they'd known each other, but that was so long ago. They'd been little more than children. He was a different person now, and the last thing he needed—the thing he'd carefully avoided—was belonging to anyone. At least exclusively.

Boon hadn't shied away from his new responsibilities. Hisoka had watched him ease Pim's fears, draw her close, and encourage the bonds of trust. The very sort of thing he should be doing now.

"I can't …." Hisoka cleared his throat and tried again. "I'm not sure I can be yours."

They came close, reached out, set their fingertips against his chest.

Unsure what else to do, Hisoka let it happen.

Slowly, cautiously they slid their arms around his torso. It brought Nemi to mind. This was how she and her child had waited for rescue, safe in each other's arms. By contrast, Hisoka stood awkwardly, arms upraised as if in surrender, even though it was resistance.

But then it struck Hisoka that Michael would be ashamed of him right now. Slowly, he enfolded the fragile life that Nemi had protected. Wearily, he confessed, "I don't know what to do."

They pressed one pointed ear over his heart and murmured, "Neither do I."

Without Novi, Hisoka had known he was facing an uncertain future. Now, that uncertain future had a face. And a voice. And a snug hold on him.

Falling back on the simplest of protocols, Hisoka asked, "Do you have a name?"

"She said you would ask." The beginnings of a smile showed on their upturned face.

"It's only natural. Is not the exchange of names the beginning of peace?" And because he really, *really* didn't want to have to give this person a name, he pressed, "What did your mother call you?"

In a sing-song lilt that was particular to stars, they answered, "Celestoria to Dayith ni Twineshaft no Rhomiko." There was something sad in their lusterless gaze. It pleaded with him, perhaps for peace. Perhaps for more. "My name is Rhomiko."

48

THE FIRST RULE OF DRAGONS

Pim peered intently into the room below, determined to fulfill this role to the best of her ability. That she had any part to play was staggering. She'd been so sure that the end of her television series had put an end to her ambassadorial status. It wasn't as if her line of lingerie was ever going to count for much in the peace process.

Yet she'd run with Hisoka Twineshaft and come out to Elara as a wolf. She'd worked alongside a real taskforce, and lives were being saved. And connected.

She leaned into Boon's considerable bulk. Since Elara's ears weren't as sharp as an Amaranthine's, Boon had taken it upon himself to relay the goings-on. His gruff words and paraphrased explanations made it possible for Elara to fulfill her role, too.

Because the stars foretold two moons.

Because Futari needed two sisters.

"The winds have returned!" Kodoku railed. "Begone, so I can sing! I will have four brides!"

Juuyu grimly asked, "Are you fool enough to sing death to your side? Listen to them. Their every voice accuses you."

"I was wronged first!"

The more Pim heard of Kodoku's raving, the more convinced she became that he was addled—by ego, by hatred, by envy.

Linlu suddenly said, "He was broken by a beacon long ago. It left him more vulnerable to the influence of stars and moonbeams and trees and stone."

Had he known what she was thinking?

The moth clansman shook his head. "You have an expressive face."

Which left Pim even more convinced that Linlu could see straight into her soul.

She returned her attention to the scene below and thought something was strange. Juuyu seemed to have forgotten that Futari was there. She'd spoken a few times, but she mostly stalked the perimeter, as if waiting her turn. At the moment, Futari was behind Juuyu, and that made Pim uneasy. Mostly because Sinder had given her a list of dragon basics alongside his repeated insistence that she touch his nose.

Tapping Boon's arm, which still held her around the shoulders, she asked, "What's the first rule of dragons?"

"Never lose sight," Boon replied. "They're way too good at fading from notice."

Yes. That's the gist of what Sinder had said. "What are you supposed to do when there are *two* dragons?"

He grunted and asked, "Do you have eyes on the daughter?"

"Futari," she reminded. "Yes, I do."

"Watch her. Closely. I'll keep my eyes on Kodoku."

She pressed the flat of her hand to his forearm. "What am I watching for?"

Boon's chin came to rest on top of her head, like he was trying to match her line of sight. "If she goes for Juuyu, stop her. I'll back you up, so get there."

"She wouldn't!"

"You don't know that." Boon quietly pointed out, "All the things that cracked Kodoku? She's been exposed, too. They're not any kind of balanced."

Elara softly said, "Juuyu isn't the one in danger. Not unless he gets between her and her father."

"But he *is*," Pim hissed.

Boon growled softly. "Juuyu's no fool."

Still, he let Pim slip free to crouch on the verge, ready to fly.

Juuyu's questions were orderly, meticulous. He asked about avenues of communication, the connections he'd used for hiring staff, and the provenance of his captives.

Sometimes, Kodoku boasted at length. At others, he grew cagey. "What we catch, we keep, and what we do not eat is still fair game." With a sneer, he added, "Times have changed. These days, people pay me to take them."

"Smell that?" asked Boon.

Pim inhaled deeply, seeking a change in the air, but nothing stood out. She glanced over her shoulder to say as much ... and paled. Several figures stood in midair above and behind them, gazes fixed upon the hole in the roof. Their flowing hair and fluttering clothes gave them away.

"Dragons?" she whispered.

"Dragon lords," Boon confirmed, his gaze never leaving Kodoku. "They're as anxious as we are for answers."

Pim couldn't believe she'd missed their approach. Then again, the winds seemed to be in their favor. Her gaze jumped from face to grim face, and she wondered what they meant to do with Futari. But then she caught another flutter of movement. An instant later, she scooted backward, crowding against Boon's legs as she craned her neck upward.

Boon's gaze flicked to hers. "The dragon lords are here for peaceful reasons. I know their scents. They're not bad guys."

"Not them," Pim whispered, inching an arm around Elara's knees. "*Them!*"

Frowning, he looked up. "Huh. Okay. Well, that's not something you see every day."

In another ring, fanned out above and behind the dragon lords, shining figures looked on. They had to be stars. Or some other members of the lost clans of the sky.

"Can you see them, Elara?" murmured Boon, who'd gone right back to keeping watch over Juuyu.

"Not exactly." She squinted skyward. "But I can tell something's there. Like lightning dancing in my peripheral vision. And the air's ... charged. It's fizzing and popping, but silently."

Boon tapped Pim's head. "Careful. I know it's hard to look away. What goes for beacons goes double for imps. Go in unguarded, and you'll come away Broken. If you make it out at all."

Pim dragged her gaze back to the lab, which seemed dim by comparison. It took a while for her dazzled eyes to adjust. And several seconds longer for her to relocate Futari.

Juuyu posed another question that had gone unanswered earlier. "Are you a father?"

"I have no harem," Kodoku spat. "And the winds are retreating."

It was true. Were the dragon lords calming them? Had the stars played a part? Maybe the wind imps were being held back by whoever brought them.

"At least one dragon calls you father. And there are many half-dragons on this island."

"I never mingled with humanity. That was more to my brother's taste." A hiss of pain, and a peevish confession. "I did some personal experimentation with golden seeds, so yes, I am a parent. What of it?"

"How many children?"

"Two," he spat.

"Three!" shrilled Futari. Both Juuyu and Kodoku started, as if they'd forgotten she was in the room. "What about Kaneko?"

Kodoku rolled his eyes. "She hardly counts. She's gone."

With a wordless cry, she lunged for him with her borrowed blade.

Yipping with fear, Kodoku shifted. Lab tables were either shoved aside or shattered as purple scales rippled outward. Pim lost sight of Futari in the muddle, which became even more confusing when Juuyu also took truest form. Feathers blazed, and wings beat as Juuyu's talons caught and held one of Kodoku's forearms. The other scrabbled against the floor, gouging and flipping tiles. Soon, the scent of poison burned Pim's nose.

Boon's growl intensified, but he stayed where he was.

"Can't we do something?" Elara asked.

"Not us," Boon grumbled. "Give him a chance."

"Sinder said this is Juuyu's area of expertise," said Pim.

"It is."

Kodoku writhed, as if trying to throw the length of his body over the avian, but Juuyu clamped his beak over a point at the base of Kodoku's skull, and his squabbling cries quickly tapered to intermittent kreeling. He'd given up.

"Where's Futari?" Pim asked worriedly.

All at once, the dragon jerked violently. Juuyu's wings flung wide, trying to bear Kodoku back to the ground, but something was wrong. The phoenix released his hold and hopped back, feathers dragging through debris. Kodoku's legs twitched, claws dragging ineffectually across stained tiles. A new scent welled up. Blood.

The dragon stilled, and Juuyu resettled his feathers, lifted his head, and launched into a mournful song.

Paltry spoke then. "I was there when his brother met a similar fate."

Heads turned.

Postures shifted.

Questions came from the dragon lords, asking *where* and *when* and *how* and *who*.

But Pim was more worried about Futari. Where *was* she?

That's when the weeping began.

Pim sprang.

She found Futari huddled under one of the lab tables, a bloodied sword abandoned on the floor at her side. Then Pim did something Aloora Longstride had never done whenever she cornered a murderer. She gathered the dragoness into her arms and rocked her while they both cried.

49

WOLVES ARE TERRIBLE ACTORS

Pim had *no* intention of letting Futari go, so when a group of honest-to-god dragon slayers showed up, Pim hissed at them. They tried to reason with her, and things got ugly.

They backed off fast.

Her yowl brought Boon, whose tail was puffed double. Elara was with him, and she crawled right over, dipping her head to try to catch Futari's eye. "Oh, god. That must have been tough. You're my hero."

Futari reached out and gently pulled Elara into their huddle.

"My turn," coaxed Elara. "Come here, pretty lady. I'm sturdier than I look."

After some rearranging, Futari sat across Elara's lap, her head on the woman's shoulder. Elara kissed her brow and pet her hair, and Futari sagged into her. Silent tears still traced her cheeks.

"Easy, now, ladies. It's just me and Juuyu." Boon sat on the floor at the far end of the table. "Gotta take care of some formalities before we can get you outta here."

Juuyu crouched near where Futari huddled. Warbling softly, he said, "Pardon me."

Pim saw what he intended, and quickly nodded. "It's okay, Futari. He's helping."

The dragoness raised her head to glare at the phoenix.

He calmly offered a handkerchief.

"Such a gentleman," Elara crooned, taking it on Futari's behalf.

Juuyu had removed his shirt and lifted it, brows arching. "If you will permit this, my bondmate and I can give you sanctuary. Otherwise, I fear you would be consigned to one of the harems."

"After this, you think they'd welcome her?" challenged Pim.

"A dragoness is always in demand." Juuyu sighed. "I would *greatly* prefer to bring you to Fumiko and Zuzu. You would not be among dragons, Futari, but you would be with other tree-kin."

The silence stretched, and Pim intervened. "Do you want to stay?"

"I hate this place."

"Will you trust me and mine?" Juuyu inquired solemnly.

"Yes," Futari whispered, "Please."

So Juuyu draped his shirt over her shoulders. Lifting his voice so it would carry, he said, "You may consider yourself in my custody." Rising, Juuyu faced the room at large, dignified, even in his undershirt. "This tree-kin is under the protection of the Kazuki Grove, whose existence is currently undisclosed. All the rules and rights of sanctuary do apply."

"We yield," called one of the dragons. And more gently, "We are sorry for your loss, Kindred. Your sister will be remembered in tonight's song."

"Kaneko!" Futari cried, "Her name was Kaneko!"

Linlu padded closer and promised, "Already, the stars are tuning their voices to your cry."

Pim looked to Boon, who tugged wearily at his ponytail.

Looking to Juuyu, he asked, "Where's Sinder in all this?"

"Called away." Juuyu indicated a direction, then pivoted to point another way. "I would be grateful if you would escort Futari to where Colt is organizing the healers. The mares will look to her needs until my section is ready to depart. Unless ... you are also bound for America?"

"Nope. Other plans," said Boon. But then his expression went oddly blank. "Should I have checked first? I should have. Hell and hellions, this is going to take some getting used to."

Pim scooted out, then offered a hand to Futari.

Elara gave her a little boost and asked, "Did he just call us hellions?"

He'd had his back turned, hand over his mouth, but at that, he pivoted, eyes wide.

"Would that be so bad?" Pim asked lightly. "It might be a compliment."

Boon snorted, and his tail started moving again.

Which made Pim wonder why it had been still.

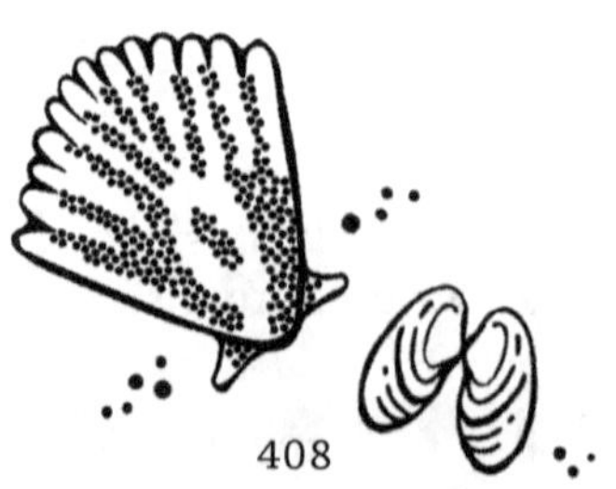

Several healers wearing the Alpenglow crest had taken over the assorted huts in the grove, where food and drink were being served to an odd mix of lab employees, tree-kin, and crossers. Pim kept an eye on Elara, who moved with ease from group to group, acting as a liaison between the island's residents and their rescuers.

Boon stood a little apart, and Pim went to stand with him. "You should probably eat something."

"Not hungry," he mumbled.

That's when his stomach growled.

Pim eyed him suspiciously. "Why has your tail gone still?"

"Take a wild guess."

"You're ... uneasy?"

"Hell, yeah."

Which couldn't be the whole of it. "Are you regretting your choices?"

"I will be if I can't get the both of you to someplace quiet, like ... now."

Boon's tail puffed, and there was pleading in his posture.

She offered, "I'll bring Elara."

He pointed toward the beach. Jaw clenched, he whispered, "Hurry."

Extracting Elara took longer than Pim expected, but she eventually led her onto a stretch of black sand that was mostly unoccupied. Reavers wearing the Spomenka crest patrolled the shoreline in groups of three, many with Kith companions. Boon stood with his arms tightly folded and his tail switching as he gazed out over the water.

"We're here," Pim softly called, since he didn't seem to notice.

He beckoned them closer, and ... he looked miserable.

She traded a look with Elara, who was similarly concerned.

"Is it poison?" Pim ventured. "You're sweating."

He growled, reached for her, and retreated, all in quick succession. Then he glanced over his shoulder to check if anyone was watching.

"What *is* this?"

"This is me, trying to be subtle." He spoke through his teeth. "I need to touch you."

Pim eased into a receptive posture, but he was making her nervous.

"Don't freak out." Hands closed around her shoulders, and he dipped closer. "Don't bite down. Just swallow, 'kay?"

Then his mouth aligned with hers. He was going to kiss her?

She froze, eyes wide. Nascent trust might have been the only thing holding her there.

Boon whined. "Come on, Pim. Let me in. Just for a sec."

"Why?"

"I need to pass you something. Let's call it a souvenir." Even more softly, he added, "Akira's dad helped me pick them out. Only the best for my girls."

She jerked back, eyes wide.

He looked relieved and nodded.

All hesitation gone, she guided him to her parted lips.

Boon's eyes were half-lidded with concentration as he carefully pushed something into her mouth. He quickly pulled back, gaze searching.

She gulped, and her breath started hitching. "Was that ...?"

He nodded and pulled her into a long embrace, then gently kissed her forehead. "Elara next, yeah?"

Pim twisted in his arms and held out a hand.

Elara stood a little apart, expression fragile.

"Your turn," Pim hissed urgently. "Please, Elara. You're next."

She crossed to them, her gaze troubled. "Are platonic kisses an Amaranthine thing? I have mixed feelings."

Pim realized that she couldn't have heard what they'd said. She pulled the woman in. "Let him do his thing. Don't bite down. Swallow."

Elara favored her with an arch look. "I can tell you're serious, but ... oh, god, there is *nothing* platonic about the image that painted."

"Boon is attempting to be subtle, and he's terrible at it. Let him kiss you, and when he passes you something, swallow it whole." Pim smiled shakily. "You're smart. Put it together."

Understanding sparked in those wide brown eyes.

Pim eased back so Boon could reel Elara in.

"Okay with this?" he checked. "Because I really, *really* don't want to swallow it myself."

"Can I kiss you for real?"

Boon's tail tucked. "You get that this is platonic, right?"

"Remind me later." She touched his scarred cheek. "If you're going to get me pregnant, I want there to be a kiss involved."

"Elara," he whined. "This really isn't my area of expertise."

"Not going to matter," she promised, pulling him down.

Pim tried not to laugh, Boon's tail was so tightly tucked. But Elara treated him gently, and he let the kiss linger, even after she'd swallowed her seed.

Then Elara pulled back, smiled tremulously at him, then turned into Pim's embrace, shoulders shaking as she softly sobbed.

Boon wrapped his arms around both of them. "Okay. That was nerve-wracking. Not the kissing part. I kinda wanted a taste, anyhow. Instincts, and all that. But better you than me."

"Taste is important to wolves?"

"Most of us will steal a taste when we're learning a scent. The more senses involved, the better you know something. Helps for tracking, too."

"Please don't lecture all the romance out of this moment," begged Elara.

"Think of it this way," suggested Pim. "He wants to memorize us with all his senses."

"Ideally, not out in the open where anyone and everyone might be watching." He gruffly added, "Save it for the den."

"Is that where you're taking us?" Elara asked.

"Not exactly. I mean, I've never had one of my own. But we'll need one, for us and for our ... huh. Guess they're not technically cubs."

"*Sprigs*," whispered Elara, whose smile was beautiful. "Oh, god. Pim, we've just been sprigged!"

50
MISSING PERSON

Juuyu gazed skyward. The storm's fury had abated, but the winds hadn't gone far. They looped in lazy swirls around the island, dancing to the ongoing songs of dragons. To his relief, the dragon lords weren't trying to woo these winds, merely thank them. Their interwoven melodies promised peace.

Linlu Dimityblest pulled him from his thoughts with a gentle clap of hands. "Your dragon needs you."

"Then I will go."

The moth clansman murmured, "Then all is as it should be."

Juuyu might have taken to the sky, but for a niggling recollection. Diverting to where Colt was assisting the healers in checking over the children, Juuyu touched his arm. "I am going to where Sinder is."

"Need a healer?"

"I might. He mentioned Jacques."

"Better safe than sorry," said Colt. "Let me grab one of the kits."

Juuyu was startled when, a moment later, one of the children collided with his leg, wrapping himself around it. The dragon crosser's tail lashed, and his glare was fierce as he announced, "I'm going, too."

"You are not being abandoned." Juuyu indicated the healers. "All who can leave will be escorted to a windship for transport in the near future."

"Oh, I know. I paid attention. I always pay attention." The boy brandished a monogrammed handkerchief. "I want my uncle."

"You ... have a relative here?"

"I sure do! He's my new family. He promised."

Juuyu wasn't sure what to make of his claim, but he gently caught the corner of the handkerchief, tilting his head to study the fussy monogram. He warbled softly. "You met Jacques."

The boy's grip tightened. "Bring me to Uncle Jackie!"

He wondered how to dissuade the boy, but then Colt was back. Picking up the boy, he lightly inquired, "Your name, young sir?"

"Sibley."

"Hold my kit, Sibley." Colt arched his brows at Juuyu and cheerfully asked, "Shall we?"

Juuyu's necklace included crystals that were tuned to each of his teammates, so he knew their general directions.

Hallow was at the fertility clinic to the south.

Moon had accompanied a team to the resort on the eastern shore.

Boon was nearby, probably sorting things out with Pim and Elara. But Sinder was somewhere north of the garden. It didn't feel far.

As they flew over thick jungle, Colt coaxed the boy into conversation. He'd always been good with children, and this one was surprisingly helpful. Juuyu soon fell back in order to ask his own questions. "How many Amaranthine trees are on the island?"

"All together? Or do you only want the ones who'll talk to you?"

"All. Even a stump can send up a shoot."

"There's seventeen in the garden. That includes the lopped one and a couple of stumps. They don't talk to us, but I don't blame them. What he did … it looks like it hurt."

Juuyu asked, "Are you familiar with bonsai?"

Sibley clearly was. "All the potted trees are in Dr. Naoki's greenhouse."

"How many?"

"Six pots, but it's seven trees. He grafted Quade and Valo together, so even though it looks like one tree, there's actually two of them."

They reached the shoreline, and Juuyu frowned. "We are close. There! The sand changes color just there."

Choppy waves preceded them onto a hidden beach, where a tight ball of abrasions trembled.

Colt hurried to kneel beside their teammate. "We're here, Sinder. Let us remove the worst of these slivers before you move."

A muffled warble promised cooperation.

Juuyu realized that Sibley was hanging back. He curled his fingers, beckoning him forward. "This dragon is my partner. If he were in speaking form, he would tell you that he is one of the good guys."

"I'd appreciate your help, Sibley." Colt held up a hand. "My nails are blunt, and my fingers are too large for the smallest slivers"

The three of them picked and flung until it was safe for Sinder to uncurl. He shuddered and hissed as his coils unlooped, revealing the unconscious man clasped to his breast. Without letting go, Sinder shifted. He winced, but only said, "I need to get him to Argent."

"Allow me." Juuyu knelt to take Jacques.

Sinder cradled him closer. "I want to do it."

"You are injured."

"Argent needs to know what I saw. And about who did this to Jacques. Plus, I think this answers another looming question." Sinder took a pleading tone. "Let me see this through."

"You are hurt," Juuyu protested.

"I want to anyhow."

Inclining his head, he warned, "I *will* step in if your strength flags."

Colt opened his kit. This time, Sinder didn't protest; he was worried about Jacques. Colt checked the basics, then sniffed lightly. "I wish either Boon or Moon was here. Or my brother. He's better when it comes to pollens and the like."

"There was a tree here." Sinder angled his head toward a barren formation that might have looked like a winter-bare tree if it hadn't been made of stone. "Well … half-tree."

Jacques' eyelashes fluttered, and he blinked hazily. "Hallo."

"Do you know who I am?" Colt asked.

"Rrricker Thunderhoof. Lovely to see you. Do you like to swim? We have a club." Switching his gaze to Sinder, he loudly whispered, "Wouldn't you like to see that in a fundoshi?"

"I know you have filters," Sinder complained. "Use them."

"Uncle Jackie! Hey, are you okay?"

"Sibley!" The man writhed so much, Sinder had to let him down. On his knees in the sand, Jacques pulled the boy close. "You came to rescue me, this time? I'm touched."

The boy sniffed and scowled. "What did you eat? Don't you know better than to dally with trees?"

"I do. Truly. But I made an exception."

Colt hunkered down and tipped Jacques' face up. He could smell the sweetness on the man's breath. "You ate pollen? That's madness."

"*Non*. They fed me flower petals." He swayed in place. "Suuzu will be so furious."

"Why?" Juuyu knelt and took a turn inspecting Jacques. "What have you done to anger my brother?"

"Oh. Oooh, my. You're a bloody rainbow." Jacques gazed at him raptly. "Marriage suits you. Or have you always been like this?"

Sinder cleared his throat. "Whatever they did, it affected him. He's seeing things. He's hearing things. He's gone all reaver-ish."

"I'm a *Smythe*."

"Yes, yes, you are. First of Smythes."

"I like that. Put it on my calling cards." Then the man's eyes rolled back, and he slumped to the side.

Sibley hauled back, holding him up until Colt lent a hand, easing the man to the ground.

Sinder wasted no time reclaiming him. "Say, Colt. Get a sample of this sand for me? A big sample. Use a shovel. Fill your pockets. Something."

"*Something*, he says." Colt dragged his fingers through the fine, green stuff, which sparkled against his skin. Definitely worth a closer look, but it wasn't as if he'd brought saddlebags. So he wrestled out of his boots and nodded to Sibley. "We'll fill these, then follow."

Sinder strode to the water's edge, then waded out past the cove's entrance before shifting into truest form and taking to the sky. Colt could understand the choice. Jacques was bigger than Sinder in speaking form, so the man was more secure in dragon claws.

Sibley scrambled, clearly anxious to stick with Jacques. Colt could sympathize. He knotted bootlaces together and slung his burden over one shoulder. Pulling Sibley against the other, Colt carried him aloft. From the looks of things, Sinder was already struggling, but he was also singing softly. Winds rushed past Colt, chasing after Sinder in order to buoy his flight. But there was only so much they could do.

Juuyu stepped in, shifting into truest form, which earned a whistle of surprise from Sibley.

"Never seen a phoenix?" Colt asked. "I'm not surprised. They don't range much."

"Can we get closer?"

"A little," he agreed, though he didn't like to get too close.

The partners were struggling to find their rhythm. Flying in tandem can't have been easy, but Juuyu was adjusting to Sinder, and with matched wingbeats, they gained a more comfortable distance from jittery waves.

A sudden sense of déjà vu sent a thrill down Colt's spine. It was just as Fira had always described it—a fiery bird tangling with a winged dragon. Storm clouds beyond. Uneasy seas below. They were natural enemies, yet they weren't fighting. Instead, they worked together to carry something.

"How about that?" Touching the remnant stone woven into his forelock, Colt murmured, "So that precious something was you."

"What? Did something happen?" Sibley demanded. "Who's precious?"

"Your Uncle Jackie."

Colt was glad to have caught the moment foretold by the remnant song in Fira's stone, because it was fleeting. Indeed, it's end was near, for an enormous silver fox with his flourish in disarray was streaking their way.

With a low chuckle, Colt said, "Precious, indeed."

51
ALTERED STATES

When Argent was able to return to the room he'd secured for his denmates, he found Akira sitting on a stool beside Jacques' bed, holding his uncle's hand.

"*Tsk*. You are meant to be resting."

Akira ignored the reprimand. "What's wrong with him?"

"Pollination, probably. Colt also mentioned something about consuming flower petals. It would account for his inability to focus on any of us for more than a few moments."

"His tattoos are gone."

Argent knew this, but he was surprised Akira did. "You checked?"

"Well, when I noticed that one was gone ...." He shrugged. "I was worried."

"You checked *all* of them?"

"Yeah. I mean ... all the ones that were inked, anyhow." Akira tangled his fingers with Jacques'. "He won't like it. He was proud of them."

Again, this is something Argent already knew. And apparently, something Akira had learned.

This stirred up a confusing clash of instincts. Argent wanted to protect Akira for several reasons, and for many other reasons, he wanted to protect Jacques. He'd never imagined a circumstance in which he'd feel the need to protect them from each other.

Shaking his head, Argent said, "You should be lying down."

"All right," he sighed.

To Argent's mounting bafflement, Akira slid in with Jacques, fussing over him without a trace of hesitation.

Roles. That must be it. They'd adopted these roles for the ruse. And Akira had always been affectionate with those he considered family.

"Your uncle is fine," Argent tried.

Akira asked, "Is it true that Jacques is a reaver now?"

"Who told you that?"

"Sinder may have let something slip."

But Argent was more interested in Akira's slip. "You are on a first name basis, now?"

"It would be odd if we weren't."

"Granted." Argent couldn't decide if Akira was preening his manservant because he thought it would do any good ... or if he was actually avoiding eye contact.

Something had happened. Well, many things had happened. But something had happened to these two, and Argent had never been fond of unforeseen consequences. He drummed his fingers against the side of his leg. "Is there anything I should know while

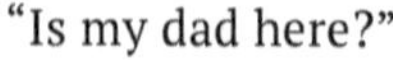

we have some measure of privacy?"

"Is my dad here?"

"Naoki is safely aboard, yes."

"Did he tell you about me …?"

"Yes. He asked if he could check on you at regular intervals. Naoki seems prone to fussing."

Akira hummed vaguely and kept right on fiddling with Jacques. Clearly, it was a family trait.

"Once we're home," Akira began. "Once things settle down enough, would you give some thought to where I should plant my seed?"

Argent blandly replied, "I had already given the matter considerable thought."

"Because the Scattering will arrive in the spring?"

"Groves *do* require planning." While not a lie, the remark was such an enormous sidestep, it barely counted as subtle. Jacques would have noticed in a heartbeat and demanded to know what Argent was hiding.

Akira only asked, "Will it cause trouble that my twin is going to be a tree like Tabi-otosan?"

"Do you really think I would pass up the chance to hide Stately House even more thoroughly, since people will forget where we are?"

"I suppose that would appeal to a fox." Akira's smile faltered. "But what about our friends?"

"Hajime assures me that there are ways to inure someone to the scent, much as you would build up an immunity to dragon sway."

"That's good then." A shy glance. "One other thing?"

"Certainly."

"Are Eiji and Anjou here?"

"As it happens, they are. Juuyu entrusted them with the island's wardstones, which I believe will interest Michael."

"Would it be all right if they came in here? With us?"

Argent didn't mind putting all the precious things in one place. "I will let them know that they would be welcome."

"Thanks."

Then Akira nestled against Jacques, who turned in his sleep, pulling Akira into his arms. They looked so at home together, Argent had to confess himself uneasy. For them. And for Suuzu.

"Excuse me, sir?" Tenma had never really considered how difficult it could be to find a dragon who was trying not to stand out. "Are you Opulence Windlore?"

Blue eyes lifted from a page crammed with writing, and pale lashes fluttered. "You have need of a bard?"

"Not … immediately. Maybe eventually?" He figured it didn't hurt to ask. "Do you ever sing at weddings?"

The white-haired dragon set aside his quill and folded his hands together. "You employed a tracker to carry you aboard a covert windship filled with refugees escaping the tropics … to secure my services for your upcoming nuptials?"

"No, sir, not exactly. Although I *did* need Merit to find you." He nodded gratefully to his guide. "He knew your scent, which helped. I guess you're acquainted …?"

Opulence spared the dog clansman a fond look. "I sang at his father's wedding. How *is* Harmonious?"

Merit frowned. "You're asking after Da? Not Mum?"

"Let's blame the resemblance. You look very like him."

Arms folding across his chest, Merit's tone sharpened. "Isn't it *Mum* you're actually curious about?"

Tenma eased onto the seat next to the dragon's and quietly waited his turn.

Merit's frustration was plain. "You've always known where to find us, but we've had no idea what became of you. Where have you been the past few hundred years?"

Opulence lowered his gaze to his quill, running his finger along the blue feather's edge. "Here and there. A bard is wont to wander."

"Hiding?" he accused.

"Let us say ... I am uncomfortable being something Anna regrets." With a rallying sort of smile, Opulence said, "Far better that she devote herself wholly to that smitten dog."

Merit snorted. Then he knelt before the dragon's chair. "Do you really think she would forget her mentor?"

Opulence fluted mournfully.

"Mum is tired of wondering. She's on her way."

"Anna never leaves the safety of Harmonious' den. That fact is sung far and wide, not unlike the ballads of Opal the Sage."

"Da knows when to give in gracefully. He's taking her to Stately House." Merit gently warned, "She's furious with you."

The dragon hugged himself. "I am in no fit state to withstand her wrath."

Tenma said, "If you'll permit it, sir, I can help."

Opulence glanced his way, then really looked. "Are you the one who inspires the stars to song?"

"Hardly the *only* one, but … well, I wouldn't be surprised."

His gaze jumped from Merit back to Tenma. "At last? Is this to be *my* confluence of destinies?"

Merit said, "Da brought Tenma into our pack when he was still a boy. While no one would credit it as foresight, he will be pleased and proud once someone points out that he has been protecting the means for you to be mended."

Then Opulence was reaching for Tenma's hand, and he confessed, "It is as he said. With one thing and another, I am a trifle Broken."

"Yes, I know." Tenma looked to Merit and asked, "Can you make sure no one interrupts?"

He stalked off, only to return a few moments later with Argent, who inclined his head to Opulence, placed a crystal in Tenma's hand, and set about filling the vicinity with sigilcraft.

"A convenient friend to have," murmured the dragon.

"More than a friend. When I marry one of the daughters of Stately House, I will officially move from Harmonious's den to Argent's." And then, "Umm, Merit? Can you help with these?"

Merit considered the heavy protective bangles around the dragon's wrists and grunted. "Argent, this is more your thing."

The fox finished his illusion with a flourish, then traded places with Merit. Argent fussed for a scant minute, and the first heavy accessory came away. As he set to work on the second, he spared the dragon a considering glance. "If you need respite, you are welcome at Stately House. We recently added a Song Circle. If you are not already spoken for, Lady Mettlebright and I would be delighted if Opal the Sage were to add his sagas and songs to our first Dichotomy Day celebrations."

"Very generous, I am sure."

Argent huffed. "Very greedy. I would love to present you to my bondmate. She has long admired your work."

"You are too kind."

"*She* is kind, as is Tenma. I am less so, but that may yet work in your favor. Many secrets are kept safe at Stately House." Setting aside the second bracelet, Argent inclined his head and stepped away, joining Merit outside the barrier.

"Formidable," remarked Opulence.

"Famously so." When they clasped hands around the crystal, Tenma could tell that the dragon was trembling. "I won't hurt you. I *can't* hurt you."

"This is not fear. You see, my star is singing, and I am quite affected."

"Are they happy for you?"

Swallowing hard, he nodded and scooted closer. "What must I do?"

"Tend me."

Opulence's mouth formed a soft *o*, and he whispered, "Is that the way of things?"

"As simple as that. Try and see."

Tenma guided and encouraged, and Opulence soon draped against him, crooning softly as tears of relief slipped down his cheeks. And when all was whole and well and the weeping was over, Opulence snuffily vowed, "I will sing over all your generations."

"We plan to be as ordinary as possible." With a little shrug, Tenma said, "Lilya and I want a quiet life. Hardly the stuff of songs."

"Impossible," he scoffed. "The stars say you will build a dynasty."

"Oh!" Tenma laughed. "That part's already true. But it's not *my* dynasty. It belongs to Lilya's parents, Michael and Sansa Ward."

"And you will add to it?"

"That's Lilya's plan. To raise our family at Stately House."

"I shall consider it settled." Opulence beamed at him, repeating, "I will sing over all your generations."

Tenma nodded and shook his head. "Maybe you should tell me what that means …?"

"Opal the Sage is renowned the world over for epics and ballads and thrilling tales of half-forgotten lore. But for you, I shall try my hand at something new."

The dragon was clearly pleased by the idea, so Tenma eased into a receptive posture. "And that would be …?"

"Cradle songs." Opulence glanced at the room beyond Argent's barrier. A room filled with weary children. "For yours and for these and for those to come, I will dedicate myself to the gentle sway and peaceful promises of lullabies."

Jacques woke with Akira in his arms and gave in to relief. Pulling him into better alignment, Jacques kissed the top of his head and basked in the prospect of a proper lie-in … only to realize—by some sense that was new and novel—that he had an audience.

Lifting his head enough to peer around the unfamiliar room, he first spotted Anjou, then Eiji, who sat on the floor, flanking the door.

The bed was exquisite, draped in sequined silks that wafted with the slight roll of ongoing movement. Were they at sea? He was about to ask when Anjou pointed.

Only then did Jacques locate the fifth person in the room. "Sibley?" he called softly. "Are we safe, then?"

Staying seated upon a small heap of gauze-wrapped bundles next to an enormous pair of boots, he said, "I'm not sure, exactly. Nobody says much to me."

"Lord, boy. You're part dragon. Do they even know you're here?"

That earned a grin. "That healer guy knows. And your stately fox. And this lot, though they pretended not to notice when I squeaked through their barrier."

The felines traded smiles.

Sibley's gaze drifted to the man in Jacques' arms. "Is that him?"

"Yes. He's your Uncle Akira."

Finally, the boy eased off his seat and approached the bed. Tipping his head to one side, he ventured, "I've been wondering for a while now. How come I smell blood?"

"*Mon dieu*! What? Where?" He flung back the blankets and patted Akira down, finally locating a patch of gauze. Peeling it back, he bared pink skin marred by a neat row of stitches. Jacques was speechless.

Akira, who'd naturally woken, rubbed wearily at the side of his face, even as he submitted to anxious inspection.

"You're cut," Sibley announced. He dipped down to lick the spot. "Don't think it's infected. No poison, either. You're lucky. That means he used a scalpel instead of his claws."

"Yes. He was careful."

Jacques was more than a little rattled. "That dragon put his hands on you? He cut you?"

Akira summoned up a smile. "I'm fine, Jacques. You're the one I'm worried about."

"But this! It can't have been elective surgery."

"No."

"What did that monster *do*?"

"Kodoku took a golden seed out of my side."

Jacques' fingers trembled as he traced the cut. "He *took* it?"

"It's okay. I took it back." Akira flopped back on his pillow and fished Suuzu's necklace from under his nightshirt. Tapping the reliquary, he said, "Right here. My twin is safe."

"Good for you," said Sibley. "And good for them, having you for a brother."

Akira turned to the boy and smiled. "Hello. I'm your Uncle Akira. Budge over, Jacques. Make room for more family."

Jacques did, and Sibley piled between them. "Are you really my uncle?"

While Akira cheerfully explained the convoluted bond they shared, Jacques flung his arm over both of them and tried not to think about what would happen once they reached Stately House.

He should be distancing himself right now, readying himself to give Akira up. Suuzu was waiting. Their pact would end, and Jacques could go back to devoting himself to Argent.

Except … he wasn't sure he *could*. And that was unsettling.

52

LORD METTLEBRIGHT AND HIS MAN

Argent peered for a long while at the tangle of people on the bed. He had no idea if it had been Jacques or Akira who'd invited the two feline guards to abandon the floor. Either of them would have insisted. All of them—including the outspoken young crosser—looked happy.

With a sigh, he stepped inside and cleared his throat.

The purring stopped. Heads lifted. Certain gazes lowered guiltily. Interestingly enough, Jacques' was one of them.

"I am borrowing my manservant." Argent haughtily added, "Come along, Smythe."

Jacques extricated himself from the others but hesitated on the edge of the bed. He'd finally noticed that he was wearing little more than ointment and gauze. One of the cats shed his sashed coat, retying it around Jacques before kissing his cheek and whispering encouragement in French.

Argent simply waited.

Jacques tottered slightly but found his stride, and he trailed after Argent without a word. The silence was unusual, but he approved. He wasn't in the mood for inanities, and secrets were better shared in seclusion.

"I managed to secure a scrap of privacy."

There wasn't a door, but he'd warded the alcove nearly out of existence. Even if Sibley had his older brother's penchant for barrier-wrecking, he wouldn't be able to follow Jacques here.

Taking Jacques by the hand, Argent guided him through.

The man gasped. "Oh, lord. A bath."

"It is makeshift, but it is better than nothing. Hurry along. I doubt the water will stay hot at this altitude."

Jacques cast aside his borrowed shirt and inspected the various bottles on offer. "These are *mine*."

"Nonny weighed me down with an excess of absolute necessities." He indicated the garment bag hanging against the wall. "He is incredibly stubborn."

"I apologize for any inconvenience."

"Not at all." And weary of polite nothings, he grumbled, "Let me help, Jackie."

Jacques blinked hard and took a receptive posture.

Argent peeled away the bandaging, annoyed that the healer's ointments mostly obscured any scents Jacques might have carried. The man scratched at his hair, and sand pattered to the floor.

As Argent steadied him into the meager bath, he grumbled, "You look naked."

"All the better for bathing …?" Jacques lightly countered.

"I meant that my sigils are gone."

"Eaten. Dayith was grateful for them." Jacques' shoulders hunched. "He said they were beautiful. Full of love."

"I suppose a person who subsists upon sigilcraft *would* have a discerning palate."

Argent set to work washing Jacques, who lapsed into another silence.

"You have sand in your hair."

"Sand gets everywhere during a beach holiday."

"It appears to be … green?"

Jacques hummed, and Argent sighed. "Sinder's version of events raised more questions than it answered. Will you tell me what happened?"

"You want me to file a report?" he asked wearily.

"No. We can decide what to put in the official report later. What is said here is between us. Think of it as the sorts of confidences a man shares with his valet. Or … the secrets one only shares with their closest friend."

Jacques' chin trembled. "Dayith wasn't alone. He has a son … a crosser. A tree."

"Is that where this is from?" From his pocket, Argent produced the crystal flower that Jacques had been clutching to his heart when Sinder brought him in.

"*Oui.*" Jacques' fingers twitched, and his glance was anxious.

"I only took it for safekeeping." Argent reached for Jacques' hand and placed the flower there. "Confide in me?"

And so Jacques spoke of being foretold. About the beach under a green bower that glittered like a cathedral. About the call for winds and the dire consequences. About the taste of flower petals and the rock imp's tending.

"You carry Dayith's remnant song?"

"His very words."

"All so they could give you this." Argent skeptically indicated the crystal flower.

"It seems smallish as legacies go."

"*Legacy*?" Argent asked sharply.

Jacques traced a delicate edge. "This is all that's left to show that they were here. I would have liked to bring them to Stately House, but ...."

"Most trees do not wander."

"*Non*. They were convinced I would get home again. Carrying this, I guess." He blinked and refocused on Argent's face. "Did I mention that Solace is half tree?"

"You implied it, yes."

"He's family. He even looks a little like Akira. And Papa Socks, of course." With a smile that trembled somewhat, Jacques confessed, "He kissed me goodbye. And Dayith ...." Jacques' gaze drifted out of focus, and he touched the back of his neck.

Argent berated himself for not making a thorough inspection. "Show me."

"Is something there?" Jacques pulled straggling curls away from his nape.

"Did you know that it is considered a great honor to be kissed by an Impression?"

"I did. Isla went on an imp kick after Mikoto Reaver's wedding, and you know how she gets. One long info dump." Jacques peered over his shoulder and repeated, "*Is* something there?"

"Yes." Argent lightly traced the edges of the mark. "You now have what looks like a blaze. This flower is a match for the one in your hand, both in shape and in hue."

He searched for it with trembling fingers. "I wish I could see it."

"How strange." Argent leaned closer, sniffing lightly. "There seems to be a scent."

"I smell strange?"

"Hmm." Leaning closer, his nose bumped skin. "It is not unappealing."

Jacques went very still. "Argent? Did you just lick me?"

"Perhaps a seal would be in order."

"Would it?" Jacques' eyes were wide.

Argent backed away and pulled at the air between them, weaving a small sigil. "I am shuttering you now. That should serve until we have more time to explore your impish legacy."

Turning to face him, Jacques' lips twitched into a smile. "I can see it. Your sigilcraft."

"Bright sides abound." Argent may have added a little extra finesse to the process.

The water cooled, so Argent shook out a towel. Wordlessly, he helped his manservant into his own clothes and oversaw the little routines that were so important to Jacques.

The man's mood lightened, his soul brightened, and the air freshened with that same intriguing scent. "*Tsk.* Let me check my seal."

Jacques crouched. "Didn't it take?"

"It did." Argent's thoughts raced. What was he missing? Only one possibility came to mind. "They *both* kissed you?"

"*Oui.*" Touching his nape, he said, "Dayith, here."

"And Solace?"

Jacques pointed to his lips.

With a sigh, Argent ordered, "Open your mouth."

Jacques stood with Akira at one of the windows, mostly watching the scenery flow past, but also watching Akira's face. The man was as presentable as Jacques could make him, under the circumstances. His borrowed finery—mostly draconic in origin—draped and fluttered and clung in ways that weren't his first preference, but Akira had been more than ready to shed his pastels.

"Lord, it's cold," Jacques casually remarked.

"There's snow," Akira noted.

"Are you warm enough?" Opening his suit coat, Jacques moved behind Akira and pulled him close, enfolding him.

Akira leaned gratefully into him. But he was being too quiet.

"Do you still have our rings? He's sure to be wearing his."

"Oh! I almost forgot." Akira coaxed Suuzu's necklace out from under filmy, sequined layers, but he turned to Jacques for help. "My hands are shaking too much."

Jacques' weren't much steadier, but he found the twist of ribbon on which two glass rings softly jingled. He passed them both to Akira. It was foolishness, but he wanted to see what he'd do. Akira first slipped on the amber ring. Then quietly, deliberately, he placed the green ring on Jacques' finger.

"*Merci*," Jacques murmured.

Akira simply patted his hand and went back to leaning.

"Nervous?"

"I'm so nervous, I'm queasy."

"I'll grant you this has the markings of a monumental day, but it can only end well. Your news is good. Suuzu will be glad. Lord, he'll probably sing for days."

Akira clasped the reliquary in one hand, as if trying to keep it warm. "I probably can't plant my seed during winter."

"Spring will come." Jacques smiled wistfully. "He'll be doubly clingy in the meantime."

"I know."

"Has anyone mentioned what happens once your twin is snugly planted?"

"I'll learn as I go, I guess." Akira tipped his head back. "What about you?"

Jacques suspected he was in for long months of withdrawal, but he wouldn't ever say as much. "Oh, look! I see home!"

Michael must have adjusted the barriers to permit the windship access. The dragons slowly descended toward the outdoor stage beside the large, circular meadow that was to be their Song Circle. The meadow was under the care of a trio of mice who'd promised a bounty of wildflowers once spring arrived, but for now, it was a field of snow.

Akira pulled open their window and leaned out to wave. Jacques kept his hands on his shoulders, knowing Suuzu would have done the same. They were close enough to make out members of their welcoming party.

Deece, flanked by two of his Kith sons. Michael, looking dignified with his cloak and crystal-topped staff. Andor, his big arms folded over his chest.

Tsumiko was there, standing amidst the mares. And there were Ginkgo and Kyrie, already hurrying forward as the dragons set the barge down with nary a bump.

"Do you see him?" Akira asked, upon tiptoe.

"Your comely bird is here. He's at the very back, next to Lapis."

Akira looked for all the world like an amateur actor with stage fright.

Jacques supposed it was up to him. "Mind if I add a touch of drama to our reunion?"

"You think it'd help?"

"Immeasurably."

"Sure. Okay. Yeah."

Jacques drew him away from the window, kissed him lightly, and murmured, "I'll miss you." Then he swept Akira into his arms and marched for the door, just as it opened. He strode out, head high.

"You won't have to miss me, Jacques," Akira quietly argued. "We both live here."

"You won't be playing footsie under the table with me. Or sleeping in my arms. And you won't need me to dress you or undress you or take you to dinner." He kept his voice low, his tone light. "My courtship fell rather flat, and I'll probably always regret giving you up."

Akira looked ready to cry.

"Lord, don't look at me like that," he chided. "Smile for your pining nestmate and go back to calling me Uncle Jackie."

"I can't!"

"*Certainly* you can. That's always been the plan, so we'll see it through."

"That's not who you are to me. Not anymore."

Jacques shushed him because Suuzu had finally stopped holding back. Dropping from the stage, he stumbled to a halt. Then Jacques was transferring Akira into rightful arms and stepping back. And stepping back. And stepping back again.

Suuzu sank to the snow with Akira and began a litany of crooning, clucking, and preening.

Akira chuckled and touched his face, and Jacques stepped back again, right into the burly wall that was Andor. The surly bear took one look, hauled Jacques into his arms, and trundled toward the woods.

Akira had been away long enough that Suuzu seemed strange and changed ... yet achingly familiar. He knew the scent of him and the sound of him, and he knew that Suuzu was barely holding himself in check. The phoenix probably wanted to carry him off, and Akira forced himself to relax in case that's how things turned out.

But his best friend settled for an awkward embrace in the snow, right there in front of everyone. He found Akira's tattoo, as if needing to reassure himself that this was really, truly him.

Tutting and crooned notes.

Sniffles and shy glances.

"I'm home," Akira said with a smile.

Suuzu's warble wobbled, only to end in a sob. Akira wasn't sure if he was shaking from the cold or if he'd reached the limit of holding himself together. Then Lapis was there, murmuring comfort and draping his cloak around the both of them.

Deece came to gather up Suuzu, who let it happen once Stately House's bodyguard spoke in his ear. Eiji knelt to lift Akira, and Anjou hovered at their side.

Casting about, Akira whispered, "Where's Jacques?"

The two felines traded a worried glance, then looked toward the woods. Eiji leaned close to ask, "Which do you want us to follow?"

Akira pointed after Suuzu because he needed to be with Suuzu. But at the same time, Akira was keenly aware that it was the answer Jacques would have wanted him to give. In his own heart, he was torn two ways. Maybe *this* was what people meant by heartbreak?

Eiji carried him one way, but Akira looked the other.

53

HOMECOMINGS

Pim lingered on the bench she shared with Elara, who slept with her head pillowed on Pim's lap. Most everyone else had left the dragon's windship already, leaving them in peace. Boon had pulled strings to get them aboard the first ship out, but none of those strings had included permission to rove freely at their destination. Stately House was world-famous, as was Argent Mettlebright's protectiveness of his holdings. Pim could only assume that Boon was lobbying on their behalf.

She left off stroking Elara's hair when the woman stirred. "We've stopped?" she murmured.

"Yes. We're here." With a faint smile, she said, "Welcome to Japan."

"Oh, god. I did *not* miss winter."

"I can hear the ocean. Maybe there's hope for a beach."

"Are we sequestered?"

"Mm-hmm. We're little better than stowaways."

Elara sat up and asked, "Where did you find a blanket?"

"Anjou smuggled it to us earlier. He's taken a liking to you."

"Jealous?"

"I intend to keep you, though not entirely to myself." Pim resituated so the blanket draped around both their shoulders.

"Speaking of Boon …?"

But before any more could be said, Dr. Naoki stepped through the arched entrance to their section. His expression brightened, and he hurried forward. "I hadn't even realized you were aboard, Dr. Perrine, or I would've sought you out sooner!" Including Pim with a small smile, he added, "Boon asked me to check on you."

Elara whispered, "You *know*, Naoki-san?"

He beamed. "How are you feeling?"

Her gaze turned inward, and she slowly shook her head. "Fine? I mean, I need food and warmer clothes, but … I can't tell anything's different."

"Entirely normal. It can take days for the first physical changes to manifest." He checked her pulse and smoothed his hand over her forehead. "Nothing seems amiss. I've been through this myself, so don't hesitated to seek me out if you have questions."

"You have?"

"You met Akira. He's one of mine." Naoki showed his palms to Pim. "May I?"

She placed her hands in his and reported, "I don't feel any different, either."

His touch was light, careful. With a hum and a nod, he said, "If you're comfortable with the idea, I'd like to watch over your progress. Both of you.”

Elara reached for his hand. “Would you?”

Naoki looked to Pim, quietly waiting for her decision.

She could tell how much respect Elara had for this man, and that swayed her. “Please.”

“We’ve apparently arrived at an exciting time. My son-in-law spent a goodly portion of the ride quizzing me about the needs of Amaranthine trees and their kin. Stately House will be fostering a grove, you see. This will be a good place for your children to put down roots.”

“That is meant to be a secret, Naoki.”

Pim and Elara both startled and stared at the person who was suddenly *there*.

A bower of small red flowers cascaded with his hair, and a tiny bell chimed when he took a step forward in wooden sandals that clacked softly against the floor. “I know how to be patient, but Tsumiko is trembling with eagerness to see her father again.”

“Hajime,” Naoki breathed.

His tone made Pim’s whiskers twitch.

“You’re a *tree*!” Elara softly exclaimed.

“He’s *his* tree,” Pim realized aloud.

The tree winked at her, acknowledging her remark, but he wasn’t done scolding Naoki. “Argent will be displeased if you talk openly about the secrets he keeps.”

“Not with these two.” Naoki found his feet. “They’ve been sprigged.”

Hajime’s gaze immediately softened. “More of mine?”

“No, they carry seeds from Second Try and Trinity.”

"Welcome news."

"Am *I* welcome, too?" Naoki asked softly.

"Am I forgiven, then?" Hajime countered.

Pim waited to see how the man would answer, but he must have decided words weren't enough. In two long steps, he had his arms around the tree, but before things could progress any further, they winked out. Only a few red flower petals remained, twirling to the floor.

"Do you think he kissed him?" Pim whispered.

Elara's brows arched. "Who's kissing whom?"

"I'm ... not sure ...?"

"Do you mean us? Because that was definitely Boon."

Pim hesitated. How strange. She'd been so sure a moment ago.

Leaning into her side, Elara asked, "This is nice. Say, where did you find a blanket?"

Jacques clung to Andor while everything caught up to him in ways he really didn't want Argent to see. Not because he didn't trust his lord and master. Far from it. He simply didn't want Argent to regret sending him into danger. Lord Mettlebright had a passel of traumatized crossers to win over. He didn't need to fret over a traumatized butler, as well.

Chances were good that the fox would never know Jacques was bawling like a child by the time the bear clansman bent to enter the squat cabin where he, his pactmate, and his twin brother made their den.

"Cry," Andor gruffly urged. "No one will hear."

Permission helped Jacques catch his breath. No need to rush. A long cry suited him fine.

Andor brought a warm cloth to wipe his face, and he wrapped him in a fur blanket before tucking him between Doran's forepaws. The big bear snuffled and grunted. When Andor returned to Jacques' side, he offered his arms.

Jacques climbed into them and mumbled, "How did you know?"

"Eri knew."

He fisted Andor's tunic and let himself be thoroughly, enormously sad. And angry in places, and frightened in others, before cycling back to all the ways he'd left himself open to heartbreak. He didn't regret anything. He wouldn't change anything. But this was the beginning of consequences.

Hooves clattered across Andor's porch, and Jacques groaned.

The door burst open, bringing a gust of cold air and an outburst of swearing.

"Door," growled Andor.

It slammed and Jacques braced himself, figuring Nonny would chew him out. But his apprentice flung his arms around Jacques's shoulders and demanded, "Who hurt you? I'll kill 'em!"

Jacques heaved a shaky sigh. "No need, but I do appreciate the sentiment."

Nonny complained, "You were supposed to come home!"

"And here I am. I did promise to survive."

"You're nowhere near home, and you know it." Nonny demanded, "Look at me."

Jacques reluctantly faced the goat-crosser who knew him better than most.

His blue eyes held a fierce light that quickly faded, softening to sympathy. "You utter idiot," he whispered.

He reached out, catching the end of a long, blond braid and testing its texture. "You haven't been conditioning properly since I left."

Nonny scowled. "There's no way I'm going through that whole long-arse routine on my own. And don't change the subject. I *saw* Akira."

He tried not to react.

Nonny wasn't fooled. "Damnit, Jacques. I told you not to go and fall in love with him."

"I remember."

"You shoulda listened! And now look at you." Pulling him into a much gentler embrace he asked, "Want me to get Cat and Canary?"

"Deferring to your old rivals? Never thought I'd see the day."

Nonny thumped his shoulder, then patted his scruffy cheek. "Geez. What's going on with your scent?" He bent closer to sniff. "Did you switch out one of your products?"

Jacques laughed a little, then lost it a little.

Another soul entered the room, then. Eri didn't usually show themself to others, so Jacques wasn't sure if Nonny knew that the star was part of Andor's den.

The goat-crosser's soft oath suggested not.

Eri knew right where to look. A slim hand lifted hair from Jacques' neck, exposing Dayith's mark. Their voice was light and lovely as it slipped into Jacques' soul. *"Precious are the gifts of trees.*

Rare is the favor of mountains."

"That does seem to be the rumor going 'round," Jacques managed.

The star smiled. *"I will guard your sleep."*

"Does that mean … no nightmares?" he asked hopefully.

Nonny stopped goggling at Eri long enough to ask, "It was that bad?"

Jacques shuddered.

Biting his lip, probably to keep from swearing in front of someone who looked for all the world like an angel, Nonny dredged up something to say. "Orders?"

Eri smiled.

Jacques snorted.

Nonny demanded, "Wha'd they say?"

"That you know what I need better than I do myself."

"Ain't it the truth?" Nonny squared his shoulders. "Right then. Lie low here until the rest clear out. Then it's straight into the bath."

"Privately?"

"Just us." Nonny's brow furrowed. "Should I let the guv know where you are?"

Just then, the door swung open. Kyrie paused beyond the threshold, belatedly rapped on the doorframe, and dipped his head. "Good evening, Andor, Eri. May I go to Uncle Jackie?"

"Peace, child," rumbled Andor.

The boy nodded once, politely stepped out of his shoes, and quietly closed the door behind him.

Kyrie crossed to Nonny's side and tapped his shoulder. "May I have a turn?"

"Knock some sense into him for me?"

"Father says that love is *rarely* sensible."

"Huh? What's this? Did *you* go and fall for somebody?" the older boy teased.

"No." He patiently, pointedly explained, "But the people I care about sometimes do, and I was curious."

Nonny blushed to the roots of his horns and made room.

Kyrie wriggled into the bundle of bear fur draping Uncle Jackie, who murmured, "You were always too good at hide and seek."

"Some winds followed the dragon lords here, and one of the scents they carried was new. But it was also yours. So I came to see."

Uncle Jackie's red-rimmed eyes looked so old. And sad.

Kyrie brought out his handkerchief and patted fresh tears from his cheeks.

"Lord, you still carry one? Somebody raised you right."

"That was *you*."

"Shouldn't you be helping your mother welcome home the newest members of the family?"

"I never knew I had so many sisters and brothers." Kyrie would get back to them. Soon. But he was very sure that this was more important. "You first."

"I'm afraid I didn't bring back any souvenirs."

"You did." Kyrie spoke softly, soothingly. "Your scent has changed, and you have shine now."

"Someone meddled," Uncle Jackie admitted. "Does it suit me?"

"You will need warding."

He frowned at this. "Your father already did that."

Kyrie fidgeted. "I would feel better if you let me add more."

"Right. If it'll put you at ease, carry on."

"Shine? What do you mean *shine*?" Nonny asked, his gaze bouncing from face to face.

Kyrie hadn't realized Nonny couldn't tell. He tried to think how to explain. "You know how Tenma is like a reaver, and yet he is not a reaver? And no one can account for his existence, yet they are grateful for it?"

Nonny rocked back on his hooves. "Jacques isn't a reaver."

With a trace of a smile, Jacques said, "I'm a Smythe."

Kyrie asked, "May I see?"

"See what?" his uncle asked warily.

"Inside your mouth."

"Lord, you're sharp," Uncle Jackie murmured. But he opened.

Kyrie peeped inside. Nothing on the roof of his mouth. Nothing on his tongue. "Lift?" he suggested. And there it was, on the underside of his tongue. "Does it match the other?"

With a bemused smile, Jacques said, "See for yourself."

Permission.

Kyrie found the second mark and traced it with the tip of one claw. "It *does* match," he reported. "They are both green flowers. Very good."

"What's good about them?" Jacques asked softly.

"They are your favorite color."

"Serendipitous."

"Lemme look." Nonny crowded close.

Jacques let him see, and the goat crosser swore softly, like he was impressed instead of angry. "How'd they get there?"

"Such a mark is the sign of an imp's favor. An Impression kissed him."

Nonny's eyes narrowed. "How come there's two marks?"

"There were two of them," he answered, still so quietly.

"Jacques!" exclaimed Nonny, looking shocked.

"It wasn't like that."

"This time," grumbled his apprentice.

And just like always, Jacques smiled and agreed, "This time."

Kyrie began weaving some of the sigils that were considered his specialty—tiny and tenacious. But he adapted them to Jacques' need, changing their shape so that a handful of flower-shaped anchors soon drifted around their heads.

Eri touched Kyrie's shoulder. "Weave my light into the pattern."

He'd never thought of trying that before. The next several sigils were easier to align. They even took on a greenish hue when they touched Jacques' skin. They shimmered there, then faded from view. Essentially invisible.

His uncle followed his every move, and Kyrie could tell that he was really watching. He now had eyes that could see. Mother would be pleased once she knew. Actually, Father had probably already told her. Because this could mean keeping Uncle Jackie for good.

With his hands busy and his focus mostly on protecting his uncle, Kyrie found the courage to ask a very different question.

"Did you see my sire?"

"*Non*, but I met your grandsire."

"What was he like?"

"Dreadful."

Kyrie considered the weight of that word for several long moments. Nodding, he asked, "Did the others find my sire?"

"*Non.*"

"Is he still ... doing bad things?"

"Probably."

"Then I will add more." Kyrie wove Eri's light and gave it shape. He flicked a few of the tiny sigils at Nonny and added more to Andor, too.

Jacques was mostly calm now. He asked, "Did you put sigils like this on me before I left for my holiday?"

"Yes." He frowned at Uncle Jackie. "But they are all gone."

"The one who took them ... he said he could tell they were full of love."

Kyrie felt his cheeks warming.

"Oi." Nonny was still stealing shy glances at Eri, but he'd noticed the sigils. "How many of us have you warded like this?"

"Everyone." Now that he knew what he could do, there was no way he wouldn't defend his family. Kyrie gravely promised, "I will protect *everyone.*"

Akira found himself at the kitchen table, with Tsumiko's chair pulled right up against his. She'd taken a break while their healers saw to bathing and outfitting the first wave of crossers. With Sonnet's help, Sis was trying to pack *welcome back* and *thank you*

in between all their other responsibilities.

"Did you get breakfast?" Tsumiko asked.

"Not really. Just some of those fruit and seed blocks that the healers serve with their medicinal teas."

Sonnet set baskets at the center of the table, then pushed a squat mug into Akira's hands. "Eat your gruel, dear. You look as if you need it. Do try, Suuzu. You're looking peaky."

Suuzu's chair was crammed close on Akira's other side, and the phoenix kept bumping against him with light touches, as if needing constant reassurance that Akira was there. Every time Akira met his gaze, Suuzu looked like he wanted to say a thousand things, but he didn't know how to start.

They'd have a good long talk eventually.

Actually, it'd probably take days to explain everything.

For now, Akira settled on something simple and straightforward, at least where avians were concerned. Fishing a scone out of one of the baskets, he broke off a corner and pushed it into Suuzu's mouth.

He gave a weak chirp, then wilted into him. It would seem their relationship had progressed to hand-feeding. Akira didn't mind. This sort of thing was easy.

Ginkgo ambled over and dropped onto the chair opposite them. "Don't stop. He's barely eaten since you left."

Suuzu mumbled a vague protest.

Akira added a little challenge to his posture.

His phoenix lowered his eyes and mutely accepted another morsel.

"Dad wants a meeting. Later, though. Don't rush through your gruel." With a quirky half-smile, he added, "Hey, Sonnet. Got any more of the good stuff? Because that guy's gonna love it. You wanting your uncle, little bro?"

Akira hadn't realized they had a tagalong until Ginkgo crooked his fingers. Sibley eased into view, just like Kyrie sometimes did. Like holding still was enough to camouflage his presence. Akira beckoned to him, saying, "Sibley is American. English, please."

Fists balled, glare wavering, the boy asked, "Where's Uncle Jackie?"

"I'm not sure," Akira admitted.

"He was *crying*," Sibley snapped.

"Oh." And Akira felt like crying.

Suuzu warbled uneasily.

Sibley pointed, "Who's *he*?"

"Suuzu is my nestmate." Indicating Tsumiko, he added, "And this is my sister, Lady Mettlebright. Do you know Ginkgo? And this wolf is Sonnet."

Sibley scowled. "We should go find Uncle Jackie."

Ginkgo raised a hand. "I'll go. Provided Uncle Akira can hold onto this for me." He sauntered around the table, dropped a kiss atop Akira's head, and lowered a bundle into his arms. "Welcome home. And meet Mercy."

Akira traded a look with his sister. "Brings back memories."

"I barely see her during the day, since everyone wants a turn holding her."

"Everyone will have their hands full, now. Plenty of dragon-crossers to go around. And other crossers, too, assuming we're taking them."

Tsumiko said, "Argent asked for all of them, so they wouldn't be separated. We'll welcome the rest in another hour or two."

Meanwhile, Sibley pointed at him and Suuzu, demanding, "What's *with* them?"

"Akira and Suuzu?" Ginkgo propped his hands on his hips. "Well, let's see. You know anything about avians?"

"What's that?"

"Bird clans."

"Oh. That's a good word. Nope."

"Well, you're in luck. Suuzu lives here, so you'll have plenty of chances to learn all about avian habits and mannerisms."

Akira glanced at Suuzu. *Lives here* made it sound very … full-time. But his work on the Amaranthine Council had never permitted more than monthly visits so Akira could watch over Suuzu while he went deep.

Sibley had already moved on. "How come you call me *little bro*?"

"Because I'm your big brother." He offered his hand.

"You don't look it."

"It's simple. My dad's your adoptive father." His silvery fox ears dipped. "Unless you have family back in the States?"

"I'm staying wherever Uncle Jackie is," the boy staunchly declared, finally taking Ginkgo's hand.

But before they could go out to track down Jacques, the back door opened, and Kyrie stepped inside. Tapping snow from his shoes, he announced, "You do not have to worry. Uncle Jackie is with Nonny."

"Yeah? That's all right, then," said Ginkgo.

Sibley wasn't convinced. "Who's that?"

"Nonny is Uncle Jackie's apprentice." Offering his hands,

he said, "Hello. My name is Kyrie Hajime-Mettlebright. We are brothers."

"You sure about that?" Sibley challenged.

"I know that I *want* to be your brother." Kyrie tapped a finger over his heart. "Something here is clamoring for more of my clan."

"I'm not blind. I can tell we're related. But brotherhood is more than bloodline."

"And bloodline alone does not guarantee closeness. But Mother says that it is all right to be greedy, so long as I am also generous." His hands remained on offer. "Will you let me be your brother?"

"What's that look like, to your way of thinking?"

"I would prefer friendship to rivalry. I like companionship and conversation, and I am curious if you can keep up with me in the sorts of training games we play." Flipping his hands over, he shyly added, "Since we are both dragons, we could engage in grooming sessions. Lapis has been teaching me."

Sibley's eyes widened, and he finally reached for Kyrie, fingers trailing over his older half-brother's painted claws. "What *is* this?"

"You like it?" Kyrie smiled shyly. "I do, too. Would you like me to adorn your claws?"

The littler boy edged closer, and his tail snaked around Kyrie's calf. "Yes?"

"I would like to hug you now, please," Kyrie announced. "Is that all right?"

Sibley answered with a mute nod.

Kyrie pulled Sibley closer and slipped his fingers into wavy purple hair, searching for any budding horns. When he began fluting one of Lapis's draconic lullabies, Sibley went up on tiptoe and touched Kyrie's long, sleek hair and tapped the line of larger horns.

Sibley gruffly announced, "I'm glad I'm not the oldest anymore."

"And I am glad I am no longer alone."

Akira glanced up to see if Suuzu was similarly touched by Kyrie's words, only to bump noses with the phoenix, who took advantage of everyone else's inattention to brush a hasty kiss across Akira's lips.

Suuzu softly declared, "I am *also* glad that I am no longer alone."

As soon as they could manage a few minutes alone, Akira hoped to add to that gladness. In the meantime, he contented himself with feeding Suuzu another piece of scone.

54

IMPISH LEGACIES

Lapis returned to the Song Circle, joining the welcoming party for the second windship, and breathed a little easier when none of its attendant dragons showed any interest in approaching him. He might speak for his clan, but that didn't mean he wanted to have to make polite conversation with any of them.

Lord Trystholm noticed his gaze and dipped his head, arching carmine wings in greeting. The gesture would have stung less if Lapis could have answered in kind. But he was nonetheless grateful. Ever since leading the song that wooed a wind imp to Mikoto Reaver's side, the dragon lords had been treating Lapis with a modicum of respect.

He hung back, leaving greetings to Stately House's capable healers. These children were escaping a dragon. They weren't likely to appreciate finding another waiting. Pulling his cloak more snugly around his body, he contemplated returning to his favorite parlor and its fire.

Argent inspired confidence. Tsumiko exuded kindness. Michael was the embodiment of good cheer, and Ginkgo won hearts at every turn. They trailed toward the house while Canarian Evernhold strode forward, inviting the dragons inside his theater, where a banquet room had been readied for their comfort after the long journey.

Normally, that task would have fallen to Hisoka.

Lapis glanced back toward Stately House, wondering if he should check on their illustrious leader, only to spy a forlorn figure standing alone in the snow.

"Hello, Isla," he called.

"Oh!" She squared her shoulders and hurried over. "I didn't notice you. But of course I wouldn't have. Why are you out here instead of mingling with dignitaries?"

"I'm not here for their sakes." Catching an artfully arranged curl with the gilded tip of one sapphire claw, he lightly added, "Just as you are not here for mine."

Isla didn't pretend. She never did with him. "Have you seen Hisoka-sensei?"

"Is he being elusive?"

"More than usual." Gesturing in the direction the dragon lords had gone, Isla said, "He was supposed to be the one to thank them for lending their support."

Lapis tried reasoning. "Canarian often speaks for the spokesperson, and he knows how to pander to an audience. The lords won't feel slighted."

Isla whispered, "But I do."

"I understand, dear heart. I do."

"*Is* he here?"

"Ah. Perhaps if you were to ask …?" Lapis indicated the windship and the figure clinging to its doorframe.

"Isla? Lord Mossberne? Could you give me a hand?" Sinder had a smile firmly in place, but he radiated tension. "I have a late-breaking applicant for Argent's and Tsumiko's affections, but she won't … let … go."

He dragged himself across the threshold, revealing a snarl of coils encasing one of his legs.

"I thought everyone had disembarked!" Isla hurried forward over trampled snow.

"Well, she was hiding. And this kid is too damned good at it. Took me forever to find her latest hidey-hole."

"Definitely reptilian. Come here, sweetheart," Isla coaxed. "Let me see you."

If anything, the little one wound herself tighter around Sinder's leg. He winced.

"What's her parentage?" Looking over her shoulder at Lapis, she asked, "Do you recognize this color?"

"Turquoise isn't unheard of," Lapis said, lowering himself to one knee at her side. "But this child isn't a dragon."

Sinder said, "Moon's best guess is half-star, half-midivar. Not that you heard it from me."

Isla's brows knit. "Are you saying this child is part Ephemera?"

"A guess is a guess, but yeah. I'm inclined to agree." Sinder sighed and asked, "Any chance Kyrie is close by? He's good at winning over the shy ones."

"If I may?" Drawing a breath, Lapis warbled coaxingly.

A face peeped from behind Sinder's leg, revealing wide, faceted eyes of iridescent yellow. She blinked at Lapis, a small frown lending a pout to full lips.

"Oh," breathed Isla. "She's beautiful."

Lapis tended to agree, but other matters were more urgent. "Are you cold, little one?" Beckoning with a flutter of jeweled fingers, he said, "My cloak is fur-lined—a gift from an especially doting dog—and I'm not opposed to sharing it."

Blue-green scales glittered like gems as she unwound from Sinder and lifted her arms toward Lapis.

"Bless you," Sinder sighed, tapping his foot against the floor. "I'd lost all feeling in this leg."

"Does she have a name?" Isla asked.

"If she knows, she's not telling." Sinder shrugged. "One of the other kids could probably tell you, though the few I met didn't seem especially attached to their names. Kodoku basically numbered them."

Lapis drew his cloak more snugly around the little girl, who weighed no more than a spring breeze. She wound the length of her body twice around his ribs. Mercifully, she didn't try to crack them. He warbled his thanks, and she stuck her thumb in her mouth.

Isla gave his arm an approving pat, then moved on to other matters. "Sinder, where is Sensei?"

"Isla, I have a long swim ahead of me, and you already know my answer. I really couldn't say."

"Does that mean you don't know or you won't say?" she pressed.

Sinder rolled his eyes. "It means I really couldn't say."

She gripped the edges of her own cloak too tightly. "Has he done something I should know about?"

"What are you fishing for, Isla?"

"Is it true that he had that Moonprowl person brought here?"

"She's here," Sinder said wearily. "Did you want an autograph?"

Isla shook her head. "I can't believe he brought her home. Why her?"

Sinder caught Lapis's eye and voiced a silent plea. *"Okay. Now, I need help with* this *one."*

Lapis answered in kind. *"Give a little grace. She's been fretting over Hisoka."*

"Is that *what we're calling it?"*

"Gently, Sinder. She cares."

In careful tones, Sinder spoke aloud. "You know I'm not obliged to report to you about his activities or his whereabouts."

"Yes, but sometimes you let things slip. *Do* let something slip? I'm worried!"

Sinder grimaced. "We're all worried. And for too many reasons. I'm sure his office will be issuing a statement eventually."

"I *know* because that's my job! But I can't do that until you tell me what's happened?"

"He's on sabbatical. Until further notice."

"Why? Where?" And more reluctantly, "With whom?"

Sinder sighed. "It's not what you're thinking. If it's Pim you want, she's with the wolves. Oh, that reminds me." Ducking back inside, he returned with a surfboard, which he lightly tossed off to one side. "Boon'll be wanting it back."

Isla radiated confusion.

"You want details, you're welcome to pester Boon."

"I will if I have to. At least I know I'd get a straight answer." Isla looked miserable. "Why won't anyone tell me what I want to know?"

"Give the guy a break, all right. Stuff happened, and he needs time."

"How much time?"

"Until further notice," he repeated.

"And he's not with Pim Moonprowl?"

"No. He's not." Gaze skidding sideways, Sinder took pity enough to ask, "Where does he ever go when he's fraught?"

Understanding dawned, and Isla's eyes closed. "Oh, of course. He's with Papka."

Pim melted into Adoona-soh's embrace and did her best to tune out Boon's chuckle.

"Don't skimp, Mom," he urged, his tone indulgent. "She's pack."

"Oh? Does Mistress Moonprowl intend to run with us for a season?"

"Nothing like that. Here's the thing. If Argent goes along with my plan, I'll be establishing a den somewhere hereabouts. Maybe join the enclave."

There was a longish pause that made Pim's heart clench, but Boon's father broke the silence. "You're finally settling down?"

"As much as any tracker can. It'll all work out ... somehow."

Pim and Elara had both been warmly welcomed by Boon's parents. And it'd been fine when they weren't anything more than friends and fellow taskforce members. But this development set off a whole bunch of extra sniffing.

Adoona-soh put Pim at arm's length but didn't release her. Looking between her and Elara, she asked, "May I be blunt?"

"You usually are," Boon blandly retorted, his tail still at an easy sway.

"Which of them are you establishing a den with?"

"Both of them." His stance radiated confidence, even pride. "They're both mine. And I'm theirs. Or did you forget how pack works?"

"But which is your bonded?" his mother murmured, looking to her mate for help.

"Both of them," Boon repeated.

Ninook-dex Elderbough was smiling, and his tail wasn't just swaying, there was a kind of twirl happening. "Such things do happen, especially with tributes."

"Which he *isn't*," Adoona reminded.

"Close enough to count," Boon asserted. "Besides, I'm not the kind of guy who won't take responsibility. They're both pregnant."

Pim was completely enfolded again in Adoona-soh's embrace, and Ninook moved to gather Elara close. Boon's father had blue eyes, and they sparkled at his son. "I must ask. By any chance, did you encounter any trees on your oh-so mysterious mission?"

Boon jerked a thumb at his father and explained, "Dad's a dex. He knows what's what."

Ninook asked Elara, "Do you love my son?"

She was positively glowing when she lightly said, "More than he's comfortable with, but he'll get used to the idea."

Boon rolled his eyes, but his tail was still keeping up that happy sway.

Pim focused on that and did her best to match his mood, even when the question came to her.

"And you," Ninook inquired, seeking her gaze. "Do you love my son?"

"I might."

Adoona-soh asked, "You're not certain?"

"Well … I don't want him *gone.*" It had made more sense before she said it out loud.

His mother shook her head and softly promised, "All you need, he will be. *Or else.*"

"I can make my own vows. And I'll keep them once I do. Nothing to worry about there." Boon casually added, "All that's left is the singing. They'll be needing pack names."

Ninook mildly pointed out, "Plenty of precedent for that."

Adoona-soh kissed Pim's forehead and firmly said, "Tonight, the Elderbough pack welcomes a wolf and a beacon."

Pim went right back to melting. She *definitely* loved Boon's mom. And maybe—if she was entirely honest—Pim was coming to love Boon's laugh.

Michael couldn't imagine what Hisoka had faced on that island to put him in such a state, but Sensei very clearly needed him. Argent had helped to settle Rhomiko in Sensei's bed, then ensured their privacy. After that, Michael had stayed in Sensei's private suite for most of the day, holding his former mentor and serving as his confessor. And tending to a soul that trembled at his lightest touch.

Hisoka eventually calmed, but he'd still clung. And now, he slept—light and fitful—insisting he only needed a nap.

As Michael meandered toward his office, he wondered if he should have a word with Stately House's only male healer. If Sensei would allow it, Colt Withershanks could look after him and his new charge. At least until they were both on their feet.

Michael had barely eased into his chair when a knock sounded at his door. With a sigh, he recrossed the room, planning to send away whoever was there. He was emotionally spent, and he still needed to navigate bedtime stories for the new crossers.

To his surprise, Argent and two felines waited at his door, draped in enough sigilcraft to hide them from incidental notice. "Argent ...?" Michael began.

"A moment. Boon is coming."

"I'm here, I'm here," Boon softly called, catching up. "I had a thing, and now this is a thing. Have you told him, yet?"

"*Tsk*. Inside first."

Michael backed all the way to the far wall, nearly toppling a stack of communiques in the process, then lunging forward to rescue a rare pink stone from his desktop when he realized they were setting a bulky package there. It was wound in strips of gauze. "Bandages?"

"I took advantage of the lab's supply closet," said Boon. "Didn't want to risk any knocked edges."

Again, Michael asked, "Argent …?"

"This is one of the wardstones that anchored that island's barrier. I was hoping to get your opinion."

"Oh! Well, yes. Of course. I'd be pleased." Fingers poised above the wrappings, he asked, "Whose sigilcraft is this?"

"Linlu Dimityblest."

"You don't say …!" Michael glanced around, quickly tallying the bundles carried by the two felines. "Only four?"

Argent asked, "Disappointed?"

Boon said, "There was an anchor, too. But yeah. These four were placed at highpoints around the island. I could probably work up a map if that's important."

One of the cats quickly sketched shining lines in midair. A map.

"Most helpful," Michael said warmly. "And you are?"

"Eiji Woodhearth, sir."

"No need for formalities. You're good with sigilcraft?"

He simply nodded, but the other cat spoke up. "Eiji is a crystal adept. He's skilled."

That was welcome news. Acknowledging the other, Michael asked, "And you are …?"

"Anjou. A tribute of the Bonhomie clan."

With a glance at Argent, Michael inquired, "Are the two of you merely dropping by or—dare I hope—planning to stay on?"

The fox sighed. "First things first."

"Right. Sorry."

Boon stepped forward to help loosen the bindings, and the first glint of green showed through. To Michael's surprise, Boon began humming, his expression gentle. That's when the crystal picked up his tune and sang with him.

This wasn't the snatch of a forgotten song that one usually found within a remnant. This was a force of personality, perhaps even a voice. Smoothing his hands over faceted curves, Michael whispered, "This is astonishing!"

"Totally with you there. Check it out." Hefting the stone, Boon reoriented it, placing the flatter side against Michael's midriff. "You get it?"

He mightn't have, if not for the extensive collection of lore in Tsumiko's ever-expanding library. "These are children?" Michael cradled the stone to his body and turned to his old friend. "Argent, I think these are children!"

The fox hummed in a pleased way.

Boon said, "Yeah, we thought so, too. Which brings us to you."

Michael was certainly glad that they'd brought this to him. Except for one thing. "What do you expect *me* to do?"

"It's simple, really? Any idea how to hatch a baby rock imp?"

55

STAY

Nonny smuggled Jacques to his own suite, a small set of rooms that might have qualified as a palatial walk-in closet with a bed. Or possibly a boutique. A very exclusive, very expensive boutique with an entire bureau given over to neckties. The *en suite* included a claw-footed tub, and that meant a private bath.

"Do you even ever use this thing?" Nonny asked.

"Every now and again." Jacques shrugged. "I've grown accustomed to the onsen. And more in the way of company."

"Which dressing gown do you want?" He waved at the armoire dedicated to Jacques' collection.

"Too tired to care."

Jacques really did look knackered. Nonny hurried to get the water going. His hand wavered over the options. "Care about these?"

"Something floral," he said quietly.

They worked around each other for a while, and Nonny kept his gaze averted. Suit to hang. Towels to fetch. Slippers to choose. The water stopped, and he hurried to help Jacques into the bath, then gasped.

"Stop!"

Jacques hesitated. "I checked. It's not too hot."

"It is! You ... you idiot! There's like three fistfuls of salt in there!"

"So? I like bath salts." He moved to get in.

"Stop!" Nonny grabbed his arm and swore. "I'm serious. Just stop! Hold totally, fucking still!"

Then he ran to the door, leaned into the hall, and bellowed, "Argent! I need your arse in here NOW!" And sucking in another breath, he added, "Suuzu! I need you. And ... aw, hell, while we're at it, *Hajime*!"

Stomping back into the room, Nonny checked to make sure Jacques had actually listened.

He stood beside the bath, a bunched up towel covering most of what needed covering. "There's a draft. Did you leave the door open?"

Hajime arrived without any warning, Naoki in tow.

"Lord. You're lucky I have exhibitionist tendencies."

Agent streaked in, tails awry. "Nonny," he growled in warning tones.

"Stow it. I know what I'm doing."

A long jumble of running footsteps brought Akira and Suuzu puffing in.

"Close the door!" Nonny ordered.

Jacques lowered himself wearily to the edge of the tub. "I just wanted a bath. Is that so much ...?"

"Idiot. Messing around with two blokes, and one of them a tree. Serves you right!"

Hajime eased forward. "Hello, Jacques. Do you remember me?"

"Good to see you again, sir. Yes. My memories of you seem to be intact." Dipping a nod at the man he'd arrived with, he politely said, "You must be Naoki. Do forgive my ... dishabille."

"Could you lower that cloth, young man?" Hajime held up thumb and forefinger. "This much should do."

Jacques did.

Suuzu gasped.

Argent groaned.

Naoki actually applauded.

Nonny just fetched a dressing gown and held it for Jacques. He slipped into it with murmured thanks, but before he could tie it shut, Suuzu begged, "Wait. Please. I must confirm ...!"

Jacques' gaze jumped from face to face. "What? Is something ...?" He looked down running his hand over his belly. His fingers soon found the first tendril, small and green and curling tightly against his skin. Eyes wide, he whispered, "Something *is* there."

Suuzu grabbed him by the hips and sternly said, "I am going to look, and I will need to touch. You must trust me."

Jacques simply eased into a receptive posture.

Nonny grabbed his hand. "It's okay, right? Trust Suuzu. He knows all about this sort of thing."

Jacques asked, "Could someone explain?"

"You've been sprigged." Naoki beamed at him. "Congratulations!"

His face went totally blank, and Nonny started to worry. "You're not going to faint, are you?"

"I don't think so. Keep hold, just in case."

Pushing up under his arm, Nonny explained, "No salt in the bath water. No swimming in the sea."

"It's *November*."

"Yeah, well … seasons turn."

Jacques' breath hitched as Suuzu prodded him. Determinedly locking his gaze with Nonny's, he asked, "How did *you* know?"

"Who d'ya think's been helping Suuzu this whole time?"

Argent sighed.

Jacques' gaze flew to Akira, finally risking eye contact. For several beats, Akira just looked back at Jacques, all befuddled. Which could only mean one thing. This was news to both of them.

Nonny stamped a hoof. "If you've been waiting for an opening, you moody chicken, I just handed you one. Tell 'im already!"

Argent hauled up the sleeve of his tunic, fished the plug from the tub, and let it begin to drain. With a carefully neutral tone, he said, "Not a word outside this room. Suuzu, I'll leave the rest to you and Akira. Everyone else … *out*."

Suuzu hadn't been able to tell Akira *anything*, and he certainly hadn't planned to break his news in front of Jacques. But perhaps this was for the best. It would have to be. Once the others were gone, Suuzu took charge. "May we move to your bed? You need to stay warm.”

The man practically fled.

Not that he could escape.

With a weary warble, Suuzu pushed Akira ahead of him and crowded onto the bed with them. He fussed with blankets longer than necessary, and the other two huddled together in a way that made Suuzu feel left out.

“Jacques, you have received a tree’s blessing.”

“*Must* we speak in euphemisms?”

“It is the usual phrase, common throughout Amaranthine lore, for the circumstance in which you find yourself.” Waving between them, he amended, “In which *we* find ourselves.”

“Suuzu …?” Akira held up a hand and said, “Just to be really, *really* clear. Sprigged means pregnant, yeah?”

“In the sense that there will be a child … yes.”

“Ourselves,” Jacques echoed softly.

“He did say that,” Akira mumbled dazedly. “Suuzu …?”

“I am a tribute. One of my duties includes the care and protection of Impressions.” He curled a hand over his abdomen. “I found a rare seed, and I needed to keep it safe.”

Akira simply nodded.

No, he nodded … *and* leaned into Jacques.

But then his nestmate sought his gaze and shyly asked, “We’re having a baby?”

Suuzu dredged up a smile and nodded. “This little one will be a chick in our nest.”

“Lord. I’m going to have a baby?” Jacques said numbly.

Akira’s expression shifted, and he put his arms around

Jacques. The man sagged against him, and Suuzu scooted closer, putting a hand on his shoulder. And suddenly, Suuzu could feel the depths of his longing. Clear and strong and bright as the soul that harbored a song that hadn't been there before.

"Jacques, what is this?"

"I'm sorry. I've given him back, but … I just need a moment."

"Jacques," Suuzu said more firmly. "Why can I tune my soul to yours?"

"That's a longish story. Ah, Akira. I met your half-brother." With a mournful glance, he confessed, "I told him you had all my devotion, but what with the foretelling and the flower petals. Lord, he left me up the duff."

"Jacques," Suuzu repeated, firming his grip. "You are a reaver?"

"*Non.* I am a *Smythe.*"

Certain he was right, wanting to prove his point, Suuzu cautiously initiated a connection. He shouldn't have, not without permission, so he dragged himself away, even though he wanted to linger.

Jacques' eyes widened, and he grabbed Suuzu's retreating hand. "Lord," he whispered. Then, "*Lord,*" with more emphasis. "Do that again?"

"I … overstepped." Suuzu lowered his gaze. "I apologize."

"If I forgive you, will you do it again?"

Akira asked, "What did he do?"

"To use the vernacular, first taste?" Jacques' gaze was so open, so hopeful. "That was tending?"

Suuzu looked to Akira, who didn't seem bothered. If anything, he was beaming.

"I have a half-brother? And he's a tree?"

"Half tree, half stone." Jacques looked to Suuzu. "Will that cause complications?"

"I do not know." He racked his brain, but there was no precedent in the lore he'd been taught. "The child will be human, but their tree twin may be … unique."

"And yours will be a phoenix?" Akira checked. "And their twin …? You said a *rare* tree."

"I consumed one of Hajime's seeds."

"Oh! Then there will be two."

Suuzu didn't follow.

Jacques drummed his fingers over Akira's chest and said, "You haven't told him? For shame."

And then Akira was pulling Suuzu's necklace over his head, and there was much babbling about dragons and fathers and … and there was the reliquary that anchored their pledge.

"A seed?" Suuzu whispered.

"My seed. My twin. This was caught up inside me, right where you found that glow. They were with me all along."

Wonder. Delight. Relief. Suuzu's throat ached to sing.

But what he'd said. *Inside*? With a worried peep, Suuzu had Akira flat on his back, his shirt lifted, his bandage peeled back. He banished a foxish sigil that had hidden the scent of injury, and he clucked mournfully over the stitched wound.

"It's fine," Akira promised, patting his head, then squirming. "Hey, that tickles!"

"Lord, you're cute together," Jacques murmured. He sounded so lonely.

Akira reached up and touched the man's face. Offering comfort. It wasn't anything more, but Suuzu still rebelled. He didn't want to share. One bondmate was all he cared to court.

Yet things were different now. Off-kilter.

Jacques' glance held guilt. He knew his trespass and winced under Suuzu's gaze. But when he tried to retreat, Akira was right there, hanging on, bringing him back.

What a muddle. Suuzu couldn't claim Akira without hurting Jacques, and he couldn't shun Jacques without hurting Akira. How had this man wiled his way into Akira's heart? In a matter of weeks, they'd grown as close as a tree and his twin.

Suuzu blinked.

Ah.

That.

Juuyu had once said that Jacques was easier to understand if you thought of him as a tree. He flirted indiscriminately, yet his devotion ran as deep as roots.

Suuzu had seen this kind of relationship over and again. His mother, while fiercely protective of her bond with Father, understood all the intricate ways in which he needed Letik. And wasn't Juuyu maintaining a similar balance, having pledged himself to Fumiko, even while accepting Zuzu as part of their balance?

All tree-kin seemed to inherently understand what was needed. Patience. Affection. Inclusion. Jacques was a mess of unmet needs, and Akira—in the absence of his own twin—seemed to have given the man a similar place in his heart.

Shifting paradigms calmed Suuzu.

Jacques wasn't necessarily a rival. He needn't be excluded.

Indeed, for the sake of the rare children they carried, it was enormously important that they all make peace.

"Suuzu," Akira said, his gaze pleading. "Jacques can't do this alone. He needs us."

"Agreed. Our pact should continue."

"Really?" asked Akira, all admiring. "We can keep him?"

Jacques ventured, "Surely not. You're courting Akira, and I know avians don't–"

A sharp chirp cut him off, and Jacques' flinch stung. Easing off Akira, Suuzu presented his palms to the man. "Do I make you nervous?"

"Not at the moment. I did expect more in the way of pillories and pillaging once you found out ... ah. It was necessary to convince those around us that ... mmm. Perhaps the less said, the better?"

Akira piped up, "He was a gentleman."

Jacques sighed. "An imperfect one. I am sorry, Suuzu."

"Are you?" he challenged.

Several emotions flitted across the man's face, and he finally gave a small shake of his head.

"Nonetheless, our pact will continue. I am bringing you into our nest."

Jacques glanced between them in disbelief. "If I may be so bold ... in what capacity?"

Suuzu tipped his head to one side, then stated the obvious. "You will be a nestmate."

The man looked like he wanted to say something more. He even made some futile hand gestures.

Akira chuckled. "I think Jacques is wondering if you'll be courting both of us. Or maybe he should court you. He's very good at it."

Suuzu's bewilderment must have shown.

Jacques' gaze softened. "Lord, I'd be up for the challenge, but I don't think your comely bird wants anyone's devotion but yours."

"I know." Akira's gaze was starry with happiness, like he'd gotten everything he'd ever wanted ... and more. "Don't worry, Jacques. I'll be *so* good to you."

"Is that meant for revenge?"

"Mm-hmm. And all baby clothes must be pastel."

"Mean thing," Jacques grumbled fondly. And raising his gaze to Suuzu's, he added, "Not you, though. You are generosity itself."

For all his brave front and banter, Suuzu could feel Jacques underlying uneasiness, and such things didn't belong in a nest. Maybe he didn't fully trust Suuzu? Or perhaps it was nerves over carrying a child. Then again, it could be the lasting effects of something he'd endured on that distant island.

"What can I do to calm you?" Suuzu asked.

Jacques' smile faded. "I'm all right."

Akira patted the man's shoulder and rolled his eyes. "This guy. He *thinks* he's a marvelous actor."

The man looked ready to protest.

Putting a finger to Jacques' lips, Akira sternly said, "Only honesty. It's still our rule."

Jacques actually eased into an apologetic posture.

"Right. Honesty. I *am* mostly calm, but only because none of this seems real. Tomorrow or the next day, after I've been questioned and probed and warned and—if the fates allow—bathed, I will probably begin to be quietly, persistently, devastatingly frightened."

Akira scrambled onto his knees and pulled Jacques close. "We'll be here. *Right* here."

"You say that now." With a worried glance Suuzu's way, he said, "I am usually only tolerated in small doses."

Suuzu caught himself nodding.

Jacques looked miserable.

"Those others." Suuzu crawled closer, then rose up on his knees so he was able to look down on the man. "Did they make you any promises? Did they listen to the song of your soul? Did they love you?"

"*Non.*"

"Do you doubt Akira's affection?"

"*Non.*"

"Do you underestimate my resolve?"

"You *will* lose patience with me."

"Many times. But you will not lose *me*. Do you understand the difference?"

Jacques gently pushed Akira away. "Suuzu, I really don't want to come between the two of you."

"Then ... bring us together."

The notion must have appealed. Jacques' smile resurfaced, and he blandly murmured, "You say that now."

Bending closer, Suuzu formalized his vow. "You are in my safekeeping. This nest is yours, and my claim binds us until ...." He could feel the tiny tug of a hazy hope and wondered how long the man had been harboring it. Gently brushing his knuckles against Jacques' cheek, he said, "Until another woos you away from me."

Jacques trembled under his touch, right down to his soul.

Bumping a kiss to his brow, Suuzu offered words that had always comforted him. "A nestmate is here."

Abundant thanks to all who lend their support by reading, rating, and reviewing my stories, wherever they may be found. ::twinkle::

ALSO BY FORTHRIGHT

AMARANTHINE SAGA

Tsumiko and the Enslaved Fox

Kimiko and the Accidental Proposal

Tamiko and the Two Janitors

Mikoto and the Reaver Village

Fumiko and the Finicky Nestmate

Pimiko and the Uncharted Island

Rhomiko and the Confirmed Bachelor

SONGS OF THE AMARANTHINE

Marked by Stars

Followed by Thunder

Dragged through Hedgerows

Governed by Whimsy

Hemmed in Silver

Captured on Film

Bathed in Moonlight

Flattered by Flowers

AMARANTHINE INTERLUDES

Lord Mettlebright's Man

PATREON EXCLUSIVES

Bard & Barbarian

Kimiko and the Cycle of Moons

When I reach 400 patrons, I'll begin publishing a new subscription-based storyline on Patreon. Loosely based on the old Amaranthine tale, "The Wolf and the Moon Maiden," this serial will involve three sisters, twelve pledges, and the long-awaited stirring of a sleeping landmark. Become a patron at https://www.patreon.com/forthrightly

never more than
FORTHRIGHT

a teller of tales who began as a fandom ficcer. (Which basically means that no one in RL knows about her anime habit, her manga collection, or her penchant for serial storytelling.) Kinda sorta almost famous for gently-paced, WAFFy adventures that might inadvertently overturn your OTP, forthy will forever adore drabble challenges, surprise fanart, and twinkles (which are rumored to keep well in jars). As always... be nice, play fair, have fun! ::twinkle::

FORTHWRITES.COM

Readers have often asked for more of Kimiko Miyabe's courtship of Eloquence Starmark. Their grand cycle is a tale I'm eager to tell. **Once I reach my posted community goal over on Patreon**, I'll begin a serialized account that ranges from fittings in the seamstress's workroom at the Starmark compound to the forming of fresh triads at New Saga High School. And of course, all the drama at Kikusawa Shrine: three sisters, twelve kisses, and the long-awaited stirring of a sleeping landmark.

Become a patron at https://www.patreon.com/forthrightly

Bard & Barbarian

BY FORTHRIGHT

*Imber was only a boy when he met the divine beast
who would one day share his adventures.*

A serialized fantasy that's currently a Patreon exclusive. Access to the ongoing adventure is available at all tiers of support. Now with bi-weekly audio installments, narrated by Travis Baldree. Become a patron in order to read along.

https://www.patreon.com/forthrightly

One bachelor is love-shy. One is unrequited.
One is much-loved. One is blindsided.

Argent Mettlebright knows how to keep a secret safe, but it's only a matter of time before someone notices that Hisoka Twineshaft has disappeared from the political arena. With tensions on the rise, the world needs his leadership more than ever.

Nobody wants to help Sensei more than Isla Ward, but his door is barred against her. *Right, then.* She has a plan, and she has a co-writer. Maybe with their next book, her hopes will finally reach her mentor.

With spring's arrival, Stately House's enclave stands ready to welcome a Scattering. The estate has never been more secure, but Tsumiko wouldn't call the resulting sanctuary *peaceful*. Too many battered souls. Too many wistful glances. But with the help of a dragon bard's lullabies and an impish crosser's confidence, she leads her ever-growing family.

Seeds to plant. Imps to hatch. Winds to change. Rogues to lure. Hearts to win. Vows to keep. Lives to share.